CHANCE PLACE

Frankie Schelly

To Anita

Enjoy

Frankie Schelly

Also by Frankie Schelly

At the Crossroads

Honorable Mention Winner
Mainstream/Literary Fiction *Writer's Digest*
9th National Self-Published Book Awards

PRAISE FOR FRANKIE SCHELLY'S CHANCE PLACE

Schelly has made the subjective harmony and cacophony of mental illness understandable. The story shows how surrender to trust and acceptance can achieve redemption even in the worst of circumstances. –Sandy Goble, RN, MSN, member of the National Association for the Mentally Ill (NAMI)

A compelling story about the transformative power of love and friendship. Two men meet in adulthood who respectively suffer the effects of childhood sexual abuse and mental illness. Through a series of shattering events, which almost destroys one and forces the other to discover his own capacity to love and nurture, both are saved. –Margret Michaelson, BSN, PHN

Chance Place opens a door into a world far removed from most of us—or is it? As the main characters become real, we see ourselves separated only by degrees or by chance. We are indebted to the author for her keen insight into a system ostensibly designed to help the mentally ill, but more effectively designed to ease our collective guilt as we continue to avoid the high cost of effective care. –Rev. Richard Stennett

DEDICATION

To my son Tom, my stepson Ralph, and all others like them
who with remarkable courage negotiate
the daily challenges of chronic mental illness.

To my family and friends who struggle with quality of life
decisions
on behalf of those they love in the face of conflicting advice
and ongoing emotional and financial burdens.

"The moral test of government is how it treats those who are in the dawn of life—the children; those who are in the twilight of life—the aged; and those who are in the shadows of life—the sick, the needy, and the handicapped."

Hubert Horatio Humphrey (1911-1978) Vice President to President Lyndon Baines Johnson (1965-1969)

ACKNOWLEDGMENTS

The fullness of my gratitude goes to my loving husband, Cy, for his courage and understanding in times of stressful decisions on behalf of our respective mentally ill sons, for his ongoing support, wisdom, and ever reliable sense of humor. For loving me enough to share this journey.

I'm grateful to Dr. Charles M. Cutler, who offered dedication and encouragement to my fifteen-year-old son, and whose empathy turned me toward healing.

I tribute the late Gail Posner, MSW, for guiding me with rare wisdom, integrity, honor, and insight into wholeness.

I also thank the many mentally ill and addictive vulnerable adults who so generously shared of their experiences that I might better comprehend and advocate on their behalf. May life be better for you. May those who would fund research and health insurance coverage for mental illnesses prevail.

My appreciation also extends to editors and writing colleagues who contributed encouragement, knowledge, and expertise to *Chance Place*—most importantly, Anne Underwood Grant, Robin Smith, Susan Snowden, Donna Jansen, Ellie Zitin, and authors Jack R. Pyle, Taylor Reese, and Steve Brown.

CHAPTER ONE

1973

The humming silence fought for space against Roberta Flack's "Killing Me Softly." Nathan Waite wondered why they would take such a nice song away, who would take it. His eyes cruised his Princeton dorm room in search of the who, but no one was there. He knew Cheryl wasn't the culprit. She had left at least an hour earlier, hadn't she? Keeping track of time these days only added to his confusion. Cheryl wouldn't take his music. He looked at the closed door then back at the playing phonograph record. Pressing his palms over his ears, fingers clawing his curly red hair, tall, muscular Nathan stared at the phonograph needle rotating to the silent humming in his mind. Hadn't he and Cheryl decided that the mental images and sounds he was experiencing were simply due to overstudy? *Focus*, he needed to focus.

He smelled the chlorine and musk of their lovemaking. Near the closed door their skis and poles leaned against the wall, tips touching like tentative new lovers. Nathan reached for the stack of four-by-six blue cards on his desk, his notes for his upcoming debate on U.S. involvement in Vietnam. He traced his trembling finger down the list of trigger words on the first card: *why France gave up; hawk arguments; quotes.* He didn't remember writing those words, yet the handwriting was his. He heard war sounds—shots, missiles, human cries and covered his ears again. The cards fluttered into blue patches on the hardwood floor. They were no longer his cards, the words no longer his. No doubt they belonged to the same people who had taken his music. The silence roared. How embarrassing it would be to call for help only to learn it was predebate stage fright, over study, maybe mono.

Nathan hurried down the hall to the phone, inserted a quarter, and dialed his sister, who was likely still awake. Light shone beneath several student doors. Before anyone could answer he hung up. He inserted a second quarter and dialed his parents, hoping Dad would answer. When his mother uttered a sleepy "Hullo," he hung up. *She'll worry, call back, never let me off the phone.* Maybe his dad was out of town selling inventions to warring parties. *Be a good soldier,* that's what his dad always said. Back in his room, Nathan gathered the multicolored, striped bedspread to his chest and paced. *Focus. Think of Cheryl.*

Tonight Cheryl had worn the embroidered peasant blouse he liked, the *Je Reviens* perfume he had given her at Christmas. He dipped his nose into the floral scent in the bedspread and inhaled deeply. *Je Reviens* means I'll come back, I'll return, I'll haunt. Cheryl never called his dreams foolish or accused him of not making sense. She didn't make fun of his freckles or try to trim his unruly curls or try to fix anything about him. Cheryl would always be there for him. The yellow stripes were dominant in the bedspread. More yellow stripes … and bolder, too. *Je Reviens.*

For some reason Nathan thought of the pantomime he had seen Marcel Marceau perform. He dropped the bedspread on the bed and opened his hands in front of himself, moving them like Marceau's Bip character, up and down the wall. His hands followed the wall to one side, around the corner, along the back, across the other side, until he was boxed in. It felt safer inside the box. Cheryl approached him as she had earlier, his red woolen ski socks flopping on her toes. The tenderness of her kiss made him feel like an Olympiad, rich as Rockefeller, smarter than the president of Princeton. A maker of music.

"I love you," Cheryl said.

"I love you, too."

He loved the way her nipples hardened at his touch. "Oh, Nathan," she whispered, wrapping her lovely bare legs around his on the bed. Nathan saw his serious reflection doubled in her irises, drifted into the sanctuary of her dark eyes. He said, "I love you so much it scares me." He kissed her heated ears, her neck, her lips, slowly paced her passion, explored her moist folds. Cheryl quivered. He kissed down the front of her, abandoned to fervor as she gripped his head.

"Oh ... Nath ... Babe ... Hon ... "

He eased into her gently, pressing lightly on the sensitive spot she had so patiently showed him. He pressed and eased, pressed and stroked, his hands moving across the wall as he penetrated slowly, steadily, moving her up ... up ... up ... the slope, pausing only once to let her catch her breath, urging her to the crest where together they leapt into the high heat of the sun ... flying into the wind over virginal snow ... flying, soaring ... FREEEEEeeeeeee.

Cheryl landed beside him with a soft, little sigh. In all the world was there a more wondrous moment? He rested his head on her breast and wrapped his arms around her, forever. "I'll love you always," he said, "always."

That's when her question ruined everything. "Hon? Maybe it's time you saw a doctor. You know—to be sure?"

Being with you is all I need. He drew a deep, unsteady breath, and exhaled it slowly. The back of her fingers brushed his cheek. "Really. I'm okay," he said.

"Sure?"

"Yes," he lied.

They rehearsed his debate then. Cheryl failed to grasp his best argument. Sometimes his mind made him feel so isolated and alone. Sometimes he just wanted to trade it in or simply give up.

"Babe," she said, "don't pressure yourself."

Nathan saw steam *whooshing* skyward from a train's smokestack. He saw the tip of Cheryl's index finger rest on the little red bow between her breasts.

"Babe? Nathan? Are you having one of those flashes? Are you?" He couldn't remember saying good-bye. *Je Reviens.*

Nathan shuddered and consciously shook his body to free himself of the too-real dream. Cheryl said she wanted a houseful of children. He saw the scattered blue cards, stooped and gathered and put them in order. He removed the sheets from the bed and dumped them into the bathroom hamper. "Man, focus, keep your focus," he said aloud. One or two kids maybe, not a houseful. "One or two … one or two only," Nathan muttered. Experiencing an overwhelming responsibility toward their unborn children, Nathan pulled fresh sheets onto the bed. He saw himself skiing in bad form at high speed down a treacherous slope, like a black streak crossing white space.

Frightened at his inability to keep his mind at bay, Nathan reached into the shower and turned the tap toward cold. He dropped his clothes in the hamper and stepped into the spray. Only when thoroughly chilled did he move the indicator to warm. Even so, his mind remained tightly wound like a Slinky. He crawled into bed, forced his breathing into longer exhales than inhales, a rhythm meant to induce sleep.

Before long Nathan found himself hurtling from one accident to another—his canoe overturned in whitewater, he rear-ended the car in front of him, fell through ice while skating. Up! Out of the ice he bolted, then skied dangerously fast down a steep slope with only a sliver of moonlight to guide him as he *etch-etch-etched* perilously over crusted ice, *too fast, too fast*. Ahead Cheryl screamed for help, "Nathaaaannnnn. Nathan!"

Nathan threw his weight and dug in his poles. Without warning he flew through space. Instinctively he tucked in his elbows and poles. His bindings released as he landed. A sharp pain traced up his left thigh and stabbed his heart. His mind sparked into shards.

Cheryl was screaming for help. Nathan disentangled himself from twisted sheets and blankets, snatched a ski and pole, and scuttled into the night. Unaware of the snow beneath his bare feet, he scaled across the campus, yelling, "Cheryl, I'll help you. I'm coming. I'm coming."

Inside her dorm, a uniformed man ordered, "You! Stop! Stop!" When Nathan didn't, the man accosted him, wrestled the ski free. As he let go Nathan did a forceful one-eighty, and watched the uniform tumble down the stairs.

He struck Cheryl's locked door with the pole, yelling, "Cheryl, Cherylll."

Men pummeled him. Nathan punched and kicked and bellowed, telling them she needed help.

"Easy. Easy," one of the three said, pinning his shoulders.

Why is no one helping her? "Help her!"

One said, "Pity what drugs will do."

Girls wearing nightgowns and pajamas stared at him from open doorways. Cheryl stood above him, frightened, screaming with her mouth closed. *How can she do that?* Nathan summoned all of his strength to free one hand. He reached toward her only to see a handcuff clamp over his wrist. Lost. She was lost. *He* was lost.

As they carried him away Nathan dropped his head and saw Cheryl upside down, her nightgown defying gravity! *Je Reviens.*

CHAPTER TWO

1973

I ducked my thirteen-year-old ass behind the TV. Mom was yelling, "Don't, Jacques, don't, please don't!" She covered her face with her arms. Jacques Bibideaux, my old man, with tattooed arms the size of telephone poles, pounded on her. Blood ran down the side of mom's mouth. She never learned not to let him back into the house after he had been gone a long time. I couldn't stand seeing her hurt this way. Last time he was here I was eleven. Suddenly I heard the old man's motorcycle *rev-rev-rev*, saw his black leather gloves grip the handles and aim that wheel at Morton, my schnauzer, who was only half-grown. *No, Daddy, noooo,* I yelled. Morton somersaulted in the air and landed in a bloody heap at my feet. Poppy, my granddad, held me on his lap and I held Morton as we rushed to the vet. Mom sobbed the whole way. Morton didn't make it. Dad never said he was sorry, only that no kid of his should go soft. Right then I decided the next time the old man appeared, I would split.

Dad turned his back toward me now, scooting Mom into the corner. Scared, stupid, knowing I couldn't defend her, I ran toward the door, snatched my windbreaker, and took off into the cold night. Knowing I was the skinny runt my old man said I was, my eyes dropped sissy water. Would I ever grow big enough to help her?

Halfway to Sam's house, I stopped to catch my breath in the alley. When Sam first moved to Burnham which was almost out of Cook County he had never seen a paved alley. I figured if I crossed into Hammond, Indiana, maybe the police wouldn't look for me there, but first I needed the money I had stashed in my school locker. Delivering papers didn't pay much, but I saved what I could for this day that I knew would come. Lucky I was wearing a sweater and a windbreaker; it was April damp and cold. I huddled close to the garage doors and moved on, imagining myself growing a couple of feet in the next year with arms bigger than the old man's telephone poles. At Sam's, I thought of tossing a rock at his window, but with my luck I'd break it, or worse, wake his parents. I opened the side door to Sam's garage. It smelled of car grease, old oil, stale sweat. The car wasn't there; Mr. Bradley was out. I felt my way to the corner of the workbench and took the folded plastic from the couch they had delivered. As much as I didn't want to go back into the cold, I took the plastic to the grassy spot between the garage and the neighbor's chain-link fence. In my pockets I had change enough for a phone call or two, a McDonald's receipt, the photo of me at almost age eleven with my arms around Morton licking my face. Next dog would be a German shepherd or a Rotweiler with teeth big enough to tattoo my old man.

I rolled myself in the plastic for warmth, then scooched on my rump up against the garage and waited for Mr. Bradley. The plastic crackled. Small clouds floated across dim stars. I didn't know there were so many sounds at night. Guilt and shame hit me big-time. Once when I was just eight I had tried to save Mom. Dad was pounding on her. I ran out. Mrs. Lipsky was hanging her wash next door. I went into her house and picked up the phone and dialed the emergency number Mom had taught me. When the police got there

Dad was gone. Still Mom tried to keep them outside. "I d-didn't call," she said, pressing a tissue against her nosebleed. I held onto her skirt. Her ear was all red, her cheek swollen and bruised.

"Someone did," one of the two policeman said, pushing the door open. He spotted me.

I backed away.

Mom looked at me like she couldn't believe I would do such a thing.

"Ma'am, let us take you to a hospital."

"I'm all right. Nothing's wrong."

He kept talking about charges. Mom said she didn't have any. I understood that he wanted money. I went into my room and brought back my piggy bank and offered it to the policeman. Mom snatched it and pushed me aside. "Get lost, Francis," she said, just like Dad did. I ran and hid in my closet.

After the policemen left, she came after me, yelling, "What will the neighbors think? What did you think you were doing?"

"'Mergency," I stammered.

"Were you lost? Was some stranger trying to pick you up?" She punched me into the corner the same way the old man punched her and beat the shit out of me, saying, "Never, never, never call the police."

I shuddered feeling her slapping me all over again and I never called the police again, but wanted to lots of times. The old man's looks dared me to. I heard a car approaching now, wiped a stupid tear away with my knuckle, and scrunched down. The neighbors knew a lot more than Mom thought they did. *I hate him, I hate him, I hate him.* The headlights stopped at the Bradleys' garage. I sat real still when Mr. Bradley got out and opened the garage door. He drove in and turned off the engine, then lowered the door, and walked to the house, whistling. Once I was sure he wasn't coming back, I folded the plastic and put it where it belonged. I crawled into the back seat of the car, reminding myself to be up and out before daylight.

I boarded the school bus one stop after Sam's. Mary June was sitting next to him. "Sam, come sit with me," I said. I followed him to the back. Sam had hair dark as mine, but his eyes were gray, not brown, and he was a lot taller than me. Both of us wore tie-dyed tee shirts because our moms hated them, and scruffy shoes. I tore the knee in my jeans when they were new. Sam's mom sewed patches on his.

"Where were you last night?" Sam asked. "Your mom phoned twice. Where's your knapsack?"

"Got anything to eat? I don't want her to know where I am." I felt guilty as I said it. Mom would worry. She would be lying on the bed with an ice bag on her face.

Sam gave me a green apple.

"Thanks." I took a bite and puckered against its sourness. "I need you to get something from my locker for me."

"It's a blue zippered pencil case on the top shelf behind a book. I'll wait behind the dumpster. Don't ask," I said, raising my hand to stop him.

Sam held my eyes in a clinch. "Okay," he finally said.

With the blue case tucked safely in my windbreaker's inside pocket, I headed for the railroad tracks. I couldn't risk going to any of my usual places. I wondered if Mom would call the police and if she did, would they help her when she had refused their help? Next time I ran away, I'd have food set aside, too. It drizzled. I knew I was walking toward the state line.

It was raining steadily. I walked a long, long time before I came to a town crossing. I shivered from wet and cold, found a White Castle in the town, and snarfed down a couple of dime-sized burgers. I drank water even though I would rather have had a Coke. I wondered if Mom had called Dad about me. I didn't want to think about what he would do to me the next time I saw him. The White Castle manager, an overweight guy older than my old man, kept staring at me. I thought about calling Mom, to say not to worry. I got up, chucked the paper cup and wrappers in the waste disposal, and headed for the can. I didn't want to go back out but going home was a bad idea.

That night I slept in a railroad car, one that looked like it wasn't about to take off. While I wanted to disappear, I didn't want to end up where I didn't know how to get around. I saw lots of people under railroad bridges and in places people shouldn't have to live. I didn't want to become one of them.

At a McDonald's I ate pancakes, scrambled eggs, and a sausage biscuit, then figured how many meals I had money for. Not as many as I thought. A woman with three little kids was trying to gather them and their trays to leave. There was a lot of food still on those trays.

"I'll take care of these for you," I said, rushing to her side.

"Why, thank you," she said, flinching when she looked at me. "Caught in the rain," I said, piling stuff onto one tray. As soon as she left, I wrapped the food in papers and stuffed it into my damp pockets. In the can, I splashed warm water onto my face and wiped it with those brown sandpaper towels. I had a blister on my heel. Next time I ran away I would set aside clothes, too. Who was I kidding? There wasn't going to be a next time.

By the end of the second day of rain, I huddled under an awning against the cold door of a storefront, too tired to trot back to the railroad tracks. Maybe leaving hadn't been so smart. I was feeling sorry for myself, thinking they should never have named me Francis, a sissy girl's name, full of bad luck. I bet as soon as he could talk Sinatra turned it into Frank. At school kids called me Frenchy because of Bibideaux, my last name. Mom didn't like that nickname. I missed Sam. Never trust a policeman, my old man said. Headlights approached. I pushed flat as Gumby against the door. I wondered if Mom was all right, if the ice helped her face, or if she should see a doctor. I could convince her if I had to.

"Hey," a man's voice called from the car that had stopped. "I thought I saw someone. Need a ride?"

I shaded my eyes with my hand. Not a police car.

"Get in. It would be a sin not to stop for you in weather like this."

The promise of warmth drew me. Being picked up by a stranger was an emergency, but not someone beating up my mother. I looked right, left, darted into the car's open back door. "Thanks," I muttered.

A dry cleaner bag hung over the back of the passenger seat. The man reached up inside it and pulled out a bulky jacket and offered it to me.

"It'll get wet."

"You'd rather catch cold?"

I took off my windbreaker and wet sweater and put it on. I hadn't realized how cold I was, hugged myself.

"Name's Peso," the man said, extending his hand.

Fear crawled up the back of my neck. The hand belonged to a black man.

"F-Frenchy," I said, taking it not too firmly.

"Hot soup's what you need. Why are you out on a night like this? Hot soup, then get you warm. Those are the priorities."

I tried to sit in as small a space as possible to keep the seat from getting wet. Peso turned the car onto busy Calumet Avenue. I felt better. At least if I needed help, someone would hear me. Peso pulled into a convenience store/station and turned off the ignition.

"Take this," he said, offering an umbrella. He flashed a smile, then opened the door and ran.

It looked safe enough. People moved about inside. Peso waited at the four-stool counter, his coat over a stool. He wore a dark green suit with a light green button-down shirt, a ring on his right hand with a blue-green stone that matched the stone in his gold tiepin.

"Chili or vegetable?" Peso asked, nodding toward two paper bowls the attendant waited to fill.

I never saw no black man dressed this good before. "Chili." His shoes were polished. Taking charity from Peso scotched anything I knew about blacks not being nice to whites.

"Careful," Peso said. "You'll burn your tongue."

The man could have been purple for all I cared. I downed two bowls and lots of crackers.

Peso smiled at me like he had spent all day making the chili. His skin was the color of light caramel, his hair trimmed close to his head. His dark, bloodshot eyes seemed kind.

"Do you have a place to stay, Frenchy?"

I didn't know what to say. It was hard not to like the guy.

"Ever hear the story of the Good Samaritan? Do you have a place to stay? I can put you up in my guest room."

I played with the plastic spoon, thought how warm a bed would feel, how dumb it would be to go with a stranger. Peso's jacket clung to me.

"Listen, Frenchy, before inviting a stranger home, I need to know a couple of things. Like, are you part of a gang? I don't want trouble with a gang and certainly not with the law. Are you in trouble with the law?"

"No! I'm not part of no gang neither."

"I could drive you home."

"Got no home."

"Then you need a place to stay." He smiled the smile of a movie star. Man like him had a pretty wife or too many girlfriends.

"I know about the Good Samaritan."

"That's good. You've been to Sunday school." He pulled out more bills than I had ever seen in one lump and left two dollars on the counter.

I thought about snitching the tip, but someone would see me: it wasn't right to steal.

Peso set a pack of BIC throwaway razors on the counter. He said, "My momma would say you need a warm bath before you get the mean chills."

"Priorities," I mumbled.

"Yeah," he said, a twinkle in his eye.

I couldn't help but smile. "You live in Illinois or Indiana?" I asked, my stupid voice cracking. I never knew whether a boy's or a man's voice would come out.

"Does it make a difference?"

I had to decide to stay where I was, to go with him, or where to be dropped off. I didn't want to give up his jacket.

"Naw."

We shared the umbrella to the car.

"You got a CB!" Peso could talk to truckers, to police, to anyone who had one, too. "Cool. What's your handle?"

"Roadrunner." Peso turned on the radio. He said, "When the fuzz is around, I stay within the speed limit. Diana Ross, now isn't she some kind of lady? You like the Supremes? Ever notice her earrings?"

I didn't notice earrings, tried to pay attention to where we were going 'cause maybe I would have to find my way back alone. Peso turned down a long, rutted lane. Floodlights came on as we entered a big yard. There was a big two-story, dark shingled house with an automatic garage door. He pulled the Buick in beside a groovy black car.

"Wow, look at those wheels!"

"It's a Mercedes, named for the daughter of an entrepreneur who said he'd buy thirty-six of the first babies off the line *if* they were named after his daughter."

"What's an entre, entre—"

"Entrepreneur. A guy who starts his own business. You're looking at one," Peso, said, taking the keys from the ignition. "Fingerprints are not allowed," he said, tilting his head toward the Mercedes.

I didn't touch it, but wanted to. Peso opened the door to the house and flipped on a light. We stood in a kitchen with cupboards that had doors like church windows. Alone with him now, I felt antsy. I thought about sleeping in the back of his car.

Peso said, "I'll show you the bathroom. You can soak in the tub and wash that grit out of your hair." I followed him upstairs. It was the biggest green tub I'd ever seen, square with holes on the sides of the inside.

"Towels," Peso said, pulling two dark green ones and a washcloth from a closet. He sure liked green. "Shampoo's on the rack." He pointed. "Dump your clothes in that basket. Want bubbles?" He held up a bottle of pink stuff.

"Naw."

"I keep it for the ladies," he said, turning on the water. "Bet you clean up real handsome. Jacuzzi timer's here. Just turn the knob to the number of minutes you want. Guest room's through that door. I'll set out a pair of pj's. They'll be too big, but you'll grow into them," he joked.

I stood there clutching those towels like a safety net.

"See you downstairs in the morning."

"Th-thanks."

How could a black person have a house as nice as this one? Steam rose from the water. I locked both doors and used the john. Before I put my clothes in the basket, I took my only photo of Morton and set it on the bedside table. I removed the tattered brown scapular I wore around my neck—two dark brown squares of cloth held by two cords that I had knotted to make it shorter. I wore the St. Francis of Assisi patch in front, him in a dark brown robe surrounded by baby animals, Disney birds flying overhead.

On the back patch St. Francis prayed under his halo. Poppy, my granddad, gave it to me the day Morton died. I wished I had snatched something to remind me of Mom. I checked the bathroom doors to be sure both were locked, then poured in some bubble stuff. Peso's wife would be mad when she found the puddles we trailed into her clean house.

Never did a bath feel so good. Maybe St. Francis was looking out for me after all. I plopped into bed, didn't even miss watching the blob in my lava lamp rise and fall. Same as life, sometimes it was ugly, sometimes like a nice dream.

CHAPTER THREE

I woke smelling coffee and bacon. The sun had been up awhile. It seemed right to make the bed, something I never did. The basket where I dumped my clothes was empty. The bedroom was neater than my whole house on days my grandparents were coming to visit. I rolled up the legs of the pj's, clutched the too-big waist, and hunted the stairs. Halfway down, I stopped when I heard a woman's voice.

Peso appeared at the foot of the stairs with a big smile and a mug of coffee. "Well, look at you." He wore dark slacks with a zigzag pattern and a crease that looked like it would cut a finger. Two gold chains hung around his neck, one on his wrist.

"Your wife," I whispered, pointing at my pants.

"Nothing my main woman hasn't seen. Coffee?"

I didn't want any strange woman seeing me this way. Peso nudged me forward.

The woman wore a white apron over a black dress. She was about my mom's age, a little on the plump side.

"Lily, this is Frenchy, our guest."

"You an orphan?" she asked with a smile. A slit of gold along a side tooth glinted.

I held on tight to my pants.

"Don't be shy now, boy. What you want for breakfast? Pancakes, waffles, grits?"

Peso sliced a finger across his throat, mouthing, No grits.

I pressed my lips to keep from smiling. "Uh—you know how to make French toast?"

"Sure enough. Bacon? Sausage?"

"Both," Peso said. He moved into the next room and came back with my folded clothes. "Lily washed these for you."

Great. I thought I would have to try to eat holding my pants. "Th-thank you, Lily."

"Okay, Champ," Peso said, "now that you've ordered breakfast, let's go up and shave."

Shave?

"Unless you are deliberately growing that mustache."

I touched my upper lip, did have one. "N-no."

When I finished dressing I found Peso waiting for me in the bathroom with shaving stuff, a new toothbrush and comb. He opened the pack of BIC razors and handed me one, saying, "It was nice of you to make the bed, Frenchy; however, no guest of mine need do that." He took my chin and moved my face to one side and another, checking my excuse of a beard. I did have a couple of chin hairs. "Someone's not doing right by you," he said. "A man's got to work up to using an electric. Skin's bound to be tender. Sit on the stool."

Peso draped a hot cloth over my face. I tilted my head back so it wouldn't fall off.

"Lily doesn't appreciate her food going cold. We need to move along." Peso removed the cloth. "Do as I do," he said, squirting shaving cream from an aerosol onto his face, then handing the can to me.

It tickled, sort of.

"You have a girlfriend?" Peso asked me in the mirror.

"Naw."

"Girls are particular about facial hair."

That would be the day when a girl noticed my facial hair. People always knew when I was embarrassed. I hoped Peso didn't notice. I copied his moves.

"You've done this a time or two."

"Uh-uh." I wouldn't let Dad near me with a razor in his hand. "Uh-uh." I concentrated.

I found an inch-long hair near my right cheekbone that I didn't know was there. Like Peso, I bent over the sink, cupped my hands, and splashed a rinse.

"You are one handsome young man," Peso said, looking pleased. "Are you sure no mama's waiting on your call?"

My face went hot. I pressed my lips, shook my head.

"Some girl's missing a big opportunity." Peso pushed three bottles forward. "Aftershave seals the deal."

My nose pulled back at the first one; it smelled like a closed-up basement. Peso laughed. The second reminded me of apple cider and the third, the one Peso was wearing, sweet perfume. If it was good enough for him, it was good enough for me.

"You have taste," he said.

I began to wipe down the counter.

"Lily will clean up."

He sure expected a lot of his wife, but he was right about getting to the table. Lily acted huffy when she lifted the cover from my plate. The French toast wasn't burned like Mom did it. I asked for cinnamon and mixed a bit of it with sugar at the side of my plate and sprinkled it on. Mom said syrup cost too much. Lily hummed under her breath as I wolfed down six slices of French toast, four sausages, four pieces of bacon, and kept good manners by saying, "No," when she asked if I wanted more. I downed two orange juices and tasted the coffee Peso insisted I try black because, he said, I'd be freer that way. I supposed that was the kind of thing my old man should be teaching me. I wondered what I should do for Peso in return.

I was thinking about having to drink the coffee when Lily swooped up my cup, saying, "That too cold to drink now," and tossed it into the sink. She looked at Peso in a way that said, Don't make him drink what he don't want.

Peso laughed.

"Best breakfast I ever had," I said, uncomfortable over their exchange.

Lily put one hand on her hip, and said, "Thank you kindly for making that bed." She turned to Peso. "You be gettin' him a haircut and some decent clothes?"

Peso turned to me. "Frenchy, will you please us by staying a day or two?"

It was the oddest invitation I ever heard. "Okay," I said, not too sure.

"Lily, how lucky can we get?"

Lily turned her back and got real busy wiping the counter.

"Frenchy, do you by any chance play table soccer, foosball?"

"Sure," I said, thinking Mom would say I was taking advantage. I heard my old man say in his gruff baritone, *Go find a dog to play with.* Peso exchanged a look with Lily, then put his hand on my shoulder. "No bad things are going to happen to you here, Frenchy. Come, m'boy. The sooner we get you a haircut and some clothes, the sooner we can play."

"I d-don't know," I said.

"You'd be doing me a favor. I've got a regulation table and no one to play with! I'll be right back," he said.

Lily said, "How that man loves to play foos. You got a mind of your own, Frenchy?"

I nodded.

"That's good, real good. Use it," she said, like she was warning me about something. I figured Peso must be a good player.

19

"Ready?" Peso said. He herded me into the garage. I wanted to touch his Mercedes, but didn't. He backed out the car. Behind the big, dark-shingled house we had been in were a couple of smaller houses with cars parked by them. Two workers moved about the yard.

"Your neighbors live close."

"Those houses are mine. I store merchandise in them."

I was thinking that I liked my hair long, that I didn't want a haircut.

Peso bought me mostly Sunday clothes—white dress shirts, ties, colorful polos with a stitched-on guy sitting on a horse, hitting a ball with a long mallet. Peso said how you dressed and how you talked made first and lasting impressions by which people judged you. He bought me two pairs of jeans. I told him it was too much and felt bad about hoping to take the clothes and receipts when I left, so I could return some of them for cash. He bought me dress shoes that I'd never wear and new sneakers.

The bald barber seemed to know Peso. I hung back like a whupped dog.

Peso said, "Short and standard."

Feeling ungrateful, I muttered, "I like it long."

"That's shaggy, not long," Peso said.

The barber pushed his fingers through my hair. "There's a bit of natural wave. It'll look okay styled," he told Peso.

I watched hair drop away, wondering what styled meant. Peso paced and fidgeted. In the corner a woman filed a man's fingernails.

"You're looking older," Peso said, smiling at the barber. "Fifteen any day."

I couldn't help but smile. Sixteen even.

"Next time," Peso told the barber, tipping him.

Peso took me to a restaurant where I ate the biggest hamburger I ever saw and a huge chocolate shake. Then we went back to his house.

Peso's basement game room was far out. I set the bags with my new clothes and old shoes on a chair. Floodlights shone on barbells and a bench. There was a punching bag in the corner and one of those walk-walk-walk machines. A billiard table, a round poker table, and a foosball table with rods that shone like Peso's Mercedes. A guy could win a satin jacket or two off a table like that one. The guys at Greased Lightning—the corner arcade where I play—would be jealous of the slick slaps and shots I could make on this table. "Cool," I said, turning the handle. Peso must be rich. I asked, "What kind of work do you do?"

"Sales," he said. "Jewelry. Well, now." Peso slid his hands against each other competitively. "Let's see what you got." He had wrapped his wrists with athletic tape.

We smacked the ball back and forth. Soon he speeded up and stole my man before I even knew what happened. I was going to be an easy kill. Peso stopped and wiped his forehead with a hanky. "Hey," he said, waving it, "we didn't buy you any of these."

"Don't use 'em," I said.

"What if you find yourself with a pretty girl, ideas on your mind, and no way to nab a bugger?"

"Yuk!"

"That was a rhetorical question," he said, "a question to which no answer is expected. Would you like a couple of tips?" Without waiting for an answer, Peso stood behind me and showed me. "First lesson is how to stand, yeah, like that, second how to hold your wrist. Looser. Practice moves in slow motion before you turn on the speed. Practice passing the ball as slowly as possible."

The rods pushed, pulled, and rotated. Control wasn't easy. I slapped the ball with the foot of a rod man when I had meant to use his head. Slowing down helped. I actually moved the ball all the way down a lane. Practicing slow would make me good.

Peso watched me with his feet wrapped around the legs of a stool and a bottle of spring water in his hand. He asked, "Are you good at defending yourself?"

I got beat up quicker 'n any slap shot. "Rhetorical, right?"

I could tell Peso liked me playing back what I had heard from him. His face lit up like Mom's when she was carrying in my birthday cake. "Let's see," he said, pointing to boxing gloves hanging on a peg.

I couldn't get my sneakers on fast enough.

CHAPTER FOUR

Once I agreed to stay, Peso didn't ask a lot of questions
and neither did I. Soon after, Lily and Peso must have settled
something about me because Lily stopped scowling at Peso. It
turned out that Lily was Peso's hired help since before the day I
was born. When Peso was out of town she stayed overnight. "You
got a good mind," Lily said more than once. I liked her
encouragement. "Don't do anything you don't want to." She
listened close when Peso corrected my grammar like she was
learning, too. In time, he suggested I needed something that
sounded awful—erudition—which turned out to mean learning.

Peso enrolled me in Catholic school because he said probably
no one would look for me there; that's how thoughtful he was.
Catholic school is what Mom had wanted for me, but the old man
said we couldn't afford it. I thought of her often, wondered how
she was doing, if she got over me, or if she was still looking. I
wanted to call her, but knew it was a bad idea. I had left and was
doing okay. Peso even let me drive his Mercedes twice around his
half-mile racetrack before washing and waxing it.

The one rule he had was to stay away from trucks that came and
went during the night to other houses on the property. I wasn't
going to disobey. I liked learning driving tricks, but would have

skipped the grammar lessons. Peso said acne was ruining my good looks and took me to a derm ... a skin doctor. Peso told the doctor he wanted it cleared up by my fifteenth birthday. That's today and my acne's gone; that's how convincing Peso was.

I could hardly wait to see my birthday presents because Peso had a knack of knowing what would please me. We were almost done with dinner in the dining room. When we ate in the dining room, Lily had to act like the servant she was. She had cleaned the house until everything gleamed, even the hardwood floors around the rugs in the dining and living rooms. Lily poured my coffee, which I had learned to drink black. She rested her hand on my shoulder and addressed Peso, "I'd like to say somethin'."

"Go ahead."

"Frenchy," she said, "I want you to know you do us proud, real proud."

"Thanks," I said, feeling warm all over. Peso said Lily fussed over me too much. Then Lily got up and strode through the swinging door into the kitchen.

Peso said, "It's been really good having you here."

I could spar good now, uh—spar well—and was fast on the foosball rods. Peso said I was not to be discounted as a driver, though I wasn't eligible for my learner's permit until today. I hoped we would get it tomorrow. "Thanks," I said, feeling mushy.

The kitchen door swung open and Lily appeared with the biggest lit-up birthday cake I ever saw. Chocolate didn't go good with acne, so inside the cake would be white or yellow. Both of them had better voices than I had. Peso cut the first slice and Lily gave it to me. I waited until we were all served before digging in.

"It's real good. I mean ... really good, Lily." I glanced at Peso.

He smiled like everything was a-okay. I ate a second smaller piece of cake and finished my coffee.

Peso said, "Lily, two of the large brandy snifters, please."

Her hand went to her heart.

Peso's expression was stern as an old nun's. "The man's fifteen. We're going to drink a toast."

Lily's expression took on the kind of crampy look you get when Milk of Magnesia's working faster 'n you'd like.

"Lily," Peso said, stern as I ever heard him.

Lily unlocked the cupboard with the frosted glass doors and took out two snifters. I had wondered what was inside it. Her hand shook as she placed one in front of me and one in front of Peso. She went back to the cupboard and brought out a bottle of VSOP cognac spelled C-o-u-r-v-o-i-s-i-e-r and set it down beside him.

"Thank you, Lily. Dinner was lovely. You may go."

She turned and looked at me like I was drowning and she didn't know how to swim to save me. "Frenchy—"

Peso snapped his fingers.

Lily darted away.

Peso studied me like a book he had meant to read for a long time, and now was going to read all the way through. No one was more surprised than me—than *I*—that I had learned to like reading. Then his expression softened and he asked, "Do you know what oxymoron means?"

"A moron with moxie?"

Peso threw his head back and laughed. "Not too far off."

"Frenchy," Peso said with a strained smile, "Let's take our brandy by the fireplace."

Excited—it was time for my present—I followed him.

"Like this," he said, showing me. He rolled the glass between his palms. "It's a ritual. Your hands warm it; then sniff, inhale, let the scent please your nose so you will savor its taste." Then Peso, who seldom touched me, reached out and brushed my cheek with the back of his fingers, triggering the memory of him touching me that first night. He said, "I thought you would grow taller."

I tucked in my chin. Five-feet-six added up to runt, making my old man right.

Peso saw my disappointment, tousled my short hair, and said, "There's still time."

"Hope so."

I was anxious to see my present, but knew Peso did things at his own pace. I had learned not to push him. He produced a small gift-wrapped box. I tore the paper off. A Pet Rock, a smooth pebble about an inch-and-a-half long on a bed of straw with a little book on the care and feeding of this pet.

I looked up and smiled and said a sarcastic, "Thanks."

Peso laughed. "You wouldn't want to be the only one in the world without one, would you?"

I thumbed through the miniature book, looking like I was too interested in it to pay attention to him.

"When you can care for a pet," Peso said, sounding very pleased with himself, "you're ready for more responsibility." He reached inside his suit jacket pocket for an envelope.

Inside was a plastic card that at first I thought was a credit card. Then I saw that it was an Indiana driver's license with my birth date wrong.

Peso had deliberately made me three years older. "Is this legit?"

"I thought someone might be tipped off if you applied for a learner's permit. I hope I did the right thing."

I couldn't believe it. I moved my thumb over the birth date. "Thanks," I said, feeling real grown-up and grateful.

Peso took my face between his hands and smacked me hard and wet on the lips. "You're welcome," he said.

My dad would never kiss me on the mouth, but the old man sure didn't know much about being a dad. I didn't know what to say or do. My fingers touched my lips. I felt odd and confused. "Thanks," I said, grinning uncomfortably. I took out my billfold and carefully slid the license under the plastic window.

Peso watched me, rolling his snifter between his palms.

I copied him, inhaled its scent.

Peso raised his glass and waited for me to raise mine. "Cheers," he said.

"Cheers," I said.

The cognac was still burning a path to my stomach when Peso refilled our snifters and we toasted again. Then Peso pulled out a set of keys and dangled them in front of me.

"Really? A car? Mine? " I wished the old man could see me. "You mean it?"

"Well," Peso said, "the title's in my name—for insurance purposes. However, m' main man, you may consider it yours." He stood and I thought we were going to wherever the car was but he cuffed me lightly on the chin and said, smiling, "In due time. In due time."

Peso sure knew how to make a guy happy. I latched him into a hug, realizing I couldn't tell the nuns or any of the kids at school, which made me sad. "Thank you, thank you. Can I see it?"

Peso sparred with me, deliberately delaying. I felt a warm glow. *What kind of car is it? A clunker?* Peso wouldn't give a clunker.

"There's more," Peso said, his eyes teasing now. He dug deep into his pocket for a small, silver-wrapped box. This was a birthday of small boxes. What else could be so small?

An earring?

"It's a diamond," he said.

The few guys I knew who wore earrings were black. Unsure, I looked up, questioning. "Does it make us engaged?" I asked, trying to cover my embarrassment.

"You can get your ear pierced," Peso said. "Or put it in a bracelet or a tie tack, whatever."

I didn't want to hurt his feelings. "I'll think about it," I said, making it sound important. I expected we'd go look at my car, which was probably hidden in one of the garages to the other houses, but Peso's attitude changed.

"Kick off your shoes," he said. "Get comfortable. Drink your brandy." He moved to refill my snifter, paused, and asked, "Maybe you'd prefer champagne, something else?"

I never tasted champagne, nor cognac neither. I had snitched the old man's beer and liked the warm, cozy feel a couple of beers gave me. I would have liked a Coca-Cola. "Cognac's cool," I said, not wanting to hurt his feelings. I drank quickly, hoping to see my wheels sooner. "You're teasing me," I said.

"It's intentional." Peso got up and unlocked a double door closet I'd never noticed before because the doors were part of the paneling. He took out a white bear skin rug and placed it in front of the fireplace.

"Wow! Did you kill it?"

Peso chuckled. "No. I reserve it for special occasions, though. It's especially nice with a fire."

I caught the oversized pillow he threw at me. Two more followed. I felt a little woozy.

"Bathroom break," he said, putting his arm around me. I laughed.

We stood side by side and targeted our spray. We returned to the fireplace with our arms around each other. I spotted the keys on the table, knew better than to push Peso.

"I didn't forget," Peso said, laughing at me. He tugged at my belt. "Loosen it. Take your shirt off. Get comfortable."

"There's another present?"

Peso draped his tie and shirt and belt over the back of the sofa. I hadn't seen his biceps before. The man worked out all right. I draped my shirt and belt over the chair, propped a pillow against it on the floor, pushed the bear rug near and sat on it. Soft and thick, it scratch—tickled. I swirled the cognac in the snifter, inhaled, drank, felt like a kite reaching for the sun.

"Frenchy," Peso said, toasting me for the umpteenth time, "It's time for your sexual initiation."

That got my attention. I didn't see no girls.

He studied me. "Sex is about a lot more than masturbating and wet dreams. A man needs to learn about everything, starting with jewelry."

I must've looked blank.

"I mean you need to recognize and cherish the real thing when you have it." I didn't know where they came from, but Peso began putting on necklaces. One looked like diamonds. Then there was a short one with red stones that he called a ruby choker, and a light green rectangular pendant on a black cord that dangled below his belly button. Maybe he was leading up to my working in his jewelry investment, which is how Peso referred to his business. He pushed bracelets up his arms.

Peso said, "It's warm in here," and took off his briefs. He lay beside me on the soft fur, one elbow on the pillow propping up his head, the other fingering the necklaces. "Can you tell which of these gems are real, which fake?"

I felt strange, but then I had felt that way at the beginning of many of Peso's lessons. I learned in time. I touched the stones in the necklaces, moving them toward the light of the fire, expecting a hint from Peso about what I was supposed to learn. The necklaces lay against his caramel-colored skin, chest hair poking through. His eyes were hard as those gems. Unfamiliar feelings bounced around inside me. My heart *thump-thumped*, probably too much cognac. I was aware of his hand on my thigh. I remembered—red stones, rubies, clear ones, diamonds. The heavy green pendant felt more like rock than a gem. I let go of it, said, "I can't tell."

"Drink." Peso handed me my snifter and waited for me to empty it, poured more, then put his hand on the back of my head and drew me close. "Let me show you."

I resisted, not knowing what he intended.

29

"Hey, buddy, loosen up. The clear ones can be zircons, fake diamonds. Good fakes. Diamond-cut glass. These," he fingered the choker, "are real. Such gems are valuable and can be yours."

What would I want with jewelry? I didn't have a girlfriend. Peso took my hand and pressed my index and middle fingers down on the green pendant. I saw his hard-on. A ball of fear roiled in the pit of my stomach. I pulled back. Peso held my hand tight to the green rectangle.

"Jade," he said. "Plastic stays cold when you touch it, jade turns warm. That's how you tell real from fake. A better test is to touch it with your lips."

I tried to pull away.

"Frenchy, Frenchy, don't ruin my best birthday present. Do you want to be a virgin forever?"

His tone suggested if I wasn't ready for initiation, I wasn't ready for a car either. I remembered Lily's warning, Don't do what you don't want to, which didn't make sense until now. Peso was telling me jewelry was about sex, kissing jade was about sex. I tried to think, but my penis knew something I didn't. Peso touched my hard-on. I snatched a quick breath.

"That's it. Pants off." It sounded like an order, yet he didn't make a move.

The guys at school didn't know nothin'. The nuns sure didn't talk about sex. Sooner or later I needed to learn. Peso hadn't steered me wrong before. He watched as I stepped out of my briefs. My eyes glued to his hard-on.

"Magnificent, isn't it?" He turned and showed me his profile. "M'boy, that's love. Rod up, ready for action." Peso took hold of my ready-for-action rod and squeezed. Pain-like pleasure shuddered through me. "Lie down," he said. "Lie down."

I did.

He stroked me gently a couple times, then removed the bracelets and two short necklaces and lay down beside me. "Tell

30

me if the jade's real. Kiss it." He pressed my lips to the jade below his belly button. I smelled his man smell. "Warm," I said, wanting him to touch me that way again, not wanting to admit it.

Peso pressed my lips to his erection. "Feel the heat? Warmer than jade. That's what you do to me." His eyes burned with ... want. "Scoring, Frenchy, is about how long you can wait and how many times you come." He traced the rim of the head of my penis with his index finger, then rolled his fingers across the head, squeezed, and let go.

"Jesus!" I swallowed, wanted to jerk off.

"Frenchy, there are two of us. Always put your partner before yourself. Always."

He pressed his body against mine and peered into my eyes and moved closer and covered my mouth with his mouth and sucked until I felt my tongue struggling for air inside him. Peso pressed me against the bear rug. I pushed against him. Finally he raised his head. His skin glistened. Panting, I reached for him.

He said, "Easy. You don't want this over too soon."

He picked up a small plastic bottle I hadn't noticed before and squirted clear liquid onto my chest, his penis. "AstroGlide," he said, straddling me and slathering the stuff around my chest, down across my stomach. Then before I knew what had happened he slid his penis up the length of my body right into my mouth. He held his weight with his hands on my arms, said, "You won't choke."

"Slow, real slow ... that's it. Show me how you would like it, exactly how you would like it ... ahhhh ... that feels so goooood. Ease up. Don't let me come … that's it, that feels ... goooood, that's uh, Uh-U-UH-HH-HHH-HHH." Peso pulled out before he came and bent to me. "Bend down on me, boy. It's called 69. You know what to do."

In no time I couldn't hold back, I humped-humped-humped and he let me. Just as I peaked like a house afire, he pushed deep into my throat. "Open your throat, tighten your lips. Open. Tighter. Tighter. Uh. Uh. Uh.Uh. Uh. Uh."

I turned my head, trying not to swallow. Peso clapped up my chin holding my mouth closed until I did, then he relaxed, face red, panting.

Confused, mind a-jumble, I snatched the snifter and swished cognac in my mouth and downed it all.

Peso chuckled and said, "You'll get used to it."

After a bit he handed me a clean, folded handkerchief. Before I had even wiped my mouth, he was at me again, saying, "I waited a long, long time for this." I didn't want him to stop.

Peso pulled me up on all fours. "Grab the bear's head," he said, lathering me with AstroGlide. I felt a shot of pain, grabbed onto the bear's head, and held on for dear life as it slid around the floor. Peso told me to count to myself. "Maintain control," he said.

Then before I knew it we had switched places and I was the one zapping Peso like he was my old man—bam, bam, bam—shoving that bear around the room until I fell limp and spent and ... initiated.

Later when I opened my eyes Peso was wiping my brow with a warm cloth, looking like the happiest man in the world. I wanted to think, but couldn't. My mouth felt real dry. I licked my lips. I was sore. He offered the snifter. Possession filled his eyes. I didn't like it.

"Remember the first lesson with the Mercedes?"

First he had taught me how to brake. I nodded.

"Knowing when and how to brake with sex is important too. Unless you're willing to risk getting VD or worse." He paused to let that sink in. He narrowed his eyes, which meant whatever he was going to say was important. "Stick with one clean partner, only one. It could mean the difference between life and death."

I wondered how many only-one partners he had stashed away, then realized Peso didn't want VD any more than I did. He came to me and soon had me glowing again like a burning kite flying into the sun.

Later I remembered Peso saying, "You're my one and only now, Frenchy, my one and only."

I had forgotten all about my best present.

CHAPTER FIVE

The occupational therapist stood behind Nathan,
watching as he pounded dents in the square of copper. Her
nearness invaded his space like she expected him to somehow
make more room for her. Each time he struck the chisel with the
wooden mallet, geometric planes sent particles of light bursting
against a dark red sky. His parents had brought him home to
Minneapolis for *this*?

He didn't even know why he was in the hospital. Back when
they had met with the doctor in Princeton, his parents already
looked twenty years older. Dr. Tennstedt, whom Nathan had never
met before, asked, "Nathan, do you know who these people are?"
In Admitting they had asked him what day it was, what month it
was, who was president of the United States. He had questions of
his own: *Where is Cheryl? Is she all right?*

Dr. Tennstedt's words sounded electronically altered and his
clothes looked like he had slept in them. The man turned to his
father and said, "We're still testing. It's too early to say."

"What did we do wrong? What?" his mother asked.

The doctor said, "We don't know what causes episodes like
this."

You are in an episode. Get in there and fight, telegraphed his father.

Nathan raised the mallet and hit the chisel. At age six he had glued wood-shaving "hair" onto a plywood dog that Uncle Carl had shaped with his jigsaw, a dog he named Hovander, a name that made him giggle. Unlike his father, Uncle Carl complimented his work. What good was it to be in Minneapolis if he couldn't canoe or sail on the city lakes or go to a concert at Orchestra Hall? They kept him locked in the mental illness ward. He was supposed to bring out the hidden image in the copper.

At first they had given him a very personal multiple-choice test: When I think of my mother I hold my urine. I am more often constipated than not. I would rather be a forest ranger than a nanny. *Was Cheryl safe? How had she screamed with her mouth closed?* He had a shelf covered with trophies for ice skating, wrestling, and debate and they treated him like he had no skills. Though he would never sing a solo on a stage, he played the guitar moderately well.

"Tuition's paid for the semester," his father told Dr. Tennstedt, as if that explained everything.

Listening, Nathan patted his hair, a new habit he seemed to have developed. It consoled him. His mother's hanky *flapped,* noisy as a big flag in a strong wind. A hoarfrosted branch *click-click-clicked* against the window. His father's anger buzzed the room.

"To answer your question, we suspect schizophrenia, an illness that occurs with little or no warning. Advance signs are insomnia, difficulty with concentration, hallucinations of sound and sight, which might explain why Nathan thought his girlfriend was screaming when she wasn't."

Cheryl *was* screaming. They weren't being honest. When the clerk at Red Owl tried to give a homeless person change for a ten when he had given her a twenty, Nathan, who was bagging the man's groceries, had simply reached into her cash drawer and

35

given the man the ten. Honesty made you feel better about yourself. This doctor certainly needed to feel better about himself!

"Schizophrenia can be triggered by illicit drugs. Nathan's blood tests showed no drugs."

"Nathan would never do drugs," his mother said.

"It's a thought disorder that affects more males than females, usually persons with high IQ. Stress is also a trigger."

Stress! Nathan tried to make the copper square disappear. It stayed where it was.

"Messages misfire between left and right brain. One-third of patients live adequate lives. One-third eventually lead reasonably satisfying, productive lives."

By age five Nathan could stop his favorite marble shooter at nearly the same spot every time. Why was making dents so difficult? *I've lost my marbles.* Nathan cut his thumb on the edge of the copper. A drop of blood appeared.

Nathan struck the chisel HARD, HARD, HARD for his dad, for his mom, for Debbie, for all the doctors who kept him locked up. For not helping Cheryl, he struck it HARDER, HARDER, HARDER, muttering obscenities until two attendants arrived and took him by the elbows, and escorted him back to his room with his feet barely touching the floor.

CHAPTER SIX

I needed to crack the books. This was the last Saturday before final exams and graduation. A part of me wished Mom could see me get my diploma. Peso never tried to find out about my family and I didn't volunteer anything. Mom would be proud. Peso had promised me a job after high school. Early in the evening I dropped off Sandy, the girl I had been seeing on the sly, and turned the Jaguar toward home, not paying attention to time.

The first time I saw this black 1972 XJ12 Jag four-door sedan, I was disappointed, thought it an old man's car. I would have preferred a late model sports car, but Peso said no one would suspect this car, whatever that meant. The guys at school thought power steering, power windows, and standard AC were cool, and my driver's license opened doors. Once when I drank too much, Peso said, "If a cop shows up here, Frenchy, you're history."

As long as Peso didn't find out about Sandy and I didn't bring friends home and kept my grades up, and gave good head, he would stay off my case. I had learned not to cross him. At the beginning of the school year, Peso said, "Wednesday, Friday, and Saturday nights, don't come home before midnight." Why would I argue?

I could defend myself with my fists, had won the regional foosball tourney, and knew four ways to tie a tie. Sandy was the only glitch. I wanted to do more than feel her up, but if Peso found out, I would be on the street without that diploma.

I turned up the volume of the radio—Elton John's "Captain Fantastic and the Brown Dirt Cowboy." He was one of a kind, Elton John. I wondered how I had ever worked up the courage to ask Peso if I could take a girl to the prom. He mussed my hair, laughed, and said, "Choose your jewels," meaning I could wear any piece of jewelry he owned. He even reserved a tux and a limo for me, told me to ask the color of my date's dress and order a corsage. "What else do you need? Disco lessons?"

"Thanks, but no, thanks," I said.

Instead Sandy and a couple of her friends giggled to death teaching me disco routines. I was quick on my feet, an unexpected payback from jumping rope forwards and backwards like a banshee. Sandy made me feel important in a way Peso didn't and I liked it. I turned the Jag into the lane. A truck I hadn't seen before was backed up to the front porch of one of the other houses. Curious, I parked the Jag in the garage, got out, and moved toward the truck. Slits of light shone alongside the window shades. I heard what sounded like sobs ... a girl's sobs. I stopped when I saw Peso's silhouette on the back porch, waving his hand like trying to move traffic along.

Then the silhouette of a female appeared, head tucked low. Behind her was another girl, and another shuffling—six, seven, eight, nine girls strung together at the wrists. Peso turned and looked in my direction. I ducked behind a shrub. My heart drummed. The girls were thin. Peso shoved the last one into the back of the truck, closed the door, and slid a padlock through the loop on the door, then punched it with the heel of his hand. When the truck turned around I would be spotted, so I ran toward the Jag, intending to hide in the garage, but the truck's headlights caught me first.

Peso yelled, "What are you doing home?"

I couldn't see my watch, figured it must be earlier than Peso's curfew. My breathing raced to hell and back. I made fists to hide my shakes, wondered what was going down, said, "Got to hit the books. Exams." I could feel Peso's eyes boring through me. The sound of the truck tapered off. I ran into the house and up to my room. The images of the girls kept replaying in my head. I wanted to study, but couldn't.

Later Peso came to my room. His body was rigid, his expression a mix of anger and dread. He looked at me and said slowly like he had rehearsed the words, "Frenchy, I thought I was clear that you were not to be home before midnight on my business nights."

I shook like a sissy, wanted to deck him and cry like a kid.

He said, "You wouldn't so upset if you hadn't come home."

"Don't blame me for what I seen!" I picked up the stupid Pet Rock and threw it over his shoulder. It hit the wall before the floor.

"*Saw.* What you *saw.* What do you think you saw? What?"

This was no time for a friggin' grammar lesson. I knew what I saw, but didn't know what it meant, was afraid to know what it meant.

"It was just business."

"What kind of business?"

Peso narrowed his eyes. "The kind that feeds you."

I couldn't concentrate, spent Sunday at Sandy's. She drilled me on history stuff. I kept telling myself I didn't need an A or a B; all I needed was a pass. I left home early and returned late. Lily sensed the rift between Peso and me. Maybe Peso would explain what I saw, in a way I could understand. Who was I fooling? I needed to graduate and get out.

When prom night arrived I put on the tux at the rental store, called the limo service and told them to pick me up there. Even seeing Sandy with her long blond hair piled high on top of her head, wearing a pale blue gown that showed every curve, didn't make me forget. Twisting and turning her on the dance floor, I found myself adding up what Peso had done for me, working back from the tux, the corsage, the limo, Catholic school, boxing lessons, safe sex, the early driver's license, the Jag. There was no end in sight of what he would do for me, if—

On a syncopated beat, I whirled Sandy away from me, caught and squeezed her tight before I spun her out again. A part of me wanted to parade her in front of Peso to make him jealous. I'd be on the street without wheels. I resented Peso keeping a big secret. Still, a part of me resisted knowing. The music stopped. I pulled Sandy close and kissed her hard.

She appeared surprised, confused. "I can't breathe," she said.

I kissed her again, this time tenderly. "You look beautiful," I said. "Really beautiful."

She turned bashful. In that moment I found myself asking why I resented Peso's big secret when I was keeping such a big one of my own?

I didn't know what to do with Sandy later in the evening or what she expected. As the evening wore on, I became glad for the limo and the driver because I doubted, even if I wanted to, that I could get it up for Sandy. I figured that Peso had ordered the limo as insurance against me being alone with a girl. That's exactly what he had done! On the way home I held her hand. Aware that the driver was watching, I walked her to the door and kissed her lightly on the mouth and waited until she was inside and I heard the door lock. No one needed Peso for an enemy.

When I got home Peso was sitting in his big leather chair, shoes off, feet on the ottoman, brandy snifters, one empty, one with brandy in it, and the bottle on the table beside him. His silence lasted into the next century. I fidgeted, didn't want to be out, didn't want to be in.

Finally Peso said, "Frenchy, I don't like how we're treating each other. Let's not go to sleep without resolving this."

I moved over to the table, poured brandy into the empty snifter, sipped it.

Peso looked hard into my eyes. "You saw what you saw."

"Jesus, that's a relief! I thought you were going to turn me into a blind man or try to convince me it was my imagination."

He rolled his snifter between his palms. "Frenchy, there are some things a white man can never know, not *know*, because a white man's experience is not the same as a black man's experience."

We had never discussed race. What did that have to do with anything?

"When I was your age," Peso said, "I sold used cars in our neighborhood and was a pretty good salesman, but soon learned that my customers couldn't afford the rundown cars they bought. When they returned them I had to return my commission. Before long, I ended up owing more commission than I had earned. I wanted—needed—to sell something that would bring a bigger return."

"So?" Whatever it was, I knew I wasn't going to like it.

Peso said, "I looked up because looking down was no way up. Figuring people die and, one way or another, folks bury 'em, I tried selling caskets; those commissions arrived on the installment plan. I saved up and took the Dale Carnegie course, which is how I learned the importance of grammar in the white world. I hired someone to teach me manners, how to dress, and thought I was on my way."

"What about the other night?"

He raised a resentful eyebrow, sipped and thought. "Let me tell this in my own way."

41

He waited for my reluctant agreement.

When I nodded, he continued. "I phoned potential employers, shared my sales history, and asked for an interview. The man usually said he could really use a salesman like me, wanted to meet me ASAP. When I arrived he would take one look at me and say, 'Sorry, the position's filled.' It didn't take too many rejections to figure out no white man was going to hire me."

I understood rejection. My old man rejected me until I felt like a reject. But what did that have to do with putting girls tied together in a truck?

"Until then, see, I was thinking of success like a white man. I decided to start thinking like a black man. Where is the money I can get? That answer was plain enough—drugs, gambling, weapons, lowlife, women. I parsed the possibilities. Unreliable people dealing in drugs, gambling. Weapons promised scrapes with the law, a no-win in any double cross. That left women. You might say, I happened into my business by research and default. I spotted some sad runaway girls who needed a meal and a helping hand and that got me started."

I guess I knew, just didn't want to believe it. I thought of Dad pounding on Mom. How could anyone hurt someone else like that?

"It's simple economics, supply and demand. I helped them live; they helped me live. The girls wanted to look pretty, to feel grown-up, to be on their own."

I had tons of questions, didn't know what to ask first. I dropped my bow tie on the table, asked, "Is that what you had in mind for me?"

"I don't do boys. Never." The way he forced eye contact, I tended to believe him. "You and I were a sure-win cinch. Something good for both of us."

What I had seen was no-win. "If they're so grateful, why were they crying? Why were their hands tied?"

He sighed as if he were tired of all this, said, "I pick up runaways, feed and shelter them until I have enough for a class with Miss Edie. Miss Edie teaches them how to dress, how to walk, basic etiquette, and the math necessary to serve high-class, wealthy johns. What you saw, Frenchy, were young women awakened in the middle of the night. They were sleepy, scared, and tied only for transportation purposes. Later they'll be grateful, beholden. When that happens there is no need for … curtailment."

I could ask to talk to some of the girls, but he wouldn't introduce me to anyone not grateful. The part about finding the position filled happened, I knew. Peso had taught me how to make fast starts and take tight corners in the Jag, how to get in and out of skids. This was one of those tight spots. I wanted no part of his work.

"Do you expect me to help with this … business?"

He swallowed and cleared his throat and shook his head. "For you, I have a driving job in mind, was going to tell you when—"

"Shuttle girls? That's against the law! No thanks."

Peso's eyes filled with pain. I didn't like hurting him but I wasn't going to get hurt because of what he did. "Tell me I can leave anytime I want to."

"Oh, Frenchy, you are not a prisoner. I love you. Don't you know that?"

I had waited to hear those words and now I wasn't so sure I belonged here. I wanted to take off and never come back, was well aware that Peso owned the Jag.

To satisfy me he said, "You may leave if you want to."

That felt like a Mack truck lifted off my chest. I knew to press the point now or forever hold my peace. "What happens to the girls?"

"After they complete Miss Edie's, I give each of them a dowry of jewelry so they can dress every bit the part they have been

43

taught to play. Clearly they have the means to leave if and when they choose."

That painted a slightly different picture. "Can they really leave? Who, where is this Miss Edie?"

"Yes, they may leave. I won't tell you about Miss Edie."

Was he protecting me, or her, or all of us? I didn't want to be on the street without money and food and clothes ever again. Neither did I want to break the law and end up in jail because I was too stupid to know what was going down.

"I won't drive tied-up girls. I won't take minors across state lines."

He breathed into next year. "I said I would keep you out of Nam and I did, didn't I?"

Since the war had ended how would I know? Peso seemed to have contacts where even God didn't. He would have kept me out. I nodded.

"Are you willing to make maps?" Peso seemed more confident now. "Decipher and drive discreet routes, say, to out-of-the-way places, mark where it's safe to stop for gas, food, sleep?"

There was nothing illegal about that. "Alone?"

"Yes."

I felt some relief. That would buy me time to decide what I really wanted to do. "Put the Jag in my name."

Peso acted as if he hadn't heard me. "Pay's better than you'll find anywhere else." Then he hesitated, said, "In due time."

I considered asking if I could date Sandy, figured I'd better quit while I was ahead. Peso didn't want me to push him any more than I wanted him to push me. "Okay," I said. *For now anyway.*

Peso's movie-star smile broke free. "To the future," he said, handing me the snifter.

"The future," I said, thinking, *God help me.*

CHAPTER SEVEN

After our talk Peso was especially nice to me. He even threw a graduation party and invited my friends. The guys went ape over the game room and gym equipment. My new job paid more than I thought possible. With my first paycheck, I signed up for a credit card and purchased a ring—mini full-cut diamonds around a sapphire—a friendship token for Peso. I wanted him to know I was grateful for all he had done for me. While I didn't see any more signs of girls on the property, each time I took to the road with the atlas and the list of state highway department phone numbers to check on construction delays, I promised myself this trip would be my last. I was saving money to buy my own wheels. From time to time I drove past Mom's with the hope of catching a glimpse of her. I didn't know if she still lived there or even was alive. Then one day I caught sight of her just as she was going in the door. I knew it was her by the curve of her shoulders. Her hair had some gray in it. I thought about knocking on her door, decided it would only complicate things. I didn't want to explain where I'd been or about my job. Even though I was doing nothing illegal, I couldn't shake the notion that someone would nail me for something somewhere, somehow, some day. My job proved drab and boring and—Peso's word—lucrative.

I traveled northern Minnesota, northern Montana, the Dakotas—Grain Belt Beer country—flat hinterlands with amber waves of grain, listening to Canadian radio stations that came in clearer than our own. I drew detailed maps of places no one wanted to visit. At the end of the day I made small talk with farmers in roadside taverns. They discussed different kinds of balers that left hay in round or square or cylinder shapes, subjects that made me itch to get on with life. But whenever I thought about leaving, I found myself asking, Where else could an ambitious, inexperienced high school grad make cash so fast?

I kept seeing Sandy on the sly, which was easier now that I was working. I kept wondering if I made love with her, what it would feel like. Before Sandy left for college, I invited her to come along for a week. I don't know what she told her mom, but she came. Tooling north on a deserted east/west Iowa two-lane with her beside me I felt like I owned the world. Sandy wore her bleached hair in pigtails coiled on top of her head. I reached out and tugged one free.

"Ow," she said, laughing.

The way her eyes lit up, my pants tightened. I said, "There's a lot more I'd like to touch."

She twisted the end of the pigtail around her index finger and smiled and looked straight ahead. Tasseled corn swished by on both sides of the road. Her hair was as gold as those tassels.

"What do you see in me anyway?" I asked.

She smiled, didn't say anything. Her home wasn't any more heaven than mine had been. On that score, we meshed. We talked about school, sports, classmates we knew, and laughed a lot. I certainly hadn't mentioned anything about life with Peso. We liked some of the same books, though she read romances and deep stuff while I liked westerns and adventures. She introduced me to Holden Caulfield, a character that reminded me of myself, except he acted out his rebellion while I stuffed mine.

She said, "I like the way you dress, your good manners ... your independence, the way you dance, your smile."

My chest swelled, taking credit, even though deep down I knew Peso was the one she should thank.

"Thanks." I could hardly get the word out. We passed a dirt lane between two cornfields. I braked and backed up to it.

"Frenchy?"

I liked hearing her say my name.

I said, "I just want to check something out," and could tell she knew what I had in mind. "Okay?"

She lowered her gaze, pulled in her chin, and seemed suddenly shy. "Okay."

I parked in what, judging by the tracks, was a tractor turnaround. I got out and walked down the lane to be sure no one was about. I removed a blanket from the trunk and some AstroGlide, which I had brought along just in case, and took her hand. We walked into the corn. A few rows hid you from everyone and everything. I stopped and counted the number of rows we had walked in, not to lose our bearings and get lost. Pleased as a bee sinking into a flower, I beamed at her. Sandy's breasts rose and fell with her breathing. Sunlight lit the freckles across her nose.

"I missed you," she said.

"I missed you, too. Let's try not to break plants," I said, knowing how hard farming was, how little farmers made. I took off my shoes, pointed the toes in the direction from which we'd come, a clue I'd taken from Hansel and Gretel's breadcrumbs. I stuck my billfold and keys inside one shoe. We folded the blanket long and narrow and laid it between rows. Sandy kicked off her sandals and took off her jeans and folded them. I resisted grabbing and saddling her. She seemed tiny as a doll. "Let me," I said, touching her shoulder. I kissed it, slid the straps of her bra down, and squeezed her breasts.

"Um," she said. "Not so hard. "Do you have protection?"

47

"Yes."

I remembered that scoring meant control even if I felt like pummeling her, to put my partner first. I turned her around and let her bra straps drop and held her so her elbows were pulled back and looked into her blue-as-the-sky eyes, and slid my other hand inside her panties. I hoped it wouldn't be too obvious that I hadn't been with a girl before. Old Glory stood proud with want. I hoped I'd know what to do and when. My fingers fumbled for her opening.

"Not so hard. What are you doing?" she asked.

I withdrew my hand. "I want you so much." I undressed. She looked at my penis like she had never seen a hard-on before.

"It's ... b-beautiful."

I pressed it against her, bent and bit her nipple.

"Frenchy—"

I covered her mouth with mine and sucked like I hoped to pull her tongue free. I slid my hands over her body, down her sides, across the flat of her tummy, up the inside of her legs, explored the secrets of her folds.

"You're hurting."

"Sorry." I took one nipple into my mouth and sucked.

"Ow!"

I sucked the other, kneaded her with my hands. She felt so soft and warm and moist. I liked the way she squirmed and tried to push me off. I wanted her, all of her. The more she tried to push me away, the harder I clasped. I rolled her over on her stomach.

"Don't! Don't do that!"

Her tone stopped me even though it sounded like I wouldn't get another chance when I wanted lots of them. I turned her over and pushed my fingers into her with my thumb on top and made like the vibrator I had seen in magazines. I liked the way she tried to ease up and away, the way she arched her back, her feminine sounds. No matter what I did or wanted, Peso pushed on, so that's what I did. I knelt with my butt in her face and bent down on her. She fought at first, then her breaths came short and fast and I knew I was onto something. I turned around and kissed her on the mouth and explored her moistness with my fingers, trying to learn what parts did what. I had never seen such soft eyes. Peso's eyes were distant and hard, like he couldn't see me. She was moist and ready, breathing in spurts. I slid on the condom and moved into her, easing slow at first to give her time to get used to me, then bammed high into the home prairie, golden tassels dancing in the wind, giving her every ounce of pleasure I had. I released with a loud cry and dropped my weight onto her.

"Get off."

I figured I would catch my breath and we'd go at it again. I saw my teeth marks around her nipple.

"Get off!"

Confused, I rolled off.

She reached for her shorts.

"Don't," I said, touching her arm.

She was crying. "That was awful. Just awful."

"Sandy, what's wrong? Give me a minute. I'll try again, do it right."

She was examining her nipple.

"Please. I didn't mean to hurt you."

She picked up both pairs of shoes and started toward the car. I could tell by the way she walked that she hurt. I grabbed the blanket and my clothes and stumbled after her. "Wait! Please. I didn't mean to hurt you. I didn't. I promise I won't touch you, not unless you say it's okay."

She stood in the lane and turned toward me. Tears dropped from her chin. I pulled on my pants, my shirt, didn't even know what I had done wrong. I couldn't bring myself to tell her I didn't know what I was doing. "Sandy, I'm sorry, let me—"

She took my billfold and keys out of my shoe and dropped the shoes and moved toward the car. "Take me home."

Moments ago I couldn't have felt higher; now I felt like scum of the earth. In addition, I felt guilty for betraying Peso, who would ask for an explanation about why my work wasn't done. Sandy sat in the back seat and wasn't going to forgive me because nothing I could say could make a difference. Remorse filled me, and fear—*can I ever make it with a woman?*

CHAPTER EIGHT

After I took Sandy home I phoned Peso, told him I was holed up in a motel with food poisoning, which was true. Full of guilt for how I had hurt Sandy, even though I didn't exactly know how, I got and stayed drunk on Grain Belt. I was still pissed at Peso for not telling me about those girls until I saw them. One moment I knew I'd shed Peso once and for all and the next I still wanted to stay to earn enough to buy my wheels of freedom. I trekked through Nebraska, Kansas, and Missouri, and stalled returning home until the leaves were almost off the trees. The kitchen door opened as I eased the Jag into the garage and Peso stood there bare-chested and barefoot, looking like he hadn't slept in awhile.

Without meeting his eyes, I bent for the cooler on the passenger seat. I didn't feel like making any intimate move. Peso usually waited for me to make the first one because it made him feel wanted. He followed on my heels like Morton did, wanting to be petted.

He asked, "Are you still angry about what you saw?"

"Just tired," I said, setting the cooler by the fridge. In my dreams, I couldn't defend Morton against the wrath of my father

51

any more than I had defended my mother in reality, any more than I could defend myself against Peso's lust.

"I'll shower with you," Peso said, sounding pitiful.

I muttered, "No, that's okay. I need to slosh away the grime."

Peso took hold of my chin, forcing me to look into his eyes.

I laughed uncomfortably, said, "I'm getting countrified. Put the beer in the fridge, okay?" and slipped away before he could object. I had never asked him to do anything like that before. It gave me satisfaction. I lathered, shaved, took my time. Sandy was right; one thing I had gained on the road was independence. A part of me felt like calling the shots; another part of me was afraid to. I wanted to curl up in front of the fire alone with a cold G-Belt and a plate of whatever Lily had in the fridge, yet I knew there would be no rest until after sex. I splashed on aftershave and slid my arms into the terry robe Peso liked. The bear rug waited in front of the cold fireplace.

Peso approached me with hungry eyes. He rested one hand on the side of my face, the other on my thigh. "Frenchy, I missed you."

I didn't feel like rough and tumble foreplay, the kind of sex no woman would give me. What was wrong with me? Resigned to the inevitable, I put my hand over his, and said, "It's lonely on the road."

His eyes narrowed. "Are you banging someone else?"

"Wouldn't be safe," I said, sounding earnest.

Peso looked intensely into my eyes. Finally seeming satisfied at having found what he was looking for, he said, "You've been away too long. You're due for promotion."

Guilt overwhelmed me. Still, I was grateful. "Peso, listen." I needed to hide my nervous hands. "When I check into some crummy motel, I slide my slacks between the mattress and box springs to press the crease. That's the extent of my night exercise."

He grabbed my face between his hands, squeezed, and kissed me hard. My tongue bammed around inside his mouth like a lost soul pounding on the gates of heaven. I panted at his mercy. He wouldn't let up. He seemed to want to show me what I would miss if I ever, ever—the bear's head slid along the wooden floor. I would be sore into next year.

Afterward I covered my eyes with my arm. His hand rested on my thigh as he reached for the snifter.

I said, "I'd rather have a Grain Belt," and got up and went into the kitchen and poured Mazola oil on my fingers and spread it over my burning hole. I washed my hands and splashed water on my face and opened a beer and took a long drink. Then I opened two more bottles and carried them into the living room where Peso sat in the leather chair with the towel across his lap. I slid into my robe and put my feet up.

"You'll gain weight," Peso said, looking at the beer.

I toasted him with the bottle, swallowed, said, "I'll buy bigger pants." If right now he asked me what I wanted, I'd say: Out. I wondered if he slept with women, what kind of women?

Sounding distant, Peso said, "I need you to drive me to Minneapolis tomorrow."

What was I thinking to sound so cross? He had kept his promise, not involved me in anything illegal, and he had been generous and kind. For my part, I was glad to have the tension broken.

"Sure," I said, wondering what was in Minneapolis.

CHAPTER NINE

In the morning, I woke disgusted with myself. Despite all her faults, Mom had given me a conscience. When we got back from Minneapolis I had to tell Peso that I wanted out. In the meantime, I dressed to please him—tan silk shirt, silk-blend dark brown pinstriped suit, crisp teal, tan, and white patterned tie, tacked with a diamond stud, polished loafers. I cleaned my fingernails and packed my small suitcase, then put an extra suit on a hanger because I hadn't asked how long we'd be gone.

Lily said, "My, aren't you pretty! Smell real good, too."

Peso didn't look up from his newspaper.

"It's good to see you, Lily. How are things?"

"Okay, now that you're back." She poured my coffee.

I smiled when I saw the French toast. "Thank you."

"You welcome."

Lily left the room. "Peso, about last night—"

He raised his eyes. Nothing soft there. Fear brought goosebumps to my arms.

"You drink too much beer."

It was best to calm him. "I was tired, out of sorts. I'm sorry. Can you overlook it?"

He pinned me with a stare. "Frenchy, do I have your loyalty?"

"Hands down. No bones about it." Lily returned. I silenced. They exchanged looks. That pissed me off.

Peso said, "I'd like to get an early start."

I nodded, needed to watch my manners, my grammar, not displease him, most of all, hatch a plan and stick to it. I followed him to the Jag. When he saw the road dust on the car he winced.

"I'll stop at the first carwash we come to."

"You do that," he said, putting his suitcase and briefcase in the trunk. Tension heated the car like fresh asphalt.

"Have you had a recent tune-up?"

"Yes." At the gas station, I filled the tank, paid with the credit card Peso had provided; then we sat through a car wash and wax. Once city sprawl lay behind us, Peso asked if I had kept my driving skills honed.

How many hours did I spend on the road? "Sure," I said, sounding huffy. "Nothing wrong with my instant reactions." Since Peso wasn't one for idle chitchat, first chance I got, I would hone those skills.

Fallow cornfields flew along Illinois 51, about to become Interstate 39, some with stalks stacked, reminding me of my failure with Sandy. Moving away from a subject that might betray me, I asked, "What's in Minneapolis?"

"Jewelry." A beat passed. "I ever show you my sapphire necklace?"

It was a tired subject. I said, "I don't think my father ever bought my mother any jewelry, except her wedding band."

"His biggest mistake. "Give a woman jewelry, she'll eat out of your hand and beg for more."

I stopped at the tollbooth, threw a quarter, dime, and nickel into the basket, said, "I appreciate what you've taught me."

"You should."

Soon after entering Wisconsin we passed a Grain Belt billboard. If I were alone I would have already downed a couple. Obviously,

Peso didn't intend to tell me the reason for this trip. We checked into the downtown Minneapolis Radisson. Traffic noises rose from the street; airplanes flew overhead. I realized I liked the quiet of a country mom-and-pop. My asshole was sore; sitting all day hadn't helped. As the ten o'clock news drew to a close, partly in defense against sex, I said, "Guess I better practice those driving skills."

Peso smiled a crooked smile.

"When you talk, I listen," I said.

Down at the desk I asked about a racetrack; then, given the hour, and the thought of finding my way in the dark through streets that meandered around lakes, I plucked a Mall of America brochure from a rack and headed for it. There in a parking lot that went forever, I skidded and screeched. On the way back to the hotel, I filled the tank and limited myself to two beers.

Peso directed me to a deserted warehouse on the
Mississippi riverfront.

"No one's here," I said, still grumpy from sleep.

He said, "Pull in front of that one, the one with the awning." Peso seemed more awake than usual. He got out, slapped the top of the car with the flat of his hand, and said, "Keep it running. I'm meeting a friend. We'll be in a hurry."

"Okay." In the rearview mirror I saw a man appear from beside the building. He wore a dark overcoat and hat and moved into the building with Peso. I turned on the radio, moved through stations until I found Donna Summer singing "Love to Love You, Baby." I was tapping my fingers on the wheel to the music when suddenly Peso dashed in beside me, yelling, "Take off! Take off!"

Like a greased pig I did.

"Head for 94 east," said the guy I didn't know had landed in the back seat. "Sixth, take Sixth!"

I braked, backed up, nearly collided with a station wagon filled with kids. "What the hell's going down?"

"Listen to Eddie, he knows his way around."

Eddie said, "Drive like your fucking life depends on it."

Peso said, "Don't exceed the speed limit by more than ten miles."

Fear pumped my adrenaline. No way was this legit. If no one was after us, we sure looked like they should be. We passed a St. Paul sign.

Peso fumbled under the floor mat, said, "Stay calm. Everything's okay." In the rearview mirror I saw a police car enter the freeway. I set my lips tight, passed cars steadily. Up ahead a line of police cars was parked across all lanes, blocking the Snelling Street exit. Behind us, police cherries *blip-blipped*. "Now what?" There was no way to cross the median. Peso and Eddie were yelling, Do this, do that, when there was nothing to do but fake our way. That's when I spotted police behind the barricade of cars aiming guns in our direction.

"Shit," Eddie said, pounding on the back of my seat. I braked toward a stop, turned to Peso. He smiled slow-like, and said, "If it's any consolation, Frenchy, you passed the loyalty test."

My old man was right about one thing—never trust a policeman. They searched the Jag, didn't find anything until later when they uncovered the welded hold under the passenger floor mat where Peso had stashed stolen jewels. No one believed me when I said I didn't know what Eddie and Peso were doing in the warehouse. After Peso's conviction the Feds nabbed everything Peso owned for back taxes, including my Jag. You'd think with all of that snooping they would have discovered what Peso really did, but they didn't. Peso and Eddie drew time. Me, I ended up convicted on a temporary insanity plea—don't know how Peso's lawyer wrangled it—except at the scene I turned into a blubbering idiot, wet my pants like a sissy kid afraid his old man was going to pound him to pulp. When I learned that people like me could stay in the looney bin a long, long time, I fell apart. Once I decided to earn my way out, it was slow, steady work, all the way.

CHAPTER TEN

In 1990 I was paroled to Chance Place, a halfway house
in a downtrodden section of American Siberia, Minneapolis. The
prison offered me a suit. Instead I opted for long underwear, a
long-sleeved black tee, heavy slacks, a bulky sweater, and a
red-and-black-checked woolen jacket. Still I wasn't warm. I pulled
my knitted hat down over my ears, and traced my gloved finger
along the line I had drawn on the map. I had x-ed Chance Place
and the Humane Society. Peso said when I got settled Lily would
send my clothes. Even from prison, people in five states did Peso's
bidding. His bidders had located my dad and said Mom still lived
where I had lived. My fingertips were numb. I couldn't stop
shivering. As soon as I could afford a real winter jacket, I would
get one. I glanced at my watch. If I didn't sign in by 5:00 p.m.
some big Blue would track me down for lockup.

In front of the Humane Society I brushed snow from my newly
trimmed, waxed mustache. I removed worn gloves and smoothed
my not-too-good haircut.

The girl behind the counter said, "I beg your pardon?"

I said, "Some dogs come in here old or sick and you put 'em to
sleep, right? How much for a dead one?"

Dread showed in her eyes. Young kids were asked to do too much too soon these days. Maybe she was too young to know anything.

"Look," I said, not meaning to frighten her, but I was losing patience, "how much would it be if I wanted a pet, a regular pet?"

"Well, for adoption—shots and all—between fifty and a hundred and thirty, depending—"

"On?"

"On the breed and the age of the dog."

"Great," I said, straightening and sending a right hook into the air. "If a live mutt's fifty, then a dead one can't be more than that, can it?"

She turned skittish again, parts of her bumping into other parts without knowing where they were headed. "Let me get someone else to—"

"It's okay. Don't bother." I could tell she was afraid. I said, "I don't hurt fleas. Not a one. I'm going now. Thanks."

I boarded another bus, heading for Dayton's department store at Nicollet and Eighth. Gabe, the prison chaplain, had warned me: Failing to plan is planning to fail. Take charge, Frenchy; you are not helpless. Easy enough for a man wearing a backwards white dog collar to say. The guys easily conned Gabe: "Pray for me, Father." "A blessing, Father." How much could a priest named after an angel, advising what the books called the *non compos mentis* to pray, know? I needed a friend at Chance Place or I *would* go nuts for sure.

Once inside Dayton's, I scanned the upper regions for the down escalator sign and headed towards it. A baby wailed. I spotted the kid bouncing at his mother's shoulder, pointing his tiny finger at a fluffy gray toy animal kersplunked on the floor. The kid was near to fits while his mother talked, ignoring him. I scooted over and picked up the dingy lamb. "Ma'am," I said, wanting to bop her on the head with it, "your little boy dropped this."

Her red mouth formed an *O*. "Thanks," she said, taking it, bouncing her kid. "She would've cried all night."

Lamb in hand, the kid's fluid eyes pierced my gut. "Don't count too many sheep," I said to the watery-eyed kid and moved away. When a kid lost a pet, even a toy one, the hurt stayed with him—her—forever. Any mother should know that. I never dreamed the kid was a girl!

The escalator took me down to the budget level where I located the toilet paper near the stacks of paper towels and private women's stuff. I'd probably never be a father, that's what I was thinking, the image of the girl kid's painful, teary eyes still in my head. If I were, I'd be nice to my kid. A kid deserved more love than anyone could give him.

Toilet paper came in four-packs and six-packs. I carried a four-pack to the idle, overweight clerk who looked Indian—uh, Native American—in the joint you didn't make that mistake more than once.

"How many of these in a case?" I asked.

She looked blank.

I wedged the toilet paper between my knees and outlined a big box in the air. "A case. A case. How much?"

She shrugged and reached for the phone. "I'll find out."

That's what Peso always said: I'll find out. If Peso hadn't hired that lawyer for me, I'd hold more serious revenge. I couldn't cross Peso, not now. I chose a baby boy blue toothbrush.

The clerk said, "Forty-eight rolls to a case, seventeen-fifty. Plus tax."

"Do you deliver?"

"If you got a charge or pay two-fifty. A case?"

"I'll be back."

"You don't want a case of toilet paper?"

Don't take up a war dance. "Just this," I said holding up the toothbrush. "A man's got to plan. Today teeth, tomorrow—"

* * *

Liking freedom, stalling, I walked and walked until
cold penetrated my soles. Finally I purchased two small pull-tab
cans of pork 'n beans in a SuperAmerica, tucked the bag under my
arm, and headed for the bus stop. It was almost 5:00 p.m. and dark
when I got off. I spotted Chance Place on the corner across the
street with the porch light on. Given the street light, I saw a
three-story framed monster, sporting froufrou around the windows
and upper deck—the kind women liked to brag about and men
hated to paint. The neighborhood was big rundown houses, homes
that once belonged to high-class folk, with no tavern in sight. To
my left, an orange Burger King sign teased my mouth to salivating,
but I needed what little money I had for my project. Hoping for
better than beans, I negotiated the narrow, cracked walk between
mounds of shoveled snow. If I was going to live here, I needed to
make a good first impression. I stomped snow from my shoes,
drew a deep breath, and cracked the door open.

Beyond the archway to the right, men hovered in a haze of
cigarette smoke, ghosts watching the TV that provided the only
light. Dan Rather questioned why President Bush, who took the
initiative in the Gulf War, didn't respond the same way in Bosnia.
Rather wondered what changes Bill Clinton would make after
inauguration. He said economists believed now that the cold war
was over, hot markets would turn into cold cash.

I hung my sweater and jacket in the coat closet, hoping they
would be safe there. When people weren't at home upstairs, you
never knew what might happen downstairs. I moved into the living
room and tried to start a conversation.

"Hey," I said, "turn on a light, why don't you?" *Dumb.*

No one looked up. My spirit drooped low as a basset hound's
ears. Above the pay phone in the hall hung a foot-square bulletin

board with pink slips of paper tacked on it. Below the bulletin board stood a small table with a pink slip pad and a pencil hanging on a string. To the right of the stairs, a light shone under the closed kitchen door, which from the food smells I suspected was the kitchen. To my left, two closed doors, one had a name on it, a resident's room, the other, the basement. Could anyone sane make it here? Would I be lucky enough to make even one friend?

I heard jangling keys and turned to see an overweight guy in slate-gray work clothes unlocking what I figured was the kitchen door. He poked his tight ass toward me as he wedged the doorstop. No doubt the house manager. His belly hung over his belt. Strands of thinning blond hair pulled back over his bald crown. I needed him to know I had arrived on time. I knuckled my mustache and approached him, "I'm Frenchy Bibideaux."

The man stood two heads taller than I. His pulley chain keys snapped back into the big ring on his belt. Weak handshake.

"Dave McMaster. I run the show here. After dinner I'll show you your room. Tomorrow you get the grand tour. Welcome." He moved to a phone near the sink, not a pay phone so it must be the house phone. Sure as sheep screwed, when McMaster locked the kitchen, no free phone was available.

The residents had shuffled into a haphazard single file moving toward the kitchen. Not knowing the pecking order, I headed for the end of the line. Already I didn't like McMaster. His body language suggested class bully, a threat to runts like me who needed to use the balls between our ears to survive.

The men were a motley crew, except for two whose neat dress separated them from the others: the first, a freckled, curly-haired redhead in his forties, wearing a blue plaid shirt, navy corduroy slacks, and polished shoes; the second, a black giant of a dude with biceps that said he pumped iron. Peso was right about appearances. Judging by the scruffiness of the others, the only guys I wanted to hang with were these two. The redhead peered sideways at me, suspicion mixed with curiosity. The dude hung on his heels like a puppy.

"I-I'm Nathan Waite," the redhead said, offering his hand like he was afraid I might take it.

For someone so shaky, his handshake proved firm. "Frenchy Bibideaux," I said. "The new guy. Not as good as some, better 'n most."

In Nathan's eyes was a glimmer of presence. Nathan aimed his thumb over his shoulder. "This is Emory."

In Emory's slanted-eye scrutiny I felt reduced to the size of Tom Thumb.

"Baby do," Emory said in a deep baritone. His grip left my hand numb. I'd need to take up judo or weightlifting to hold my own with him; I should never cross Emory. The man had plum-colored skin and wore a starched lavender dress shirt, a vest of geometric, probably African, design. No doubt a Muslim. Most of the blacks in the joint were Muslim. Meticulous, that's how Peso would describe Emory.

"These are not my regular clothes," I said. "They're coming."

"Mr. Bibideaux lives here now," Nathan explained to Emory.

"Baby do," Emory said.

"Call me Frenchy."

The line advanced. Nathan indicated an older, gaunt guy who lagged behind, keeping his distance. "That's Jupiter, my roommate."

I could tell Jupiter was paranoid and close to breaking. I spent my initial stint at St. Peter's Hospital for the criminally insane. There, the library that was supposed to be for patients had only books about mental illness. To pass time I read a lot of them. The staff called the books that listed symptoms for every mental illness DSMs—Diagnostic and Statistic Manuals. There was nothing else to do except smoke. I never took up the dirty habit. Guys who smoked wore clothes with burn holes in them. While I didn't understand everything I read, one contradiction bopped about in paragraphs like a bad yo-yo. Illnesses seemed to go in and out of style like women's hemlines and I never found one definition of mental health. Not one! That translated into: Getting the kind of help anyone needed offered odds greater than those for winning the Publishers' Clearinghouse Sweepstakes. It was clear that Jupiter wasn't getting the kind of help he needed. The man's slumped posture and fragile frame and tremors suggested a vulnerability that made me turn away. I didn't want to get suckered into nannyhood? Not here. *Never.*

Nathan patted his hair the way I used to pet Morton to comfort him, gently, slowly. "Let Jupe be," he said. Nathan leaned forward and confided, "McMaster listens to the news while we eat, then locks the kitchen."

"Yo," I said. Locked kitchen, a dead giveaway; the house manager was siphoning money from the food budget. If I wanted food, get it at mealtime. "Thanks," I said.

Beyond the large kitchen table flanked by unmatched chairs, men helped themselves from dishes on the counter—some kind of noodle hot dish in a pale thin gravy, canned peas, which I hated, green Kool-aid, and boxes of diddly vanilla wafers. I counted men, spotting various side effects from meds—rigid posture, tremors, an occasional jerking limb, shuffling. Some patients claimed that the side effects were worse than the hallucinations and voices the meds were supposed to squelch. Guys were squinting; the Gestapo must've designed the fluorescents overhead, because some meds caused light sensitivity. From the smell I couldn't guess what kind of meat, if any, was in the hot dish.

McMaster cupped the phone like he was talking dirty. Clearly the man was also saving money on heat. Managers qualified for mortgages on halfway houses faster 'n popcorn popped. With what the government paid them per resident, plus the money they saved on the services they didn't provide, a guy could rake in a fortune.

Emory sat across from Nathan, smiling at Jupiter with a row of light yellow teeth even as corn on a cob. I wondered if Nathan and Emory were tight—lovers. Nathan helped Jupiter, who sat beside him. I took the one remaining chair.

"Butter nutter," Emory said.

Nathan nodded.

Oh boy.

Spoons scraped. Was there a rule against talking? McMaster *kiss-kissed* into the phone and hung up. I had expected the residents here would be able to converse, play cards, offer companionship. McMaster cast a look of disgust at us and exited toward the living room, where some guy on TV was hawking Kentucky Fried Chicken.

"Hey," I asked, glad to have him gone, "anyone here play poker? Euchre? Hearts?" When no one answered, I felt downright depressed. "Tomorrow," I said, still trying to get a conversation going, "I'm starting a carpentry project in the basement. Anyone want to help?"

No reply. "You know, hammer and nails? How about you, Nathan?"

Nathan flushed, stammered, "I d-don't know."

My shoulders drooped. From Chance Place I was supposed to move out and up to something better. None of these guys, including me, looked like we were going anywhere anytime soon. How could I get out of the system without blowing my cork or going off my rocker? There was no justice; otherwise I wouldn't be here. I swallowed hard.

Men scraped their scraps into a large, plastic-lined wastebasket, then rinsed and stacked their dishes on the drain board. I looked around for coffee, found none. Caffeine, that's why. No caffeine, no sugar. Neither went with meds, yet that never stopped the cooks at St. Peter's, where desserts were cheaper than meat and patients bartered them same as cons. Instead of snafuing Medicaid, the government should find out where its money went. Never to miss an opportunity, the government might even be supplying surplus sugar to guys who weren't supposed to eat it. Nathan was still force feeding Jupiter. The sad little guy probably looked a lot older than he was. I popped a vanilla wafer into my mouth, wishing I had a Grain Belt.

After dinner, with no one to talk to, as I unpacked my duffel bag in my room, I kept telling myself that Chance Place was notches—notches—above St. Peter's, and that I'd damn well better make the best of it. I hoped Lily didn't forget to send my things.

Without being criminal or insane, I had graduated from the so-called criminally insane of St. Peter's to the insecurity of minimum security, when I was innocent in the first place. And now I had moved up to Chance Place for the mentally ill, which I wasn't either. I put the framed wrinkled photo of Morton on the bedside table. My total life experience added up to the likes of a bug creeping along minding his own business, who'd been slurped into a Venus flytrap when he wasn't looking. Seeing Morton alive gave me a glimmer of hope that one day I would feel like me again. What I wanted was respect. *Self-respect.* The baffler was, how to get that. For sure, first thing in the morning I would ask my parole officer for a transfer out of Chance Place.

CHAPTER ELEVEN

Usually it was too cold for snow in January, but Santa's
machine had gone berserk. I walked against the big flakes bent like
an old woman, working up enough courage to face my parole
officer. Who needed to take on an opponent so early in the
morning? The red brick building proved to be a no-count,
one-story in the no high-rise fringes of downtown. The warden
said the nuns at Catholic Charities were a desirable backup to
Hennepin County's burnt-out social workers, that I should be
grateful. The place smelled of fresh coffee and old paint. The
receptionist directed me to an office with a hissing radiator. I
knocked on the open door.

"Good morning. I'm glad you're prompt," the woman said,
half-rising.

Now here was a surprise! Instead of the old biddy nun I had
expected, Sister Kathleen stood thin and young with hair shiny and
dark as a silk nightie, eyes afire. She wore a plain white blouse
with a black cardigan, and dangly earrings. She smiled and touched
the silver cross hanging between her breasts. I focused on her pink
lips, on her bright, lilting voice.

"It gets us off to a good start, doesn't it, your being prompt?"

Lost in the sudden blight of unexpected lust, I nodded, sat, and watched her fingers flit through papers that told her more about me than anyone should know. I wanted to explain how I had been set up and falsely arrested. No one believed me; she wouldn't either.

I said, "One of my two new roommates snores like a rhinoceros." *Stupid.*

She peered at me like I was some kind of quiz she had to figure out. Gray, her eyes were gray.

My fists found the inside of my knit hat and stretched it this way and that. I added, "I couldn't sleep," to explain my nerves.

The way she shook her head and touched her cross with her fingertip reminded me of Gabe. "Frenchy," Gabe had advised, "you've got to get past your old life. Put Morton to rest."
I would never get over Morton.

"You're settled in at Chance Place?"

"Huh?"

Sister Kathleen looked wavy like she was under water. I sniffed, knuckled my nose, and dropped my hat. Fumbling for it, I hit my head on the edge of her desk. Definitely, I wanted her to believe that I was not a valid candidate for residency. I wondered if I could have a pet wherever I was going to live. There was a box of Kleenex on her desk. No matter what, I wouldn't take one. Sissiness had a way of backfiring; you got called wimpy and you got walloped or worse. It was hard to know when to challenge authority, when to back off. On that score I was one tooth shy of a set. Swiping my eye with the back of my hand, I sniffed and said, "The cold. I found the address all right."

"Francis Bibideaux. Am I saying your name correctly?"

"Uh-huh. Yes. I mean, yes. Sister. Right, but call me Frenchy."
I moved my knuckle across the front of my nose. *Take control.*

"Frenchy," she said.

I shrugged my arms out of my jacket, crossed my legs, snatched a tissue, and blew. "The cold," I said.

She smiled a warm, overpolite smile. She had dimples!

"All right. Frenchy. Let's see. You signed a work contract. Have you a work plan?"

"A guy's got to plan," I said. Those dangly earrings were garnets when she was a ruby kind of woman. I could give her rubies, thinking like Peso now. Peso knew how to get around and through, that's for sure. Peso had made me the happiest man in the world; Peso had made me the most miserable man in the world.

"Please," she said.

I saw my signature on the paper in front of her. That contract she would hold me to restricted my inalienable freedoms.

"Monday," I said, shifting, wanting the interview over. "Monday, I report to Olson Electronics." I had decided I wanted a transfer even though it probably meant I'd be slotted into the less desirable Hennepin County social service system. Now my mind did a backwards tumble: Sister Kathleen would no longer be my parole officer. My job would get me out of Chance Place eight hours a day, five days a week. My hat lay limp as a used condom on my knee. "Uh—" I said, trying to remember what we were talking about. "Bring my lunch, ask for Otto, for Mr. Otto Olson. Eight a.m."

"And?"

I felt a rush of rebellion. What did she want? I said, "Do something with microchips until I ruin my eyes." I poked my fists inside my hat and pulled them as far apart as I could, then recited the don'ts: "Don't drive. Don't go out of the state. Don't carry a weapon."

"And?"

Zircons would be too good for her. I heard my old man's voice say: *Get lost.* Feeling defeated, I added, "Be here next Friday; stay clean."

"Clean?"

I should have studied Peso closer. Peso could charm a lady in an eye blink. "Listen," I said, trying to soothe her. "I thought Chance Place would be ... nicer. I'm ... uncomfortable there. Isn't there someplace else?"

Sister Kathleen fingered the Christ figure on the cross between her breasts. "Your temporary insanity conviction pretty much dictates where you can live. It must be difficult," she said, making eye contact.

My knee took to bobbing like I was on medication—on meds—like the guys at Chance Place. I willed it to stop. Not wanting to look into her eyes, I peered up over her shoulder where I saw the picture of the poor suffering souls in purgatory, hands raised to a nasty cloud that was about to dump a deluge that would drown them into kingdom come.

"Mr. Bibi ... Frenchy," Sister Kathleen said. "You've listed your religion as Catholic. Chance Place is in St. Joan of Arc parish. Is that where you'll go? The congregation has a carpool cooperative. I can arrange transportation."

"No! I'll walk. I mean, it's good for the heart, Sister. Exercise. I need more of it."

Peso said I would receive an updated driver's license, not that having it would give me wheels. I wouldn't steal a car. Definitely, I wanted to stay out of trouble. I said, "I like to pray when I walk." Inspired, I reached inside my collar and pulled out the scapular, "I wear this, all the time," I said, extending it on my palm.

"Why, I haven't seen an old-fashioned scapular like that for ... forever," she said. "May I?" She took the patch on her palm.

Glee, I felt glee.

"Where did you get that?"

"Just a minute." I slipped the cord over my head and gave the scapular to her and smoothed my hair. "My granddad," I said, feeling self-conscious.

"What happened here?"

71

"My dog chewed it."

Sister Kathleen returned it with a gentle smile. "You like dogs?"

I pushed the last of the cord into my jacket breast pocket and patted it.

"No."

I must've sounded aggressive the way she pulled back. Her index finger flipped the corners of the papers on her desk twice.

"Prescriptions?"

"Sister, that's one thing you don't need to worry about, 'cause I don't take meds. None. Never."

She stared at me.

"Sister, these guys hear themselves and they don't even know who's talking!" I stopped, put a lid on my opinions.

Her eyes softened. She said, "It must be hard living with the mentally ill."

Her softness made me shifty-assed. I got up and moved over to the hissing radiator. A drink, that's what I needed. Nothing made for happy like booze.

"What about leisure?" Sister Kathleen asked.

"Oh, I don't know," I said, twisting my hat. "Maybe ask a girl out to a movie, afterwards order Coke and—whoops—Coca-Cola, Sister, that kind of Coke." I knuckled my mustache and sat down again. "I'd just like to take ... someone ... out on a date to a movie and then go for a Coca-Cola and a double Whopper and fries, and make it home before curfew. All in one night. Sister, I'd sure like to be able to do that." Right now she was the only woman I knew. "You like malts, Sister Kathleen?" Her name sounded nice coming out of my mouth.

She looked like somebody had stuck a pin in her. Awesome how my cells were manufacturing loneliness on the spot. "Maybe you and me, we could have a bite together. A chocolate malt? Sometime," I hurried to say when she moved her hands to the arms of her chair, "when we know each other better." She was too thin, could use a malt. I swallowed, changed the subject. "I like to work with tools. I have a building project in mind. I mean everybody's got to eat. That's what I mean, meant."

"Frenchy, I was asking about AA, about Alcoholics Anonymous."

"AA. You bet," I said, hanging a right hook in the air. The price of getting out of the system, make no mistake about it—sobriety. *Dry mouth. Dry gut. Dry dock.*

"Which AA meeting will you go to?"

"Tomorrow," I said. "It's on my plan to get an AA schedule tomorrow."

She studied me, said, "AA answers its line twenty-four hours a day. Here." She handed me a three-by-five card. "Have the leader sign this and bring it with you next week when we meet."

My mind did miles because she didn't know that the person who led AA meetings wasn't called a leader; he was a trusted servant, which meant she didn't know a lot of other things. She was new at this! I looked down at the card in my hand. On the blank line next to Name, she had written Francis B. The rest of the sentence said, "attended AA meeting." There were spaces for Place, Time, Date, Signature. Her handwriting flourished up at the ends.

She said, "AA leaders are used to signing these cards for the courts. It's not like announcing you're on probation. Traffic violations, driving while intoxicated—DWIs—there are all kinds of reasons."

I slipped the card into my pocket and pulled my hat down over my ears and stood up. She seemed surprised that I thought we were finished; then her expression changed as she realized we were, and she stood, too.

Sister Kathleen proved taller than I had guessed. She came around the desk; her legs went on forever. I fantasized her legs squeezing around—someone—and summoned a poker face. Emeralds. No doubt about it. She was an emerald kind of woman.

To put space between us, I backed to the door and extended my hat toward her. "Sister, you think about meeting somewhere. If you'd rather have something other than a hamburger or malt, that's okay." And I was outta there.

Making tracks in the snow, I thought about how Peso had organized his fellow cons into Ambassadors for Jesus Christ who visited churches to tell others how they had found Jesus in prison and were now saved. I thought about how much power a parole officer had and decided I mustn't fantasize about Sister Kathleen's legs or about any other part of her body, as if life without sex was goin' to go by quiet and easy. I had executed a jump-shift to learn how to get along with Peso and how to get along in prison. Now I needed a jump-shift to learn how to get along at Chance Place.

CHAPTER TWELVE

Frenchy was staring at Murray like he'd never seen a man pour from a teakettle with a sock over his hand before. Imagine Frenchy saying, "You know, hammer and nails?" as if Nathan didn't know that carpentry meant using tools. It had been a long time since anyone had extended an invitation to him; on and off all night long he thought about doing a carpentry project. He just didn't know what to think of the new resident. Instead of sitting down to lunch with them, Frenchy stood and ate pork 'n beans out of a can. The man read their work assignments on the kitchen bulletin board like he was reading the newspaper. Frenchy didn't smoke. Except for Emory, who obsessed over neatness, all the other residents smoked.

"Mosquito torpedo," Emory said, smearing peanut butter onto toast.

"Yes," Nathan said.

"Court short?"

"It'll go okay."

Emory was inquiring about Nathan's upcoming court hearing. The government had canceled his Social Security benefits, probably because he hadn't opened the envelope with the letter advising him about it. Sister Angela, his social worker, said the cancellation was a computer error, that correction required a judgment. Nathan didn't need any more judgments, especially not from a stranger. After Reagan took office, computer errors happened to too many disabled persons to be mistakes.

Frenchy had no paunch, no bloat, no shoulder slump. No stammer. No tremor. The man's eyes darted about without shame. Frenchy wasn't one of them. Maybe Frenchy carried a new strain of illness. If not, why was Frenchy here?

When Nathan first arrived at Chance Place, such unsightly side effects of meds depressed him. It took courage for him to risk even trying to understand; when he did, a sense of closeness resulted, but also the kind of anguish that came from caring. In time, he found each resident to have, if only pieces of mind, both personality and heart. It would be nice to work with tools again.

Nathan used to be good at friendships, but not anymore; he was too scared and meds slowed his physical reactions and robbed him of intellectual sharpness. Meds gave him dry mouth and an awful preoccupation with the real possibility that one day his tongue might go in and out on its own like a tentacle. Meds stiffened his muscles; for that he took Cogentin. Doctors claimed meds weren't addictive. Then why were they forever trying to strike a balance between excessive dullness and an agitated manic state? If he helped Frenchy, would his shakes get in the way?

Doctors always erred on the side of dullness—that big gray void that stole away the highs and lows, leaving only blahs. Would Frenchy ridicule him?

At the sound of Jupiter's shuffle, Nathan stood to help him. Jupe's muscles were already quivering like guitar strings about to break in his jerking limbs. Jupe didn't go out anymore because people stared or turned away. When your meds got out of sync, your brain chemistry went out of sync, too; horror movies played in your head; voices told you to do absurd things—like move a chair in and out three times before sitting in it. You slept by day and stayed awake all night.

Jupe slid the chair next to Nathan in and out three times. The man hadn't shaved for two days and his blond hair lay matted for want of a shampoo. With so much mental distraction, who paid attention to grooming? It was a miracle his roommate still got in bed at night.

The way Frenchy gawked, Frenchy couldn't possibly be one of them.

Jupe dipped the stem end of his spoon into the Red Owl grape jelly. Nathan, alert but passive, maintaining unintrusive-intrusive, captured a J from his alphabet soup on his spoon and held it on his tongue, praying—J for Jupiter, J for Jesus, J for Justice. He looked up, saw Frenchy staring. Frenchy might say or do something to disturb Jupiter. Nathan released his spoon, got up, and moved to the new resident.

"Hey," Frenchy said, backing up as if threatened. He said, "I'm ... not interested in your roommate. Really I'm not. Uh, tell me, can you sneak a chick into this place?"

Emory appeared behind Frenchy, sandwiching the man between him and Nathan.

"It's okay," Nathan said to Emory.

Frenchy held up the empty can, and said, "I need to get rid of this." He pelted the tin into the wastebasket. Leaving, he said, "I sure could use another pair of hands downstairs, anyone who wants to help."

Nathan waited until he heard the basement door close, then returned to the table. Frenchy was a mystery—a man saying "Come here" and "Go away" at the same time. "Jupe, you sure about eating that jelly? That's a lot of sugar."

Jupe ignored him. Zookeepers and vet helpers made more pay than mental health aides.

Jupe didn't need deinstitutionalization, not the kind of government help that changed human beings into helpless, homeless, reviled persons. Jupe needed TLC, a guardian angel, the role Nathan had chosen, hoping that when *he* needed help, Jupe or someone would care for him.

When Nathan's illness struck twenty years ago, he had been taught what meds could and could not do for him and that meds worked best with balanced nutrition. His mind flashed an image of himself sitting in occupational therapy, pounding dents into copper as his mind perched on that razor's edge between tragedy and comedy. Suddenly it struck him as funny that he could neither count on his mind—which for starters was above average—nor on his body, which no longer felt familiar. The brochure had said Chance Place offered him another chance. *Some chance!* Nathan snickered. Jupe was playing with grape jelly. Jupe was making a mess.

Emory said. "Fake take."

"It's okay," Nathan said.

He tried to feed Jupiter; Jupiter shoved the spoon away. McMaster wouldn't help, but Nathan would ask anyway. He crossed to the windowsill, picked up the heavy green glass ashtray, and leaned against the refrigerator and smoked, hovering over Jupe like a protective father watching his son about to take his first step.

Nathan's dilemma always came down to: *Why do I seem to know what others need when no one seems to know what I need? When the time comes, who will take care of me?* Messages came in threes. Take his latest preoccupation with purple—he didn't know where or when this purple business had started, maybe from being around Emory or from Jupe dawdling in grape jelly. A dot of jelly hung like a purple tear from the big eye on the Red Owl jar label now. What could a person be thinking to name a supermarket chain Red Owl?

"Thick dick," Emory said, fanning Nathan's smoke.

Nathan refused to be distracted while tending Jupiter. He closed his eyes, saw a purple screen, and heard a clear, vibrant, baritone voice recite the "Parable of Purple."

Once there was a person who believed purple
to be bad, a color worn only by bad people.
Since few people wore purple, this was not a
problem. But purple came to be "in" and
purple-wearers were everywhere! The bad-purple-believer
grew uncomfortable inside his own skin.
Avoiding purple-wearers became a full-time job.
When the discomfort of being alone equaled
the discomfort of being around purple, it came time to act.

Nathan opened his eyes, smiled, nodded encouragement to Jupiter. He closed his eyes again and returned to the pleasure of the story.

The-bad-purple-believer worked to persuade
all others to stop wearing purple.
The purple-wearers wanted to feel they belonged.
Next, the bad-purple-believer tried
to change his own feelings, tried not to be
uncomfortable around so many purple-wearers.
It didn't work; he still felt alone. Finally, when
he couldn't stand being alone anymore,
he knew he had to test his belief.

Feeling heat near his fingertips, Nathan startled, then extinguished his cigarette.

To test just how bad a person it would make him,
the bad-purple-believer put on purple.
And guess what! Purple didn't make him a bad person at all!

Nathan heard Jupiter's chair sliding in and out.

Each day after that, the bad-purple-believer
wore a touch of purple. It taught him that risk
and welcoming real truth only produced more freedom.
Truth was: Morals called beliefs can be lies.

Nathan swallowed and set the ashtray on top of the refrigerator. He took Jupiter gently by the wrist and walked him to the bathroom. By the time Nathan finished washing Jupiter and wiping down Jupiter's chair and place, only Emory, who had dishwashing duty, remained.

"Scutt butt." Emory deliberately bumped Nathan's hip with his.

Nathan threw the purple-stained cloth he had been using into the sink. "What?" he asked, not wanting the pleasure of his purple story disturbed. He moved to the work roster and squinted at the words to be double-sure he didn't have dishes this week. He knew he didn't, but then you never knew when someone changed what you already knew. Maybe Emory would take the hint.

Emory bent close to Nathan's ear and said, "Some Wayzata woman surprised her husband, took coffee out to his fish house on Lake Minnetonka, and caught him," he raised his eyebrows and gestured jerking off, "with someone else's woman."

Nathan glanced sideways at Emory.

Emory nodded. Yes. Hookers were working the ice fishing houses on the lake.

"That's fu-fu-funny," Nathan said, sliding into laughter, visualizing the small, rectangular icehouses on the frozen lake looking like miniature Monopoly houses against the shoreline of expensive homes. Inside the fishing house was a heater, maybe a wooden crate for playing cards, a fishing line twitching in the ice hole while a man and woman tried to make it on a cot. He envisioned fur-wrapped hookers, tiptoeing like merry ghosts from house to house, and doubled up with laughter. Emory's guttural laugh punctuated his own. Nathan clutched the table.

"Wh-where did you hear that?" he asked, trying to catch his breath.

"Mi-Mi-MIBCA," sputtered Emory, who dropped in at the Minnesota Institute for Black Chemical Abuse like it was his second home. Emory found a sense of family there.

Nathan shook his hands in an effort to rid himself of built-up energy. He jogged in place, wiped the outer corners of his eyes on his sleeve. "Like before meds," he said, grinning.

Emory smiled with satisfaction.

They slapped high-five.

"Affable laughable," Emory said. "Riffraff, hobnob, and hoi polloi."

"Yes," Nathan said. Then, because he hadn't stopped to think about it, he asked. "Emory, you got anything purple I can wear?"

"Sock frock."

"Sock," Nathan said, accepting the reminder, not believing he had asked. If Emory smoked he could repay him in cigarettes, he thought.

"Soon," Nathan said, as Emory cleaned the tabletop, "they're going to give me a judgment. I will get my money and pay you. Save that milk carton, okay?"

"Never ever," Emory said. "After laughter. Lake make."

Nathan broke up again, knowing life had become too serious to be taken seriously; one did not overdose on this best medicine. Humor was laughing at what you didn't have when you knew you ought to have it. They sure got a lot of smileage out of that one.

CHAPTER THIRTEEN

On the bus Nathan played peek-a-boo with a little
Ojibwa boy until the boy's mother jerked her son's arm and gave
Nathan that look. Nathan shrugged an apology and eased his gaze
over her shoulder, out the filthy window, across the
snow-mounded curb into the false promise of Dayton's store
window—mannequins in bikinis. He deboarded in what they called
Nordeast Minneapolis, zipped up his navy blue down jacket, and
pulled on his mittens. Nathan had to visit the Center for Universal
Awareness, even though it would make him late for work. He was
considering helping Frenchy and wanted some assurance. What
would the message say?

Back when Nathan first visited the one-story blond brick
building between white frame homes, it had been Mayslack's
Restaurant. When Nathan's wrestling team came to celebrate wins,
Mayslack, the Wrestling King himself, piled their sandwiches high
with thin-sliced, garlicky beef. One day, the team arrived to new
green letters outlined in gold on the window that said, "Center for
Universal Awareness."

At first Nathan came to the center and prayed silently with
others. Then he attended discussion groups during which he
remained silent. Sometimes he reposed under the different-colored

healing lights. People were kind to him even when he didn't respond to their questions. Then it happened. Swami, the man who wore a turban wrapped around his head, took Nathan aside one sunny day and said, "Nathan, I sense you are a seeker, that you want answers, yes? You are shy, yes?"

Excited that someone understood, Nathan nodded.

"Follow me," Swami said, leading Nathan to a small office where photos hung on the wall of Swami with the Dali Lama, of a much younger Swami with Pope John XXIII, of Swami in front of the Taj Mahal. Nathan was impressed.

Swami held up what looked like a credit card and said, "We have this for people who are ... shy. It is free," Swami hurried to say.

Debt was not free.

"It's a way," Swami said, "to get answers to your deepest longings, anytime of the day or night, free."

"H-how?" Nathan asked, suspicious of anything that sounded so good; no one gave anything away.

"This card is for the ATM outside."

ATM sounded like something a doctor tested him for.

"That stands for automatic teller machine, but that is not what this is," Swami said. "No. It is a way for our members to feel our presence without coming to a meeting, a way for you to get in touch with God's universal energy, the Force, awareness, however you name this common experience."

Nathan had paid no dues. "I-I'm not a member," he said.

"Oh, my friend, you are, because you have that very special sense of connection to the greater universe. I see that clearly. This is your card," Swami said, offering it.

Nathan felt so excited. He moved his thumb over the silver card, admiring the golden rays radiating from its center.

"Come. I will show you how it works."

Nathan followed Swami outside to the ATM. He had seen people using it.

"This," Swami said, pointing to the row of numbers and letters on the card, "is your personal code. It says this card belongs to you. On the back is the center's address, so if you lose this card, it can be dropped into any mailbox and returned to us and we will send it back to you. The machine reads the black line on the card. This illustration," Swami pointed, "shows how to insert the card."

"Wh-what happens?" Nathan asked.

"You are going to find out, but not with me here. Your messages are private and change depending on the day, on your openness, on your willingness to receive, on all sorts of conditions. Think of this as an alternative to I Ching or consulting astrology."

Nathan knew about I Ching and astrology, though he had consulted neither. "Are you sure this is mine?" he asked, holding the card as if it were sacred.

"I have entered your name in our book as an honored member."

"Th-thank you."

Nathan couldn't believe his good fortune. He watched Swami retreat, then looked to the right, to the left. The message depended on his state of mind, on his openness. Nathan swallowed and closed his eyes and pried his heart open, which since his illness had become much harder to do. He looked to the right and left again, took a deep breath, and inserted the card. The machine whirred with electronic sounds; words appeared on the screen:

Your Personal Daily Message from the Center for Universal Awareness—

No one is more or less equal.
You are Wholly and Equally Channeled into the
Universal Source of Energy.

The idea of having the same chance as everyone else—that was enough for Nathan to think about for days. And he hadn't had to expose his worst fears, which sometimes made people laugh. The screen turned blank.

Nathan tried to remember the words exactly as they had appeared. If he put his card in again, the message would be different. Next time he would memorize the words. He turned toward the bus stop. The card gave him a way not to have to decide things alone, a means of control over wanton destiny, not that he needed to act on the message; he could always choose. If he felt lost inside himself, the message could act as a compass, an answer to his prayers.

Snowflakes tickled Nathan's face and clung to his eyelashes. He smelled kolachies baking in the Polish bakery. Emory had suggested in rhyme, of course, that the ATM was nothing more than a dispenser of fortune cookies. However, those messages had guided Nathan through bad times, and he needed one now to help him decide about Frenchy's request. He thought, *If ever I get to start over, maybe I can grow up in a different life.*

Now in front of the ATM, he patted his down hood and looked right and left. Those days when Mr. Mayslack shook his hand and slapped him on the back were gone, part of another life. He swiped the black line of the computer card across his thigh. Once when it was this cold, he hadn't done that and the machine consumed his card, which came back in the mail. As the computer whirred, Nathan stomped snow from his shoes. The words appeared:

Your Personal Daily Message from the Center for Universal Awareness—

All life is a balance of opposites,
Harmony in four parts ... with you
As an audience of one.

He memorized the words. How did this answer, Should he or shouldn't he help Frenchy? The meaning must be there; he just had to decipher it. His mother used to say, "If God gives you only half of what you need, it's up to you to supply the rest." By the time

Nathan arrived at his volunteer job at Abbott-Northwestern Hospital's coffee shop, he had decided that his body carried his life and his mind—two of the four parts. Unfortunately, his life played a simple folk melody while his mind played a fugue.

In the coffee shop Mrs. Simpson bustled with the kind of energy he used to have, wiping a table he was supposed to keep clean. She was a small-boned, wrinkled woman with eyes as mellow as his sister's cat when it first woke up.

"Nathan, I didn't think you were coming. The cold."

"Sorry," he said. "I'm out of harmony." He went to the back room and hung his jacket and hat on a peg. "Pretty soon," he said, returning, "I'll get my money. Then I can be a customer and buy a sandwich from you."

"Why, Nathan, such a nice thought." She held a pair of aluminum salt and pepper shakers in one hand, pushed her glasses higher on her nose with the index finger of her other hand. She watched him tie on the white butcher's apron and begin wiping tables.

Maybe somewhere he could find a many-layered Mayslack sandwich, but he wouldn't say that to her, not hurt her feelings by suggesting that he didn't want her sandwich. "Or maybe I can buy a flower," he said, gesturing toward the gift shop. "I have to wait and see." Flowers made him think of Cheryl, who had promised to marry him and love him forever. For a fleeting moment Nathan saw Cheryl standing in the lobby and blinked her away. It hurt to see her. He said, "Maybe I don't remember how to count past fifty."

"Are you that old?"

"I didn't mean age. I meant money. Everything I'm entitled to, except for fifty-six dollars and ninety cents a month, goes to the halfway house where I live. Regardless of my expenses, I get fifty-six ninety." He tilted his head to catch the light to check the shine on the tabletop, which reminded him of a pearly gray shooter he had once owned. "Mr. McMaster cashes my checks so I don't have to pay the check-cashing service. Sometimes it takes many days because he doesn't have the right change, so I lose some."

An odd expression crossed Mrs. Simpson's face. "Why don't you take your check to the bank?"

"I don't have enough money for an account." Maybe he could get one when he got his judgment. Sister Angela said they would give him back pay.

"Nathan," Mrs. Simpson said, standing much too close to him, "that's terrible. What does it cost to cash a check?"

"Depends on the amount of the check. More than five dollars. Should I do the sugars?"

"Why, the bank knows they're good! They're government checks, aren't they?" she asked, following him.

She should know it wasn't good not to let go of things you couldn't change. He felt her aura. She hadn't answered about the sugars. He saw the crusted edge of the almost empty macaroni and cheese pan on the counter. He went over, picked up the pan, and carried it to the kitchen, and said, "Social Security. State of Minnesota. Hennepin County."

Her tone turned real light. "What do you spend your money on? Movies, bowling?"

"Movies?" He was tempted to turn the pan around three times. "Not movies." His left hand squeezed his right biceps in search of the kind of tightness a bowling ball would put there. A warm wet spot formed on his sleeve. He picked up the plastic Scrubbie and pushed hard against the crust on the pan. He didn't know what to tell her. Thankfully, customers arrived and saved him from having to try because Mrs. Simpson went to wait on them. Every Friday they served macaroni and cheese and every Friday he faced crust as hard as his life. He needed something stronger than a Scrubbie. When he got money, he'd buy something more practical, also a nice smelling aftershave, something with a sophisticated name. British Sterling maybe.

Mrs. Simpson piled plates of sandwiches along her arm and picked up a glass of milk, and headed for the dining room. She came back and poured two cups of coffee. "Father, mother, and son. Daughter's in surgery," she said.

In spite of his decision not to, Nathan supplied the facts. "My fifty-plus dollars are supposed to go for clothes, toothpaste, personal items, whatever I need, entertainment, gifts, everything except food, lodging, and meds. I use the house bus card to get here. If it's not food, lodging, or meds—" The pan clattered to the floor, spouting an awful mess he would have to clean up. He turned to her, trying to keep his tone anger-free. "I have my own entertainment list, which is more than buying a cup of coffee for a date, if I could ever get lucky enough to find someone who'd go out on a date with Nathan. Cigarettes are not on *their* list." Life was cacophony. He threw the pan into the sink.

Mrs. Simpson stood still as a statue, eyes wide, one hand on her throat, pale.

"Oh, Mrs. Simpson, don't be scared. You've seen too much TV. I'm not violent. Please. Most of us are not violent. I'm okay with anger, at not having any of my own money. People get frightened of us because they don't want to think about mental illness; they don't want to think it could happen to them. That's what they tell us. I wouldn't hurt you. Not anyone," he said. He pushed at the burnt cheese with the spatula, but his strength had left. Frenchy was quick with words. Maybe if Frenchy were here he could help. Nathan said, "Even on a good day, we're scared of everybody else." He tried not to make any more noise with the pan.

Mrs. Simpson had poured coffee for herself and held out an empty cup. "Would you like some?"

Nathan shook his head and rinsed the pan and turned it upside down on the drain board. The bad air lay between them and he wanted to fix it.

She did, too, because she asked warmly, "If you could afford anything, what would you buy for yourself?"

Suddenly Cheryl's lovely, youthful face transposed itself over Mrs. Simpson's. Cheryl had made him laugh and feel important. Emory could be a stitch, too, but Emory didn't make the kind of sense people understood. Nathan said, "Time with someone who could make me smile and laugh." He peered down at the pan, thought of Frenchy, who maybe hid a good heart under his false bravado. There was a tongue-in-cheek quality to just about everything Frenchy said. Anyone could turn on you. He wouldn't really know about Frenchy unless he gave the man a chance. The man's paradoxical attitude attracted him. Maybe Frenchy would be the one to rescue him if he ever needed it. Nathan said, "Making friends is all elbow grease."

"I need to check on the customers."

For the remainder of the work shift, Mrs. Simpson smiled often and Nathan was extra polite. When he put on his jacket to leave, she put two dollars and fifty cents in coins on the counter. "For you," she said.

Nathan looked at the coins, saw twenty-five phone calls. AT&T provided the only bargain they had: halfway house pay phones took dimes.

"I don't think so."

"Nathan, meager as it is, that's half of today's tips. We both deserve better." She looked into his eyes. "I'd like us to be friends, Nathan. Is that all right? Can you agree?"

"Agree?" He shifted his weight. How could he disagree? "Well. Yes."

"You and I, Nathan, we do a lot of good being nice to customers who are visiting sick people. Friends share. Do you agree, friends share?"

He patted his hair, looked at the macaroni pan. He didn't see or hear any sign of pity.

"It would make me happy if you took it."

That clinched it. He would go home the long way, browse among normal people at the armory flea market. Doing that would keep him away from the house longer. It would be a real treat.

"Thank you," he said.

Out in the lobby Nathan looked into the floral shop window, thinking how Jupe would like a flower in the hospital. He fingered the coins in his jacket pocket for a long time before he moved his thumb along the Velcro, sealing the pocket.

The armory smelled of hot dogs, popcorn, and cotton candy. Nathan slid his fingertips along the smooth, wooden handle of an antique tool, knowing how Uncle Carl would appreciate it. He moved a fingertip down a shiny ceramic parrot. Its curved lines reminded him of an angel his mother kept on her bathroom shelf. She had Dresden, Dolton, and Hummel figures all over the house. It angered him that he no longer lived at home.

He saw the home-canned tomatoes and green beans and corn relish and thought of his mother's pantry. To dissipate the anger that filled his chest and pressed him like a weight, he turned his mind to Emory. Emory put sugar on sweet corn, on lettuce, and salt on bananas and cantaloupe. Emory liked corn relish. Emory's favorite commercial was "the incredible edible egg."

Inadvertently Nathan found himself strolling among a family with three children until the woman gave him that get-lost look. He hesitated, then turned to a display of secondhand cameras. "Say cheese," a bearded man wearing bib overalls said. The man clicked the shutter on the Polaroid and they watched Nathan's photo emerge. "Give you a good deal on this camera," the man said, handing the photo to Nathan. Nathan saw a more rounded body than he thought he had.

"Need more light," the man said.

Nathan extended the picture to him, shook his head.

"Keep it."

"No," Nathan said, his hand on his protruding mid-section.

"What would I want with a picture of you?" The man turned and aimed the camera at a little boy. "Say cheese."

Nathan put the image of himself behind his cigarette pack in the pocket next to his heart and moved on. The little boy exclaimed, "It's me. It's really me."

Nathan's last posed picture had been taken at his high school graduation, before Princeton, before Cheryl. "Babe, I love you," Cheryl said now. Where was she? Did she have a houseful of someone else's children? To quell his rising emotions, Nathan drew slow, tremulous breaths. He passed a display of terraria, told himself he needed to stop living like a plant cooped up in a snifter surrounded by chopped up bits of bark off a dead tree. He needed to save himself before it was too late. But how? He spotted a display of novelty clocks and hurried around passersby to get to it. There were clocks shaped like Texas, like Mickey Mouse, houses with cuckoos locked inside them.

"They keep good time," the vendor said. His eyes receded under thick white brows.

Nathan pointed to a large cat clock.

"Ah, that pussy purrs," the man said. The cat's eyelashes blinked over goo-goo eyes that rolled left and right. "Eyelids blink by the half-minute, curlicue tail swings by the second. A doozy, this one. Lots of character."

Nathan felt a chuckle rippling up from deep inside. It was the kind of clock Dr. Seuss would invent. Glee dizzied Nathan. He pressed his hand over the pocket with his money.

The man located a floor socket and plugged in the cord. "Takes a bit of precision to work on a ticker like this one."

"Does it meow?" Nathan asked, patting his hair.

The man unplugged the cord and wound it around the clock. He said, "Gimme a break."

Guilt made Nathan edgy. If he spent the money, he couldn't buy Jupe a flower. "Two dollars and fifty cents."

The man's eyes narrowed.

Nathan said, "That's all I have."

"Oh, what the hell," the man said. "It's not exactly a high demand item." They shook hands.

Afterward Nathan looked down at his hand still tingling from the man's grip, wondering how long it had been since anyone other than a government worker or someone at Chance Place or his parents had voluntarily touched him. He had actually negotiated for something he wanted and the man was wrapping it in brown paper.

"Ought to be good for a time or two," the man said, laughing at his own pun. "My card's in there. If it ever needs fixin'— 'Does it meow?'" he said. "I'll have to tell that one to my wife."

Nathan's chest swelled with pride.

Aware of the photo in his pocket, Nathan rode the bus with his cat clutched against his chest. He would never own a real pet again, not unless his mind played a trick and returned. Emory would like this pet, but as an audience of one, he didn't have to share it; he could keep it to himself. "Harmony," Nathan whispered, naming his clock. "Harmony." Houses whizzed by. He felt like a new man who could keep time in four parts: lashes blinking, eyes rolling, tail swishing, whiskers whisking. No—he had made up the whiskers. What was real was that he had laughed twice this week—temporarily ending emotional constipation.

CHAPTER FOURTEEN

Suitcases and boxes of residents' belongings surrounded
us. Like two dogs circling each other to establish the alpha male,
Nathan and I considered each other across the island workbench in
the basement. An unshaded light bulb burned overhead. Lily had
sent my clothes, but because we were working I wore jeans and a
blue and green striped, long-sleeved polo. Nathan wore corduroy
slacks and a matching shirt; his colors were always coordinated.

"You dress well," I said, pencil poised over the slab of
plywood. "I like that."

Nathan lowered his gaze. He said, "Emory's mother comes
every Saturday for his laundry. She irons his shorts and socks."

I said, "Anyone could use a mother like that." Lily had taken
good care of me. I measured and marked a spot and bent and
eyeballed the edge of the board to be sure the lumberyard had cut it
straight.

"E-easy for y-you to say."

"Will you hold the board steady?" I picked up the handsaw and
moved my thumb over the jagged edge. "That stammer. Meds,
right?"

Nathan wilted like a sad, dying flower. Big mouth, the disease
of my life. "Hey," I said, trying to make light, needing to recover

from my blooper, wanting to make a friend. "Goes with the territory. Couldn't do this without you. I really appreciate your help."

Nathan gripped the wood so tightly his knuckles turned white. He pulled his body back as far as possible.

"Don't worry. I won't slip."

"I don't want sawdust on my clothes."

"Oh."

When I stopped sawing he looked at me, then away, shifted his weight, asked, "Why don't you shake?"

God, I hated being so desperate for a friend.

Nathan lit a cigarette and waited for my response. If he knew I wasn't bonafide, would he change his mind about helping?

"I have only a mild case," I said, flexing and spreading my fingers and looking at them. Needing to change the subject, I latched onto the first thing that came into my mind. "Smoking's not good for you."

"Sorry." Nathan dropped the cigarette to the cement floor and stepped on it.

Strike two!

"I didn't mean you shouldn't smoke." I swished sandpaper over the edge of the wood.

Nathan picked up the butt, examined the tip of it, then inserted it into his pack and put the pack in his shirt pocket. Guys like Nathan treasured butts like C-notes. Tobacco companies should forget about teenagers, just concentrate on dedicated mentally ill customers. Tactless, that's me. Smoking was probably Nathan's only pleasure. Stupid beyond belief.

"Hold this," I said. "Please."

"W-what are we making?"

"A box. Foot-and-a-half by four. Tell me," I said, making sure not to sound offensive, "you have a mom?"

"She lives in Deephaven near Lake Minnetonka."

"But she doesn't iron your socks. Mine's dead," I said, not wanting to explain why I didn't see my mom. I sawed.

Nathan said, "My mother and dad are divorced. She says it's good for me to do my own laundry."

"You seem like the kind of guy who can do a lot of things."

Nathan made brief eye contact, shifted, and accepted the compliment like a kid who had waited a long time for one. "If I tell you something, it's true," Nathan said finally, breathing shallowly. He hesitated, then said, "I like working with tools."

I tried to imagine what it would be like to live in a world where everyone told the truth. "Glad to hear it," I said.

"C-can I ask you something?"

"Shoot."

"Where'd you get that?"

I followed his pointing finger to the rose-colored scar on my left arm, like North America, only squished longer and narrower, Mexico's tail curling down over my elbow. An ugly souvenir from the joint I didn't want to explain. "Stuck my arm where it didn't belong," I said, gesturing for him to hold the wood.

As Nathan gripped it, I saw the muscles of a former athlete. His physique had once been well-oiled and strong. The guy was built, handsome, the kind of guy Peso would have been attracted to. I finished sawing and caught Nathan waiting for approval the same way I waited for it from my father. I turned the saw around and extended the handle to him.

"I'll hold. You saw."

"You mean it?"

"Why not?"

Nathan measured this way and that, tested the edge of the saw, the edge of the wood, moving everything around into the best light, perfectionism to crack the patience of Job. Sawing made him so damn proud. Watching, my chest swelled. Then the etchy sound suddenly turned into a ratchety motorcycle's *rev-rev-rev* and my body took to shaking.

Nathan lowered the saw. "What's wrong?"

I wiped my forehead on my sleeve and swallowed. "You're doing fine, just fine." Nathan's eyes pleaded for something more from me, like Morton's dead open eyes. I pushed my thumb along the newly sawed edge. "This is good. Sorry. Great job. My mind's just a Mexican jumping bean today."

"Th-thanks," Nathan said, reaching for a cigarette, then stopping.

"Smoke," I said. "We'll die together."

"I know about jumping bean minds. It's hard," he said.

Here was the perfect opening to ask him anything I wanted to know about Chance Place, about other guys, even McMaster. But right then I was wondering if my father had killed Morton to get back at my mother, if killing Morton even had anything to do with me.

"You're right. Smoking's not good for you."

I said, "Let's put this thing together." With tremors I squeezed a transparent stream of glue between the edges of two corners. "Push 'em together," I said. "Hold." The smell of the glue hovered over the cooking smells seeping down from the kitchen above. I said, "If we had a vise we wouldn't have to do it this way."

Nathan said, "If we had a lot of things we wouldn't have to do without so many."

We squeezed corners waiting for the glue to bind.

"What's this for anyway? Why can't you use a cardboard box?"

"Can't, that's all." After a minute I tested the glue. "Okay," I said. I tipped the paint thinner can and dampened the edge of a cloth, then cleaned the screwdriver tip.

"McMaster likes things clean."

"He's not exactly man's best friend, is he?" I picked up the aerosol can of black lacquer and tipped it to the light to read the directions. "You ever have a dog?"

"Go-fer, a black Lab. She used to fetch in the lake. My mother has a collie named Lady. Debbie, my sister, had a gray cat. It was real friendly—for a cat. It got run over." Nathan's eyes took on the sense of longing.

I wanted to say I knew how that kind of longing hurt. "My dog got run over, too. Heads up." I sprayed black circles onto the plywood. "You have a girlfriend?" I asked, moving to the other side of the box.

Nathan lowered his eyes and pressed his lips together.

"You do!"

"I d-don't know."

I flashed a knowing smile. "Good for you." I sprayed small circles giving way to bigger ones. "What color's her hair?"

"Long. Dark." He patted his hair. "Soft," he said wistfully. "I don't know. Girls are always changing their hair. Maybe it's changed."

Not sure of what I had tripped into, I changed the subject. "What's it like having freckles?"

"Kids used to tease me." A couple of beats passed. Nathan said, "You have a job. I have cigarettes."

An unexpected spark! "Listen, Nathan. You're ... likable and helpful. I bet you could hold any number of decent jobs." A twinkle flashed through his eyes, then changed to fright.

"When I do what I know how to do, people won't let me," he said. "They want me to work for nothing. There's no dignity in that."

"Nathan, there're too many don'ts around here, but getting a job's not one of them." I wondered if I should introduce Nathan to Big Swede, a guy who definitely couldn't hold a job. Maybe I could convince Larson, Olson, whatever my boss's name was, to hire Nathan. "What d'ya think? Would a small spaniel fit in this box? A schnauzer?"

"You're not going to kill a dog!"

"Do I look like the kind of guy who'd kill a dog?"

Nathan patted his hair and stared at me. "A porcupine. A skunk, maybe?"

"A joke," I said. "Nathan, do you have plans? Dreams?"

He burst out laughing.

"What's so funny?"

"I-I could maybe grow a mustache—not one as nice as yours—th-that's the kind of dream I can make come true."

There were footsteps overhead.

Nathan sobered and said, "I used to dream of winning the Milk Carton Boat Race. Kids—grownups, too—race boats built out of milk cartons on Lake Nokomis in the July Aquatennial, some big enough for people to ride on like parade floats."

"Why didn't you ever make one?"

"I couldn't save enough cartons."

People were always discounting the mentally ill. Before long they couldn't believe in themselves at all.

"You want a boat, make a boat."

Nathan looked up at the sound of footsteps. "What time is it?"

"What difference does that make?" I was enjoying talking.

"Whether we eat or not. If I don't eat— Hurry! Hurry!"

I followed him, taking two steps at a time the same way he was.

"We didn't know it was so late," Nathan said, stopping so abruptly I tailgated into him.

McMaster said, "I've heard that one before."

"We lost track of time," I said, rubbing my forehead.

Jupiter stood in a corner of the living room, moving his thumb up and down the crease in the wall.

Nathan said, "Jupe's bad."

"So let him call his social worker. Ten minutes."

"He's scared of his social worker," Nathan said, following the man. "He hasn't seen him for months."

McMaster jerked his thumb in the direction of the kitchen. "Vamoose. Ten minutes."

I clenched my jaw to stay out of a fight that wasn't mine. Most of the men had already eaten and left. Nathan pinched spaghetti between tongs and dropped some onto two plates. A few kernels of corn remained, some Sunbeam bread, and no dessert, though there were apples, oranges, and bananas in the bowl.

"Here," I said, taking the pitcher of strawberry Kool-Aid from Nathan's shaking hand. "I'll pour. Don't let him get to you."

Nathan glanced around, then unbuttoned two buttons of his shirt and slid four slices of bread inside it. "He's trying to impress you because you're new."

Gummy, the tepid spaghetti.

McMaster entered the kitchen, strode to the house phone and punched in numbers. "Leaving in four minutes," he said. Then he turned his back, lowered his voice, and said, "Oh, yeah?"

Nathan and I exchanged glances. Nathan half-stood and took an apple and a banana from the fruit bowl and covered them with the paper napkin in his lap.

"Me, too," McMaster said. He hung up and rubbed his hands together.

"Please," Nathan said to McMaster. "Jupiter may need help tonight. Leave the kitchen unlocked so we can use the phone."

"Hell," McMaster said, digging into his pant's pocket. He pulled out a dime and held it up like a priest offering communion. "Here." He slapped it on the edge of the drain board. "Call me on yours. If you don't use it, I'll collect in the morning." Then he picked up the dime, came over, and dropped it behind Nathan's cigarette pack in his shirt pocket. "See how I take care of my boys?" he said, addressing me. He went over and removed messages from the assignment bulletin board.

Nathan was looking out for me, but I didn't exactly know why or what he was protecting me from.

"Time," McMaster said.

Nathan huddled the fruit wrapped in a napkin against his chest.

"You're lucky I don't have time to mess with that," McMaster said, indicating the bundle. He followed us out and locked the door, then gestured at Nathan with the key, a one-two kind of gesture, like shedding the last drop from his penis. "He's nuts," McMaster said to me, then waved his hand to take in the whole house. "They're all nuts." He moved to the closet and pulled out his jacket, then sauntered out the door, leaving us in a cold draft.

Shivering, Nathan extended the apple and banana on the napkin. He had bitten into the apple. "I didn't bite the banana," he said. "I just broke off the tip so he couldn't make me put it back."

There must be some law against guys like McMaster getting caught because they never were. My blood boiled. Underdogs like Nathan were expected to take such guff.

Emory said, "Blood cud."

"Yeah, well," Nathan said.

"No thanks," I said, regarding the fruit. Then noticing Nathan's disappointment, I took the banana anyway. "Thanks. I owe you."

"Wait, wait!" Nathan stuck the apple in his mouth, unbuttoned his shirt.

I took a slice of bread. "Next time, I'll wear my watch," I said. Rules or not, I intended to stash peanut butter and jelly in my room.

Emory said, "Smite bite."

"Yeah," Nathan said. "Smurf turf."

CHAPTER FIFTEEN

The men had retired except for Nathan and Frenchy, who watched TV, and Jupiter. Working with Frenchy had proved easier than Nathan had expected, except for that disturbing question about fitting an animal into the box. Nathan buzzed with a sense of accomplishment. He had even acquired a nail with which to hang Harmony, his clock. He watched as Jupiter felt along the wall of what used to be the dining room, moving hand over hand, passing through, Nathan knew from experience, the third eye, the third ear, into the fourth and fifth dimensions.

Dimensional experiences, like those Jupiter was currently into, used to seem far out to Nathan, too, until someone pointed out that shamans and aborigines and Native Americans and saints and Buddhists and Maharishis had them. Well, drug addicts and mentally ill people had them, too; you didn't have consciousness; consciousness had you. Some people claimed that when you were dying your mind expanded out of your body, allowing your whole life to pass before you.

Frenchy said, "Hey, I'm grateful for the banana and the bread." He nodded toward Jupiter. "Is he all right?"

"I don't know."

They watched Jupe trace the edge of the ledge of a curtainless window, then move on to other ledges, always maintaining contact as if something terrible might happen to him if he didn't. Actually Jupiter was maintaining contact in order to keep track of himself. Then a tire backfired on TV and Jupiter put his hands up against the wall. Nathan half-stood to go to him, but Jupe slid his hands down and continued in the lost pursuit of himself.

At 2:17 a.m. Nathan woke in response to Jupiter's guttural animal sounds in the other bed.

Nathan whispered, "Don't get scared. I'll turn on the light. I'm going to turn on the light, Jupiter." Nathan crept from the bed to the light switch. "Okay? I'm going to turn on the light. Now."

Jupiter lay rocking in a fetal position on the bed, eyes wide with fright.

Nathan pulled on Emory's purple sock, then one of his own. He donned his flannel robe, keeping distance, cautioning himself against terrifying Jupe into an imagined need for defense. The law said an adult had the right to help himself, that you couldn't take away that right or force help. Still, whether Jupe liked it or not, he needed help. Nathan held up the dime McMaster had given him so his roommate could see it and asked the futile question.

"Will you call for help?"

Of course, Jupe didn't answer.

The sicker a man got, the more rights he had to overcome in order to get the help he needed. Keeping his eyes on his roommate, Nathan inched to the door. Once out of the room, he bounded down the stairs to the phone. With trembling fingers he inserted the dime and dialed McMaster.

After the third ring, he heard a click, then, "This is Dave McMaster. I can't come to the phone right now … "

Nathan banged the wall with his fist, but remembered to wait for the beep. He said, "It's 2:25 a.m. Jupe needs help NOW."

Three floors up Jupiter let out a bloodcurdling yell.

Nathan slammed the receiver down and tried to focus on one thought at a time. Men appeared on the steps. He ignored them. "Anyone got a dime?" No one did. He mounted the steps two at a time.

"Wake up," he said, shaking Emory, who could sleep through a tornado. "I need a dime. Do you have a dime?"

"Go away," muttered one of Emory's roommates.

"It's Jupe. I need a dime for the phone. I need a dime."

Murray turned on the light. Nathan blinked against its sudden brightness.

"I don't have one," Emory said, sitting up, pulling pants on over lavender pj's.

Jupiter howled again.

All of the men, now awake, looked ceilingward.

"Five smokes," said Murray.

Nathan extended his shaking hand.

"Smokes first."

"I don't have them with me!"

"Smokes first. I'll meet you at the phone."

Nathan turned and bounded up the steps. Jupiter lay on the floor of their room like a bug on its back, kicking. Nathan moved slowly as fast as he could to get his cigarettes.

Emory and men in various stages of dress—Frenchy in long johns—waited by the phone. Nathan exchanged his cigarettes for Murray's dime. Except in cases of failure to breathe or excessive bleeding, they were forbidden to call an ambulance.

"Crisis Center?" Nathan asked the others.

"First Call for Help," Emory suggested.

"What if they won't come?" Nathan asked, jittery as a gnat.

"Loose noose."

Nathan patted his hair and turned full circle. "If I sound scared," he said, "they won't believe me. If I sound crazy, they won't come. You do it," he said, extending the coin to Emory.

Emory shook his head and stepped back.

Frenchy asked, "What's going down?"

"I am scared and I am crazy," muttered Nathan. "We need cab fare," he said to Frenchy. "Do you have cab fare?"

Frenchy shook his head.

A wild howl.

They all looked up.

Someone said, "He's not bleeding."

Someone else said, "He's not suffocating."

Emory said, "Wolf-wolf."

The chances of finding another dime were slim. Nathan asked, "What if I dial 911 and no one comes?" He swallowed and explained for Frenchy's benefit. "Murray's called 911 too many times. Police," he said, lifting the receiver. Nathan swallowed, breathed slow and deep, shakily inserted the coin, and dialed.

As soon as the woman answered, he said, "Th-this is Ch-chance Place. One of our residents needs help BAD. No one here can help. Come right away. Please." He hung up before there were questions for which he had no sane answers.

The silence charged with tension. Then the kitchen phone rang and the men stared at the locked door.

"I c-can't," Nathan said. He slid to the floor, drew his knees up into his chest, and covered his ears with his hands.

Frenchy stooped beside him, asked, "Why didn't you call McMaster?"

"I did. His machine's on. He never returns calls."

"Jesus."

"Rub-a-dub-dub. Rub-dub."

Frenchy kicked the kitchen door. He backed up and took a run at it and rammed it with his shoulder. "Damn," he said, rubbing his shoulder. "Damn, damn, damn."

Jupiter wailed. Men scattered, retreated, shook in place. Emory sat on the bottom step, humming, "Jericho, Jericho, Joshua fit the Battle of Jericho."

Nathan reached for a cigarette. He didn't have one. Murray did. Nathan's mind split like atoms in search of a corner on the round earth.

CHAPTER SIXTEEN

Nathan removed his roommate's soiled sheets. Images of attendants strapping Jupe down roiled inside his head. He took the sheets to the basement and left them soaking in the laundry sink. Motivated to nurture something if not someone, he returned to their room and tended to the two sweet potato vines which were growing in cutoff milk cartons on the windowsill. He took them to the bathroom down the hall and watered them, then set his poor excuse for a garden on his bedside table because they needed more sun than the windowsill offered. Given enough sun sweet potato vines grew and grew.

Filled with concern for Jupe, Nathan didn't know what to do with the energy bouncing around inside him. Where had they taken Jupiter? How was he being treated? Nathan entered his closet. Nearly two decades ago, Uncle Carl had installed this wall of boxes that came from an old post office. Seeking the kind of comfort that came from touch, Nathan touched the individual garments in each box one by one. He came to his Rubik's cube and picked it up and turned its different-colored sections until three greens aligned: Proceed. That was the message of green. Get on with life.

He carried his green shirt to his bedside chair and hung it over the back of it, then took the purple sock Emory had given him to the bathroom and washed it and draped it over the radiator. Nervous from no smokes on top of everything else, he got into his bed and tossed about. Was Jupe in the unlocked ward or in lockup? Was he comfortable or fighting demons? It was hard to be mentally ill. He mustn't think about Jupe. Jupe was where he needed to be. Nathan drew long, slow calming breaths. He wished he were back in his room in Princeton with Cheryl making love to him. "Oh, Babe," she said, arriving as she often did when he didn't want to be where he was. He looked into her eyes and saw his reflection doubled. He was safe. Cheryl would be with him always.

CHAPTER SEVENTEEN

Otto Olson, my new boss, looked me over starting with my Gucci loafers, up my charcoal pleated slacks and suit jacket. His eyes stopped at the diamond tie tack and again at my mustache before they met my eyes. I had just had my hair styled and looked like a pot of gold.

"Tie might get in the way. We're casual here," he said. "You'll be standing and stomping, so wear practical shoes. Don't want worker's comp claims."

I could tell I had made a good impression, knuckled my nose. "Sure," I said.

His knobby features suggested a Marciano who should've quit a few fights sooner. I dubbed him Zero, Double Zero, on account of his initials. No taller than me, Double Zero sported a football build that, because of the way his tight short-sleeved polo shirts showed off his oversized biceps and taut torso, reminded me of a sausage. The man's voice had a squeaky quality, like he'd taken a hit in his larynx or been sniffing helium.

Double Zero opened my workstation drawer. "Job's simple. These white gloves, wear 'em. Take a microchip, set it on the inverted V-frame like so." He placed the diddly chip sealed in a protective case. "Insert the casing under it, then press the pedal with your foot. *Whump*, clip's installed."

All I had to do was wear gloves, line up a tiny microchip, and whump it. To think I once resented traveling country roads. This work, beneath me by scads. Playing poker in prison would be more lucrative. Robotic equipment hummed and moved parts automatically from one place to another. The place didn't even smell like work, just like some antiseptic cleaner hanging in the air. My workstation testified to ancient times—an isolated set of small wooden drawers in an outdated cupboard filled with diddly parts.

"Good ones here. Rejects there," Zero said, hands on his hips. "You can do that?"

Any idiot could. "Sure," I said, resisting the sounds and pictures in my head left over from Jupiter's outburst. *Poor guy.* I hadn't slept well. I wished I could have helped. The sirens and shouts and psychotic stuff bouncing off the walls like ping-pong balls left me edgy. Was there no justice? I gestured to one of the movers and shakers, asked, "How come I don't have a robot?"

Double Zero said, "The robot for your station's due in late spring. Each is custom order."

Obviously a man not overskilled at conversation. I didn't know whether to believe him or not, set to work. At the end of the room my boss's glassed-in office gave him a clear view of me. Before long, he noticed that my reject pile was higher than my keeper pile. I aimed to please, yet him watching made me nervous. Finally Double Zero tossed papers onto his desk and headed my way. He stayed beside me like a guard expecting a payoff.

I felt his breath as I concentrated and stomped. I finally said, "With practice I'll get the hang of it."

Zero said in the kind of tone a guy could do without, "Careful is as careful does."

I realized Double Aught wasn't going to go away anytime soon; a sudden craving for liquor overtook me. The diddly part shook in my fingers. The man was an ambulance chaser in pursuit of an accident. I bit down, lined up the chip like drawing a stripe on a skunk, and stomped.

"Better. Secret's the line up."

"Thanks."

So this was how it was going to be—McMaster and Aught Naught Double Zero, Jupiter, and nut cases. Peso and Gabe were smarter than any of 'em. I flexed my fingers. The skintight gloves slowed my circulation. I had done some pretty dumb things, but was no dummy. I placed the chip, trying to ignore the craving only liquor would satisfy. Nathan had suggested a skunk or a porcupine for the box. Come summer, those animals would be dead on the road, free for the taking, but I couldn't send just any critter. I wanted to send a clear message. Zero was still watching me. I spotted the pay phone near the rest room doors. Didn't he have anything better to do? If I had a quarter, I could call Gabe. But I didn't have a quarter and was already bored with this job. The task required more patience and more stupidity than I could ever summon.

Underneath my thirst oozed anger that Jupe, or anyone as vulnerable and needy as he, should be so mistreated and abused. I wiped my mouth with the back of my hand. I had to get through this day and every day hereafter, over and out. Zero was right about one thing: Guccis were no match for the stomper. My foot slid off it. At coffee break when the boss vacated his office, I walked right into it and dialed Sister Kathleen.

"I got the shakes," I said. "I need a drink. I want a drink. So I'm calling."

After a pause, she said, "Have you been to an AA meeting?"

Telling her about Jupiter would take too much time. My mind, which I thought was trained to handle anything, failed me. I didn't want to get caught in Zero's office.

She said AA meetings took place night and day in every part of the city. Recovering drunks—she called them alcoholics—were on call twenty-four/seven for the likes of me. I had already learned enough lessons in the last twenty-four hours.

"You should be calling a sponsor, Frenchy, not me." She said it was up to me to save myself.

Was I or was I not the sanest person at Chance Place? I gripped the edge of Zero's desk and pleaded without pride. "Sister, this just sneaked up on me. I didn't think it would get this bad so soon," I said, slipping into despair. "Guess I don't have enough willpower."

"It's not a matter of willpower," she said. "Scientists have identified a cluster of genes guilty of alcoholism. It may help to think about your ailment like having diabetes; you need to pay attention to what you can safely ingest."

I didn't know that about genes.

"I'm glad you called, Frenchy, but it's not a good idea to mix my parole office role with acting as your counselor. Find an AA group and a sponsor. You'll get a phone list with lots of people to call when you find yourself in this situation. What if you needed someone in the middle of the night?"

I wanted to tell her how last night McMaster had done a first class Judas kiss-off, that there was no cause for hope in the world for Jupiter or Nathan or anyone like me. I wanted to save all of us; then I got practical, wondering how long Peso would send what I considered palimony.

"Sister, thanks for talking to me. I feel better. I'll find an AA group."

"Good," she said. "Frenchy, the men you live with suffer chronic irreversible illness. You don't. Alcoholism, Frenchy, is something you can do something about. No one forces you to swallow. No one raises a bottle to your lips."

My emotions rumbled like a Rip Van Winkle volcano trying to wake up. Inside me a hurt little kid cried. I hated that she was right. She was still talking.

"… my job is to say how it is. I don't need failures either."

I heard Gabe's voice saying, *You're not responsible for being down; you are responsible for getting up.* Now *I* was hearing voices!

I said, "Sister Kathleen, I don't think I'll ever be a father. I gotta go," and hung up.

At Chance Place I stuffed myself with instant mashed potatoes, sauerkraut, and cheap hot dogs; then, without speaking to anyone, I marched my anger through the cold dark, across the bridge over I- 35W. Slippery-soled Guccis weren't good for walking in snow or over metal bridges either. My feet were cold. I needed to buy boots with my first paycheck. Not much for hats, I kept wearing the knitted one because my ears got cold. St. Joan's School basement smelled of chalk and brewing coffee. I followed the smell to the meeting I didn't want to attend.

It began with the stupid Serenity Prayer that made no sense: "God grant me the serenity to accept the things I cannot change, the courage to change the things I can, and the wisdom to know the difference." After repetitive, routine preliminaries, a guy who looked like a truck driver talked about powerlessness in his life. Powerlessness was something I didn't think much about except around my old man and right after being falsely arrested. I wasn't powerless about getting away from Peso; I just didn't like the price of letting go of all the goodies he provided that I was still taking from him. Basically I counted myself as a take-charge kind of guy. Now powerlessness threatened to stretch over the rest of my lifetime when what I needed was a renewed sense of power. Action, that's what I needed and I wasn't going to find it here.

When it came my turn to talk I didn't know what to say. How can anyone hide in an open circle? I wrestled down anxiety and tucked my Guccis behind the legs of the metal chair. The guys waited; there was nothing to do but plunge in.

"Name's Frenchy. Alcoholic."

"Hi, Frenchy," they chorused. What a crock of NutraSweet. The greeting was supposed to make me feel okay about being here, okay about being an alcoholic, get me good and used to the idea when I had better things to do than listen to a bunch of confess-alls. In spite of my best intentions to keep quiet, I said, "I'm new in the neighborhood. Thirsty."

They already knew that; otherwise why would I be here?

"You came to the right place," Ernest, the trusted servant, said. Lanky, ruddy-faced Ernie wore a wrinkled, polyester-blend pinstriped suit and a loosened tie.

"Listen," I said. "Day at a time, stinkin' thinkin', runnin' and gunnin', first things first. I don't need fuckin' slogans—I want a drink. I *need* a drink." Before I even knew what happened, I was on my feet raging, zinging words quick as rocks zapping out of a slingshot. "What good is powerlessness? Serenity? I'm up to my ears in crazies! Where's the higher power?" I spun around and kicked my chair. It collapsed dead as a dog. I kicked that chair around the floor, couldn't believe I was ruining my Guccis. The chair clattered for my father beating on me, for him beating on Mom, for him beating Morton, for being told to stop crying when he was hitting me. A kid, a mere teenager, pulled a phone from his jacket, a damn phone!

"Hey," I said, putting my hands up. *Not the police! No police!* "Am I hurting anyone? If I'm boring you, I'll stop, okay? Or maybe you're calling your girlfriend?" I swiped the back of my hand across my mouth. Blues, not now or ever. Slowly the acned kid lowered the phone.

The gray-headed fella they called Gramps asked me, "Are you all right?"

I wanted to smash the chair over the kid's head. "Yeah, yeah. Sure."

I bent and picked up the chair. Who the hell did that kid think he was pulling a phone out? I sent him a poisonous look. I tried to pry open the chair; it was stuck closed, the metal bent. My big toe throbbed and my chest hurt from breathing. My blood pressure must be off the chart. I felt the same kind of hurt I had felt when they slapped the handcuffs on blubbering me. *Stupid, stupid, stupid.* Why was I here with ... drunks? Disgusted, I dropped the chair. It hit the floor.

After a moment of silence Gramps said, "We don't tolerate inappropriate behavior."

"I know, I know," I said, wishing I were dead. Everything I did was inappropriate. I waved my hand toward the chair. "I didn't mean to—"

The man who had been sitting next to me got up and came over and took my hand and pumped it. One by one the men paraded past me like I was father to the friggin' groom, shaking my hand, hugging me, telling me how glad they were that I had come. By the time they finished, I felt reduced to the size of a peeled Spanish peanut.

Someone brought another chair and I sat down on it and the meeting continued like I hadn't maimed the one that lay in the middle of the circle reminding everyone.

Ernie droned on about how he missed Russell's Bar where he used to be the life of the party. The guys laughed at tales of their own grandiosity. I didn't let on that I knew they were trying to teach me a lesson I neither wanted nor needed. I wasn't much good at this thing called sharing. I stretched my hat this way and that, could never laugh at myself that way. An obese guy talked about making amends. After him it got real quiet.

I looked up to find everyone looking at me. Was I supposed to say something?

"Before we close," trusted servant Ernie said, "is there anything you want to say, Frenchy?"

What was there to say? I shook my head.

"Okay," Ernie said, rising. We stood and joined hands and repeated the mumbo jumbo, "God grant me serenity … Amen." Everyone headed for the coffeepot like school was out.

"This is for you," Ernie said, handing me a phone list. "Stay. Have a cup of coffee. We're complimented you trusted us enough to let go, even if we objected to how you did it. Call anyone on this list day or night. If one guy's not home, another will be." He waited for something. What?

"We expect you to call the church and pay for the chair."

Fair enough. I nodded.

When Ernie saw I didn't intend to hang around for palsy-walsy, he said, "Go in peace."

I shivered all the way home, not so much from the windchill as from having been physically touched. Those handshakes and hugs triggered feelings I thought were long gone. Not to mention how much I missed the pleasure and thrill of Peso's hands on my body—though not the depression Peso also brought on. How could anyone so confused as I was stay in charge of himself? A rush of anger at Peso coiled in my chest. That man could put me down with a smile smooth as silk. When someone loves you, aren't you supposed to feel one-up? With Morton I had felt safe. Once in awhile with Lily. AA had de-fused me; I no longer wanted a drink!

CHAPTER EIGHTEEN

Nathan stood smoking in Jupiter's favorite dining room corner, paying tribute to his roommate, whose absence filled the atmosphere like a bad smell. He had waited for Frenchy to come home from work, hoping that talking with him would alleviate his own pain. At times like this Emory resorted to rhythm rather than rhyme and made even less sense.

When Frenchy finally appeared, he said, "Not now," ate in a hurry, and left immediately, giving Nathan no alternative but to sit and wait and hope things would work out for the best. Frenchy returned just after 8:00 p.m. Nathan was sitting in the living room, smoking.

"Listen," Frenchy said, his face red from the cold. "Get a couple of bus passes. Let's get out of here."

Eager for a change, numb, Nathan readily complied, but if Frenchy had said where they were going, he would have declined.

Nathan slowly moved down an aisle, peeking furtively at pictures of naked women on magazine covers. Breasts came in more sizes and shapes than he had ever imagined. Women did unbelievable things on some of the covers—with pets, candles, cucumbers, zucchini, each other. At the back of the store, overcoat slung across one arm, Frenchy leered at a foldout. Frenchy kept shifting his weight and appeared as jittery as Nathan felt. Nathan wanted to leave, yet he liked that the pictures awakened sexual feelings he had feared were long gone, feelings that could erase the pain he felt and from which he wanted relief.

He fantasized Cheryl lying beside him, felt her nipples hardening under his fingertips. Trouble was, Cupid could kill with that arrow of his. The farther back in the store Nathan moved, the more bizarre the pictures in his head became; Cheryl should never have betrayed him, not deserted him when he needed her most. He never would have guessed she would do that. It still hurt. He edged toward the front of the store and picked up a magazine, flipped pages, hoping to find something less prurient. If Cheryl returned to his life, he would forgive her.

Nathan looked up at the sound of a throat clearing and saw a tall blond man, an Adonis as Scandinavian as they came, with strong, chiseled features, wearing black leather pants so tight they made Nathan want to cough. The man smoked a brown cigarette. Suddenly relieved to know he could smoke—there were hardly any public places left where you could—Nathan set the magazine back on the rack and lit up. Exhaling, he saw the photo of a man and woman spraying whipped cream on each other. He smiled, imagining how cool whipped cream would feel, how sweet it would taste as he licked it from Cheryl's body. The Nordic man bumped him.

"E-excuse me," Nathan said, backing away, his reverie fading.

The man's fingernails were manicured. Nathan grew confused at the question in the man's eyes, hesitated, then extended the magazine. "Y-you want this one?"

"Hey," Frenchy said, slapping Nathan's back. He snatched the magazine and set it back on the shelf. "We're together," Frenchy said to the man, steering Nathan toward the door.

"Stop pushing! What're you doing?"

117

"Keep moving. Don't look back," Frenchy said. "If anyone asks what we're doing here, just say we're from the Antiporno League." Before Nathan knew what had happened they were outside, his breath rising in the air like steam as he tried to keep up the clipped pace Frenchy had set.

"You'll get pneumonia. Zip up," Frenchy said.

"I can't walk and zip."

"Okay, okay." Frenchy stopped and danced against the cold, hands in his pockets. He looked back toward the store. "Let me do that," Frenchy said, taking hold of the zipper. "You gotta be careful with strangers. That was a cop back there."

"How do you know?"

"Listen," Frenchy said, still walking too fast for Nathan to keep up. "Look for signals. What pretty boy's going to risk nicotine brownout on his teeth? He was a cop. A cop."

After sorting through sordid photographs and finally finding one he wanted to relish, Frenchy had insisted they leave. Nathan felt miffed. He didn't know if he should say so or not.

"You ever think of leaving Chance Place? Getting out?"

Every day he dreamed of leaving. Nathan stopped and stared at the man who kept moving, hands deep in his pockets. How could he make that happen? Like all those other unrealistic dreams, this one was just another delusion. Once he tried skipping his meds for a few days and had ended up in the locked hospital ward.

"Keep up," Frenchy said, dancing. "It's too cold to stand still."

Nathan didn't move. Did Frenchy know a way out that he didn't?

Frenchy crossed to him. "Take charge before the system eats you alive. Walk, why don't ya?"

Nathan moved along Hennepin Avenue. It was unfair to say the system would destroy him. Still, it was unlikely they'd find a cure for his illness during his lifetime. They were looking for one, weren't they? Was there even a slim chance?

"You think you're astute," Nathan said, using a word he doubted Frenchy knew. "You're not."

"I may not have gone to college," Frenchy said, keeping his pace, "but I acted smart on an occasion or two. C'mon."

Nathan skipped a step to keep up.

Frenchy walked past their bus stop and turned on Eighth; Nathan stayed on his heels. Since Frenchy had come into his life, his own dull existence had taken on borrowed interest, like a fresh shine on old shoes. They went into Dayton's and down to the budget floor where Frenchy filled out a mailing label and a gift card for a case of plain white toilet paper. The black woman who took his order seemed as wary and as curious as Nathan. Neither asked: To whom do you send a case of toilet paper as a gift?

This transaction proved to Nathan beyond any reasonable doubt that indeed Frenchy was one of them.

Afterward Frenchy ran up and down the up escalator, sparring and joking like he'd just won the lottery. Even without asking, Nathan could tell Frenchy wasn't going to reveal anything. If he did, it probably wouldn't make any sense. As with Emory, Nathan might, in time, decipher particular patterns. Figuring out such patterns added interest to life. Sometimes Nathan thought he was better at this than the doctors who were supposed to know the patterns they were looking for. He followed Frenchy into the better men's clothing department where Frenchy tugged on his sleeve, and said, "Nathan, buy something."

"I don't have any money."

"I do," Frenchy said, waving his charge card. "Anything you want. Anything."

Nathan remembered that morals called beliefs could be lies.

"Purple socks," he said boldly. "I want a pair of purple socks." His words surprised him.

CHAPTER NINETEEN

Nathan attended mass at St. Joan of Arc Church with his father, who criticized his socks and reminded him to renew his driver's license because it served as his ID. A plain photo ID flagged you as retarded or mentally ill, or not normal somehow. Nathan sang extra loud even when people turned and looked at him. After mass, his father dropped him at the foot of the steep driveway on Ravenscroft Ridge where his mom still lived. "Th-thanks," Nathan said, waving.

He turned toward the cedar split-level house, put two fingers in his mouth and whistled. Lady, his mother's half-blind collie, appeared amid the gone-to-seed, wheat-colored weeds at the side of the house, nose high, sniffing for his scent.

"Over here. I'm here." Nathan whistled again and started up the driveway. When he had lived here he was too young to appreciate the beauty of the wooded setting, the oversized downstairs playroom that opened into the backyard, and the treehouse he and Uncle Carl had built. Nathan used to take Mogo, Debbie's cat, whom he called Fluffypuss, up into his treehouse just to annoy her. From his perch, Mogo in his arms, he would watch boats skimming across Lake Minnetonka a couple of blocks away.

Lady waited at the back door, as excited as she could get these days, tail wagging. She couldn't jump higher than his knees. "I feel old, too," Nathan said, rubbing behind her ears, moving his face close to hers so she could smell him.

The door opened and Lady wedged her nose in.

"Outside, Lady, outside," his mother said, already spying the brown bag Nathan carried, the cartons of cigarettes his father had bought him. "Shouldn't you be wearing boots? Where are your boots?"

Nathan didn't answer. Lady's sad expression reminded him of Jupiter. His mother, short, shaped like Minnie Mouse, wore a dark dress with a lace collar, a bibbed apron of tiny yellow flowers. She took his gloves, his hat, and coat, moved slower than Nathan remembered. Did she still have friends? He never saw them. She used to have so many.

"I prayed for you," he said, setting his cigarettes out of sight on the seat of a chair at the table. "I prayed for you."

"St. Joan's," she said in a tone that suggested Father Harrigan, the liberal priest, might be responsible for his illness. "Sausage, the kind you like," she said, going to the stove and pushing her glasses higher on her nose. She beat eggs with a fork, then poured them into an omelet pan.

Nuthatches flew to and from the feeders. The oak oval table stood in the crescent alcove in front of the large window overlooking the back woods. If only his mother could realize that he was still the same person—not different—only jumbled. He had never stopped loving her. Or his father or his sister. Why couldn't she still love him, them, the same way?

"Spanish omelet," she said. "Belgian waffles. Strawberries and whipped cream." She was always too busy to look at him.

"Like I like," he said, preempting her. A nuthatch pecked at the suet. In saner moments, Nathan knew she, too, wanted their relationship better. "I'll wash my hands."

When he returned she was sitting at the table with a cup of coffee.

"Jupiter's in the hospital," he said.

"Such an unchristian name." Then she turned sad and took out her handkerchief and touched it to her cheek. "Hope it's not serious."

"Serious enough for the hospital. Aren't you going to eat?"

"Just grapefruit. Calories," she said. She got up, went to the refrigerator, and returned with half a grapefruit and a bowl of whipped cream, which she set in front of him.

Nathan suddenly saw Cheryl, naked, covered with whipped cream, and smiled.

His mother said, "Doctors are supposed to know what to do."

Cheryl disappeared.

"Jupiter's meds need fine-tuning, that's all."

His mother sighed, softened, and changed the subject. "You'll do well by the judge," she said. "I'm sure it will go well."

A knot formed deep down inside him. He didn't want to think about judgment.

"Your waffle's keeping warm in the oven."

A squirt of grapefruit juice landed on her lens. She took off her glasses and wiped it on her apron, saying lightly, as if making up for hurting him, "Belgian waffles come frozen at Byerly's now. I still make my own. We're lucky to have such a good supermarket. Foreign visitors are always strolling through, learning how to be successful."

A downy woodpecker backed down the trunk of the white oak, the dot on its red head bobbing as it snitched bugs from the bark. *Woodpecker takes in bug, energizes bird. Bird drops seed. Seed becomes flower. The flower, maybe a rose or a violet, blooms and creates happiness. Everything recycles. Even love.* He should have saved his money for a flower for Jupiter. Jupiter was hurting.

Nathan said, "Officials tour our place, too." Then, seeing that she didn't want to discuss where he lived, he said, "I helped a new resident build a box."

"For what?"

I wish I knew.

His mother got up and opened the oven and produced a waffle on a plate. She brought it to the table and piled berries on it and a dollop of whipped cream. She knew better than to ply him with so much food and he knew better than to eat it. If only they could stop this game.

She said, "The Sample boy visited with his wife and new baby, their fourth."

Hearing about old friends only reminded Nathan that their lives had continued after his had stopped. Les Sample, a father of four. Imagine.

"Debbie and Bill bought a new Sirocco, or maybe it was a Jetta. Everything's foreign these days, except at the supermarket."

Nathan looked at the morsel of Belgian waffle on his fork and laughed.

His mother bunched her apron between her fingers, said, "I never know what to say or do when you act like that."

"Sorry."

"Lester Sample," he said. "A father."

A crow spooked a chickadee away. Nathan felt the beginning of low cramps, the kind that came from overeating rich food when he wasn't used to it.

He said, "I can't save money."

"Don't give that leftover egg to the dog. You'll have some money soon. I suppose Dayton's bridal registry helped Debbie and Bill, though, Lord knows, they accumulated too much stuff that didn't match."

He hadn't seen Debbie and Bill's home. His sister's wedding happened in Bill's hometown, in Superior. Debbie knew he was too afraid to travel and Bill was uncomfortable around him. Maybe Debbie didn't want to be embarrassed in front of her friends. And maybe Bill didn't want to think about having a child turn out like his new brother-in-law. Before marrying, Debbie and Bill had lived together, stressing his parents.

Nathan said, "I don't know what a bridal registry is."

"A couple signs up and makes a list of gifts they'd like to receive. All guests have to do is ask the store what the couple wants. Dayton's even gift-wraps and sends out presents."

They would even include a gift card and not ask questions that should be asked about the kind of message Frenchy had sent.

Nathan reached for a cigarette, then remembered he couldn't smoke in the house. He didn't know what got into him to ask, "Does Debbie still like Bill?"

"What an awful question! They're married!"

His mother and father had married and they no longer liked each other. Nathan turned to look out the window, wished he could leap free as that red squirrel. Once he had known the names of all those weeds, which he preferred to think of as field flowers. If there were a registry for bachelors, he'd request a shoe polish kit, a sewing kit—maybe an iron. Lots of cigarettes—no generics.

"I'll walk Lady," he said, rising. "That was real good." As both of them pretended he wasn't going out for a smoke, she made him feel like a bad boy, guilty for feeling guilty, ashamed. Unlike most of the men at Chance Place, he ought to feel grateful to have parents who still saw him. Frenchy's mother was dead. Few had visitors.

Lady couldn't walk much faster than he could and had to sniff her way. Nathan bent his head low into the wind, hoping he wouldn't meet anyone he knew. He was indebted to his father—for boots, shoes, jackets, coats, hats, his mother for slacks, shirts, underwear, pajamas, socks. He had to be grateful for the things he needed and couldn't afford, items other residents did without or stole or got used from Free Clothes.

A surge of angry energy flung his left arm out. He arrived at the frozen lake. A ways out two men sat on camp stools—one wore a red-and-black-checked jacket like the one Frenchy wore when he arrived at Chance Place—held sunken fishing lines down through holes drilled in the ice. Smoke rose from the chimney of their fish house. Nathan strode the snowtrodden path toward them, but forked off before he got close. Lady had chosen not to follow him onto the fresh snow. He approached a cluster of seemingly deserted fish houses and peered sideways into the small window of one. Seeing no movement inside, checking to be sure the fishermen couldn't see him, he used his hands like blinders beside his eyes, and pressed his nose against the window. It was empty. He retreated along the path, belching the acid taste of strawberries.

"I feel like I've had a ride on the Whip," he confided to Lady. Cataracts made her eyes milky. Frenchy's question resurfaced: Do you ever think about leaving Chance Place? He certainly hadn't resigned himself to living there for the rest of his life, yet he didn't exactly know how not to.

Back on shore, Nathan leaned against a Norway spruce and waited for his wave of nausea to pass. A junco, a bird plumaged like a penguin, pecked in the snow after seed. Watching it presented Nathan with an idea for a gift for Jupiter. He turned and set a faster pace toward his mother's house.

As Lady headed for the back door Nathan trudged through deep snow to pick brown, dormant evening primroses, peppergrass, and curly dock, proud trumpet-shaped pods on long stems, wispy aster to breathe air into the bouquet, Queen Anne's lace, finally a large prickly sunflower. He had reached down deep into the snow for longer stems. Snow dampened his socks and his sleeves. Once he got excited about an idea, he couldn't stop.

Lady lay waiting for him with her chin on her front paws. Nathan set down the bouquet, blew on his cold fingers, and unlaced his shoes.

"Look at you," said his mother. "You need socks!"

"Yes ... no," Nathan said, removing them. "I'd like to take a bath. I picked flowers for Jupiter. Can I use your hair spray to fasten the seeds?"

"I'll throw these socks in the dryer," she said, holding them out in disgust, shaking her head at their color.

Nathan's room basked in the glow of setting sun. He took out the photo the man at the flea market had taken of him and tacked it on his bulletin board next to the newspaper clipping of him accepting a skiing trophy. The memories here seemed to belong to someone else—the boy proud of his four-pound walleye beside his father. The group shot of neighborhood fathers and sons camping for a week in the Boundary Waters. When had he last pleased his father? Nathan sighed and turned away. Like him, the trophies on the shelf were out of date. Not that he had aspired to become a full-fledged professional athlete—but a man, he had expected to become a full-fledged man.

Trying now not to focus on the past, but on the present, Nathan put on his favorite Benny Carter jazz record and arranged his clothes neatly over the back of a chair. Then he locked the door and got under the blanket. In spite of his meds, in time to the music, he, as an audience of one, tried the best way he knew how to make himself come.

Later that day Nathan approached the clerk in the Hennepin County Medical Center floral shop and asked for colored tissue to wrap around Jupiter's bouquet to make it look like a real present. At the request the young man began moving things here, there.

"I-I'll pay."

"You didn't buy those flowers here."

"I picked them," Nathan said. "Broke snow, got my feet wet—had to polish my shoes."

The young man took up a broom and started sweeping.

Nathan patted his hair and said, "I'd rather have purple tissue, but green's okay."

The man wouldn't look at him. In a similar situation, Emory would make a purchase at Dayton's, get a free box from gift-wrap, then return the purchase. Nathan knew about a family on welfare who without transportation to the laundromat, resorted to taking garments from Free Clothes because they needed clean clothes.

Nathan looked into the lobby, then back at the stack of green paper. If he left without tissue, Jupiter, who sat lost in a colorless world, would have no color to help bring him back. He felt guilty about buying his clock. Miffed at his own thoughtlessness, Nathan flung himself across the counter and in one swift movement took two pieces of tissue.

"You can't do that!"

"I'm doing it," Nathan said, dropping two-and-a-half phone calls, a quarter, on the counter. Then he did an even braver thing. He set his bouquet down, unwrapped the newspaper from it, and transferred it onto the tissue. Nathan cradled his gift and said, "Have a g-good day." Selfish and unkind people ought to be the ones in locked wards, not hurting, confused people like Jupiter. Nathan rode the elevator to the fifth floor. He pressed the doorbell to the locked psychiatric ward. Geoff, the attendant, peered out at him through the square of wire-meshed glass, and unlocked the door.

"Nathan," Geoff said. "Are you sick?"

"No. I'm here to see Jupiter Barnes. He's my roommate," he said, making brief eye contact. Geoff was as handsome as Nathan liked to think he used to be. He followed Geoff to the nurse's station. There, he set down the bouquet and dug deep into his pocket for matches and keys. Nail clippers were on the key ring. He set everything in the small box Geoff provided, said, "That's all."

Geoff put the box in a pigeonhole labeled with Jupiter's room number. "He's not in good shape. Just a couple of minutes."

"I know." Nathan hesitated. "Can I have a vase?"

Geoff stooped and produced a knobby, plastic green vase. "Not long, Nathan."

Nathan knew about the family-only visitor policy. Didn't roommates count as family? "Jupiter lives with me," he said.

Geoff said, "Later he'll remember you came and be glad."

His roommate wore a hospital gown, sat in the brown vinyl chair in the corner, staring straight ahead. A tray of untouched food sat on the trolley at the foot of the bed, not a good sign.

"Jupiter?" Nathan whispered from the doorway.

Nathan approached ever so slowly, speaking barely above a whisper. "I picked these for you." Careful to make no quick moves or sound, he set the vase on the dresser, then the bouquet. He tried to prevent the paper from crackling, was fully aware of the sacred presence of life residing in the seeds. He had pre-arranged the bouquet and inserted his gift into the vase. Pleased, he turned it toward Jupiter. "I hope you like it. It's a hospital vase."

Did Jupiter even know he was here? Not a flicker of recognition.

Nathan swallowed and shifted his weight. He resisted clearing his throat. "Have you been in the pink room? They say, uh, it calms you. You don't need to water these," he said, forcing a smile. "I've never been. In the pink. Room."

On top of everything else, Jupiter would be feeling the effects of withdrawal from cigarettes. There was nothing Nathan could say or do that would help that. Absolutely nothing.

"Have you called your social worker?"

There was no emergency; the social worker wouldn't be in any hurry to help. Hospitals tended to keep you until your yearly Medicaid days ran out, then discharged you in a hurry. If you needed hospitalization later that year, too bad. Mental wards were profit centers. Knowing there was nothing more he could do, that soon Geoff would arrive and shoo him away, Nathan edged slowly toward the door, thinking how lucky he was to have Sister Angela assigned to him. She cared.

Finally at the door, Nathan said, "I'm going to see my social worker. You should do that. Someone here will call if you ask. They will, Jupiter. Ask." Nathan spotted the cup on the tray. Coffee sure was Jupe's weakness. "And try to eat, but not coffee, no caffeine. In three or four days, maybe a week," Nathan said, patting his hair, "you will be as good as before."

Suddenly Nathan felt suffocated because he wasn't so sure his roommate would be as good as before. You could never be sure. Depression overwhelmed him. He said, "Don't let the devils get to you," and exited.

Out in the hall Nathan shuddered and pushed his hands deep into his pockets. Personally he'd prefer Abbott-Northwestern, though seldom did one have a choice. Residents discussed hospitals the way other people discussed hotels.

A male patient's voice pontificated from inside a room, "Save yourself from sin before lightning strikes you."

Nathan passed two older women holding hands, shuffling in disposable slippers. The system was crazier than the patients it was supposed to cure. In this very hospital Nathan had first learned how to tune out disturbances worse than those inside his own head.

Once outside, he lit up.

CHAPTER TWENTY

The old man repeated, "I can't sell you a dead dog."
    All week I dreamed of putting my plan into action and now I had run into this guy. I could have persuaded the girl who was here before. I heard Nathan say, *You're not going to kill a dog!*
    "You want me to buy one and kill it?"
    "Mercy, no! That would be against the law!"
    "The law, the law, the law," I said, punching the door.
    What a guy had to go through to get his life back on track. Disgruntled, I left.
    Shortly after that, fate dropped a gift right into my path. Crossing the bridge over I-35W at Forty-sixth Street, I spotted the body of a small white dog lying in the snow at the foot of the street lamp. A miracle, finding a white dog on snow!

My new Nikes worked well on the stomper. How I'd like to witness my old man's face when he opened Dayton's delivery of the box Nathan and I had built. Gabe was right: Put Morton to rest. Poetic justice, Peso would say. Taking charge made me feel powerful. I whistled "Ninety-nine Bottles of Beer on the Wall."

I had managed to be solemn when I filled out the Continental Mortuary Air Service destination form and watched the driver and his aide slide the box into the back of the limo.

When I had whistled down to seventy-two bottles a hand gripped my shoulder. I turned to see Double Zero standing beside me with a cop! The microchip in my hand clattered on the floor.

Zero said, "Let's go in my office." He waved his hand to tell the others to get back to work.

"Whatever it is, I didn't do it," I said. "Curfew even," I said, glancing at the policeman, knuckling my mustache, "I keep it."

"Nothing like that," Badge 522 said, extending a paper. "Is this your signature?"

The Continental Mortuary Air Service form! Pressure pushed against the back of my eyes. Sweat poured into my armpits. My body took to fidgets; I fumbled blindly for the smart thing to say, the right thing.

"I saw my dog die! I d-didn't hurt that dog."

"Of course not," the officer said.

I had paid Continental with my credit card. Wasn't the card good?

The officer rubbed the side of his neck. "Continental couldn't deliver," he said, looking uncomfortable. "The recipient moved without a forwarding address. They phoned the number you gave them. The man who answered, spoke, they said ... in rhyme. They ... called us and we called Mr. McMaster, who referred us to Sister Kathleen Lerner. She's due here."

Wasn't that like the old man to disappear just when I was trying to connect? Sister Kathleen was coming. Double Zero looked like he was holding in a fart. My stomach flipped like I was tossed from a roller coaster. I cleared my throat and hung one hand on my collar, trying to salvage what I could.

I asked, swallowing, "What's the problem? Exactly?"

"Disposal of the body."

Oh. I hooked my thumbs in my belt to try to still my tremors.

"Sir, I'm sorry to have to do this," Blue said. "It's just that since the Rodney King incident ... we're trying harder. Before that we wouldn't have followed up on a situation like this. Your departed pet is still ... they need to know what to do with ..."

Gabe was right; failing to plan was planning to fail. Sister Kathleen arrived, breathless, tweed coat open, red scarf flying over her shoulder like a war flag. "Frenchy," she said, then asked lots of questions, talking as fast as my mother did when she was upset. Blue's heavy boots reminded me of my father kicking bruises into me and Mom. His motorcycle *Rev-rev-reved* in my ears. A kid-of-a-man wearing plaid pants and clunky snowmobile boots arrived toting a camera.

"Star Trib," he said, flashing ID.

I covered my ears with my hands, backed away as my old man pounded on my mother. A flashbulb flashed. Sister Kathleen gripped my shoulders and shook me. My little boy sissy voice said, "I-I just wanted to say g-good-bye to M-Morton." I saw bloody Morton on the asphalt, broken ribs sticking out.

"Mr. Bibideaux?"

I couldn't respond. The doctor wanted to put me to sleep the same way the vet had put Morton to sleep. I fought like a banshee before the needle pricked my backside.

Zero said, "This is taking too long."

"Look," the policeman said, not unkindly. "St. Paul has a nice pet cemetery. If Mr. Bibideaux will authorize it, Continental will ... here." He picked up a pen and wrote on the form, then handed the pen to me.

I fixed my eyes on the man's penmanship: This is authorization for Continental Mortuary Air Service to inter this dog's body in St. Paul Municipal Pet Memorial Cemetery. Fearing I would dot an "i" wrong and end up back in prison, I raised my eyes in a plea to Sister Kathleen.

She nodded.

My hand signed my name.

"Great schmaltz," the reporter said, flashing another photo. He turned to Zero. "Mr. Olson, I want a shot with the dog. You'll let Bibideaux come with me without docking his pay?"

Zero practically pushed us out the door.

Zoned out, wearing Nikes instead of dress shoes, I posed beside the white dog propped up against the blue lining in the open casket. The scapular of St. Francis praying lay against the dog's chest. The flash blitzed my vision into floating dots. Sister Kathleen eased the reporter by the elbow out the door. She said, "Can't you see Mr. Bibideaux's grieving?"

In answer to the reporter's question about the scapular, she had explained that St. Francis of Assisi was the patron saint of animal lovers and of nature, that burying it with my pet was my way of wishing Morton Godspeed.

"Great schmaltz," the kid said for the umpteenth time, and left. Sister Kathleen said, "Come with me." I followed her to her car. "Where are you taking me?"

"To my office."

I didn't want to be alone with my parole officer.

One glimpse of those poor pleading souls in purgatory hanging on her wall and horror cut into my chest and gut like a freshly-sharpened knife. My body dissolved into sobs. My eyes shed waterfalls. I couldn't control myself. What had happened?

When awareness returned, my head hung between my knees. I heard Sister Kathleen's breathing. She was kneading tension from my neck and shoulders. My throat was raw and rough as a newly sawed edge. I saw a blurry glass of water, and drank all of it.

"Frenchy?" She spoke real soft.

I had made a super class sissy display. Shame filled me. I pulled two tissues from the box, doubled them, and blew my nose. *What an ass I am.*

Ever so softly, she asked, "What did you like most about your grandfather?"

When I didn't answer, she said, "Your father's father?"

I shook my head.

"Your mother's?"

I nodded and drew a quick, quivering breath in search of control.

I had slumped on Poppy's lap the same way Morton had slumped on mine. Poppy swung the chewed scapular like a pendulum over my face, trying to distract me when it only reminded me of what I needed to forget. I reached up and took it from him. It was wet.

"He held me after—" I said, not realizing I was even talking. I took a deep breath, said, "It's over. A thing in the past, Sister. All this was on the up and up."

She moved to the other side of the desk. Her eyes looked so tender. Never had I felt so beholden, so vulnerable. Not even with Peso. Without thinking, I pulled the crumpled card she had requested that I get signed at AA from my pocket and offered it to her. I thought about telling her that AA didn't have leaders, only trusted servants. She had been nice, nicer than my mother could be—

She said, "You're going to be in the newspaper."

The words dropped me into reality: *Dad and trouble, Siamese twins.* "I suppose Zero will fire me."

"Zero?"

"Mr. Olson."

"Because now he knows you live at Chance Place?"

Her softness softened me. I didn't know how to act, shifted with discomfort.

"Why would he fire you for trying to bury your pet? Frenchy, I don't know what Mr. Olson thinks. I ... urged the reporter to focus on your wishes and on St. Francis."

I took my hat from her desk and twisted it this way and that. "Olson knows I've been in jail?"

"Only if you told him."

My mind did somersaults. My parole officer hadn't ratted! My feelings spun like molten glass getting thinner, thinner. What I would give to cuddle up to someone with eyes as soft as hers and feel safe. I was very confused. My heart still belonged to Peso, didn't it?

She said, "There are laws regarding confidentiality."

Sure.

She reached up and stopped her earring from dangling. "You're not going to tell me about this, are you?"

In the silence that followed I realized she had something on the line here, too. I hadn't considered that my actions would have consequences for her.

"Sister, I swear I did nothing illegal. Nothing! I just wanted—" I stopped before my spill of honesty let her too close. "Maybe we should pay our respects," I said, joking to stop the closeness.

She smiled as I knew she would. The way her earrings swayed made me think of Nathan's clock.

"Actually," she said, "that may not be a bad idea ... later." She looked into my eyes.

I tugged at my hat. Zero would tell me to get lost. "Sister Kathleen, could you call—"

"Mr. Olson? Sure."

My heart took the kindness hit with the force of a punch. I asked and she had said okay. How many shocks could a guy absorb in one day?

CHAPTER TWENTY-ONE

Nathan drummed his fingers on the conference table in the small courtroom. Sister Angela, who was older than he, but not as old as his mother, sat across from him next to his father. Her suit matched the taupe color of her hair, which was coiled in a knot behind her head. Sister Angela's profile offered sharp, angled features; straight on, she appeared soft with sensitive eyes. She took off her jacket and hung it over the back of her chair. There had to be a message there—back of chair, color of hair. Up front, the judge and clerk were whispering to each other. Sister Angela said he needn't be nervous, but the microphone poised like a cobra ready to strike in front of him. Nathan wanted to repossess his money and go home. Changes, the kind that made him build boxes for unknown purposes, formed knots in his intestines. His mother caught him looking at her. Nathan touched his shirt pocket, pictured himself chopping poisonous lily-of-the-valley leaves into a salad for whomever decided he must be here today.

His attorney, a woman from Legal Aid, arrived and set her briefcase on the table on the other side of Sister Angela. He half-rose and greeted her. What was he thinking? He could never ever poison anyone. He patted his hair against tension in the air. His attorney seemed too young to be out of school. Nathan wanted to smoke. Against better judgment, he had worn navy socks. He turned at the sound of a thud and saw a woman stuck in the doorway carrying a book as big as a library dictionary. She backed up and entered the room sideways. Nathan pinched the crease in his navy blue slacks. When the woman dropped the book on the table her melon breasts swung under her shiny, white dress. Over each melon was a gold button on a patch pocket. "Sorry," she said, fluttering a hand toward the judge. "Traffic, Your Honor." She wore thick, false eyelashes, located Nathan. Her expression reminded him of a teacher trying to decide whether or not to punish him. Nathan clutched the microphone.

The woman covered her ears.

His chair scraped back.

Sister Angela touched her throat.

"What?" asked the judge.

"The m-m-microphone," Nathan muttered, only to hear his voice amplified. He turned to Sister Angela with a plea. "It scares me," he said. Nathan glimpsed the breasts he was trying to avoid and licked his lips, and said, "It makes everyone know what I'm saying." The woman with the book hid a smile behind ringed fingers. Nathan squeezed the cigarette pack in his pocket. Sister Angela had warned him, "Please. No undue attention."

His lawyer stood and asked, "Your Honor, may we turn off the mikes?"

"All right. Mr. Waite, slide the button to off and remember to speak up."

Sister Angela patted his arm. Sometimes he dreamed of sleeping in Sister Angela's lap—another thought he shouldn't have.

The judge squinted, straining to read the time on the wall clock behind him. "Let the record show this hearing began at 10:03."

The judge raised and lowered his glasses.

Nathan patted his hair.

"Counsel?"

"We're here, Your Honor, to reinstate Mr. Waite's Social Security income and Social Security disability benefits. They stopped by computer error ten months ago."

"If the problem was computer error, why are we in hearing?"

"Your Honor, despite the fact that no one at the Social Security Administration signed Mr. Waite's appeal, the file was sent to your office. Your office maintained that once there, you would hear the case."

The judge stared at the back of the clerk's head. He cleared his throat and shuffled papers. "Well. Did your client appeal within the allotted time?"

"No, Your Honor."

Nathan tried to retrieve a dot of lint from his cords. He should buy some of that dryer stuff which was supposed to prevent lint. He didn't want Sister Angela to scold him for not opening envelopes from the Social Security Administration. "You don't have trouble opening the envelopes with checks," she accused. Those envelopes had windows so he could tell what was inside. Secrets, especially those you weren't allowed to discuss, were frightening.

"How old are you, Mr. Waite?"

Nathan was no longer sure. "In my forties."

"Do you have a job?"

"At A-Abbott-Northwestern Hospital."

"How much do you make a month?"

Lint was caught between the tracks on his cords.

"In a week?"

He squirmed. "I work for honor, Your Honor."

The judge's eyebrows arched with expectancy.

"Doesn't everybody?" asked Nathan.

"It's a volunteer position," said the attorney, half-rising.

Like everyone else, she gave parts of him away. Soon he would have nothing left.

"Ah. Yes," acknowledged the judge. "Mr. Waite, would you like a job?"

"Yes. Yes, Your Honor. I would."

Nathan's father pinched the bridge of his nose. His mother pressed her handkerchief to her cheek. The judge smiled. Nathan tried to relax.

"What kind of a job would you like?"

The woman with the rings and breasts leaned forward and put one hand on the big book. Nathan glimpsed her cleavage, acted on a flash of inspiration.

"Yours," he said to the judge. "Not business like my father, too competitive. Not waiting on people like my mother. I'd like a job like yours. I know how to ask questions. Will you help me?"

Sister Angela crossed her lips with two fingers, paled, and shook her head.

"My job requires a law degree, Mr. Waite. Do you have one?"

"Nooooo ... sir."

"What skills do you have?"

"Skills?" It was a word Nathan hadn't thought of in a long time. A burning sensation spread out from his heart. He reached for the button on the microphone, thinking if he moved it, it might make Sister Angela sit still.

"I SKI," he said, sending everyone in the room into a downhill run. "Sorry." He slid the button to off. "I'm a good woodsman, know which plants to eat, how to survive. I used to be a fishing guide in the Boundary Waters. I know how to build model cities with popsicle sticks. Elmer's Glue works best because you can fasten them with rubber bands, and—" Nathan speeded up to get out the whole truth before Sister Angela stopped him. "I bagged groceries. I worked as a lifeguard, a ski instructor, cut lawns—course not when there's snow—well, I mean the grass is

139

still underneath." He saw their annoyance and stopped. "Anyway, for snow you need a shovel."

The judge opened a folder and flipped pages. Sounding frustrated, he addressed Sister Angela.

"IQ?"

"One-hundred-forty-three, Your Honor."

Nathan turned to the judge, who by the expression on his face had clearly misjudged.

"Not retarded," Nathan said, correcting a mistake so many people made.

The judge put his elbows on his desk and folded his hands and looked at Nathan with new respect. "Education?"

Nathan didn't want to tell what had happened at Princeton. "I'm self-taut. S-i-c," he said.

"Have you had job training?"

Nathan's mind ran through programs for which he was supposed to be eligible: I-R-C, S-L-I-C, T-A-S-K, R-I-S-E. "Spare me alphabet soup," he said.

A silence followed during which Nathan tried to gather himself, which was more than he could say for Sister Angela, whose vibes scattered like she needed help. His father's face flushed. His mother looked like she was going to cry. Everyone was disappointed in him.

"Mr. Waite, do you have a good relationship with your doctor?"

"Now that, *that*," Nathan said, rising, and pointing at the judge, "is a job I would really like. They never ask the right questions and have a lot of wrong answers." Nathan hadn't felt such energy in a long time. He slapped the table, was going to spill what he knew when Sister Angela folded her hands and squeezed until her knuckles turned white. Nathan peered at her, pleading to continue.

She pressed her lips together and shook her head, then closed her eyes.

His parents wouldn't look at him.

Nathan sat. His knees took to bobbing. Sister Angela had told him to avoid drama, to give simple answers.

"Mr. Waite?" The judge's tone offered patience for the patient. "Tell me about the last paying job you had."

Nathan crossed his arms. There were fingerprints on the table. If he told the truth, he'd be splashing in class ten whitewater without a paddle. Nathan started counting backwards from one hundred.

Sister Angela said, "Two years ago Mr. Waite worked for five months as a waiter at El Torito's."

"What happened to that job?"

"They wouldn't put me back in lettuce," Nathan blurted. He leaned forward to launch into the whole sad story, but his father's voice stopped him.

"Because he damn well dumped food into customers' laps three times in one day, that's why."

"That's not what happened!"

Nathan wanted to tell his side of the story, but first he needed to explain the context. "Your Honor, do you know how I figured your job was easy?"

"I think I do."

"You do? Then that makes you about the smartest man I know." Nathan relaxed. "Tell me."

"Why, Mr. Waite, you've already explained. You said you knew how to ask questions and I'm asking questions."

"Oh."

The judge asked a lot more questions, then turned to the lady with the big book. She said that there were no jobs for which she thought Nathan was now qualified. The judge said he would put his answer in the mail within three days and struck his gavel to end the session.

That thick book was a dictionary of jobs listing the skills you needed to do them. Nathan knew what he could and couldn't do. Frenchy dressed better and was smarter than anyone in the room.

141

* * *

As he rode home beside Sister Angela in her rickety,
yellow VW, Nathan smoked and repeated his story. "The chef
hired me to do lettuce. I worked hard. He said I did it so well I
could wait on customers. I told him I didn't want to because no one
stared at me in the kitchen, the way customers did. He had
promised lettuce. When he didn't keep his promise, I spilled food
on customers to convince him to let me be in lettuce."

Sister Angela took a deep breath and slowly exhaled. She
stopped for a red light. "Nathan, some people are … unkind. Even
some of my social services colleagues seem more interested in
making their jobs easier than in assisting clients."

Jupiter was one of those people with a social worker who didn't
care. "I know." Traffic was especially heavy.

"Nathan, I have to ask you some questions. This is as good a
time as any. Do you have life insurance?"

"You know I don't."

"Do you own a burial plot?"

"I'm not dead."

"Do you have a savings account? Own tools of your trade?"

"What tools? What trade?" This felt like his mother pushing
food into him and him eating it when he didn't want to. The
amount of money he could keep kept changing with the license of
the residence he lived in. Last year it was five hundred dollars. If
he were warehoused in a nursing home where some social workers
put their mentally ill clients, he could have up to three thousand
dollars. No matter how much money he had, the government
siphoned it to nothing. The government made people spend down
inheritances.

Nathan said, "When my January cost of living raise comes, why doesn't the amount of money I get to keep change? Where does my cost-of-living raise go?"

"To your cost of living. Nathan, I need you to come to my office this week and resign your claim to state supplementary income and county medical benefits."

"You want to stop my benefits!"

"It sounds like that, but no, not really." She looked at him like he was missing the obvious. "Nathan, when you receive your back pay, you will no longer be eligible for state and county funds."

Nathan shifted his weight. Who ever won a disagreement with his social worker? His heel took to tapping. "But I don't have any back pay! How will I—" *get cigarettes?* He asked, "How will I live?"

"You'll be getting four thousand, four hundred sixty dollars. It takes six weeks to stop benefits."

It takes six months to start them. "I don't want to stop my benefits."

"Nathan, you're allowed a burial plot, which you said you don't have. You're allowed premiums for life insurance, which you don't have. You're allowed up to five hundred dollars in a savings account, which you don't have. There are some people in social services who will intentionally do you harm. I am not one of them." She pulled in front of Chance Place and stopped the car. "Come in and sign the papers and we'll be finished."

"I don't want to be finished."

"Nathan, this is how the system works."

The system doesn't work! A terrible question formulated in his mind, one that filled him with so much fear, he could hardly ask it. "Wh-when the money you say I'm supposed to get is all gone, Wh-what happens?"

"Then we'll reinstate your benefits."

"Fill out all those forms again about having no car, no house, no real estate?" Nathan threw his head back and laughed wildly. "You are asking me to sign away money I don't even have. That's wrong." *It's crazy.* He should have worn his purple sock. "You want to take better care of me dead than alive. I didn't ask to be sick. I don't want to be sick."

"Nathan, Nathan," Sister Angela said, resting her forehead on the steering wheel.

"I'm not signing," Nathan said.

CHAPTER TWENTY-TWO

Your Personal Daily Message from the Center for
Universal Awareness—
> In the triangle of life's energy,
> Are you charged plus?
> Or minus?

This was just the kind of encouragement Nathan needed to ask
Frenchy about the toilet paper. He delayed eating dinner, waited at
the living room window to spot Frenchy. When the man didn't
show, Nathan gulped his dinner. By the time Frenchy finally
appeared, Nathan was in his room, scissors in hand, shaping sweet
potato vines. Frenchy's nose was red like he had a bad cold, his
eyes glassy and swollen.

"What's wrong? Are you okay?"

Frenchy plopped onto Jupe's bed, sat with his back against the
headboard, pulled up his knees, and lowered his head between
them, clasping his hands behind his neck.

Nathan lit a cigarette.

"That box we made?" Frenchy said, looking like a gopher
peeking out of a hole. "Tomorrow there's going to be a picture of it
in the newspaper."

"We did a good job."

"Jeez, sometimes—"

Nathan's gaze landed on the crucifix above Jupiter's headboard. Frenchy didn't have to spell it out. *Frenchy thinks I'm crazy like everyone else.*

Frenchy pulled out Jupe's pillow and punched it. He said, "For Christ's sake, I did the dog's owner a favor. A favor. If the owner claims the dog—" Frenchy strained his neck and drew his finger across his throat.

Moisture glistened on the man's forehead; his body trembled. Frenchy was hallucinating. Maybe he should be looking for a triangle here—Jupiter, Frenchy, and himself? Would Frenchy break? He didn't know if he could handle another mental breakdown, not now. Frenchy needed to see a psychiatrist.

"Frenchy, what dog?"

"Just some mutt I found at the side of the road when I was coming back from AA."

"AA?"

"Shit." Frenchy punched the pillow. "Forget that. I found this creamed dog at the side of the road and wanted to give it a proper Christian burial, that's all."

Double negative energy.

Nathan extinguished his cigarette. He moved his chair over beside Jupe's bed, sat in it, and crossed his legs. "Tell me about it," he said.

"What do you want to know?"

"What would you like to tell me?"

"Sister Kathleen. I didn't tell her nothing, I mean anything."

"Your social worker?"

"Yeah, Sister Kathleen. Dangly earrings."

"You didn't tell her?"

"No."

"What didn't you tell her?"

Frenchy's energy surged at Nathan. Nathan raised his chin and waited.

"I need a new plan," Frenchy said, popping the pillow.

This doctor job was harder than Nathan had figured it would be. He wanted to smoke, but doctors didn't smoke, not when with a patient. Frenchy had never mentioned having a wife or children; maybe he should ask.

"Your parents?" Nathan said. "Brothers and sisters?"

"Nope."

Excitement welled in Nathan. "Well, for goodness sakes, Frenchy, that's your problem. An only child thinks he deserves more than others. If you expect too much, you set up expectations and you do things you later regret." As Nathan continued, Frenchy's expressions changed the same way Cheryl's did when Cheryl couldn't follow his logic. Why did he affect people this way?

"That's it," Nathan said, trying to sound convincing. He patted his hair and straightened his shoulders. "Things come in threes. You have to pay attention, learn their numbers, know whether they're moving forward or backward, up or down, if they're charged positive or negative. The dog, Frenchy. Was it a plus or a minus? A one, two, or three?"

Frenchy's brow furrowed. He seemed to have a hard time coming up with the answer.

Hitting his forehead with the heel of his hand, Frenchy said, "God, I am dense, so dense I may not live until tomorrow. My mother hated it when Morton barked at her visitors because, she said, it called the wrong kind of attention to our house. She used to say she wasn't divorced because of something about the law. Know what? That dog sniffed and snatched their shorts, her visitors' shorts. Dense," he said, poking his forehead with his thumb. "Men who drop in and drop their shorts aren't visitors!"

Frenchy overexuded energy now, energy that Nathan found hard to deflect. In an effort to remain calm, he steepled his fingers, drew a deep breath, and risked asking the question he wanted most to ask. "Frenchy, what about that case of toilet paper?"

Frenchy bolted off the bed. Acting like McMaster, even hitching his pants, Frenchy said, "Hell, you're a Gestapo, a regular Gestapo," and walked out and slammed the door.

Wasn't the doctor supposed to be the one to end the session?

CHAPTER TWENTY-THREE

I got up early and braved ten below zero to buy the
Sunday newspaper and lie on my stomach on the threadbare living
room carpet, looking at the muddy black and white image.

"Can I see it, the photo?" Nathan asked, coming in and looking
over my shoulder.

"Back of the sports section," Frenchy muttered. "I should have
worn a tie."

"It looks good, Frenchy. Don't you think so?"

I tore the page out and gave it to Nathan. "Doesn't show off our
good carpentry."

"It's all right to be happy. Your face won't crack if you smile."

Something inside me let go. "You're right. Considering
everything, it's okay."

"We could go for a walk around Lake of the Isles, feed the
squirrels in Loring Park. A sort of celebration."

"Squirrels."

"Don't spoil a good day. Bring popcorn. It's in that cupboard."

Nathan was smarter than I gave him credit for. How many times
had I spoiled a good day?

* * *

There were dog walkers everywhere in Loring Park and loudspeakers crackling Muzak, skaters on the ice rink. Snow dropped from a low evergreen branch down the back of my neck inside my collar. I shagged it with my finger, thinking, like the snow, I would melt before I ever got out of the system. As Nathan said, I should be grateful, enjoy my good luck. I was lucky to bury that dog.

Nathan directed us along a curved path between two frozen duck ponds. "An albino squirrel lives here," he said, tossing popcorn. "Maybe we'll see him." After a beat or two Nathan said, making the statement sound like a question, "My social worker wanted me to sign a paper. I wouldn't."

Something was bothering him. "Why not?"

Nathan sighed. "This used to be the cruisers' park before the Greenery connected it with Nicollet Mall. When the high-rise condos went up, the cruisers had to move somewhere else because people who moved into the high-rises didn't want them here. It's a nice neighborhood. You can walk downtown to work or to the Walker Art Center, to the Guthrie Theater and Orchestra Hall."

"Too many spires."

"Sometimes I attend mass in the Basilica. The front of that angled office building, that was the gay pickup spot."

I looked at the angled building, then peered into Nathan's eyes until he turned away. I wasn't sure.

"Want to visit the sculpture garden? It's free."

"I need to visit a friend. Tag along, why don't you?"

Any notion of change sent a schizophrenic into charging his paranoia battery. I waited.

"If I go with you today, will you visit Jupe with me tomorrow?"

"Sure, why not? We'll take the seventeen bus. First, I got to buy a couple of Twinkies for Swede. His heart's in the right place, but his head isn't. You can learn something from Swede."

Nathan said, "After seeing Jupe we can go to my mother's. She likes to cook. She'll fix whatever you like."

The fountain at the entrance to the Greenway looked like a dandelion gone to seed, probably cost more than it would to put seats on all the toilets in the joint. They said in summer the homeless bathed in its spray. "In my house cooking was bad when my mother forgot to open the can before she heated it." I watched a fluffy dog on a leash pee on a weed sticking up through dirty snow. I was living on a leash—a dog's life.

I rested the bag with two Twinkies in it on the table and emptied my pockets and raised my hands for Marco to frisk me. "Aren't you the pretty boy?" he said.

"Yeah, moving up in the world."

Nathan turned antsy.

"Marco, Nathan. Nathan, Marco."

Marco grunted.

"H-hello."

I measured Marco through Nathan's eyes and came up with: *Slob.* Nathan retreated, saying, "I-I don't like strange hands touching me."

Marco laughed.

I looked the guard in the eye to check him. Marco shrugged and frisked Nathan quickly. Nathan survived.

I led us toward the sounds of the football game on TV. "It's minimum security," I said. "For the good bad guys."

Men clustered around the tube. Two guys I didn't know slumped over a checkerboard. Others played poker. "In a hurry," I told them, holding up the Twinkies. I didn't want to put Nathan on the spot. He had enough troubles. "Prison cake's flat as a tortilla," I explained. "Some days you can't even barter it for smokes."

Swede sat on the edge of the bed in the open cell with light causing a shine on his bald head. Here was a misdefined problem if there ever were one. I bent and knocked on the floor. "Hey, don't look up. You might get a surprise." I parlayed the Twinkies across the air, had forgotten how blue Swede's eyes were, a surprise every time, those vivid eyes.

Swede grinned at the sight of the cakes. The black space of a missing side tooth gaped. He pulled up into his fullback frame and reached for the Twinkies.

"How come you're in a different cell?" I said, releasing them.

"Nurse made me move," he said. He moved his thumb over the wrapper, making it crackle. "Thank you, Frenchy."

"You're welcome."

I turned to Nathan. "He can sit and stare and do nothing for hours." To Swede I said, "This is Nathan. Nathan Waite, a friend who needs your help."

Nathan extended his hand.

Swede didn't take it.

I highsigned to say, It's okay, don't take offense. Swede was afraid of strangers.

Swede dropped the Twinkies onto the bed. "I had to move," he said. "The nurse," his hands drew the curvaceous shape of a woman in the air, "kept walking past. I couldn't take it no more. I asked. The warden said it was okay for me to move."

Swede unwrapped the Twinkie with extreme patience. "Mama always gave me Twinkies." He held up one of the finger cakes, smiled at it, then bit it in half. Cream clung to the corners of his mouth, decorated his fingers.

"Can I smoke?" Nathan whispered.

"Why not?" I sat cross-legged on the floor, could tell from the way Nathan kept patting his hair that he felt uneasy. I motioned him to sit beside me.

"If I can help," Swede said, licking his cream-filled smile. "It's good."

"Tell you what, Swede. Nathan's not in the joint, but it's not nice where he lives either. He needs better digs. I'm trying to advise him."

Now Nathan turned edgy as a guy planning a break; he hyperventilated. Poor guy. This was for his own good. He needed to think better of himself because who could count on a social worker or McMaster to help?

"Tell Nathan why you'll live here for the rest of your life."

Swede stared at the last bite of the Twinkie in his hand. It couldn't be easy for him. I reached and picked up the other one, saying, "I'll give this to you when we leave so you can enjoy it after we're gone. Tell. Start. How old were you when you got to prison?"

"Seventeen."

"How old are you now?"

"Thirty-four." Swede licked his fingers, then wiped them on his jeans. He stared at the other Twinkie in my lap.

Nathan dropped ashes into his cupped palm as if he were counting pennies. I nudged him and pointed my thumb at the metal wastebasket. Nathan hesitated, then reached out and pressed the tip of his cigarette against the inside rim of it. He examined the butt closely, tossed it in, and wrapped his arms around his knees, like he was bracing for something long and painful. Maybe bringing him here had been a mistake. He was a good guy and deserved more.

Swede said, "How I got here."

"Fifth grade," I prompted.

Swede set his elbows on his knees and folded his hands loosely between them. His bed squeaked. Nathan's stale smoke hung in the air.

"Mama and Daddy wanted me to go to school. Mama, she fought for me to go to school. I wanted to go to school." Swede lowered his gaze and drew in a slow deliberate breath. This part was always hard for him. "On the bus, kids unzipped my fly. In school, teachers gave me crayons. I like coloring with pencils, with paint, sticks even." Swede paused and his lips silently formed the words: fifth grade.

"By fifth grade they said I growed too big for school. Mama, she fought. They still said I was too growed. Mama said feelings around girls was why. Daddy said maybe they was right." Swede looked at me with a woeful plea. "Why wouldn't they let me go to school, Frenchy? No one else was too old."

"Tough break. We all get tough breaks." At times like this I just wanted to reach out and hug the guy.

Swede's brain chewed on that for awhile before he continued.

"Daddy got me a bicycle. I helped with the cows. He tried to teach me to drive the tractor. I practiced throwing rocks better. Every day I waited for the school bus to come back and when they got off I followed the kids who were not too big to go to school. Some were bigger than me."

He peered at me again as if I could make sense of what he couldn't. Poor guy didn't know when to doubt and not doubt what was told to him. He was such an odd mixture of goodwill and dullness. If ever a man needed a dad. I sat down beside him, hooked my arm in his.

Swede addressed Nathan. "There was this girl with hair down to here," he said, touching his tailbone. "She combed." He combed. "She combed and walked. Combed and walked." The pulse in Swede's temples quickened.

It was a good story. Nathan sat mesmerized.

"One day I got them feelings—the bad ones Mama said made me not go to school. Right away I knew combing was what caused them feelings. I had to stop that combing." Swede looked at me and smiled a slow triumphant smile. "Did, too. I took a ax from the barn and chopped her up."

Nathan gripped the toes of his shoes and held on until his knuckles blanched.

"I chopped her up real good. There was no more combing, but they still wouldn't let me go to school. After that they said I couldn't go home neither." Swede drew three long breaths. The nurse makes them same feelings come. I want to go home. I don't want those feelings. I want to go to school. Can I have the Twinkie now?"

Nathan didn't speak to me all the way home. He went straight to his room and wouldn't come down to dinner. I didn't think the visit would affect him this way. I made him a peanut butter and jelly sandwich in my room and took it to him. Nathan sat on his bed holding his stupid clock, marking time. I offered the sandwich.

"How can you eat? That was a terrible story. Terrible." His eyes brimmed with gullibility, which was why they dubbed people like Swede and Nathan vulnerable adults. Somehow they were wise and innocent at the same time.

"Hey, you got the point, which is that your life isn't as bad as it could be; it can get better. Isn't knowing that worth something?"

Nathan swallowed and looked pitiful. He said, "I don't want to be alone. I put clean sheets on Jupe's bed. Frenchy, would you mind sleeping here tonight?"

My heart skipped a beat. "Sure. Why not?" Easy as opening a can of beans.

CHAPTER TWENTY-FOUR

Nathan wondered how many people in prison really belonged in halfway houses for the retarded or even at the state mental hospital in Anoka. Why had Frenchy taken him to meet Swede in that terrible place? Frenchy had tossed restlessly in Jupe's bed and kept getting up and pacing. Frenchy needed better meds.

Chance Place didn't seem so bad after meeting Swede.

At breakfast, Nathan asked Frenchy, "Do you like it here?"

"Do *you*?" Frenchy asked, making it sound like an attack. Without waiting for an answer, Frenchy said, "Listen. I don't belong here and I think you can live as well or better at some other address."

This unsettled Nathan. It had taken him years to accept his illness, even more to own the name of it. Before that, he had refused meds and his overactive mind tortured him with sounds and images, sometimes jerking him like a yo-yo from one haphazard accident to another until his parents committed him. Once stable on meds, he finally decided he would take them. Still, he didn't believe his parents were justified in resorting to such a drastic measure.

Nathan asked, "You think I'm faking?"

"No. I know the law says you're entitled to live at the highest level of function you can handle. No one's going to give that to you gift-wrapped. You have to fight for it. Do you ever fight, Nathan? For anything?"

Fighting can leave you worse off than you were before.
"Wh-what did you think I would learn from Swede?"

"How much you can do that you're not doing."

"Are you angry with me?"

Frenchy threw up his hands.

"No. I'm angry ... at myself." Frenchy let time pass. Nicer, he said, "Nathan, you've got a lot going for you. Use it. Don't hang it up like a rain check you never plan to call in."

Frenchy didn't know that the system that helped you also beat you down. It awarded a burial plot like a trophy, but was stingy with what he really needed. What he could accomplish was to seek and find patterns that lent harmony to his life. With harmony he might be able to resign himself.

Frenchy accompanied Nathan to visit Jupiter. Nathan paused outside the door of Jupiter's room and crossed his lips with his finger, saying, "Follow my lead." His bouquet stood on the dresser. The hairspray had worked; there was no debris falling from it.

Jupe sat in the brown vinyl chair in the corner wearing a hospital gown with a blanket across his lap. A hint of pink in his cheeks, was a good sign.

"Jupiter," whispered Nathan. "It's me ... and Frenchy, the new resident." Nathan waited for the slightest sign of recognition, the blink of an eye—anything. Nothing. Nor was there any indication that they weren't welcome. Using the caution of a tightrope walker inching over a deep canyon in a high wind without a net, Nathan crossed toward his roommate. Frenchy's impatient vibes mixed with his own. Arriving at the foot of the unoccupied bed took forever.

"You've had a shower," Nathan said softly.

"Lucky for us."

"Shhhh," Nathan cautioned.

Frenchy had scattered the energy in the room like particles of dust blown in sunlight; Nathan waited for it to resettle. Jupe would also be tracking the flow of energy. If Nathan hadn't known what to look for, he might have missed the slightest twitch at the corner of Jupe's mouth. Nathan waved his hand behind him to still Frenchy.

"You look like you're eating. That's good, Jupe," Nathan said after a long quiet. Jupe stared blankly ahead, and he seemed older. Nathan breathed slow and deep for three long breaths, inched again. He said, "Tell the voices and the images to go away." Not that the voices and images would obey; they had a way all their own. "Get better. Come home. I miss you." Nathan picked up a sudden disturbance in Frenchy's energy, wasn't sure, paused, until it dissipated. As he finally arrived beside Jupe, he focused his mind keenly before reaching out ever so slowly and touching the arm of his roommate's chair.

This close, Nathan felt Jupe's schizophrenic void, that inner black hole from which Jupe had to spin himself free, like a spider with the thinnest of lifelines—energy charged minus. It shorted out like a poorly wired electrical circuit. Had Jupe's chin lowered a fraction or had he imagined that? It could have been an illusion. Or a delusion. A projection of what he hoped to see. It could have been simple gravity or a hopeful attempt at communication. An important insight rose from deep within Nathan—he was on the verge of discovering something brilliant—something impressive about to burst into his awareness, he felt it, rising, rising—

"Gentlemen."

The nurse materialized from nowhere, pushed past Nathan, saying, "How are we today, Mr. Barnes?"

Nathan couldn't believe her ignorance, her insensitivity. Grace—that's what her name tag said—picked up Jupiter's wrist and clocked his pulse.

Discombobulated—all his preparation toward meaningful contact ruined—Nathan wanted to shout Grace away, which would only make matters worse. In distress he glanced at Frenchy, who shrugged and shoved his hands into his pockets.

The invasion of Jupe's personal space was a gross intrusion. Grace pumped the blood pressure band, *puh, puh, puh*. She snapped gum, which must've sounded like a gunshot to Jupiter. Then she *riiiiipped* off the Velcro and scratched her pen on the chart. "Enjoy," she said, snapping her gum again and was gone.

Frenchy's gaze trailed after her with lust held as tight as a wet suit. He shrugged as if to say: Why not? and exited after her.

Jupiter sat eyes turned inward, frozen in terror, glazed, vacant. Nathan stood there feeling inadequate, defeated, though still not accepting how his careful efforts had been so quickly destroyed. Tentatively Nathan extended his index finger toward Jupiter's fist on the arm of the chair, then lowered it without contact. "We'll try another time," he whispered. He was about to begin to back away when Jupiter's little finger moved—Nathan thought it did—a slight unfurling. On the arm of the chair under Jupe's raised finger lay a lone curly dock seed.

Jubilance whirled inside Nathan. For a brief moment he and Jupe breathed in sync. "I'll help you, Jupiter. I know you're trying. I know you can do it. I will. Please. Try to get better. Come home." It was enough, too much maybe. Nathan drew a long, slow breath and began inching backward. Eyes, like windows, had two sides It was difficult to look out when you were having so much trouble looking in. Doctors forgot; nurses forgot. Maybe they didn't comprehend that the human revue came in upside down and backwards, left and right reversed like a camera lens or the human eye. One needed to pay attention to know which lens was open, which closed, whether the mind was tracking vertically or horizontally. One had to track from the focal point, notice context within perspective. Sometimes hallucinations collided and overlapped in time and dimension. When that happened it took all the skill a doctor could muster to guide you out. Patients taught the doctors how to do that, not the other way around. Nathan arrived at the door exhausted from tedious thought and effort.

He said, "Don't be fooled, Jupe. They're just mental pictures." Aware of the hidden and cherished curly dock seed, Nathan smiled and said, "Frenchy's okay, I think." Flexible minds had to try this and that without getting fraught in fruitless, changing perspectives. He wondered if maybe Jupiter might try thinking in triangles. No. They had done enough for today.

"I'll be back," Nathan said, opening and closing the door behind him soundlessly.

Frenchy saw him coming and stopped joshing with the nurses. He followed Nathan without a word.

Once outside, Frenchy said, "Depressing. Too depressing."

Nathan's right brain said, *anomaly*; his left brain said, *not depressing—regressing.*

CHAPTER TWENTY-FIVE

Nathan's mother said, "I have just about anything you'd like. Sausage, ham, bacon."

"I like them all, Frenchy said." His gaze took in the shelves of knickknacks, the expensive porcelains in the next room, which Nathan had never been allowed to touch.

Nathan watched a red squirrel leap from one branch to another. On top of monitoring Jupiter—minus Grace had done enough damage—he didn't feel like monitoring Frenchy, too. Nathan turned back, said pointedly, "They're not for touching."

His mother said, "Oh, that's a handsome tie. It's nice you could come." She sliced Jimmy Dean sausage into patties.

"Thanks."

"It's been a long time since— Well. Eggs. Scrambled? Over easy?"

She fawned over Frenchy the way she fawned over Debbie. Frenchy grinned like he had just tasted cotton candy for the first time.

Nathan said, "Red squirrels are territorial."

His mother said, "I'll make some of each," and took out two frying pans.

Frenchy moved into the dining room, picked up a Hummel figure, and turned it over. "French toast," he said. "You know how to make that?"

Nathan expected his mother to say, Be careful, put that down. She said, "Sure."

Frenchy was wearing a pair of new suede shoes. He had bought new boots. How much money did Frenchy make? He even sent clothes to the dry cleaners. Nathan's knees bobbed like teeth chattering.

"Nathan, dear. What would you like?"

"Oatmeal," he said. "Toast."

That deflated her enthusiasm. She stopped what she was doing and looked at him, while Frenchy continued to handle her precious porcelains as if this were *his* house. Raccoon tracks trailed to the garbage can.

Nathan suddenly stood. "I'm going out for a smoke. Frenchy, come with me."

"Fifteen, twenty minutes," his mother said, moving her finger along the print on the upside-down oatmeal box, pretending to read. Nathan hadn't intended to hurt her.

"We won't be long," Nathan said, trying to make up.

Nathan raised the garage door so they could stand inside away from the wind. Lady growled at Frenchy. "It's okay," Nathan said, scratching behind her ears. The space beside his mother's Honda, the one his father's car used to occupy, remained empty.

Frenchy moved around touching ice skates, baseball mitts, tools, whatever hung on hooks, as if he lived here. Nathan had little energy left for confrontation or anything else.

"My mother likes to cook," he said.

"Good. I like to eat."

Nathan's canoe hung overhead on the rack he and Uncle Carl had rigged. Debbie's dollhouse hung up there, too. Frenchy considered the silver, two-door Honda like he was thinking of purchasing it. "With a car like this and a house like that, why don't you live here?"

Nathan turned away. The Wilsons across the street had moved to Utah, which they said was beautiful. Maybe he'd visit them sometime. More than once Nathan had discussed where he lived with his mother and his father. Sister Angela had told his parents that schizophrenics fared better away from family. She had even given them copies of studies. They had all betrayed him.

"Is it all right if I look under the hood?"

"I suppose so."

Frenchy opened the driver's door and released the latch, then walked around to the front of the car.

Nathan thought perhaps he should have told Sister Angela that he owned a canoe. When she was asking all those questions, he hadn't thought about it. What he could and couldn't own complicated matters. He had no interest in a burial plot, but owned a canoe he never used. She would have told him he had to sell it.

He said, "The canoe rides on top of the car on that rack."

Frenchy closed the hood. He tested an ice skate blade with his thumb.

"Do you skate?" Nathan asked, lighting another cigarette.

Frenchy shook his head and continued snooping.

Nathan needed to get him out of here. He tipped his cuff to see his watch. "There's sure to be a pair that'll fit you. We'll skate after our food settles."

"I don't think so."

The man in the porno store, the one Frenchy had claimed was a cop, came to Nathan's mind. The man's feet were as big as Swede's. Nathan tried to calculate Frenchy's shoe size. He dropped his cigarette, stepped on it, went over and took down a pair of skates, turned and asked, "Frenchy, why that porno place? How did you think Swede could help me?"

Frenchy kicked a pebble and watched it disappear beneath snow.

"Nathan, your mind works—at least part of it does—part of the time. You're good with your hands. You're good with Jupiter. Swede can't— Listen," Frenchy said, knuckling his mustache, "I wanted you to notice the difference between why Swede can't hold a job and why you can. He can't help himself. You can. Don't blow it. You've got a lot to work with."

Nathan looked at the skates in his hands. Frenchy wasn't exactly the most successful human being he'd ever met. Yes, he could do carpentry and a lot more that Frenchy didn't know about. The compliment challenged him. He said, "I must remember to pick up my cigarette butt. Let's measure your foot."

"I'll be too cold. I'm not wearing the right clothes to go skating."

"I have a sweater you can wear, even a down jacket from when I was smaller."

Nathan ate his oatmeal halfheartedly while Frenchy stuffed himself with French toast, sausage, bacon, and ham. That's what stubbornness wrought in the face of his mother's fawning over Frenchy. Foolishly, he had taken his own jealousy out on himself. When his mother turned gullible with Frenchy, it only reminded Nathan of himself, and he didn't like it, not one bit. He swallowed several pills with water.

Nathan turned to Frenchy, who was a guest, he reminded himself, and said, "I need a short rest. You can nap in my sister's room. After that, we'll skate."

"Frenchy," Nathan's mother said, "don't go. Keep me company. Have another cup of coffee."

Nathan left them with their heads together like conspirators.

CHAPTER TWENTY-SIX

I smoothed the newspaper clipping on the table in front of Mrs. Waite, and pointed to the photo. "Nathan helped make this box."

"Oh. Really? I'll get my glasses."

"I had just come from work, so I didn't have a tie."

"Nathan always liked making things," she said, peering through half spectacles. "Oh, my. It's a nice cemetery, the one over to St.Paul."

Her kindness made me uncomfortable, like I might turn to mush. I had not expected Nathan to come from such a nice house, not that I had thought much about it. His mother cooked and cleaned and acted like a mom. I could grow used to that kind of mom. Still, it gave me the creeps. I folded the clipping and slid it into my shirt pocket.

"Red squirrels," I said, aiming my thumb toward the window. "Do they really get into the house?"

Mrs. Waite took off her glasses, sighed, and laid them on the table. "Chuck, my husband used to— Well. Now I pay someone to set traps in the attic." She studied me as if I might set a few traps. Then I figured maybe she was looking for signs of my illness.

"I have only a mild case," I said. "Don't take meds."

A red squirrel took a flying leap, landed on a birdhouse, then dropped. "I plan to move out of Chance Place."

"I didn't know Nathan could still build," she said, peering at my shirt pocket. "I'm sure he liked helping you."

"Yeah. He's a good guy, one of the few I can talk to." I took a squirrelly leap. "How come he doesn't live here?"

Mrs. Waite busily pushed crumbs into a little cone with the side of her hand. Pretending it was something else, she brushed away a tear from the corner of her eye. She moved her trembling hands to her lap.

"Chuck, Nathan's father, and I argue about that. Nathan and I tried it for awhile."

She appeared guilt-ridden, like I felt a lot of times.

"He'd stay in his room and smoke. I didn't dare leave him alone or invite anyone in, was afraid he'd burn the house down. I became a prisoner in my own house." She poked a hole in the cone of crumbs, looked up. "Nathan left after he burned his own arms. He's much better now."

That was not the Nathan I knew. I felt for the guy. He had come a long way.

"After several weeks in the hospital, it became clear that Nathan couldn't go back to school. That's when the insurance company said we could no longer claim him as our dependent."

They didn't let Swede go back to school either. How lucky I was.

"His father and I fought all the time about what to do. The insurance company actually kicked Nathan out of the hospital by refusing to pay for what he needed. That happens a lot." She covered her eyes with her hand. "The only new thing Nathan learned in the hospital was obscenity."

God, this was like the disasters AAers repeated. I felt spacey. Each story different, but the same. I thought of my trapped mother. Mrs. Waite turned into a spigot. I didn't know how to turn her off.

"Listen," I said, swallowing.

"Before Nathan's illness Chuck and I were happy. We got conflicting advice from doctors and social workers and fought with each other over what to do. We couldn't comfort each other. The gap pulled us apart. Soon there wasn't enough money; no amount's ever enough to fight mental illness."

Life was unfair, unfair. I smacked my palm with my fist. Peso did me in, yet I was the lucky one here. "Listen." I cracked my knuckles, tried to get up, walk away, but my body wouldn't move.

She said, "They determined what was wrong with Nathan by what he *didn't* have!" She held up a teaspoon. "This is not a knife. This is not a fork. Therefore, it must be a spoon." She dropped it. "They ruled out drugs, alcoholism, manic depression; by default Nathan must be schizophrenic."

I'm not heterosexual. I'm not gay. By default I'm bisexual, nonsexual? I found myself wondering how my skipping town had affected Mom? How could I have been so ignorant? Did she hurt like this?

"One doctor advised us against spending money on Nathan, said we'd only go bankrupt, that his condition was futile."

Judges came in different titles, sizes, and shapes, none of them good. Mrs. Waite was going to crumble if I didn't stop her.

"You know what? Nathan's going to teach me to skate."

"It's hard to watch someone you love disappear before your eyes, to watch someone who's capable and smart and fun-loving turn helpless."

The way her tones went up and down reminded me of Nathan's speech. My gut wrenched into knots. Instead of a can of worms, I had opened a bucket of snakes. I couldn't help her and I couldn't stop thinking of Mom missing me, fearing the old man's return.

"Mrs. Waite, listen—"

"Relatives suggested everything from hypnotism to ignoring Nathan. They said he was just acting out."

"Listen. Mrs. Waite—"

"We didn't know how to help him. Nathan acted weird and out of control. Sister Angela said families break up over crises, that everyone's suffering so much there's no energy left for comfort and support. Before long Chuck and I couldn't be in the same room."

"Don't meds help?" I asked, attempting to bring her back to the here and now the way I would bring Nathan back. Birdseed sure made a mess on snow.

"You live with people on meds. What do you think?"

I took my cup to the sink and rinsed it, then filled it with water and drank. I felt as trapped as when I was trying to get away from Peso, except there wasn't an ounce of meanness in Nathan's mom. I had come to understand that Peso wasn't exactly made of milk and honey.

"Frenchy, maybe you can help. Nathan's entitled to drop in at the Vail Center anytime to talk to a counselor. Could you convince him to do that? Social workers have so many clients. If he doesn't show initiative, they'll write him off, move on to someone else." She inhaled a quivering breath. "When Nathan got sick, he was number 137 on the Crisis Center's emergency waiting list!"

I needed to get away. "Mrs. Waite, I can try, but don't expect it'll help. Could I rest now?"

She looked up slowly.

"Sorry. I got this sudden tiredness."

She nodded, raised herself as if she weighed a ton. Upstairs, she crossed her lips with a finger and pointed to a closed door and took me into a pink room and pulled a pink blanket from a drawer.

"Just lie on top of the spread," she whispered, and left.

I took in the white, knobby furniture, the ruffles, opened a dresser drawer—shiny, lacy, thin-strapped things, the kind my mother wore when "visitors" dropped in, the kind Peso gave to the girls he escorted across state lines. Mrs. Waite's pain had opened up some deep hurt inside me. I kept trying not to feel it. I opened a jewelry box, picked up a pair of dangly blue earrings and held them up to the light. I thought of Sister Kathleen. I futzed around until my fingertip found a pair of silver split bells. I considered wrapping them in toilet tissue and taking them with me, but put them back. I was not a thief and wouldn't start now.

I moved a chair over to the window, turned it around, and sat on it. Birds, squirrels, bugs—dullsville. My eyes followed foot tracks in the snow, maybe from when Nathan picked those weeds for Jupiter. A guy could go crazy living in such quiet. Down the hall a door opened. I heard Nathan's shuffle, a door close. The toilet flushed. He knocked lightly.

"Yo."

Nathan's eyes were swollen from sleep. He looked at me a long time before he spoke. "Don't worry," he said. "I'm a good teacher."

CHAPTER TWENTY-SEVEN

It was Sunday so there weren't many skaters. It felt good to see Frenchy so unsure of himself. Frenchy scrutinized two giggling teenage girls. In the distance beyond the rink, men sat on upside-down buckets and on campstools, ice fishing.

"Like this," Nathan said, standing on his skate tips. "Your brakes." He extended his mitten-covered hand and Frenchy took it and they wobbled along.

"Just a minute," Nathan said. He moved behind Frenchy and took hold of Frenchy's hips. "Like this," he said, moving them.

Feeling a dash of negative energy Nathan didn't understand, he let go. "It's easier than walking. Bend your knees. Not so much. Torso, back straight, head up. Up. Okay. Push and glide. Glide. Glide," he said, demonstrating.

Arms out like a toddler's, Frenchy tottered trying to stay up. "Sure," he said, as Nathan rescued him from falling.

Seeing Frenchy so vulnerable opened Nathan's heart. He stayed close and helped Frenchy up until he thought Frenchy could manage without breaking an arm or a leg.

"You just need practice," Nathan said, and then, because he knew it felt better to be embarrassed alone, he skated away. From afar, he watched Frenchy's flow, jerky and staccato as an old movie. Satisfied that his pupil would, for the most part, stay upright, Nathan free-skated. His muscles remembered old patterns. He did a double figure-eight, stopped and appraised his etching on the ice—objective proof that he could still do this. Primed, his body warmed, sprinted and raced, breaths coming hard with each stride. He felt like a man in a man's body. Exhilarated. In charge. Noble. His cheeks burned. Pausing to catch his breath he spotted an icehouse and discreetly peered inside the window. It appeared empty. Whoever told Emory that hooker story must have made it up.

Two giggling girls had hooked arms with Frenchy's and were ushering him around the rink. Stifling envy, Nathan flowed free and smooth as air across the ice. He spun and did maneuvers that had taken him more discipline and practice to learn than Frenchy would ever have. He hadn't felt this good since taking second place in the Northeast Amateur Competition, which Cheryl had convinced him to enter. Suddenly Nathan filled with renewed resentment that Cheryl was no longer in his life. Ice chips flew. Still, he could summon Cheryl whenever he wanted to feel her warmth. Who was he kidding? He would never make love again.

He might find sex in a porno store, but not in real life. Images of burning triangles floated through his vision. He had overextended. Regardless of how much time remained, he needed to stop and take care of himself before the images that pressed hard as rock against his forehead turned into hallucinations. The sky had become gray and ominous. Frenchy toggled alone now, his arms out as if around barrels.

"Hey," Frenchy said, smiling broadly. "Did you see me with those girls? I'm a regular athlete." He lost focus, stumbled, and grabbed Nathan into a bear hug.

"Whoa," Nathan said, releasing him, but Frenchy clung on.

Nathan said, "You're doing all right without me."

"Not as good as some, not better 'n most," Frenchy said, turning sad.

Frenchy's forehead was white from cold, his cheeks red. Feeling sorry for him, Nathan extended his elbow. Frenchy hitched on.

"Those girls turned me on," he said. "They turned me on."

Nathan didn't know what to say. He moved them to the side of the ice near the two evergreens where they had left their shoes. Nathan gained speed. Frenchy got an attack of beginner's fear, wrapping himself tighter around Nathan. They tussled, fell, rolled. Nathan saw Frenchy's strained, distant eyes, then before he knew what was happening, Frenchy clutched him tightly and was humping his hard-on in sexual frenzy against Nathan's hip bone.

"Hey!" Nathan pushed. "Stop! Quit it!" Nathan couldn't believe what was happening. His mind flashed floating neon triangles: obtuse, acute, right. He tried again to yell Stop, but the word wouldn't come out. *This isn't right, not rite.* He summoned the latent wrestler in him; with an act of will, he gripped and overturned his opponent.

Frenchy's eyes widened in surprise, then narrowed.

Nathan's heart thumped; his mind presented triangles a-whirl in space, neon minuses, choruses. He knelt on all fours, drawing cold air into his lungs. Like names of diseases, a baritone chanted: *isosceles, scalene, equilateral, obtuse, acute.*

Frenchy lay on his back, panting, with his arm up over his eyes.

With his fantasy of friendship with Frenchy now dredged in the slime of disgust, feeling violated and fraught with confusion, Nathan still couldn't grasp what had transpired. He looked about. No one seemed to have noticed. Frenchy, his parents, even Sister Angela, everyone who said they wanted to help him, added up to one big minus zero. Frenchy sat up and put his head between his knees. Nathan sidled backwards on his rump to his shoes. This is what resulted from his mother's powder-puffing Frenchy. Frenchy should take a powder all right. Triangulation is how you located points from the base.

Nathan couldn't tie his shoestrings.

"Want help?"

"No!"

Frenchy started to say something, stopped. His face looked sunburned.

Nathan stood and slung his skates over his shoulder. He smothered the urge to throw back his head and howl like a lost coyote, had half a mind to abandon the man. One slight bit of sanity stopped him; he didn't want to be guilty of making someone lost, not of aiding disorientation even of an enemy. *If Frenchy boards the wrong bus*—Frenchy seemed to be putting on his shoes in slow motion. Like the increasing, rumbling vibration in a railroad track before the engine arrives, energy escalated inside Nathan.

Nathan surrounded himself with an aura strong enough to keep Frenchy at bay and walked. He would shed the negative, latch onto the positive, forget Frenchy, who was trying to keep up. Nathan concentrated so fully on not allowing his mind to betray him that he didn't stop to light a cigarette. He walked faster. Some day he hoped to discover a friend who would not take advantage of him, someone who would look nothing like Frenchy. Frenchy tugged on his sleeve.

"L-listen. B-back there—"

Nathan pulled his arm free and kept walking. "I invited you to my home. My mother cooked for you."

"Let me explai—"

"Not now. Never."

At the bus stop they waited, not speaking. Nathan insisted that Frenchy board ahead of him, then selected a seat two rows behind him. Nathan's knees bobbed, his hands twittered. Out of habit, his mind sought stability by summoning Cheryl, but this time Cheryl did not come. Nathan reached out and drew a triangle in the condensation on the window. Forcing focus, wanting to understand, he projected full-sized, miniature images of Frenchy, Swede, and himself onto each point of the triangle. He tried Frenchy, Emory, himself. How were pluses and minuses clues to what he needed? Nothing computed. Lights swished by. He erased the triangle with his elbow, and peered out the blurry oval. The world was passing him by. Nathan snatched a quick, involuntary breath, glimpsed Frenchy ... Jupiter ... himself.

Back at Chance Place, with not so much as an eye blink, Nathan strode to his room and closed the door. Every part of him felt dirty. He perched on top of the radiator and chain-smoked, feeling no heat from below, no cold from the window, letting the sound of Frenchy's pounding on the door pass through him out into the universe. When Frenchy went away, he would shower.

Nathan shuddered. Frenchy pounded. Nathan put himself inside a phone booth made with walls of lead.

CHAPTER TWENTY-EIGHT

My knuckles grew raw from pounding. The loss of friendship thudded like a fucking sledgehammer in my head. I leaned my forehead against Nathan's door. There was no lock; I could open it. "Nathan," I pleaded. "Be a sport. Let me explain."

Someone in another room yelled, "Get lost."

If Nathan told McMaster, McMaster would tell Sister Kathleen. One minute I was trying not to fall on the ice and the next I ranked number one super first-class shit. What made me do it? Nothing had made me think Nathan could care about me that way.

"Nathan, please." The girls had turned me on. "It was an impulse, a bad impulse" I waited. "Please believe me."

I kicked the door and left.

"I'm thirsty," I admitted to the certified, bonafide, confessed drunks, twisting my hat between my knees, willing to take any help they could give. Nyquil would help, Sterno strained through bread.

"Do you have a sponsor?"

I didn't know who had asked the question, shook my head. There were a couple of women present who I could do without.

Junior, the kid with acne, the one with a phone in his pocket, said, "I used to think I was unique, that I was in control of my drinking and my life."

I crossed and uncrossed my legs, hid my shakes inside my hat. I didn't like asking for help. Instead of helping, they looked at me, expecting more. It was none of their business; they had no right to pry. "I pissed off someone big time, that's what."

"And you wish you hadn't?" The older of the two women.

The other woman said, "Someone you care about?"

I hung my hat on one finger like a chicken head whose neck I could fracture in a second. "Not exactly," I said, plopping the hat on my knee. "It was a man."

"Nothing wrong with a different orientation," Junior said. "Drinking stole my sense of morality Easy as plucking a rotten apple off a tree."

Gramps said, "Let's not take that tack."

My head throbbed. I knuckled my mustache, set my jaw. Not only had I made every homosexual in the world look bad, I had acted like a bully, thumping on an innocent, hurt someone vulnerable, who by definition couldn't take care of himself. *I'm the worst, the worst. Why even try?*

Square, football stud Duke, the voice of reason, said, "We can't help you unless you let us."

I cracked my knuckles. "Let me explain—"

Ernie said, "Keep it simple."

This from the resident vaudevillian at Russell's Bar. To be simple meant I would have to be explicit. I put my elbows on my knees and punched my palm, couldn't find words to tell them how despicable I had been. *Why am I here?*

Gramps asked, "Do you believe you were at fault?"

"Are you guilty?"

"Premeditated?"

The questions came too fast. I didn't even know who asked them.

The hint of red in Ernie's hair reminded me of Nathan. "What business you in?" I asked Ernie.

Not that it matters, advertising. "We're talking about you. Have you made amends?"

The questions, tough ones, were coming too fast. I felt cornered. I looked at the door, wondered what would happen if I just got up and walked out. I remembered the last question. "I tried to fix it, but couldn't pull it off."

"Making amends helps me," Ernie said, "especially the part that means forgiving myself."

I would never forgive myself. Nathan would never forgive me.

Duke said, "Whether or not the other guy forgives you, you can make amends, forgive yourself, and go on."

In prisons there were no heterosexuals. They wouldn't understand. I looked around, might have earmarked the guy with the flushed, pockmarked skin and dead, bloodshot eyes as a drunk, but mostly they looked like any men you'd pass on the sidewalk. They weren't going to let me sidle by.

I turned to the pitiful younger woman. "Be my sponsor?"

"Guys have male sponsors," Gramps said.

Ernie said, "It works better that way."

If he knew me he wouldn't say that.

"Big Book says," Gramps said, "those incapable of self-honesty won't succeed in this program." The man finagled for eye contact until I felt forced to give it to him. Gramps reminded me of Poppy. Poppy sniffed out a lie, sure as a dachs kept a rabbit down a hole. If I kept quiet maybe they would take the hint and move on to someone else. Gramps said, "Frenchy, any male in AA can be your sponsor, though it's best to pick someone who's experienced. You could ask someone tonight and visit with him before our next meeting."

The older woman said, "You'll like yourself better if you do."

A cold hardness pushed against the back of my eyes. The last thing I needed was another mother who didn't know which end was up. Still, I had asked for help and they were trying to give it to me.

"Okay," Gramps said, his tone losing patience. "Let's continue around the circle."

I had known, but forgotten that business about sponsors—males for males, females for females. When the going got tough, everything came down to sex. If I agreed to ask a sponsor, he'd ask me to talk the talk and walk the walk. If I didn't, he'd set me on the carpet in front of the circle. If I stayed away, Sister Kathleen would be on my case. Either way, I was fried. I wanted relief and got the hot seat. I didn't know how long the loud quiet went on before I noticed everyone looking at me, expectant. *Shit.* I closed my eyes and did a mental eenie-meenie-minie-moe around the circle. I pointed, opened my eyes, found my finger aiming at Ernie, who sat legs stretched out, ankles crossed, hands clasped behind his head. I asked the first thing that came into my mind, "How long you been in AA?"

"Twelfth medallion coming up in June."

A dozen years.

I tried to sound sincere when I was more afraid than anything else. "Will you be my sponsor?"

"Ernie's tough," someone muttered.

With my luck, what else?

"I'm not one to mince words," Ernie said.

"Me neither," I said.

"Stay after. We'll start."

Tonight! I couldn't back down, not now in front of everyone. How many ways could a guy shoot himself in the foot?

* * *

As soon as the last guy left, Ernie straddled a chair and said, "Tell me about yourself, Frenchy."

I gave him the short, smooth version, leaving out some details like jail, probation.

"Do you really want help?" Ernie asked, appearing suspicious.

"Sure."

"Frenchy, I'm not subtle. My wife, God love her, threatened me with divorce if I didn't stop drinking and see a therapist. I did both. The therapist confronted the shit out of me. I hated him for it. Now I know in my marrow that was the best thing that ever happened to me."

There was no turning back.

Ernie asked, "What would you say is the core problem? What bothers you most about yourself?"

"I thought we were going to talk about drinking."

"That's the drill. You think because you dress well, you're somehow protected? That you're better than any of us? This isn't a program for cowards. What lies do you tell yourself that make you drink? What secrets do you keep from yourself that turn you to drink? What steals more than its fair share of your mind? What really, really bothers you? That is talking about drinking."

Sex! Am I wired for guys or gals? Or both? How can I know? I squirmed. "Sometimes, uh ... I wonder about—" I was struck dumb.

"Won't kill either of us if you say it."

I looked up at a corner of the ceiling, was out of my element. "It's ... well, it's been a long time since ... I've made it with a woman."

Ernie's eyes made contact, killing any bravado I might have had. I tossed my hat into the air and caught it. "'Course I can anytime I want," I said. "I-it's just that I haven't wanted to." Who did I think I was kidding? My foot tapped.

"What's the underlying problem?"

When I didn't answer, Ernie said, "I guess you don't know what you think."

"Shit," I said.

"Frenchy, since I've quit drinking, I've discovered my family's a lot of fun and that they still like me. I don't deserve it and I don't know why, but they do, and I'm grateful. If you'd rather not use this time constructively, I'm going home to them."

"Is the sponsor supposed to be a cop? Is that what you are? A cop?"

"Sometimes I feel like one. With my kids. With guys I sponsor."

Already I had said too much. I didn't know how to say what I needed to say without telling him too much. I danced, sparred my fists into the air, one-two, one-two, said, "The reason I brought the subject up is that I'm living only with men. Not by choice."

"Oh. DWI. Jail? Why didn't you say so?"

"Not jail. Mental case." One-two, one-two.

Ernie slid lower in his chair. He shook his head with a sly smile. Not for a minute did he buy mental case. He raised one eyebrow. "All right, Frenchy, it's been a while since you've been with a woman. That could make it pretty scary."

"Naw." I advanced, one-two, one-two.

"Are you going to take this seriously or not? What problem wants to kick you off the wagon?"

I dropped my fists. Making amends to Nathan was impossible. I knuckled my mustache, sat down and drew a deep breath. I told him about getting arrested because Peso had turncoated on me, but left out that I lived in a halfway house for the mentally ill, because Ernie had already proved he wouldn't believe that. Hard as it was, I told him about the ice incident.

"Let me be sure," he said. "You're ice-skating, the girls give you the hots, you hump your friend's ... hip, then he bars you from his bedroom and you don't understand why?"

His dark eyes burrowed through to my conscience.

"Frenchy, you're lucky you still have your front teeth. My father beat up my mother for a lot less."

A guy could suffocate in here. I got up, a lion circling in a cage.

"Booze and bravado and beating up women often go together."

I needed to MOVE.

"Your mother or your father drink too much?"

"The old man," I said, wishing I hadn't. "I don't want to talk about it."

"Of course you don't. Me, I'd rather drink than deal with the pain."

I kicked a chair. It collapsed. *Shit, another chair.* I said, "He beat on her, okay?"

Ernie clasped his hands behind his head, laying himself wide open. He said, "I didn't like coming to AA, then I figured I owed it to myself to at least give it a try. I'm living proof that there's hope for you, too."

I wiped my forehead on my arm, wanted to punch him, but that would be a sissy thing to do. He was open, defenseless.

"Awhile ago this room was full of people who used to think they didn't need anyone or anything. We all thought we could go it alone. Dead wrong. Frenchy, you get out of the program what you put in. Believe me. If it works for me, it can work for you."

I was checking likely spots and crevices for spider webs, anything to keep the heat of my thermometer down.

"Did he beat your mom often?"

"Only when he came home, okay?"

"Ever put her in the hospital?"

"No." I willed my temper down, sat.

"She ever call the cops?"

A vise tightened around my temples and squeezed. Pressure pushed down on top of my head, a hot, heavy iron lid.

Ernie leaned forward. "I didn't hear you."

My voice, a barely audible boy's pip-squeak voice, said, "I did. I called the cops."

"Oh, how awful for you," Ernie said, putting his hand on my shoulder.

I swallowed and stared at it.

"How old were you?"

"S-seven, eight."

"What did your mom call you?"

"F-Francis. She called me Francis."

"Francis," Ernie said gently. "Did she tell you you were a bad boy for calling the cops? That you shouldn't have called them?"

I shucked his hand off. "She told 'em it was a big fuckin' mistake, that's what! And when they left, she beat me like he beat her, you smug son of a bitch." I pushed my fist under Ernie's nose.

"I won't play this game," Ernie said evenly. "If you want a sponsor, I'm here. If you don't, I'm gone." He turned his face away from my fist, and said, "I'm not a punching bag. There's no self-respect in letting you treat me this way."

Squelched, I withdrew my hand, muttered, "Sorry."

Ernie was quiet a long time. Then the man's syllables landed on me like separate, slow punches. "How did you feel about your mom betraying you?"

"I wanted to smash her face!"

"Understandable."

Understandable!

"Only seven or eight and you tried to protect her and she beat you up for being brave, for defending her, for acting like a man."

This was a new twist. I tasted sour mixed with salt, couldn't say anything.

"Maybe you'd benefit from talking to someone in MI, a mental illness counselor, a therapist."

I was steeped in enough mental illness to last me three lifetimes.

Ernie deliberated. "Frenchy," he finally said, "you frighten me. Working the program takes courage and guts. I don't want to get decked and I am concerned for you. I don't know if you have what it takes. Are you willing to name and confront what's underneath your anger?"

I sat stiff as a dog in *rigor mortis*. I had chickened out lots of times, but no one had ever said they were frightened of me before, not frightened of the runt. Pain oozed into me, first in trickles then in a rush. My breath clutched, my shoulders drooped. For the first time in my life I didn't feel like I had to be stronger than everyone else.

"Ah," Ernie said. "The first step. It's a beginning. Now let's discuss what a sponsor can and cannot do."

Afterward, I walked blocks and blocks in the cold dark until my toes numbed beyond feeling. The big surprise was that I no longer felt like punching anyone out. When I finally trudged up Chance Place steps, I found Nathan sitting alone in the living room. I stood in the archway wanting to say I knew a little bit more now about why I had done such a stupid thing—not that I could take it back or really excuse my behavior—just that I understood a splinter's worth more. Nathan wouldn't acknowledge my presence; he stared at the TV pretending I was not there.

I wanted to say: I'm sorry. Please, forgive me, but pride clutched the words in my throat. I mumbled, not intending for it to come out so lame, "I don't know what came over me."

Nathan stiffened.

Dejected, feeling worse than ever, I trundled up to bed. Once under the covers, I tried to masturbate but couldn't even succeed at that.

* * *

In the days that followed, I twitched with nerves,
expecting Nathan to break down or the dog's owner or the law to
appear with handcuffs engraved with my name. If Nathan fell apart
because of what I had done, I wouldn't be able to live with myself.
I approached him more than once, but, slippery as an eel, Nathan
always disappeared. As far as I could tell, he showed no sign of
deterioration, only an acute awareness of how to avoid me.

At work, every stomp triggered my thirst. Stomp, stomp.
Glug, glug. *Stomp, stomp.* Glug, glug. One beer. That's all I
needed to ease the pain.

"Bibideaux!" Double O snapped, pointing at my rising reject
pile.

In defiance, I placed the next chip with exaggerated
concentration. Double Zero watched the clip glom onto it, huffed
and left.

Like him, every guy in the joint acted as if *he* were the one who
totally owned or disowned the world, the only one in control. Once
I asked a guy in St. Peter's how he survived and he said, "Life's
more interesting inside myself." That surprised me. I had survived
the joint; I could survive Chance Place. Everything went back to
the old man, didn't it? Act tough; get lost. If Ernie was right, I had
to do something different. But what?

If Nathan had ratted, I'd be behind bars. That made me even
more beholden to him. Emory had taken to peering at me through
those pubic eyebrows of his. Most of the men I lived with were
capable of sieving psychic lint out of the air and weaving whole
blankets with it. Truth was, not having someone to talk to
blowtorched a hole in my gut too big to accept, deny, satisfy, or
fill. "Shit," I muttered, tossing another chip onto the reject pile. I
didn't miss Poppy. I told myself, *I don't miss Poppy, I don't miss
Peso, and I sure don't miss Nathan.*

* * *

Soon I developed a plan to outwit Nathan: Lay low, catch
him alone, accidentally bump into him, and make amends—get
him to accept my stupid apology. I staked out the stairs, the
bathrooms, the refrigerator. Such stealth reminded me of Morton,
who managed to avoid my dad while tracking his every move.
After days of Nathan successfully avoiding me, I was standing in
the hall near the pay phone, considering giving up the whole game,
when the phone rang. I answered. A woman asked for Nathan. I
covered the receiver and yelled, "Natha-an. Phone," recognizing
this was my best chance.

Without a nod, Nathan appeared and took the receiver from me.

I moved to the L-shaped landing on the stairwell and waited out
of sight. After he hung up, I would skip down like I was in a rush,
smack into him, step back real quick so he wouldn't get the wrong
idea, then spit out my say. Nathan would hear and accept my
apology and we'd be talking again.

Nathan said into the phone, "I d-don't know. I have to work."

It wasn't my intention to listen; I just couldn't help it.

"No," he said. "With an 'e'. W-a-i-t-e. Sister Angela is my—"
Pause. "Go slower. S-t-i-l-t-s-e-n. Government Center. Two
o'clock. She asked me to sign, but I didn't."

Poor kid was being conned.

"I'm sort of happy," Nathan said. "Yes. Okay. Yes." He hung
up.

I crouched and bounded.

Nathan sidestepped me easy as a fly missing a swatter. To keep
from running into the front door, I swerved and bammed into the
back of the overstuffed chair. My breath *whooshed.* I bent over,
hugged my middle.

In the kitchen I heard Nathan say, "Government Center,"
probably to Emory, who was the only one he seemed to converse

185

with, unless you counted Jupiter and that didn't sound like conversation. I hobbled into the kitchen.

Emory held a stack of plates, was setting the table with Nathan following close behind. McMaster was sweet-talking someone on the phone. Disappointed—defeated—I stood, trying to catch my breath.

Nathan said, "She wants me to come to her office to sign—"

"County bounty."

Nathan saw me and turned back to Emory as if I were invisible. He said, "I'm wearing tan socks."

It was hopeless, a no-go. I left.

CHAPTER TWENTY-NINE

Dinner, if that's what you want to call it, was
tuna/noodle slop, beets, sliced bananas daubed with peanut butter,
and green Kool-Aid. I heard every slurp and swallow. Nathan
stood beside the refrigerator, his half-empty glass on top of it,
eating from a plate in his hand. Maybe I could soften him up by
asking about Jupiter.

I asked a bit too loudly, "Anybody know how Jupiter is?"
Slurp. Swallow.
"Doesn't anybody care?"
Emory held a chunk of beet on his fork, said, "Cud blood."
"No," Nathan said. The tension in the room turned thick as the
goop on my plate. Nathan said, "Jupiter will be back before the
weekend."
"That's great, hey! Great!" Perhaps that overdid it. After all, I
hadn't got to know Jupiter before he went to the hospital. "Uh,
how do you know he'll be home?" I asked.
By not answering, Nathan blew my short fuse, and I blitzed
him, said, "Yeah, yeah, I know, psychic. Purple socks."
How could I open my big mouth that way after pining for a
word or two from Nathan? *Dumb, dumb, dumb.* Backtracking, I
swiped my mustache with the paper napkin, dug in my pocket, and

187

pulled out the newspaper clipping, sad and wrinkled as old money now, and offered it to Nathan as a peace offering. "I thought you might like this."

The man could have been a statue. Beet juice colored the edge of my noodles. I got up and slid the clipping on the top of the refrigerator, and said, sounding gruff when I wanted to sound—one of Peso's words—conciliatory, "It's my only one."

Nathan left the clipping where it was, took his plate over to the sink, and scraped food into the garbage.

I wanted to deck him.

Afraid now of what I might do since I had already done enough, I left the kitchen for the basement. Shavings lay on the workbench in the outline of the box we had made. I paced, thinking, *Rye whiskey, that's what I need. Not smooth bourbon—the nip of good strong rye. I tried to make amends. Nathan wouldn't let me.* With one swift movement I sent the shavings to the floor and pressed the top of my head against a stack of boxes and zapped them with my fists, one-two, one-two. I needed a friend, deserved a friend, needed a bottle, deserved a bottle, and, for Christ sakes, a good lay—one-two, one-two.

That night I waited on the last step of the landing, elbows on my knees, chin in hand. One by one men passed me on their way to bed. I was obsessed now, had to try one more time. When only Nathan remained in the living room, I pushed my fingers through my hair and coughed to warn him of my presence. I made like a brave man and moved into the living room.

"Let's be men . Can't we get past this?" I said to Nathan's back. He didn't respond. I crossed to the TV and turned it off.

"Please. I need to talk. We need to talk."

Nathan tried to pass by me, backed up and tried again. He wobbled like a spinning coin not knowing quite where to land.

I stuck myself between him and the stairs.

Nathan sidestepped.

So did I.

"I was dumb," I said.

Nathan twitched. He touched his shirt pocket. The cellophane on his cigarettes crackled. Nathan said, "N-not dumb. Your message, l-loud and clear. A vio-vio-violation."

"Nathan, it didn't have anything to do with you. Not really. It had to do with those girls, the ones who were teasing me, and with other ... things."

Nathan peered at the ceiling.

This was further than we had ever got and I didn't want to blow it. I shifted my weight. "Nathan, I didn't know what I was doing. I acted on instinct. Instinct. Haven't you ever done anything you didn't understand and later regretted it?"

I saw an eyelash flicker as if something had registered. Couldn't he tell how miserable and desperate I was? *Aren't you going to say anything?* "I feel alone here. I want to make it right. What do you want? Name it, you got it."

Very deliberately Nathan lit a cigarette and exhaled smoke away from me. Looking at the floor, he said, "I thought you were half-a-friend, maybe two-thirds." Finally he made eye contact. "Frenchy, I invited you to my mother's house." Then he exhaled patiently. "You can't have what you want, Frenchy, not with me."

Stunned, hearing him this way, realizing how bizarre my behavior must've seemed, made me speechless. Nathan extinguished the half-smoked cigarette and dropped the butt into the heap in the ashtray. He said, "I want nothing from you. We are now 'past this.'"

"No," I said, following him. "Buddies. I want to be buddies."

Nathan paused with his hand on the banister, turned, and said, "That's just more budding than I want to do," and headed up the stairs.

CHAPTER THIRTY

Time dragged like misery. Nathan and I both worked at avoidance. Me, I got up early, skipped breakfast, made my bag lunch, and left for work. As soon as I got home, I disappeared into my room until dinnertime, and then stuffed food down sitting as far away from Nathan as I could. After dinner I descended to the basement where I planed scrap lumber into shavings until bedtime. Doing this, I managed not to see him for days. Disconnected from everyone and everything, I lived a no-life life, and didn't like what it was doing to me. The thought of going back to prison began to seem better than staying at Chance Place, that's how out of it I was. I heard shuffling footsteps, shoved the peanut butter sandwich into the paper bag, rolled it closed, ready to hit the road, before I saw ... Jupiter!

"Yo. I didn't know you were back!"

Awareness lighted the man's gray eyes; color flowed in his cheeks now. I doubt I would have recognized him anywhere else. Weak, but well-groomed, Jupiter nodded in a way that suggested talking took more effort than he could make. I didn't want to stare. Since it wasn't Nathan, I turned and tucked vanilla wafers into a sandwich bag.

Jupiter foraged in the corner cupboard and pulled out a blue vase. He said, "For the flowers Nathan gave me." I had heard him holler before, but not speak. His voice sounded rough as gravel. "Thanks for coming to the hospital."

"Sure. You bet."

Jupiter set the vase on the counter with both hands. He gripped the ledge and, veins pulsing, raised himself. I wondered if I should offer help.

Jupiter said, "If it weren't for you and Nathan, I'd be in Anoka State Hospital."

"I can't take any credit," I said, rolling the top of the bag. "It was Nathan's doing." Although my relationship with Nathan had proved anything but common, Jupiter and I had Nathan in common.

Vase under his arm, Jupiter slowly trekked across the kitchen. At the doorway he paused, turned back, and said, "Do you know where Nathan is? He hasn't been sleeping in our room."

Nathan wasn't the kind of guy who would punish his roommate for what I did.

Jupe said, "I miss him. Can't sleep."

A lump of worry chunked up inside me. When a vulnerable adult disappeared, it was bad news. Pedestrians frightened them; they got disoriented. Police could be unkind. Questions popped into my head: Where could Nathan be? At his mother's? His father's? Lost? McMaster should know.

"Listen," I said. "I don't have time to talk now. I have to go or I'll be late for work." By the time I put on my new Thinsulate jacket and hat, Jupe was ascending the stairs on his rump, cradling the vase like a baby.

I warned myself not to sweat Nathan's absence. Still, I plugged a quarter into the pay phone at work and dialed Chance Place. McMaster answered.

"Jupe says Nathan hasn't been home at night."

"So?"

I hoped I never built a fortress around me as tough as McMaster's. "Do you know where he is?"

"Why should I tell you?"

I jabbed a left hook at the wall. "I just wondered if he was sick, that's all, like maybe in the hospital. I'd visit him."

"French, with these guys, it's cock-a-doodle-do all the time. Take my advice. Forget it."

So much for caring cooperation.

Nervous as an ant who'd lost his antennae, I worked the day. First thing when I got home, I asked Emory about Nathan. Emory led me to the phone bulletin board and pointed to several messages there for Nathan. I took them down. There were three from a Mrs. Simpson and two from a Sister Angela, whose phone number was the same as Sister Kathleen's, but a different extension. I questioned Emory with a look.

"Boy toy. Tad had," he said, his thick brows knitted in distress.

"Do you know where he is?"

Emory took a step back.

Scaring these skittish guys was easier than drinking water. Would I never learn? Nathan could be lying in a gutter freezing to death.

"Where's the phone book? I'll call his mother."

As I dialed Emory stuck to me like a tongue frozen to a metal fence.

Mrs. Waite said, "I expect Nathan on Sunday. Is something wrong?"

"N-No," I said, not wanting to alarm her. What if Nathan reverted to what Mrs. Waite had described as his first line of defense? What if he needed help? "I just need to talk to him. Could he be with his dad? Mr. Waite, he works downtown?"

She hesitated, then said, "Communications Inventions. In the IDS Center. Are you sure nothing's wrong?"

"Listen. That was a great breakfast, Mrs. Waite. The best. Thanks again. I really liked it."

I dialed Communications Inventions and got an answering service. Mr. Waite was out of town and wasn't expected for several days. That smacked me exactly where I didn't want to be, between a missing Nathan and his social worker.

I lugged my pain and discomfort to Russell's Bar where Ernie used to go, kitty-corner from the Grain Exchange Building. Unlike the bars I used to haunt, women wore tailored suits with high-collared white blouses, and classy jewelry. Odd, there seemed to be about an equal number of men and women and hardly any smokers, music softer than I associated with bars. The attitude suggested some cozy school reunion or a big business party after closing an important deal. The bartender was a woman, a young woman.

I snitched peanuts from a wooden bowl on the bar and ordered a bottle of Grain Belt. Beside me sat a woman with short, neat, honey-colored hair. She had glossy red lips.

"Frenchy," I said. "New in town."

"Diane." Diane had wide-set, soft eyes, a firm chin, fetching features. One by one, they didn't impress me; put together they sang a pretty tune.

"What do you do, Frenchy?"

I gave her my best smile. "As little as possible."

"Original."

She had a lean, exercised body, firm thighs. I thought her eyes were blue; it was hard to tell in this dim light. I drew a nice, cold swig from the bottle.

"Aaahhh," I said, "been waiting a long time for this."

She laughed lightly. "You should be more generous with yourself."

"You know it," I said, raising my finger to order another.

Diane worked for Pillsbury, was saving to buy one of those expensive gabled homes on the Greenway, preferably facing Loring Park. By the time four empties stood in front of me, I had met Diane's roommate, Kimberly Stanapoulos, who worked for Control Data Corporation, a company, Kimberly said, that had preceded IBM. We bantered. I must have passed some sort of roommate test, because when Kimberly disappeared Diane was still there.

"Actually, I said, picking up on Diane's earlier question, "I'm not allowed to talk about what I do." I tapped the tip of my nose. "Confidential."

"Really?"

"Puts a dent in a guy's social life," I said, ordering a white wine for her. "In Illinois, I worked in interstate commerce. Here—well, there's Sperry Univac, Honeywell, Federal Cartridge."

"Federal Cartridge?"

"Ammunition."

"Oh." She raised an eyebrow of intrigue and slid her hand closer to mine. Her eyes, definitely blue, soft as velvet. Ernie would be proud at how I hung in there.

I said, "Uncle Sam keeps close tabs on me."

Between sheets as slippery as the satin I had puckered and glued into the box, she smelled of some floral-scented perfume. It was everywhere. On her neck, behind her ears, between her breasts. I lapped and suckled her. Diane moaned and clung to me like her life depended on what I was doing to her. Urged on by soft feminine sounds and her passion, I moved down on her, flicking my tongue, gorging after so long a fast, unable to get enough. She clutched my head between her hands; my tongue teased her to multiple climaxes.

Flowing like the fabric of a light silk shirt, she nibbled and kissed her way down on me. Sandy had done that until— At first I felt delight, anticipation, but soon I knew I couldn't get it up. Before Diane would say anything, I took her by the shoulders and said, "Sorry. I drank too much."

"Oh, hon." She peered at my penis, lying soft as a marshmallow on my thigh.

I took her hand and kissed it, said, "Don't take it personally." I patted my shoulder, telling her to rest her head there. "It's okay."

But it wasn't okay.

She hesitated, seemed to wrestle with the challenge, finally rested her head. Good thing, too; no way was my dick going to cooperate. Damn Peso. My dick still believed it belonged to him and only to him. Would it ever be free to act on its own?

"Tell me," I said, still wishing I could spill inside her, hoping maybe she'd give me another chance, "in your business, can you get milk cartons, like by the truckload?"

She tipped her head and looked into my eyes like this was a quiz. "You're a stitch," she said.

"Research," I said, laughing. "Always research."

I hadn't laughed or felt so at home in a long, long time.

CHAPTER THIRTY-ONE

When a guy drank, detectives were everywhere. I had
fallen asleep in the overstuffed chair; McMaster woke me up
sniffing my breath. Utensils clinking in the kitchen hurt my
eardrums. I called in sick to work on the kitchen phone, then dialed
Sister Angela, who insisted on knowing who my social worker was
and that I come in for a late afternoon meeting with them. I hung
up knowing I had done the number on Nathan that made him
disappear and that something I had run from all of my life was
pursuing me. I took four aspirin and crawled into bed.

Sister Kathleen wore silver bauble earrings I hadn't seen
before. Sister Angela proved thin and plain. I tried to answer their
questions, finally said, "Sisters, I wish I knew more, but I don't."

There followed this long, tense silence. Then Sister Kathleen
asked lightly, "Might there have been any message for Nathan
from Government Center?"

I started to shake my head, then remembered. "Wait! I
overheard a bit of an odd phone conversation Nathan had. When he
hung up, he told another resident he had to go to Government
Center."

Sister Kathleen reached up and stilled an earring. Sister Angela grimaced the way my mother did when she had female cramps. Then the women looked at each other sharing something dismal.

I added, "Nathan asked the caller to spell a name. Something like … the hat, like …Stetson! It sounded like Stetson."

Sister Angela paled. "Stiltsen?" she asked. "S-t-i-l-t-s-e-n."

"Yeah. That's it!"

"Would you be willing to swear to hearing this conversation?" Sister Kathleen asked.

"You mean like in court?"

She nodded.

Thanks, Peso, for everything. I snatched my hat from the chair and pulled it over my ears, said, "Listen, Sisters, I got a dog to walk."

I met with Ernie a half-hour before the AA meeting, hoping he could free me of guilt and grief.

"Something's new," I said, sparring in the air between us. "Can you tell?"

"Haircut?"

"Jeez. C'mon."

Ernie's eyes glinted like the big crop had just come in. He stretched his long legs and crossed his ankles. "What am I supposed to notice?"

"Been with a woman."

"Well, now."

I slapped Ernie's knee and sat on the edge of my chair. "That friend I told you about? I made amends." I plopped my hat on the side of my head like a pancake and smiled cockily. "Here I am."

"You don't seem humbled. Making amends usually humbles a guy." The man's steady gaze unnerved me. Did I have to eat crow? What did he expect, a miracle? I sobered, felt my hat going around in my hands. "Which was more important, Frenchy, making amends or making it with a woman?"

Heads up all the time, that's what you had to be, heads up, because sooner or later everyone turned on you—my old man, my mom, Peso, Nathan, my sponsor.

"I don't know what you mean," I said, sounding much more smart-assed than I felt. I couldn't pick up my hat because my foot was on it.

"How long have you known this woman?"

"Long enough to get the job done, okay?" I stood and sparred, wanted to smack him in the mouth.

"So what's she like?"

"Professional. Pretty. Oh. Not that kind of professional. I mean an office type—wears a suit. That kind of professional."

"Where?"

"Where what?"

"Where did you meet her?"

"Around." I was scared as hell.

"Does she work?"

"Pillsbury. Nothin' says lovin' like somethin' in the oven." I smacked my palm with my fist, my mouth felt dry as fire. Ernie had my number and could cash it in.

"Sounds pretty safe," he said slowly. "Someone you find interesting, but who probably won't take you seriously. Notice your hands, Frenchy. They're trying to tell you something. What?"

I popped a punch in the air, danced. "Put'em up. C'mon. Put 'em up."

Ernie wouldn't move. He said, "Is that it? Get a lady into a clench and you don't have to deal with her? A ready, keep-away lady?"

"Fight, you bastard."

"I thought we'd already discussed violence. Hit me; I'll press charges."

Heat snaked up my spine, flooded my skull, cooked my brain.
Sure as if I had taken a hit in the gut my wind left. If Ernie found
out what kind of a wimp I really was he'd hate me for sure.
I didn't like that I needed him.

"Frenchy, talking about women is one of your favorite hot
buttons."

Confused, I dropped my fists.

"How did Nathan respond to your amend?"

I mumbled, "I went out on a limb." *Dangerously far out on a
too thin, high limb*—with Nathan, with Sister Kathleen, here.
There was too much to hide now and that limb could break. "I
did," I said.

Ernie put his elbows on his knees, dangled his hands between
them. "How'd it go?"

"What?"

"With the woman."

I hung my hand on the back of my neck, felt tension there. Ernie
was turning me inside out, would see me for the turd I was. What
defense did I have? "I thought we were discussing Nathan."

"You said you went out on a limb. I took that to mean you did
what you could. Isn't that what you meant?"

"Yes," I hurried to say. I felt hot, like the lie had dumped me
into deep hot water.

"Okay. You did what you could. You said you accomplished
two things this week, made amends and made it with a woman."

"Right." I kicked my hat.

"Truth," Ernie said.

"I liked it and didn't like it, okay?" I sent my hat around the
floor. "It reminded me of ..."

The hat slid in front of Ernie.

He tossed it to me.

"It reminded me of something."

"Of what?"

"A long time ago. Waaaay back," I said, returning his toss.

"The woman reminded you of someone in particular?"

I slung my hand behind my left side, tossed. "Needs more weight," I said.

"Your mother?"

I said, "'Go out and play. Wash your hands. Stay out of my way.'"

"How were you in your mother's way?"

"Underfoot. Nice ... catch. When she had company." We had a great rhythm going. I tried to put some spin on the throw. Ernie caught it anyway.

"You respected her a lot then, your mom?"

The hat fell. "She was balling half the town!"

Ernie moved toward me. I cringed.

"Tell me," Ernie said, looking into my eyes. "Where was little Francis when she was balling half the town?"

I punched after blood. Went after him. Jab. Jab. Jab-jab.

Ernie ducked to one side, instinctively blocked my punches. I advanced, jabbed, jabbed, jabbed. Ernie held his own, backed across the room

"Fr-Francis, where were you while she was ... balling?"

My uppercut landed soft. Ernie faked a punch, connected; I edged him toward the corner. Ernie evaded my plan.

"I was with my dog, you bastard." Jab, zap. "When I still had a dog." WHOP. "Where you fuckin' learn to fight?"

"Choose," Ernie gasped, feigning. "You don't like women because ... you're mad at Mommie. Or— " Ernie dropped his left and I aimed to kill the son of a bitch. "Or ... you like men because Mommie did. Or," Ernie grunted, shifted, ducked, shifted, "you want to ... suck on Mommie's sugar tit forever, even though it's dry as sunburnt bone."

"You fucker, I liked men because ... they paid. I fuckin' survived on men. I survived... fucking."

201

"Hi," Ernie said, pretending to look over my shoulder like someone had just come into the room, as if I would fall for that old trick. He protected his face. I beat his arms.

"What's going on here?"

I damn dropped my guard. Ernie moved away. Gramps and that young, pitiful woman stood in the doorway.

"I thought you'd never get here," Ernie managed to say, breathing like he had come to the end of the world. He dropped into a chair, "Awesome," he said. "Friendly sponsor chat."

Gramps looked from one to the other of us with a puzzled expression. He concentrated like he was thinking of calling the cops. I *smack-smack-smacked* my palm, thinking I should have finished the job.

Ernie shook his head at Gramps.

"Sure?" Gramps asked.

"Sure," Ernie said.

AAers ambled in and glanced at the two of us with curiosity. I sulked. They set up the chairs. Ernie picked up my hat, placed one hand flat over his heart, and moved over to me. He extended it. "Don't hurt me. Please don't hurt me," he said. I wanted to pelt him, but couldn't help but smile and snatch the hat. When I did, Ernie grabbed my shoulders and hugged me. He spoke softly into my ear. "If little Francis can forgive himself for surviving, Frenchy just might stop craving booze."

Before I could react, someone grabbed my hand and pulled me into the circle for the Serenity Prayer. The room spun like I had been clopped upside the head. Then someone was reading the twelve steps. What had happened? I sat there feeling zapped, vulnerable, naked, and, most of all, alone. Just like that, my whole outlook on life snapped into some other zone. Time must have passed because the young, pitiful woman was taking us through the ain't-it-awfuls of her life.

Gramps called her "dear" in an oozing-sap tone. He said, "Sounds like growing up you took more than your share of put-downs. Maybe it's time you built yourself up."

Ernie tilted his head at me in a way that suggested: Pay attention. Ernie said to the woman, "Put-down's just a fancy way of saying your heart got beat up. Over time, a heart can get so bruised and tender, you can find yourself striking out at imagined danger and twisted into believing you're heartless when, in fact, you might be all heart."

A technical knockout.

CHAPTER THIRTY-TWO

Mrs. Stiltsen was about the same age as Nathan's mother, only thinner, with a long, sharp nose, and a powdery complexion.

Releasing Nathan's hand, she said, "I've heard nice things about you, Mr. Waite. From Sister Angela. She works for me." Mrs. Stiltsen tugged the hem of her dark suit jacket with blunt-edged, bright red fingernails. "Sit."

Nathan felt unsafe and didn't know why. Mrs. Stiltsen closed the door. The nameplate on her desk said: Millie Stiltsen. She picked up a fat white envelope and flagged it at him. "Do you know what this is?"

"N-no."

"Can you guess?"

"I don't want to."

"How does it feel to be rich?"

"I wouldn't know," Nathan said, looking at the door.

She narrowed her eyes at him the way a cat blames you for the first snow. "Not anymore," she said in a triumphant tone. She set the envelope in front of him, but kept her hand on it.

"Has Sister Angela discussed your benefits with you?"

What did she want of him? "I told Sister Angela what I understood."

"Good," Mrs. Stiltsen said, removing her hand from the envelope. She peered at him like he was supposed to say or do something. Somehow she reminded him of the lady with the big book and cleavage, except Mrs. Stiltsen's breasts sagged and she smelled of an unpleasant musk perfume. He wouldn't want to be stuck in an elevator with anyone wearing that perfume.

She said, "I'm saving you the check-cashing fee. Not everyone in this department would do that for you." Her eyes looked like lake ice just before it melted, the color of charcoal, hard.

Nathan looked down at his boots. They needed polishing.

"Sister Angela wanted to give you this herself. I'm taking the prerogative, one of the few nice things I get to do."

Nathan crossed and uncrossed his legs. Since skating with Frenchy, he had become less able to trust anyone or anything. People like Stiltsen said they had money for you, then after what they called necessary deductions he'd be lucky if he had enough left for a pack of cigarettes. Why was he even here?

"Do you have family here in town?"

"Y-yes."

"Your mother, does she call often?"

"Not too often."

His answer seemed to please her.

"Your sister? Debbie, isn't it? How long since you've seen Debbie?"

"More than a year, maybe two. She married Bill."

"You miss her?"

He supposed he missed his sister, but Debbie was a girl. Except for soccer, they hadn't played together all that much. He always stole the ball from Debbie.

"She lives ... where?"

"Superior, Wisconsin."

"Why, Mr. Waite, this is your lucky day. Superior is as close to Duluth as St. Paul is to Minneapolis. Right here in this envelope with your money is a ticket, a Greyhound ticket, that will take you to Superior. Debbie will be delighted to see you. Bill, too. Isn't that nice?"

"Visit Debbie?"

She reached for the envelope, which wasn't sealed, poked her finger inside it, and produced a bus ticket.

Nathan's left knee took to bobbing. "I have to work," he said.

"Pooh. You can quit and start a volunteer job anytime."

His heel *clat-clat-clatted*. That isn't what Sister Angela had told him. *Nathan, if you make this commitment, keep it.* Sister Angela claimed she had worked extra hard to get the hospital to take him and he could tell he was supposed to appreciate her effort just like he was supposed to appreciate whatever Mrs. Stiltsen was doing for him now.

He said, "Maybe I'll go to Dayton's and buy a few things."

Mrs. Stiltsen arranged the bills from the envelope into a fan—tens, fifties, hundreds—Nathan had never seen so much money. "You can buy just about anything you want," she said. "I'll call Abbott-Northwestern for you, tell them you're taking a well-deserved vacation. And this ticket," she said, waving it, "is courtesy of Hennepin County. It did not come out of your money."

"It didn't?"

"No. It didn't." She pushed the fan of money toward him. "Count it, sign this receipt, and you'll be on your way. No, Nathan. You must count it. Count it!"

He didn't want to count it. There were too many possibilities for mixing up pluses and minuses. He wanted to leave. He signed the receipt and stuffed the money into the envelope. Before he could pocket it, Mrs. Stiltsen took it and they tugged the envelope back and forth. With social workers, you never won, so he let go.

Mrs. Stiltsen pulled the bills out and counted them one by one out loud like he was a first grader. It wasn't as if he had won some sweepstakes. If only she would let him take it and leave. Watching, he filled with resentment, felt ripped off, violated just as he had with Frenchy on the ice. Is that what people like Frenchy thought, that he was just some kind of animal ready for the taking? Nathan stared into the woman's controlling eyes and said, "My illness isn't a mind clarifier. There are too many angles."

She flinched.

"Sign here," she said. "It says you received your money."

Before signing, he made sure he wasn't stopping any benefits.

She shoved the envelope toward him.

"Meds?" She sounded suddenly impatient. "Do you have them with you? Nathan, don't open that envelope in public. Keep the ticket separate. Do you have your meds with you?"

He slid the ticket into his shirt pocket behind his cigarettes, then hid the envelope in the inside secret pocket of his down jacket. That didn't make sense because anyone who owned an L. L. Bean jacket, a considerable number of people, would know about it. Was he supposed to carry his meds?

"One dose," he answered. "Can I go now?"

"Debbie will be thrilled to see you," she said, escorting him hastily to the door. "Go home and get your prescriptions. Take them with you. One bus leaves at four, another at seven."

"I don't think so." Nathan patted his hair.

"Mr. Waite, be *on* one of those buses."

Nathan knew an order when he heard one. Still, he wasn't about to leave town without first getting his personal daily message. The message, as if he weren't confused enough, said:

> Because all life is circular,
> Anything taken to the extreme
> Becomes its opposite.

207

CHAPTER THIRTY-THREE

I tried to explain to Emory that the nuns knew something they weren't telling, but I couldn't tell if I had gotten through. "What can we do?" I asked, wishing I knew how to follow the dude's mind. Humming that stupid Jericho dirge, Emory pulled me to the hall closet, where he reached in and took my jacket, then his Chesterfield coat and beaver hat.

I had to take two strides for every one of Emory's, skipping like a little kid to keep up. Knowing the futility of asking Emory questions, I scuttled along beside him.

Letters on the sad storefront window said MIBCA and underneath in smaller letters, Minnesota Institute for Black Chemical Abuse. Inside was a large room of unattended, cluttered desks, and two offices to one side with open doors.

"Emory, my man," said a guy appearing in one of them. The reddish-brown man with rheumy eyes stood tall and lean as a Globetrotter.

"Name's Jim," he said, extending his hand. "Welcome."

"Frenchy Bibideaux," I said, taking it. "Not as good as some, better 'n most."

"Come on in."

Jim's long, tapered fingers tugged at his gray, tufted sideburns, which contrasted with his close-cropped hair. His dark eyes behind wire-rimmed bifocals, suggested kindness. He said, "Emory don't bring a man in, 'less it's *big* trouble. Whatever it is, we best rap it."

Emory sat stroking his coat, which lay folded across his lap. Clearly, he wasn't going to speak.

"There's this guy at Chance Place," I said, hoping Jim could be trusted. "Nathan."

"I know Nathan."

Unsure of what I was doing here, I knuckled my nose. "Well, Nathan hasn't been home for a few nights. No one knows exactly how many. When I asked Emory if he had any ideas, he brought me here."

"Clerk work."

Huh?

Jim frowned and turned pensive. He steepled his hands and tapped a fingertip against his lips, asked, "Wrap trap?"

Emory nodded.

Jim's middle seemed to cave in; he released a slow wheeze of a breath and addressed me. "Chew on this. Was there anything new or different goin' down in Nathan's life?"

"Uh." I coughed, swallowed. "Jupiter, Nathan's roommate, was in the hospital. When Jupe got home, he said Nathan wasn't sleeping in their room."

"Court short."

"Oh, yeah. Nathan went to court. I don't know why."

"A crime?"

"No," Emory and I answered together.

Jim's brows furrowed. "Inheritance maybe? Do we know who saw him last? When?"

"As far as we can tell maybe a couple, three weekends ago." I sounded anxious when I wanted to sound concerned. "When I told

Nathan's social worker that he took a phone call in which he was asked to go to Government Center, she got ... agitated."

"Oh-oh," Jim said. He moved his index fingertip slowly along the top of his hand. "Nathan get him a financial windfall?"

I shrugged.

"See, there's this jive," Jim said, "to get people off welfare. If a client be convinced to visit some relative out of state—like family—know what I'm sayin'? Maybe he never come back, lose his entitlements."

My expression must have showed how puzzled I was because Jim explained. "There's nothin' illegal, see, about givin' a bus ticket to visit kin." His rheumy eyes turned sad as a hound's who'd lost the scent. "They call it 'Greyhound Therapy.'"

Emory petted his coat faster and faster.

My mind did one of those delayed numbers it did like when I was trying to convince myself that my old man hadn't been so cruel or that it was all my fault. Then I got it. The system was giving Nathan the shaft, throwing him away like garbage!

First I felt numb, then angry.

Jim pushed at his eyebrow like trying to erase it.

He said, "Man like Nathan get pretty lost. If the po-lice pick him up, maybe they send 'im back, maybe not." His hand dropped with powerlessness.

I now had enough energy to attack. "Why wouldn't they send him back? Why not?"

Jim said, "No travel money. And," he raised his eyebrows to mean: Better believe it, and added, "Nathan's got to want to come back. Sometimes that's a tall order, know what I'm saying?"

Certainly Nathan's father or mother would buy him a return ticket! As for the kind of help Nathan needed, only millionaires and governments could afford it. That's the way it was.

"See," Jim said, "mind-sick people, 'specially paranoid ones, like schizophrenics, usually be too afraid to accept aid. They think the people trying to give it are out to hurt 'em. If Nathan's like that, no one will help; no one will want to help. Nathan's entitlements are here in Minnesota. No state is looking for more people to help. Maybe Nathan's out there refusin' contact with anyone who might help him. The law gives him the right to refuse help and no law gives us rights to make him take it, know what I'm saying?"

Not unless someone commits him.

What law ever did anything for anyone? Except maybe traffic lights, that kind of law. Guilt pushed up in me like some tired volcano waking up. I ignored it because it would only muddle my brain more. The government spent more researching tooth decay than mental illness. Nathan could be wandering homeless. Or he could land in jail like Big Swede, or on the street; any horror could happen. We needed to find whatever it would take to bring Nathan home safely. That answer added up to more amends than any one man could make in one lifetime.

CHAPTER THIRTY-FOUR

Nathan presented his bus ticket to the ticket agent who wore a green plastic visor, and asked if it was good.

"Humph!" the man said, "It is. 'Twere me, I'd go someplace warm."

Nathan touched his jacket over the pocket holding his money. "Like wh-where?"

The man rattled off names of places.

Nathan was afraid of Mrs. Stiltsen's power over him. Even thinking about going somewhere other than where she had ordered enlivened him. Nathan's mind and heart tumbled over turbulent currents. The ticket agent had mentioned a place with "beach" in its name. Nathan pictured himself fishing from his canoe, basking in warm sun. "The beach city," he said, fumbling for his envelope. "That's where I want to go."

The man cocked his head. "Son, are you sure?"

"Yes." It felt good to make this decision. Not crafty like Mrs. Stiltsen. Honorable. "The beach one."

The agent exchanged his ticket.

At the Quik Take-Out counter, Nathan purchased three packs of Marlboros—he could afford brands—no generics now. He ordered two cups of black coffee and an egg salad sandwich. Before boarding, he sauntered back to the counter and bought a Hershey with almonds, a Reese's Peanut Butter Bar, an O'Henry, and a Kit Kat, so there. Regardless of what Mrs. Stiltsen said, a visit from him was not high on Debbie's wish list.

Nathan tested several seats before settling in the middle on the driver's side next to the window, his purchases on the seat beside him. There weren't many passengers. Tall downtown buildings quickly gave way to suburban homes, then to freeway signs followed by fallow farm land and barren trees. The rhythm of the tires soothed him, but he couldn't smoke and that made him edgy.

In a couple of hours or so, the bus crossed into Iowa onto two-lane roads with no highway lamps. Here and there, a spotlighted house or a barn appeared. Seeing those lonely houses made Nathan feel his isolation, like he was traveling inside a sealed capsule. He glanced at his watch. McMaster would be locking the kitchen about now. The residents would be enjoying that best after-dinner cigarette in the living room. When Jupiter got home he should abstain from TV for awhile because he would mistake the action on the tube for real and believe it would hurt him. Frenchy, as always, would be finagling attention. Nathan hated to admit that he missed Frenchy.

He unwrapped the egg salad sandwich and ate half of it, consumed two candy bars. The coffee was tepid. He didn't mind that, but with the motion of the bus, not being able to smoke, and eating too much sugar, his stomach felt queasy. He curled up on the double seat and tried to sleep. When the driver stopped at an oasis on the Illinois Tri-State Tollway, Nathan's nerves were snapping like breaking rubberbands. Nathan deboarded and smoked three Marlboros.

Two passengers took their suitcases and left.

New passengers got on.

Inches of snow dwindled to a thin film whipped about by wind. The sound of wind and the whir of the tires kept Nathan awake.

After what seemed an interminable time, they stopped at a Day's Inn restaurant near the Indiana/Kentucky border. Nathan ordered waffles, sausage, and a glass of milk.

After two bites he swallowed his meds with milk and left the remainder of his food uneaten. He realized that Frenchy would have known what to do in his situation. Frenchy would smart off and not take guff from Mrs. Stiltsen. If Nathan had stood up for himself, maybe he'd still be in Minneapolis, safe in Chance Place, not here in the middle of nowhere. *Why am I on this ride?*

The sign over the door said: Seymour, Indiana. Catfish capital of the world.

CHAPTER THIRTY-FIVE

A new passenger, a young woman in jeans, took the seat across the aisle from Nathan. He couldn't stop looking at her long, dark hair, which fell over her pink sweatshirt. The wave and the color of it reminded him of Cheryl's hair.

"I'm going to Berea," she said, addressing him in a voice high as a child's. Her eyes were swollen from sleep. "You have artist's hands. Any chance you're going to the potter's workshop?"

He held out his hands and looked at them. "No," he said. They were good, strong hands, but artist's? "I just did a project," he said, chest swelling.

"What kind of project?"

She smiled and got up and stood in the aisle while he gathered up his belongings on the seat, so she could sit beside him. His fingertips remembered Cheryl's soft, smooth skin. He put one hand under his thigh. Outside, the fields were flat. He said, "My project was more like ... sculpture."

"It's tough, isn't it?"

"Wh-what?"

She had an overlapping front tooth, a bright smile.

"Not being able to smoke."

His fingers touched his pocket. "Yes." It was daylight now. Cheryl didn't know he smoked. He hadn't slept. "W-would you move back? I-I want to try to sleep."

"Well, okay," she said, clearly disappointed.

In Lexington, Nathan watched the young woman's red backpack move away. He heard an infant's cry of rage, but saw no baby on the bus.

The coach passed from Tennessee into North Carolina, then strained up a mountain, heading, the new bus driver said, for Asheville. Hairpin twists took them past expansive vistas that dizzied Nathan. Exhaust fumes coming from the back of the bus made him nauseous. Voices in his head chanted in the rhythm of the wheels: *inferior-superior, inferior-superior, inferior-superior.* By the time they stopped at a small country store near Gaffney, South Carolina, where the water tower looked like a peach, Nathan felt hung over. The driver announced, "Home of the pit bull and entrance to the Piedmont."

Nathan could no longer control the voices he heard. Continuing would be disastrous. Frightened of suffering a break with reality, he asked directions to the nearest park and, hearing the bus depart behind him, walked toward it. He toted his mental burden past frame houses with sagging porches and rocking chairs where, no doubt, in summer, families sat in harmony. He tied the arms of his jacket around his waist. Imagine, early April and this warm. Three, maybe four, voices warred. Soft images materialized. If he rested, he'd be okay. He needed rest.

Nathan selected a picnic table under a sweet gum tree and lay down. Birds chittered. Squirrels romped over branches with leaves fully out, creatures as free as he used to be in his boyhood treehouse, free as he wanted to be now. His left arm flung out. He closed his eyes, drew an unsteady breath, and started counting backwards to anchor himself—*ninety-nine, ninety-eight.*

After an hour and a half, Nathan woke chilled and groggy. He ate what was left of his crumpled egg salad sandwich and the Kit Kat, then located the less-than-clean rest room. He ran water over his sticky fingers, splashed his face, and combed his hair, then forced his rigid, reluctant muscles back to the highway, where he stuck out his thumb. Within an hour he was traveling east in a rattling, red pickup, beside a farmer whose cheek bulged with tobacco.

"That Randy Travis," said the man, pointing to the radio and raising his billed cap. His sentences sounded like questions that Nathan should answer. "A North Carolina boy. Made a name for hisself at twenty-one, he did. That li'l blond lady on *Wheel of Fortune*? The one that dresses so nice? She's from North Myrtle Beach near where you goin'; she's from *South* Carolina. We Carolinians make that distinction. Every year my daddy took us to the beach." Nathan was afraid to talk for fear he might not make sense. "Where you from?"

Calculating how to participate and remain removed from conversation, Nathan asked how a person could tell by looking at a leaf of tobacco whether or not it would taste sweet. After that conversation took care of itself and Nathan watched freshly plowed, red clay fields speed by.

By twilight he squinted at the sun-streaked skyline between motels on touristy Ocean Drive. High-rises stood like bookends at either end of the crescent-shaped shoreline. Between the bookends were less ostentatious one, two, and three-story motels. Though he liked the sound of the ocean and knew he should compare room rates, Nathan lacked the energy. At all costs, he needed quality rest. He selected the modest, red brick Mar Vista. When he told the woman (who reminded him of his mother, except this woman wore jeans), that he had no car, therefore, no license number, she peered at him longer than he liked. He pulled out his driver's license and showed it to her and said, "I'm hitchhiking."

She gave him the key to 310. Once inside the room, Nathan removed his shoes, got into bed, and pulled the covers over his head.

CHAPTER THIRTY-SIX

Nathan rose up on one elbow during the night, checking,
as was his custom, on Jupiter. His roommate wasn't there; Jupe
was in the hospital. Nathan lay back and listened for Harmony's
tick. Instead he heard a low, repetitive roar, sat up, and blinked.
That's when he remembered that it was he who had disappeared
and not Jupiter. He got up and felt along the wall in search of the
light switch. Finding none, he moved toward the sound of the
ocean and located glass patio doors. His fingers followed the floor
track until he came to the end and moved up and pulled the cord
that opened the drapes. Outside, he saw a row of lighted globes
mounted on a brick wall and, beyond them, the foam of the
incoming ocean.

He moved out onto the balcony and breathed in the cool, salty
air, the ocean breeze. There were two wooden rocking chairs.
Rainwater shimmered on the surface of the tarp that covered the
pool directly below. His muscles ached. Stars twinkled in a
cloudless sky. His mouth tasted foul. Insects battered the light
globes. Lighting a cigarette, Nathan felt the stubble on his cheeks.
The constantly moving water frightened him; he could drown and
no one would know. He should have headed north to the familiar
Boundary Waters where he knew how to portage his canoe from

one placid lake to another without concern about tides. He settled
in one of the chairs with his stockinged feet on the brick railing,
which, like his mind, had openings in it. Soon he knew if he
watched the ocean much more, he would suffer nausea.

He took his cigarette butt inside to dispose of it properly. When
he found the light switch, his spirits soared: He had a four-burner
stove, a small refrigerator with a real freezer compartment,
cupboards with dishes in them—pots, pans, paper towels, flatware,
two double beds, a bathroom with a tub and a shower, four huge
towels. Why, he had his own apartment!

Excited, he took a shower, letting the spray pelt first one part of
his body, then another. He didn't have to hurry; no one was
waiting in line; he could take as long as he wanted. At 4:00 a.m. he
hummed "Pomp and Circumstance."

The first extreme had become its opposite.

Nathan left his purple socks in his shoes on Mar Vista's
seawall and walked east, into the breeze. The sun lay on the
horizon like a shimmering, red beach ball. He felt as free and
content as the gulls, enjoyed watching the swooping brown
pelicans. He nodded a greeting to a woman with a black Lab on a
leash. A pelican dove and snapped up a silvery fish.

Nathan said, "Hello," to an older, barefoot couple. Sandpipers
with stilt-like legs followed the water as it receded, then rushed
away from it as it came ashore, sometimes stopping to stick a beak
into a hole. He was like those birds playing tag with life,
directionless, afraid to get his feet wet. He stooped and picked up a
tiny coiled shell and examined it. If only Cheryl were here to enjoy
this with him.

Soon sand chafed Nathan's soles. A gray cloud—an imagined
one he knew—dimmed his view. He blinked it away, spotted a real
trolling vessel with a winged rigging. He imagined floating on a
bed of milk cartons, as he, the captain gave orders to the first mate,

his father, who in turn ordered hands to do the captain's bidding—a delightful, if juvenile, fantasy. Frenchy appeared and climbed over the gunwales of the vessel, which had become a canoe. Frenchy wore a black eye patch.

Nathan shook his head to shed the image, shaded his eyes to better see the distant, long fishing pier ahead. He needed this exercise to keep his mind in tow. He focused on positives: the sound of the ocean, the breeze, the salty smell, and his brisk pace.

Out on the pier the wind blew fiercely. Two older women wearing high-top boots and gray, hooded sweatshirts were pulling a rope in from the sea, hand over hand, until each landed a birdcage-like trap. One opened the hinged top of her trap, reached inside and pulled crabs away from a chicken neck, and tossed them into a bucket.

Nathan dry-heaved over the rail. As he wiped his mouth with his handkerchief, the women were laughing at him.

He backed away, turned, and sprinted across roughhewn boards, hoping he wouldn't get splinters, ran down the steps, and onto the sand. Panting, chest heaving, he tried to escape the horror of Frenchy wanting to get at his pale chicken neck penis. Before long, Nathan dropped to his knees gasping. He made an extraordinary effort, as he had been taught at the Center for Universal Awareness, to pull light and energy down through the top of his head, to exhale toxicity out of his navel. He sensed Cheryl's presence and reached for her. She dropped a swatch of hair into his hand which quickly reshaped into a dark, handlebar mustache.

Nathan closed his eyes; he wouldn't entertain hallucination. He turned toward the sea, took a deep breath, and silently counted *one hundred, ninety-nine, ninety-eight*. The hallucination dissipated. He was close to the edge with no one to help him. Slowly, he got up and placed one foot in front of the other very consciously—not fast, not slow—one step at a time toward Mar Vista. He must shave, eat breakfast. That's what he must do next.

In his room, Nathan counted out money enough for food and lodging for two weeks, knowing it might take him that long to stabilize. He wrapped the remainder of the money in paper towels, then searched long and hard before settling on a hiding place. He went down to the motel office and asked directions to the nearest supermarket and drug store where he could buy shaving supplies. The woman was a different one from the woman who had registered him the night before, younger. She wore the kind of clothes Debbie bought at Banana Republic.

"A Red Owl," he repeated. "For groceries."

"Oh, you mean the Food Lion," she said. "At the light," she pointed to the light on the corner, "go left. At the next light, left. It's on the left next to the Revco Drug Store."

Grateful to have only lefts to remember, Nathan thanked her, and turned to leave.

She asked, "Do you know how long you'll be staying?"

He patted his hair. "No. I haven't talked with my sister yet. I have to talk to her."

She said, "Better reserve if you want to stay the next two weekends. Spring break." She smiled, intimating that he understood what he didn't. "The swimming pool opens tomorrow."

"Thanks. I-I'll let you know."

He followed her directions, walking, he knew, as a square on the way to becoming a cube, which would turn him inside out and into a whirlwind, into his minus opposite. He would run out of meds. He had to make decisions. The only resident at Chance Place with enough mettle to help, he hated to admit, was Frenchy. Well, stabilizing would take as long as it took. How had the geometry of his life yielded so much bad chemistry?

CHAPTER THIRTY-SEVEN

"Frenchy? Get up."

"Who is it? What are you doing?"

"You have a phone call."

"It's the middle of the night!"

I pulled on my trousers without zipping them and padded down the cold stairs to the phone. Peso was the only person I knew who would call in the middle of the night.

"I have a collect person-to-person call for Frenchy ... Bibidoo, from ... sir?"

"Nathan."

I straightened, alerted. "From where? I got to know from where."

Nathan's voice said, "I dunno. I'm at a pay phone."

"Are you Mr. Bibidoo? What area code?" asked the operator.

"Ju-just a minute. Eight-oh-three."

"Uh ... that would be ... South Carolina. Will you accept charges? Are you Mr. Bibidoo?"

"Can I have a number, a number?"

"Will you pay?" She sounded irritated now, persistent. "Are you Mr. Bibidoo?"

"Yes, but—"

She disconnected.

"Nathan, where are you?"

"Collect. Sorry. I didn't want to. I need favors."

"Nathan, listen." I tried to get my sleeping brain in gear. "If I'm the reason you— Come home. Nathan, you got to come home."

Silence.

I knuckled my nose, told myself to stay calm, to do good here. I tried to make my tone anxiety free. "Emory was hoping you'd call."

"W-will you water my sweet potatoes?"

"Sweet— oh. Sure. On your window sill, right?" Nathan sounded ... weak. "I don't have a green thumb. It won't be the same as when you do it." I checked my watch, snatched the pencil on the string, wrote "3:39 a.m. South Carolina" on a pink slip. I could hear Nathan's uneven breathing. "Jupe's back. He misses you." *What to say? What to do?* "Nathan, Jupe asks about you all the time. He needs you. Hey ... where in South Carolina are you anyway?"

"I need meds. Voices. Why did you send that toilet paper? It was a terrible thing to do."

I tried to think, decided only the truth would do. "I owed someone, that's all. I sent it with a card that said, 'Because you're full of shit.' I didn't mean any harm, Nathan. It won't happen again. Can't we—"

"Judgment," Nathan interrupted. "Everyone gets it. Things are cycling backwards, opposite. Can you get meds for me?" His speech sounded slurred.

Okay. Okay. "I'll sure try. Give me your address so I can send them."

"I didn't want to ask you."

"Meds," I prompted. "You been drinking? How do I get 'em?"

"Drinking? Not with meds."

Wouldn't stop me.

"My M.A. card's under the Rubik's cube. In my closet."

"What's M.A.?"

"M.A.," Nathan said, insisting.

I raised a hand overhead in a silent appeal to whatever higher power existed and tried again. "Nathan, would you like me to get your meds?"

"Yes."

"What do I do with your M.A. card to get your meds?"

"I can have a burial plot."

"Where are you, Nathan?"

"In a motel. Take it to the pharmacist."

"Okay, first thing when the drug store opens, I'll take your M.A. card to the pharmacist. It's under your Rubik's cube in your closet. Where should I send your meds?"

"Here. To the motel."

"Which motel?"

"This one. The one where I am!"

This was madness, then I remembered Nathan took a lot of pills. "Which med do you want?"

"All of them."

A moment passed. I wanted to keep him talking. "Uh, how do you like it there?"

"It's cold when the wind comes off the ocean. I wear my jacket only early and late in the day. It's loud. The ocean."

"You're close to the ocean? Hey, Nathan, that milk carton boat you talked about? Wouldn't it be great if we made one? We could sail it on the ocean."

"I don't want to make it with you."

Contempt, that's what he meant. Still he had asked me to do him favors. That was a good sign. I breathed, said, "Don't swat a stupid flea. I'm talking about a boat here. I apologized. What more can I do? You're good at building things. I'll bring your meds.

Maybe we can get some milk cartons. Tell me where you are. What city?" *Please. Please.*

"Harmony's minus. Tide's in. Extremes go back and forth."

"Na— Don't hang up! Don't!"

Click.

McMaster was stomping snow from his boots out on the porch. His key turned in the lock. I had no idea the man arrived this early. Maybe he had a wife who threw him out. A blast of arctic air shocked me.

"At this hour?" McMaster said.

"Morning to you, too." I whacked the receiver into place.

"Clean up that sawdust in the basement yet?" Without waiting for an answer, McMaster pointed at the phone and said, "You gotta tell 'em what they want to hear."

Fearful of what I might say or do if I hung around, I took the stairs two at a time. The man's voice followed me.

"Sawdust. Clean it or—"

Yeah, yeah. Or vamoose.

Peso took forever to answer his page.

"Hey, baby, what's goin' down?"

"I'm a suffering savior, Peso."

Silence.

"A friend of mine named Nathan is lost."

"I'm supposed to be flattered?"

Already I was sorry; calling him proved a big mistake. "Listen," I said. "Don't be jealous. I'm still your one and only. The guy's a mental case who needs help, that's all. A naive kid. Help me over the hump here." My unfortunate choice of word sounded more like a plea than I intended. I suspected Peso could kill wearing a grin sweet as taffy. Peso had robbed my prick's ability to point in its own direction, whatever that was. "I-I hate to ask," I said. "Got a pencil?"

"Like a scout, always prepared."

"Nathan called collect here to the Chance Place pay phone, 612-555-3436, from South Carolina, area code 803, Central Standard Time, give or take a minute, 3:39 a.m. You getting all this?"

"Do I ever miss?"

The likes of Peso thought nothing of preying on vulnerables. I certainly didn't want him harming Nathan.

"Peso, it's simple. He took me to breakfast at his mother's home. For that kindness, I owe him. He's asked me to send his prescriptions, his medicine, that's all. He's sick in some motel near the ocean."

"Pretty boy. Not quick."

Nathan was scared and alone, jittery, as lost as Jupiter had been. Or worse.

"I owe him," I repeated, feeling apprehensive. "And you owe me. He's just a lost puppy." Then truth flowed out of my mouth. "Peso, I'm the son you're never going to have."

Peso hung up.

I found Nathan's medical assistance card paper clipped to a folded slip of paper with the name of the drug store on it, the same one where I had purchased the newspaper with the dog's mug shot in it. I rummaged through Nathan's folded tee shirts, shorts, shirts, slacks, looking for pill bottles and/or prescription numbers. Who would've guessed Nathan would be so neat? I checked pockets, felt along the shelf and inside Nathan's shoes. Who knew where Nathan would keep such information? My stomach twisted into knots. If only Mr. Waite had built a stupid milk carton boat with him, maybe Nathan wouldn't be such a lost kid, and then *I* wouldn't be doing *this*. I was about to give up, when my shoulder bumped the khaki laundry bag. Something hard was inside it. I took the bag down, pried open the drawstring, and extracted a red spiral notebook. On it, written in bold black letters: Nathan's Mindbook. I moved my fingertip along the top of the book and down the side of the binding, wondering if the information I needed might be inside? If I had something called a mindbook I wouldn't want anyone looking inside it. *But what if... ?* Only laundry was in the bag. I put the notebook back without opening it.

I tipped the M.A. card toward the light—number, name, address, and thank God, no photo. I had watched Nathan earn the blue badge of honor the way he had approached Jupiter in the hospital; Nathan deserved no less from me. Okay. What if I have to sign for prescriptions? What if I get caught buying mind-altering drugs with a government medical assistance card that's not mine? I had checked every inch of Nathan's closet. Sighing, I closed the door behind me. A guy could get seasick watching that clock. A guy could get locked up in maximum security for life.

"Fill 'em," I said, extending the card to the pharmacist, a young woman with red-rimmed glasses and tight little brown curls that bounced when she moved. "Please."

She took it and typed into the computer without looking at me.

I swiped my mouth with the back of my hand, shoved my hands into my pockets, jingled change, looked around.

"Which ones?" she asked, frowning.

"All of 'em." She squinted at the computer screen. Surely there had to be some law about a pharmacist keeping what she knew confidential. I swallowed. "I mean all of the ones for my ... illness."

She sighed like it was a tall order. "Okay."

In spite of the jitters, in spite of being all dressed up, I tried to appear casual. A long line of people stood at the checkout counter. My getaway would be at a snail's pace. The pharmacist counted and pushed pills with a stick. I spotted a display of condoms and went over to it.

There were so many choices. Maybe no condom was why I hadn't gotten it up with Diane. No. She had condoms. Booze was why I couldn't get it up. Liquor advertising never hinted what alcohol could do to your wand. Would I ever see Diane again? With HIV everywhere, a guy couldn't be oversupplied. I selected Trojan Kling-Tites.

The pharmacist was still counting. How many pills could one guy take? I found the disposable razors and selected a pack and a small bottle of Mennen's and a yellow toothbrush. Nathan, wherever he was, would appreciate these things. I reminded myself that if I had to sign Nathan's name, it was "Waite" with an "e" at the end.

Three white paper bags with bills stapled to them waited for me on the counter. The pharmacist handed me Nathan's M.A. card. I waited.

"Mr. Waite," she said in the kindest tone, "pay over there."

"Th-thanks."

I knuckled my mustache and took my place in the checkout line. The clerk, a skinny boy with acne, was slow to lazy. In other circumstances I might try to push ahead, but here I tried to shrink into invisibility, thinking I could do time into old age before my turn and, if caught, after death, too. My heart thumped up into my Adam's apple and cut my breaths short. I felt lightheaded; my adrenaline *pumpety-pump-pumped. Easy does it*, I told myself. *Keep it simple. First things first.* I was reduced to boosting my ego with stupid AA slogans.

"All these yours?"

My heart zapped all the way to China. *Junior from AA!* Drunks couldn't take just any drugs—a prescription or two given by a doctor who knew what they could take, sure—but three bags full, *baba black sheep, no sir, no sir.*

Junior's nose twitched like he smelled something bad. If Junior ratted ... I looked around helplessly, couldn't summon a word. AA was probably full of guys getting high on prescriptions. When I turned back, Junior had moved the razors, the Mennen's, the condoms, and the toothbrush across the bar code. I offered the quivering M.A. card.

"Can't," Junior said. My feet cemented to the spot. I heard people muttering behind me. Junior said, "Card's good only for the prescriptions."

"Y-you bet." I caught his uneasy grin, took out my wallet and said, "My mind, a zillion miles away."

Junior pressed his lips tight and dropped change into my palm, then reached under the counter and produced a book of forms. Painstakingly he copied each prescription number in it.

"I-I take a lot of pills," I said to the person in line behind me. *Stupid.* Junior was peering at the name on the M.A. card.

"Ni-ni-nickname," I said.

Junior's thumb moved over the name.

I said, "Non, non-addictive."

Without looking at me, Junior recorded Nathan's number on the form, tore off a copy, gave it to me, and put the original under the cash tray.

I must've frozen because he asked, "Is there something else?" *How long before you tell Ernie?* I shook my head and got the hell out of there.

CHAPTER THIRTY-EIGHT

It was a miracle I had gotten this far. I hid the bags containing Nathan's prescriptions inside *my* laundry bag. If Sister Kathleen knew what I was doing ... The thought of her set the hair on my arms at static attention. Now, filled with dread and a sense of eager expectation, not knowing what might happen, I waited for Nathan to call again. He had to call, he had to.

At work I ruined microchips and even considered smoking. At home, I stayed close to the phone. I couldn't ask the police or anyone for help. Maybe this was the kind of helplessness Nathan felt. *Why am I doing this?* It was a question I had to ask; there was so much at risk.

The surprising answer came: *Because you care.*

Trapped inside a cycle of waiting, nerves on edge, I paced through two nights. That was the repeating cycle of my life: waiting, hiding, getting caught. Waiting for my father to come home, waiting for him to leave. Waiting for my mother to notice me. Now, I waited for Junior to rat, for Ernie to pounce, for Peso to zap, for Sister Kathleen or Double Zero, ole Aught Naught, to zonk me into some hellhole from which I would never dig out. I was tired of waiting, tired of hiding, tired of all of it; I wanted *out*.

Helping Nathan was no way out.

If I phoned Peso and asked why it was taking so long, he would turn it into a grudge; if I waited too long, Nathan might end up beyond retrieval. *Peso—Nathan, someone, call! Why doesn't someone call?* Did Mrs. Waite even know? Mr. Waite was still out of town, but Sister Angela had called and given me his phone number, as he had instructed her to do—just in case. I decided to give Peso until Saturday. Saturday.

On day five I skipped AA. Friday, day six, I met with Sister Kathleen, taking with me a large, brown, padded envelope containing Nathan's prescriptions and the toilet articles I had bought. I carried the envelope everywhere like a drunk carries a bottle, or one who knows at every moment where a bottle is, to address and mail it in an instant. I slid it behind my feet under my chair in Sister Kathleen's office. Her earrings were perfect-gold balls dangling on chains. First, she asked routine questions as if I weren't even there and check-marked my replies. For a moment, I figured she was the nervous one, that's how nervous *I* was. After the Q and A, I gulped and asked, easy like, "Say, Sister Kathleen, any word on Nathan?"

The way she fingered the corner of the paper and wouldn't look at me I was sure she knew something. I couldn't sit still, felt like a bug was caught in my drawers nibbling my ass.

"Sister, level with me. Nathan's ... my friend."

Sadness filled her eyes. "We're ... concerned."

"I can tell you know something."

She reached up and stilled an earring. "We know Nathan set out to visit his sister in Wisconsin and ... didn't arrive."

"Huh— " Could I possibly know more than she did? If I told her what would she say? Do?

Sister Kathleen squeezed the Christ figure on her cross. She said, "Last year someone ... like Nathan ... was traveling here by bus from Arizona. In Utah he was robbed. He—exposure," she said, not looking at me.

I pressed my soles to the floor. My gaze landed on the poor pleaders in purgatory. If that happened what could I, or anyone, do? I swallowed.

She said, trying to make it sound reassuring, "Eventually the police will connect."

Rule keepers, rule breakers, dick makers, dick takers. Blues were more like the guys they locked up than anyone else I knew. Flip heads, tails, police and cons would come up the same. I had learned social workers didn't score so well in the straight goods department either. For once, focusing on the positive, I asked, "What's the best that can happen?"

Sounding weary, she said, "Nathan returns of his own accord. There's so much red tape. Nathan's benefits ... Well," she said, like she carried the burden of it. She sealed me off, said, "I need your AA attendance slip."

I shuttled words faster than a gambler shuffled cards. "I got the one I forgot last week, but now I forgot this week's. I'm so forgetful. I swear, Sister, the guys I live with are rubbing off on me. Hey, if you knew where Nathan was, couldn't you convince him to come back?"

She fingered the AA slip, then bent and recorded the date, and dropped it in my file. She bit on her lower lip and closed the file. "Only if he wants to."

"Everything he needs is here!"

"Unless Nathan breaks a law, unless he harms someone, the police won't look for him. We don't have jurisdiction anywhere else."

Police were always there when you didn't want them, but need help and, where were they? As for the fighting for turf between doctors and lawyers, well, when lawyers were ahead, like now, the law concerned itself more with Nathan's right to refuse care than with his right to receive it. I didn't think anyone could be worse off than me; Nathan was.

"Sister. I, I ... care about Nathan."

"I know." She sighed. "Confidentiality laws are designed to protect people like Nathan. None of us can reveal anything about him or his condition."

That was her way of saying if she knew anything, she wouldn't tell me! I said, "That sounds like a cop-out to keep anyone from helping him."

She drew a shaky breath. "Sister Angela and I are worried and there's nothing we can do, except detach."

"Detach!"

"If Nathan demonstrates that he's harmful to himself or others, he can be picked up, otherwise there's nothing we can do."

My shoe brushed against the envelope. Detach was the one thing I couldn't do even if I knew what that meant.

"Sooner or later," she said, "Nathan will panhandle or loiter or ... do something socially inappropriate."

And end up like Swede. Jesus, help me. I snatched the envelope, said, "Sister, I got things to do."

Peso acted like I had been the one to hang up abruptly the last time we talked.

"You be sure? It's pretty iffy, Baby."

When Peso got nervous he spoke lowbrow.

"Time's important," I said.

"You've done a lot of it. You want to do more?"

Nothing like sticking it to a guy when he's down. I poised the pencil over the paper.

"French. Oh, French," uttered Peso, his tone suggesting that I never learned. "Well. I say, son, I sure would like to get me a su-u-n tan on some warm sandy beach."

I licked my lips in anticipation. He had something for me! At the prison, you never knew when someone was listening, which was why Peso camouflaged his message.

234

"I know a place in Myrtle Beach," Peso said. "North Myrtle Beach would be just the ticket."

I wrote down North Myrtle Beach.

"They say it's nice there this time of year, full of sweet, young, curvy bodies."

"I'm not looking to get laid, Peso, and I'm not slaving for anyone either."

He was quiet into next year. I got nervous as a randy rooster. Maybe I'd blown it and he'd write me off, stop sending my allowance. I tried, "This is where you'd vacation?"

"Me, I'd return to roots."

He's pissed. No way would I go back to Peso massaging my balls, Peso giving me more pleasure and guilt than I ever thought possible. Doing time had evened the score, over and out.

Peso said, "I'd stay at the charming Mar Vista. Oceanside."

"Really?"

"Sure."

I said, "Anyone could use a vacation. *Ciao,*" and hung up before saying something I'd regret. We were even, even, even. Except I knew we wouldn't be even until I stopped taking his money. Peso knew that, too. I shuttled up to my room, extracted the tired atlas from my duffel bag, and shoved underwear and socks into it.

I didn't know if I could find Mrs. Waite's house by myself, especially after dark in the blinding snow. The bus driver said the blizzard was supposed to last all night. The bus arrived in Deephaven an hour late. I recognized the house all right and damn near killed myself toting my duffel bag up the icy driveway.

Mrs. Waite cracked the door open with one hand clutching her robe closed, looking anxious.

"Remember me? Frenchy? I'm here about Nathan. It's important."

"Oh," she said, real soft-like, opening the door.

She seemed older than I remembered. Pink curlers all over her head, eyes puffy like she'd been crying.

"I guess you heard," I said, once we sat in the kitchen.

She sniffed and nodded.

"Nathan called me a couple of days ago."

"He did!" Her expression tried for happier.

I hurried to say, "He didn't tell me where he was."

She tilted her head like a bird. I sure didn't want to cause her any more pain, but now was no time to hide the truth. "He ... sounded out of it ... asked me to refill his prescriptions. I think—that is, generally, I have a clue to where he might be." I looked in the direction of the garage, took the risk. "I thought it might be easier ... for him ... if I would be the one to try to bring him back. He knows me. I have his meds."

The pain in her eyes reminded me of my mother's right after the old man left. I didn't ever want to see that kind of pain again. Mrs. Waite took my meaning in. Her fingers tightened on the front of her robe and her other hand reached out toward me, but no words came. Briefly I squeezed her hand. My plan was nuts. What if the police caught me? She waited for me to say more.

"Nathan's call came from ... South Carolina."

She gasped, tugged a hanky from her pocket, and pressed it to her lips.

"Don't faint on me! You okay?"

She nodded weakly and waved a hand to say she would be okay. I tried small talk to ease her back. When she learned I hadn't eaten, she insisted on fixing me "something quick." I agreed only to let her get used to the idea of me going after Nathan. Eating a chip steak sandwich and a hash brown patty while hidden animals spied from the woods, discounted any sense of control I thought I had. I was hungrier than I thought. I finished and wiped my mouth with the paper napkin. It was now or never.

"That Honda in the garage, you drive it a lot?"

"Do I drive my car?"

In some ways she seemed more innocent than Nathan. Such an expression. I picked up the spoon, set it down. "Sister Angela said she can't do anything for Nathan, him being out of state and all. On the phone Nathan sounded ... lost." Then I lied. "Nathan and I, we're close. I'm sure if I had a car I could convince him to come back." That gave me headway, so I pressed by adding what I hoped would be the clincher. "I think trying to bring him back on public transportation might be risky. I'd really like to try and hope you'll let me." I was always overdoing it, so I stopped talking and let her think.

"Take it," she said. "The car."

I breathed. "Thanks. I— Can I use the can?"

She started to point to the downstairs bathroom, but already I was backing toward the stairs, saying, "Mrs. Waite, from the first time I saw you, I knew you were the kind of mother who sticks by her kid no matter what. I knew that." I turned and took the stairs two at a time, flipped on the bathroom light switch, and closed the door without going in. I tiptoed into Nathan's room and right off spotted what I wanted—a recent snapshot, a Polaroid right there on the bulletin board. I removed it and slid it into my shirt pocket, then tiptoed back to the bathroom, used the toilet, and was in such a hurry I almost forgot to flush. I bounded down the stairs because I wanted to escape before Mrs. Waite had second thoughts or before I thought about consequences and chickened out.

"Frenchy," she said, as I stood in the doorway, blinking at the snow, "Nathan likes beer. Give him beer."

Highway 101 snaked between two narrow portions of frozen Lake Minnetonka. Snow gushed onto it like the Ivory Flakes Poppy used to pour over the Christmas village under the tree. I hunched over the steering wheel, rubbed an oval in the condensation on the windshield with my gloved hand. I cursed and tried yet another combination of heater-defroster-fan.

Mrs. Waite's last words, "Unleaded. It takes unleaded," and, "Nathan was supposed to go to Superior." She couldn't believe Nathan had ended up someplace else or that a social worker might have victimized him. I concentrated hard because I didn't need to end up dead in a ditch before I rescued him. On Monday, I would call in sick to work, and also for my meeting with Sister Kathleen. I figured I should be able to miss at least two AA meetings before some do-gooder like Ernie phoned to check up on me. Unless Junior put the bead on me first. With luck, I should be able to weasel a week for the round trip plus another to find and persuade Nathan to return.

"Damn," I muttered, swiping the condensation on the windshield. The Japs must've designed the confusing Honda controls in revenge for our winning the war, making us unsafe on our own highways. Blindly, I fumbled along the door in search of the automatic window control. Cold or not, I'd have to drive with the window cracked open or I couldn't see. Once I got on the open highway there should be less drifting snow, fewer patches of ice.

I kept pushing the worst scenario out of my mind: If I didn't find him, forget friendship, forget parole. *Forget life.*

CHAPTER THIRTY-NINE

A trail of well-spaced, twinkling headlights followed me in the blinding snow. Thank God I had bought this Thinsulate jacket. I was warm. One car length for every ten miles of speed, that was the safe following distance—double or triple in conditions like these. That was one safety rule I kept when I drove for Peso.

My headlights flashed across the "Welcome to Iowa" sign, where the road narrowed to two lanes without a shoulder. Ahead, creeping toward me was the whirling blue light of a snowplow. I experienced the oddest sensation that it would bury me. During those few distracted seconds, my wheels hit a patch of ice and the car spun out of control.

"Jesus," I muttered, remembering to turn the wheel into the skid—not away from it—to keep my foot off the brake. The car came to a stop angled sideways across both lanes, the rear wheels over the mound of snow at the side of the road. To the right of me was the oncoming whirling blue light, to the left, headlights seemed to stutter as drivers pumped their brakes. Several cars back, I saw a red blinking light. It moved into the opposite lane and approached.

I pressed the gas pedal. The wheels spun. Fighting for breath, for speed, not wanting to deal with a policeman, I bammed my forehead on the steering wheel. Soon, the patrol car's headlights were beside me. The officer got out and shone his flashlight on the Honda's front tires, then on me, as I endured chest pain equal to twenty thousand heart attacks. I watched in the side mirror as he trudged through ankle-deep snow. He assessed my rear tires, then stomped his boots. Dying—I was as good as behind bars—I lowered the window.

"Time's like this," he said, leaning in, "wouldn't you just like to give away that automatic transmission? Rock her. If that doesn't work, I've got a hundred pounds of kitty litter in the trunk. If necessary, we'll commandeer that snowplow when it gets here. You okay?"

"Sh-shook up."

"Who wouldn't be? Straighten the front wheels. Reverse first. The guys at the station laugh at me, but kitty litter works in or out of the bag." His gloved hand patted the window ledge twice; then he walked back in his tracks and beckoned me with his flashlight.

God. Oh, God. It'd be a miracle to get out of this alive. I straightened the wheels, shifted to reverse, eased my foot on the gas pedal. I shifted into Drive, touched the accelerator. Reverse, a little more gas, not too much, or I'd end up deeper in the ditch. Drive, a little more gas. Each shift rocked me closer to the circling light and The Badge. Four, five jerky starts. I *was* gaining. If I didn't get anxious, if I didn't ram into the cop, or shoot off my runaway mouth, I might make it out of here.

The car lurched onto the road and spun a quarter turn before stopping. I faced the headlights of the car that had been behind me and swallowed. Not daring to look at the cop, I straightened the wheels and began the slow process of turning the Honda around. Finally I edged into the right lane and pumped to a stop.

"You did that well," the cop said, his face in mine again. "Shouldn't be out on a night like this."

"You got that right. Officer. I need to get to a friend in trouble."

He shone his beam on the dash. "If you press AC and the outside air lever, it'll defrost."

Who ever heard of turning on air conditioning in winter?

"You bet," I said, following orders. "Thanks. Absolutely."

"Can I help get you to your friend?"

I swallowed hard. "Thanks, he's out of state."

He nodded. "Okay. Drive safely," he said, and headed for his car.

Behind me, headlights waited. My ears were going to drop off from cold. I took time to blow my nose. How much heart thumping could a chest take? Ahead, snow swirled in front of the plow. I accelerated slowly, closed the window tight to prevent snow from entering the car when the plow passed. I felt like I was leading a funeral procession.

Behind the plow came another procession in the opposite direction. Thanks to the air conditioning, the windshield was clear now and the car warm! How lucky I was, the cop could have made a big deal of wondering why I didn't know how to defrost. My breathing remained uneven and shallow; I had encountered the law and left the law, not only free, but assisted! That's when I spotted the red blinking cherry, approaching from behind again. My fear heated to fever pitch. I gripped the wheel and peered straight ahead. The cherry pulled alongside. I couldn't not look at the cop. He motioned me to follow him on the plowed side of the road. I saluted and damn near pissed my pants as I edged the car into the left lane behind him.

That night I rented a seedy motel room not far from Burnham where my mom lived. I thought about driving by the house. I pulled the chair over to the bed, sat, and tucked my feet under the covers. My mirrored image appeared as nervous as Nathan, steel nerves turned molten, leaking out all over the place. I thought of Peso, indulged the memory of being held by him, hearing his soothing voice, feeling his warm breath, his touch, the stupid bear rug. I had felt really loved, which proved that love came in lots of packages. Peso with the hots for jewelry the way other guys had the hots for women. Peso never let me use any of the derogatory terms for homosexual. I sighed and reached for my peanut butter and jelly sandwich, and turned on the TV. I had things to do before I resolved that one.

I watched two cowboys who thought they could beat the law. No one could beat the law, not if they kept testing it. I didn't want to test the law, yet here I was breaking it big-time. And I kept taking Peso's money. I wanted it both ways. I offed the cowboys, set my watch on the table. The inscription on its back said: Love, Peso. I turned the inscription away from me. Peso had helped me find Nathan. I should be grateful, really grateful. I stepped into the shower, wondering if I'd ever find a woman I'd like to spend time with, and, more importantly, who liked being with me, and, if I did, would I be able to have sex with her without thinking of him? Who knew? I roughed the towel over my skin, pushed thoughts of love out of my mind, and crawled into bed.

It wasn't long before giant police boots chased me through snowdrifts. I came upon a clutch of tied up pretty girls. My fingers dripped blood from trying to free them. Powerless, fatigued, dripping blood, a scent any hound could follow, I trudged and trudged. Swede appeared toting an ax. To hide from him, I huddled in a dark, dank cave. Soon I was calling, "Nathan. Nathan." The earth rumbled. My old man's voice said, "Come out! Come out!" Terror engulfed me.

I bolted upright. My tee shirt was drenched with perspiration.

I showered again.

In the morning, the sun shone and the roads were clear. I maneuvered through predawn Chicago traffic like a racecar driver, passing a pickup truck too close, ignoring the finger the driver gave me. Fart 'n dart, that's what driving in the Windy City was. I was in familiar territory and making up for lost time.

Mrs. Waite kept cassettes in a shoebox on the passenger seat. I tried a few of them. Either piano notes chased each other like mice dodging a broom or singers wailed like wounded cats in a foreign language. No wonder Nathan had folded. Once I had asked Nathan what his father did for a living. He said his father invented listening devices that looked like innocent, small evergreens, knickknacks, umbrellas, like all sorts of things, and sold them to border fighting countries. I didn't know whether or not to believe him.

By the time the sun hung overhead, flat plains whizzed by and I hummed to Dolly Parton singing, appropriately enough, "Afraid to Live Afraid of Dying." I could really make it with a woman like Dolly. I knew I could.

Sometimes after my father had materialized I hummed away whole days. Thinking of the old man reminded me of The Badge who had helped me last night. I felt guilty for feeling grateful to him. The guy had done his job well and I appreciated it. I wondered if Mrs. Waite might have a bottle in the trunk. If this were my car, I'd have stashed one with the spare.

CHAPTER FORTY

The woman at the motel registration desk said she
couldn't give out a second key, not to people who hadn't arrived
together. She said Mr. Waite hadn't come out for days and that he
refused to let the maid clean his room. I showed her Nathan's
photo proving I knew him. If Mr. Waite needed medicine, well, if
he were sick, that might be the exception. Mr. Waite's eyes *were*
jumpy. At Mar Vista they didn't operate this way; however, if the
man was sick … With strangers, you never knew. It wasn't as if
Mr. Waite had disturbed the peace. Yet, she had no cause for
calling the police. Mr. Waite had paid through the weekend.
However, with someone dressed the way I was, well maybe this
was the exception. She gave me a key.

I pounded and pounded on 310 before inserting it.

CHAPTER FORTY-ONE

Nathan lay trembling in a fetal position, facing the balcony doors. He peered under the seat of the rocking chair through the open spaces in the bricks at the ocean, wondering why Frenchy hadn't sent his meds. Had he contracted a case of crabs? He didn't want to be all washed up. Tides curled the ocean in and out. With canoeing, there was no roar, no swashing foam, only quiet which he would like now.

He felt cold and hard ice against his back. *Be a sport, hey. Hump. Hump. Hump.* McMaster said vamoose. His mother pushed a high stack of pancakes. His father hurried him.

Nathan flailed his arms against an attacking red owl. It passed over him, landed on the blue lion. Feathers flew. He heard *growls*. A *ROAR*. A vulture strafed his skull and scratched him. Nathan closed his eyes, played dead.

He didn't remember falling asleep, but must have, because when he opened his eyes he felt a bit rested. Gingerly he moved his fingertip along the row of fresh burns on his forearm, heard a *hiss* of pain as someone touched them. The sound confirmed what he had hoped—he was still here.

Outside, neon blue, red, yellow squares, triangles, circles changed colors like chameleons, their shapes inverting, reversing, switching from plus to minus and back again. In such a conundrum, how could anyone know anything?

He focused, trying to get a grip. He sat up and pressed the heels of his hands against his temples, then, after a moment, moved backward on his rump, trying to synchronize his breathing with the sound of the surf. A pelican dipped into the ocean. If it was real or imagined he didn't know. A red owl circled overhead, trailing something in its beak, which wound and tightened around Nathan's throat, cutting off his air, choking him. He heard gagging as geometrics darted, blurred, vanished. His mind screamed: *Angela, Sister Angela.*

Gasping, trying to hold on, he moved his fingers along the strip wound around his throat, searching for a way to pull it free. He found a notch, the notch of a priest's collar! He was being punished for not forgiving Frenchy. Punished. It was hard to breathe.

Whooooo? Whooooooo? Whooooooo?

They would give him seventy-two hours to straighten up or lock him up forever. His body felt rigid. He closed his eyes, straightened his legs. By a supreme act of will, he focused and concentrated on the image of the collar. He inhaled a deep breath, held it, counted backwards from one hundred. When he felt he would burst, he exhaled—longer than he had inhaled—as slowly as he could. The collar evaporated. Nathan swallowed.

Having a semblance of control now, he hugged his knees and tried to shrink, to become invisible, because somewhere deep inside him lurked this terrible monster that demanded life. Determined to balance his inner and outer worlds, to find the pulse of balance that lived dangerously close to the place where images reversed left and right and turned inside out as easy as pockets, he tried to stifle his hallucinations before they tricked him into believing they were real, ordered him to do strange things to himself and to others that he wouldn't remember.

Nathan knew he had spent his energy reserve, and was in serious trouble. He stroked the carpet's texture to keep in touch. He should never have counted on Frenchy. He breathed, counted, turned toward the sea, away from the sea, back to the sea. Waves moved in and out. His breathing moved in and out. He counted. He breathed. He counted. He breathed. He counted.

A milk carton floated in the waves close to him. The carton's spout sprouted a little blue flag with a big white "N" on it. Beside the carton bobbed a buoy. His sobbing four-year-old self held onto the flag. Frightened, alone, the little boy crawled inside the carton, used the flagpole to paddle, paddle, paddle, aiming for shore, for safety, because there was this persistent *knock-knock-knock* he had to get away from.

Nathan paddled furiously. He would *make it to shore, make it to shore, make it to shore.* He had *done it before, done it before, done it before. KNOCK. KNOCK. KNOCK. Must getaway, getaway, getaway.*

CHAPTER FORTY-TWO

The room looked like it had been broken into and trashed—mattresses stacked on a table between the beds, a chair on top of them—putrid smells of cigarette smoke, pizza, sweat. Open cupboards, open drawers, strewn clothing, the lid from the toilet tank off, discarded pizza boxes. I spotted Nathan sitting on the floor, knees up, arms sweeping back and forth diagonally across his chest, moving one fist above the other, repeating an odd, frenzied motion. He looked as wild and wan as a guy fresh out of solitary. I remembered how he had behaved with Jupiter. In slow motion I propped my duffel bag to keep the door open, which hopefully would keep Nathan from feeling trapped and let out the smells.

"Nathan," I whispered, "your mom and dad miss you. *I* miss you."

"You didn't miss me." He pulled back his arm to throw a cup. I ducked.

It broke on the pavement outside.

CHAPTER FORTY-THREE

Nathan bobbed aimlessly on the choppy sea. He hallucinated Frenchy on the other side of piled-up furniture.

The hallucination moved toward Nathan, saying, "I brought your purple socks."

"Stop!"

The vision obeyed.

Nathan paddled, paddled, paddled away from the vision, It wouldn't go away. Nathan dropped the paddle, crawled to the mattresses, and peered at the vision between the rungs of an upside-down chair. Nathan shouted, "Where did you put my money?"

Given no answer, Nathan directed energy minus charges from his third eye, said, "I don't have a plot."

"I have your meds."

Nathan clutched the chair. Behind the intruder, palmettos swayed. "Th-thief," he accused.

"Let me get you a sandwich, hey."

Poison. Nathan glanced at the balcony behind him.

"Smokes. I brought smokes."

Nathan crawled backwards. The hard cement hurt his knees. The hallucination advanced. Nathan shakily pulled himself onto the brick railing, shot his hands over his head, and dove.

CHAPTER FORTY-FOUR

I heard a splash, spun around, and dashed down the steps to the second floor, the first, around the corner, through an underpass to the pool. Circles rippled in it. I followed the trail of water to the beach where Nathan wobbled aimless as a drunk, scattering sand as he tried to run. I rushed, lunged, tackled him.

We grappled and rolled. Nathan was stronger than I would have guessed. He held me down.

"Nathan, you're hurting me. You wanted your meds. I brought them. Remember? You called me."

Nathan stared, released his grip.

I rolled away, knelt, spat sand, saw the burns on his arms, the glare of madness in his eyes. Seeing him this way hurt. I backed away and brushed off my clothes, tried to be sensitive and firm at the same time. "I brought your meds. I'm trying to help you. Nathan, come back to the motel."

Emotions hopscotched through Nathan's eyes: defiance, gullibility, paranoia, confusion. I tried AA talk. "Aren't you sick and tired of being sick and tired?" Knowing nothing better to try, I risked big-time, turned my back, said, "Follow me. Please."

He did.

In the room I wrapped Nathan in a blanket and helped him into a chair and told him to stay there. Glad that Sister Angela had given me Mr. Waite's number, I phoned him collect from the office and explained the situation. He said he would alert the hospital to expect us and tell the motel manager he would pay for damages and a new room. I said, "I don't want anyone to know I left Minneapolis."

"Fine," he said. "Frenchy, I owe you."

Little did he know.

All you need is a cigar and we'll call you Chief," I said, lifting Nathan by the elbow. Pitiful, how docile he was. "Come, we're going to a clean room."

In the new room, I took him right to the shower. "Drop your clothes here. I'll return this blanket to the other room and get my duffel bag. Then I'll buy some sandwiches. Will you be okay?"

He half nodded.

I didn't want to leave Nathan, but figured once he was in the shower, I'd take his clothes; he wouldn't go anywhere naked, at least I didn't think so. I shook sand from the blanket. The duffel bag stood where I had left it. The maid was inside, one hand on her hip, shaking her head at the room. She had skin darker than Peso's, large, dark eyes in a small angular face.

"Ma'am?"

"Y'all had *some* party."

"Ma'am, this here blanket belongs in this room."

In other circumstances her eyes would drown me to softness. Cute, the way she talked. I tucked the purple socks into the duffel bag and slung it over my shoulder, decided to return with a tip. "If you find any belongings, we're in 329," I said.

"Mercy," she said.

* * *

I set a dose of pills on the motel's complimentary
postcard on the bedside table and filled a glass with water and put
it beside the pills. I gathered Nathan's clothes from the floor and
carried them to the maid. She had propped the door open with a
wedge of wood and was scouring the sink.

"Excuse me again. Can I include my friend's clothes with the
laundry?"

"Ain't nothin' about that man clean?"

"I know. He's sick and can't help it. Nothing contagious," I
hurried to say. "These are his only clothes." I took out my billfold.
I had twenties, a five, and three ones. I reached alongside her and
set down a twenty, saying, "No one should have to do what you're
doing. It's a tough job."

She peered at the twenty, said, "Y'all can get his clothes from
the office."

I felt her eyes on my back as I left and found myself wishing I
had time to spend with her. Wrong place, wrong time ... story of
my life.

I got all the way down to the car, then went back up to the room
for the pill bottles, and took them with me. I bought sandwiches,
apples, Gatorade, cigarettes, and, God help me, four six-packs of
cold bottled Coors. (They had never heard of Grain Belt.) I
purchased an ointment the pharmacist recommended for burns and
a Styrofoam cooler. By the time I scurried back to the motel, I was
salivating for what I could not drink and might not resist.

Nathan sat in bed against propped up pillows, covers
tucked around his shoulders. The pills were still on the postcard.

"Your clothes are being washed," I said, offering the
sandwiches.

Nathan looked at them suspiciously.

253

"They're heat-sealed. See? Tamper proof. Ham salad, beef and Swiss, tuna salad. They didn't have egg salad."

Nathan selected the tuna.

"Got cold beer, " I said, making a big deal out of twisting the cap off in front of him. The aroma of hops hit my nostrils and sent me to crazy cravings. "Here. Wash down those pills."

I edged the postcard closer. Gratitude, that's what I thought I saw in Nathan's eyes. I could tell he wanted space, said, "I'll get some ice for the cooler."

When I returned, the room smelled of Coors. The pills still lay on the postcard. Just smelling the beer made me feel foam tickling my nose, the cold bitter bite on my tongue, the brew trickling down, anticipation of the rush. Who was I kidding? I needed to get through this sober.

I moved a chair over to the balcony doors, putting as much room as I could between me and heavenly hops. I poured Gatorade and drank it down, then poured again. I wiped my mouth with the back of my hand and opened another beer for Nathan. I had wondered if he would survive the night. Now, I wondered if *I* would. I unwrapped the beef and Swiss and chomped on it like a stupid guard.

After the third beer and no pills, Nathan's head drooped. Soon his breathing evened in slumber. I tiptoed over and tugged the propped pillow free. He dropped spread-eagle, one hand hanging over the side of the bed. The poor guy was exhausted. I disposed of the empties in the garbage can out in the walkway and lathered my hands with soap, but couldn't get rid of the smell. I plopped mini ice cubes into my glass, went out onto the balcony, and crunched on them.

A rising half moon glimmered in early dusk. On the beach a young man tossed a Frisbee to an Irish setter. I tried not to think about tomorrow or my own paranoia about what Nathan might do. My gaze followed the bouncing breasts of a jogger. An older couple walked hand in hand. I was trying not to think about getting caught, what my parole officer would do, Ernie or McMaster or Double Zero.

The globes on the seawall lighted. The residue of Gatorade in my glass looked like pee. For sure, Peso wouldn't rescue me again. In the fridge was this cold, wet Coors. How much could one beer possibly hurt?

Nathan was snoring. He looked sad and limp, vulnerable. No doubt about it: One guy over the edge, already one too many. Nathan needed me in dry dock.

A surge of tense music, the kind that comes at the chase scene in an action movie, rose from the TV in the adjoining room. A car honked. I tossed more cubes into the glass, concluding that I didn't know how to be a friend any more than Nathan did. I didn't even know the difference between sex and love. If I had to spend the whole night crunching ice, well, that wasn't the end of the world. I was about to go back out on the balcony, when there was a knock on the door. Nervous, I opened it.

The maid stood there with Nathan's clothes folded on her palm. In her other hand she held crumpled paper towels.

"Thanks," I said, pressing my finger to my lips. "He's sleeping."

"This, too," she said, extending the clump of paper towels.

They were damp. Wrapped inside was an envelope with Nathan's name on it in smeared ink. In the envelope—money.

"Thought I should give it to you, not take it to the office," she said. "Was in the freezer."

I fingered the edge of a ten.

She said, "I'm not lookin' for a reward. It's just the right thing to do."

"The right thing," I said, wondering if I would have done it. "Look," I said, suddenly feeling desperate for company. "I've had a hard day. You've had a hard day. Can I ... offer you some Gatorade?"

She faltered, peered over my shoulder at Nathan. "Man like that be no company," she said. "My feet's tired. I could use a cola."

"I'll get you one," I said, not believing my good fortune. "Tell me what kind. I'll get it." I gestured to say I'd set aside the clothes.

"Suppose," she said, her brow furrowing, glancing at Nathan, "we could set a spell on the porch of 310."

She was right—inviting her into the room was not the best idea. "Meet you there."

I wrapped the money in dry paper towels and stuffed it deep into my duffel bag. Nathan seemed zonked for the night. I pocketed the key and a couple of Kling-Tites.

"I can't believe you did all this in so short a time," I said. "The room is so clean."

She led me to the rocking chairs on the balcony.

"Tell me about your friend."

"He's sick in the mind and needs to be in a hospital. His parents are waiting."

She slipped her feet out of her shoes and pushed her toes between the open spaces in the bricks in the railing. Her profile looked like it belonged on some Egyptian coin. My fingertip traced a stream of condensation on the Gatorade bottle.

"At first," she said, "he was real polite. Then like a snail turned to sting fish. You family?"

"In a manner of speaking."

"If it weren't for family," she said, dangling her hand over the arm of the chair, "who would be there for you when you need them?"

I considered reaching for her hand.

She looked at me, then moved her hand into her lap. "Got me the most precious little boy," she said. "Come Saturday, we goin' over to Conway and ride the carousel. Love Ezra more than myself."

I imagined being a little boy on her lap, my arm around her neck, my head against her breast, listening to her heartbeat. I saw myself on the merry-go-round, riding a fancy bridled horse, her hand caressing my leg, her seductive eyes. "Uh ... your little boy, does he have a dog?"

"Uh-uh."

"He'd like a dog."

"Reckon?"

"Guaranteed," I said, easing my hand toward hers on the arm of her chair. "If he's old enough for the merry-go-round, he's old enough for a dog."

"I'll think on it," she said, removing her hand. She tipped the can up and drained the cola. "It's been a long day," she said, pressing the empty into my hand and standing. "I best go home."

"We just got here! Stay," I pleaded.

"I got Ezra. You got your friend," she said.

Lost opportunity, every chapter of my life. I could tell it would be no use.

She tested the door to be sure it was locked and let her sweet, dark eyes linger on mine for a moment.

"After cleaning that room, I be down," she said. "He seemed like such a nice man. Y'all have a safe trip home."

I watched her move away.

"Responsibility," I called after her. "A dog will teach your little boy responsibility."

She waved over her head without looking back.

Later, in bed, listening to Nathan snore and the ocean roar, I thought about what the woman—I didn't even know her name—had said: *If it weren't for family—"*

CHAPTER FORTY-FIVE

Before sunup, nervous as a tick letting go at the touch of a hot match, I shaved, showered, and took the duffel bag and cooler down to the trunk. I set Nathan's prescriptions to one side of the trunk near the front where I could get at them. I went to the desk and verified that everything was okay, that no one had a reason to come after us. The woman said she was glad I had come, that she didn't know what she would have done if I hadn't.

"Nathan," I called gently. "It's time to get up."

Nathan's eyes opened, darted about. He sat up. "What're *you* doing here?" He looked down, realized he was naked and pulled the covers up. I put space between us.

"You asked me to get your meds. You asked me to bring them to you."

Dazed, Nathan seemed to huddle into himself.

"Here. Clean clothes." I dropped them near his feet. "I'll just step out on the balcony and watch the ocean while you dress. Don't forget to take your meds."

Pink streaks radiated from the horizon. *Old man upstairs, this is more amends than anyone should have to make. Help me here.* It promised to be a long, long day.

When I heard water running, I went inside. Nathan tracked my every move.

"We can stop on the way and get a drive-by breakfast. Some coffee."

"Meds?" I pointed at the pills. Clearly, he had no intention of taking them. No telling what he would do if I forced the issue. I transferred the pills to a tissue and wrapped them, then slipped the tissue into my pocket. Nathan followed me without protest. He didn't argue at the car when I suggested he ride in the back seat. Nathan was asleep even before we hit the highway, a blessing greater than I could have imagined.

A minute at a time, an hour at a time, a day at a time. *Make time,* I told myself, *make time.*

A few hours later I gassed up at a convenience store and used the men's room. I purchased coffee and sandwiches. Nathan must not have slept for days. *So far so good.*

At dusk, the car tooled past fenced corrals in Kentucky horse country. I was telling myself how lucky we were to have gotten this far without incident when Nathan's face loomed like a horror mask in the rearview mirror.

He demanded, "Where are you taking me?"

The car swerved.

"Nathan, you scared the bejesus out of me! Home, we're going home."

"Not to my mother's."

"Home to Minneapolis. Minneapolis."

"Minneapolis is not doing so good." His eyes narrowed. He took out a cigarette.

I cracked the passenger window to exhaust the smoke.

"I'm thirsty."

"There's beer in the trunk."

I found a place to pull over and stopped. Nathan got out and urinated, then tried to sit in front.

"No. The back seat is safer, more comfortable. You can stretch out. Here. Sandwiches, potato chips, Nabs."

Given too many choices, Nathan stared at my offerings. I should have known better. "Hurry," I said. "We don't want to be late."

Nathan moved into the back seat. "Late?"

I parked the Styrofoam cooler on the front seat, walked around to the driver's side, got in. Thank God the Honda was two-door. I needed Nathan to take his meds or get blitzed. Or both. I locked the doors, then removed the cap from a beer and handed it back. I opened the tissue with the pills and extended it.

"No."

"Don't you want to feel better?" I wanted to force his pills down his throat.

His defiance said: *I feel fine.*

I rewrapped the meds and eased the car onto the road, told myself, *Better luck next time.*

"Why did you lock the doors?"

"Safety. We're in strange country here. It's yours, the beer. All of it."

"Owls are not wise. Lions don't fly."

The back of my neck prickled. Nathan hadn't buckled his seat belt; it wasn't something to raise a ruckus over. *Priorities: pills, beer. Beer, pills.* Blissful smell, hops.

"See those lights ahead? Lexington."

Traffic grew heavier. With a few beers I could find oblivion. Why had I ever attempted this rescue?

"Everybody wants a piece. Look out for soldiers, chicken necks, doctors, crabs."

"Have another beer."

"Geometry is counterpoint."

I reached inside the cooler, extracted a bottle, set my elbows on the wheel, and unscrewed the cap. My eyes met Nathan's in the rearview mirror. "Hey, you saw me open it. Don't be difficult."

He accepted it. I wiped my damp fingers on my shirt. It would be no use to push pills. I bristled with tension, kept tabs in the rearview mirror. The smell of alcohol mixed with the smell of damp fabric permeated the car. Nathan must have spilled some beer. I lowered the passenger window partway and slowed down at the city limits sign. I needed a rest room, spotted a Handy Pantry ahead. I was fatigued, would buy a picker up candy bar or two, a caffeine fix.

Nathan mumbled incoherently.

Where was that fine line between drunkenness and insanity, between insight and a mind out of bounds?

As we approached the Handy Pantry, Nathan pressed his head against mine. "You can't hump Nathan," he said in my ear. "I can wrestle Felix Helix." He armlocked my throat and squeezed. I hit the brakes. The car jerk-jerk-jerked. Choking, I turned the wheel toward the Handy Pantry. The car zigzagged, screeched, stopped. I couldn't pry Nathan off, heard shouting. Ape-strong Nathan straddled the back of the front seat now, tightening his grip. I was losing consciousness. A hand reached inside the window, Nathan howled, and I felt myself freed. I fell out of the car coughing, tears rolling, holding my throat. A siren slurred.

A policeman handcuffed Nathan. Another reached into the Honda and removed the keys. It all happened so fast.

"My friend," I uttered, holding my throat, adrenaline pumping. "Don't hurt him. He's sick."

The policeman spotted the empty beer bottles and motioned me up against the car. "You people, go about your business," he said to the onlookers, then frisked me. One minute we were tooling down the road, the next— I looked for a way out, found none.

"This your car?"

"No, sir. It's his mother's car. His name's Nathan. He's sick. Don't hurt him, please."

"Driver's license."

Shit. "I've driven halfway across the country to take him home. He's got a mental condition, won't take his meds—medication. We were fighting because he wanted to drive."

"Driver's license."

I didn't want to show it, was afraid they'd spot it as a fake. How thorough had Peso been? I swallowed. "I don't drink. Not me. He's drinking."

The policeman holding Nathan pulled out his gun and motioned me to one side with it.

The other said, "Do you or don't you have a license?"

"I have it, I have it." I dug out my wallet and flashed it.

"Take it out."

I did.

He glanced at his partner, took my license to the police car, called in my fake ID. I was already history. I considered options. Running to the interstate, no way. Nowhere to hide. The Blue with the gun guarded us like we were dangerous. Finally, finally, the guy returned, sliding my license inside his shirt pocket. I couldn't tell what he knew or didn't know.

"Blow in my face," he said.

I blew.

"Walk the line in the cement."

"I've been driving since dawn," I said, suggesting I might not be able to do it. Nathan muttered and tried to chew off his handcuffs. I walked the line, then pleaded, "Every minute counts. You're keeping him from seeing his doctor. He needs to see his doctor."

The officer moved from me to the trunk and opened it.

"See those bags? They're his prescriptions."

The man picked up one of the bags and opened it. He handled the prescriptions, reading the labels.

"Nathan's father will tell you what I'm saying is true. His phone number is in my pocket. Help us. Call him. Please."

"I know a con when I spot one." Still, he put his hand out.

I produced the paper with Mr. Waite's number.

"We'll know soon enough, won't we?" he said, heading toward the police car, all of us watching. Nathan took to acting out. While the other Blue tried to settle him, easy like, I reached up and quietly closed the trunk. What if Mr. Waite was out? I needed to go to the bathroom. If I ran, I'd be dead. I died and went to hell a thousand times while Nathan puffed on the cigarette dangling between his lips, muttering nonsense. What was taking so long?

Finally we heard a coded message on the police radio.

"Well, what d'ya know?" the officer said, returning. He tossed the car keys to me. I looked down at them in my palm in disbelief. "We best get you to a hospital."

"No! I-I'm okay," I said, stroking my throat. "I mean, I want to get Nathan back to help."

"That throat could use some ice."

"I-I've got some in the cooler."

Nathan's guard holstered his gun. He had the key to the handcuffs. "Wait," I said, drawing on guts I didn't know I had. "Nathan's had a lot of beer. I think—" I tilted my head toward the men's room.

"C'mon," said the officer, edging Nathan toward it, still in cuffs.

The other policeman opened the car door for me. I dug in the cooler for ice, held it to my throat and said, "It's important to get him to his Minneapolis doctor. Soon isn't soon enough. I'd like to use the rest room, too. If you'd watch him for me."

"I've had 'em in my car, too. I'll call ahead, tell troopers to be on the lookout for you. You could have done that, you know."

"Y-you're right. I didn't think of that."

The officer returned with Nathan no longer handcuffed.

"We're here to serve," he said.

I couldn't believe my boldness or their helpfulness. I used the can, bought sandwiches, candy bars, gum, cigarettes, more coffee. When I returned, red-in-the-face Nathan sat in the back seat, listening to a lecture.

"You do what you're told now, hear? Don't touch the driver."

"Tell *him* not to touch *me*."

I got in the car and pulled on my seat belt.

"We can call for restraints," the other officer said to me like we were friends now.

I turned to Nathan.

Nathan lowered his gaze.

My heart went out to him. *Poor beaten guy.*

"If he takes his pills, we can forget restraints," I said, holding out the tissue with the pills on it. The officer took it. I opened a Coors and handed it to the man.

"Mr. Waite, sir. Please. Take these."

Nathan washed the pills down.

"That seat belt's for your safety, sir. Put it on."

Nathan glared at me, muttered, fumbled with the belt.

"Anything else?" asked the officer.

"Naw," I said, touching my throat. "Thanks."

I eased the Honda onto the road, waved to the officers . My heart nearly jumped out of my chest. My hands took to shaking with the same kind of DT's, *delirium tremens,* I had experienced when I first landed in jail. I weighed my hands onto the steering wheel like an anchor to keep driving steady and straight.

CHAPTER FORTY-SIX

Cops emerged like coins from behind an ear to escort us.
Nathan's eyes darted like Mexican jumping beans. He muttered
obscenities that would turn cabbage into kraut. I didn't believe
anything so vile could come out of him. My throat hurt from being
strangled and inside from inhaling so much smoke. I felt like
cornered prey; Nathan did, too. I didn't exceed the speed limit,
used the directional signal when I changed lanes, held onto the
steering wheel for dear life; I didn't even spit out the window.

The Hoosiers did a U-turn at the state line, and magic-like, an
Illinois squad car pulled in behind us. Finally Nathan slept again; I
took the opportunity to pull over to the side of the road and rest.
The officers parked a respectable distance behind us. Fuzz, fuzz
everywhere. Never had my nerves run so raw. I could die of help.

Once inside Minnesota, a new police tail found us. The
lakes had thawed; it was April 20. I wondered how I would coax
Nathan inside the hospital. He hadn't taken more meds and
crackled with vengeance.

As we approached the hospital, I waved to the cops, hoping to
lose them. The driver waved back and continued past the

emergency entrance as I pulled in. Stuck on alert for too long, buzzing from lack of sleep, ready for relief, I said to Nathan, real casual, "I think a doctor should look at those burns."

"I d-don't know."

I turned off the ignition, said, "You don't want to risk infection, do you?"

Old man upstairs, help me here. Between us we didn't have a whole deck. "Maybe it's asking too much, Nathan, but I'm in big trouble for ... driving you. No one can know that I drove or that I left Minnesota. If anyone finds out, I'll be living like Swede for the rest of my life." He just stared at me. I couldn't tell if he understood. I said, "When we're done, I'll return the car to your mother," and got out.

Nathan looked at the emergency entrance. I opened his door and waited for what seemed forever before Nathan got out. He motioned me to walk in front of him. Slowly I led him toward the doors that said: Hennepin County Medical Center, the same way Morton had pretended to follow by leading, looking sideways, keeping him in my peripheral vision. Traffic buzzed by. This was my last chance.

"Nathan, I can't say it plainer. I'm sorry for what happened on the ice. I'm sorry. I don't exactly have friends crawling out of the woodwork either and I value your friendship."

Nathan stopped and turned pitiful. "Frenchy, I'd rather go home."

I kept walking. "Hey, we're in Minneapolis, aren't we?" Neither of us had shaved or washed in the last three days. We looked like bums. If a judge handed me a life sentence right here, I deserved it. Finally, finally the automatic double doors *psssted* open. I paused to let Nathan move ahead of me. He stopped and narrowed those defiant green eyes at me. I could smell Lysol, old blood, medicinal stuff. My heart *thump-thumped, thump-thumped.* I moved on. A gray-haired receptionist talked on the phone. A baby with a pacifier in his mouth crawled on the floor. Two teens wearing black leather jackets, one with a bloodstained bandage wrapped around his hand, sat beside each other.

"Nathan, remember, nothing about me bringing you back. Please. You can't be too lost in space to remember that."

"If I'm lost in space," he said, snickering into paranoia, "you're lost in time." He moved past me to the receptionist's desk.

Two, three seconds more and I could go. Hospital staff moved up and down the hall. I experienced a strong, undeniable thirst, wondered if the guys at AA were after me, if Junior had said anything.

Finally the receptionist hung up and turned to Nathan. Very slowly he rolled up his sleeve.

I wanted to leave, *not yet, not yet*. Sister Angela would be relieved to know he was back. Watching him, I thought, *Nathan's the only guy I know who tries to live the Golden Rule the way God intended. I'm a fool to think he'd want me for a friend.* I longed for the funny, smart, innocent, pain-in-the-ass Nathan.

He aimed his thumb over his shoulder at me. "He says a doctor should look at these burns."

"Oh," the woman said, tilting her head to take me in, smiling like she had just found something she'd long been looking for. "You must be Mr. Waite. We've been expecting you."

Guilt and anguish flowed into my bloodstream. Nathan did a full-body, one-eighty, fury firing from his eyes. He connected the dots, knew I had set him up the same way Peso had set me up. I heard a loud *whoosh,* sucked in my gut as air gushed from my lungs. Nathan had tackled me!

"Don't!" I yelled, pounding on his back. "Stop!" I heard screams, footsteps, the crying baby. "Stop!" I cursed, smelled Nathan's beer breath, couldn't get a grip. In no time he had twisted my arms around my back, contorted me into submission. "Stay

267

away!" he shouted at two men wearing hospital greens running toward us. "Stay away!"

The men stopped. I tried to bite Nathan's arm, but couldn't. The leather-jacketed teens stared at us with dull, drugged expressions.

Nathan yanked me to my feet.

"Ow!"

He dragged me toward the exit. One of the men in green looked about as the other tried to reason with Nathan.

I said, "They'll call the police. They won't be ... kind."

"You burned me!"

"I didn't. I didn't!" *I did.* If the police came— I had promised Nathan's parents I would get him here and I had. "Think of your future," I said, thinking of mine. Afraid for him, for me, I acted on instinct. I clenched my jaw, felt the rush of adrenaline, cranked my foot around Nathan's ankle, and jerked as hard as I could. He staggered; his grip loosened. Green streaks pummeled him.

I nearly whacked my head on the automatic doors before they opened. Behind me I heard Nathan's bloodcurdling howl. I shifted, the car into Drive, backed it out, and headed toward the exit. Having done what I set out to do, I felt shabby, ashamed of my betrayal. Nathan could lose his life as well as his mind. Nerves as jittery as bugs trapped in a jar, picturing Nathan in a straightjacket, I eased into traffic, telling myself, *Slow. Go slow.* In the last few days I had had enough police to last a lifetime. No one would understand what Nathan said or did, adding hurt to insult. If only someone else could have rescued Nathan. What I did was out of bounds and it had pushed Nathan out of bounds. I glanced over my shoulder, switched into the right lane. *I risked my life for you, Nathan, the whole rest of my life!* Who else was there? All the way down to the black hole I called my heart, I felt as guilty as sin. Nothing would change that.

I turned onto one-way Portland and calculated reality: *Nathan has to make it on his own now.* As if he could. Lawyers created whirlwinds in a system riddled with thorns. I had seen doctors and nurses who didn't know what to do in cases like his—Grace with Jupiter. The driver behind me honked; the light had changed. I pressed the accelerator. Emory, Nathan's true friend, would want to know Nathan was back.

I maneuvered through traffic perspiring, adrenaline pumping, hyperventilating. My mind kept replaying that last glimpse of Nathan. Once again I felt the same kind of terror I felt when the doctor jammed that needle into me saying he was going to put me to sleep, the same way Morton had been put to sleep. I needed to zone out into orbit on alcohol.

CHAPTER FORTY-SEVEN

As soon as I entered Chance Place, I spotted Emory and gave him a thumbs-up to say Nathan was back. Then palm down, I indicated his condition as iffy.

McMaster charged right at me. "You've been on a binge?"

"No hair on that dog. Forget it," I said.

He snorted, hitched his belt. "Dayton's delivered that mess," he said, pointing to a large, tattered box on the floor by the pay phone. "They said it returned to their warehouse beat up, which is why they won't take it back." The damned toilet paper didn't get delivered either.

"Okay, okay." Too tired for words, I trundled up the stairs and fell across my bed.

I woke during the night with a throbbing headache. I smelled of tobacco. My stomach roiled. I sat up too fast. My throat, my arms, everything hurt. Lucky for me, my roommates slept through anything because I groaned with every move. I lit the face of my watch. Past midnight. I went down the hall and shaved and showered.

Even though I hadn't consumed a drop, my nerves were doing marathon DT's. I dressed. Going downstairs I passed a resident I didn't know, someone who had arrived during my absence. The dot in the middle of the TV screen was still fading. I turned on the brass floor lamp and went out to the car for my duffel bag.

What I needed was a plan. Could I, I wondered, a guy drenched in guilt and shame, report to work in the morning and get through the day without being fired? Back in the living room, I did a few deep-knee bends and jumping jacks, trying to erase Nathan's accusation about being lost in time. Those words replayed in my head. Exercise was supposed to release tension, but my mind was stuck and my body wouldn't get the message. Okay. I needed to return the Honda. I needed a backup story for Sister Kathleen. There was nothing more I could do for Nathan. I needed to get past my homosexual fixation, *Am I or am I not?*

The house creaked and groaned with eerie sounds that freaked me out. I sat on the ottoman, *smack-smack-smacked* my fist into my palm. If Junior had snitched, I would need some kind of squelch for Ernie, too. *Doomed, that's what I am. Doomed.* I couldn't erase that last, sad image of Nathan, frightened and betrayed, his nose pressed to the linoleum. Was there a better way out for Nathan? None that I knew.

Energy drained from my body, leaving me feeling dead and empty as a ghost. I needed to talk to someone, someone I trusted, but who? Gabe would say: *"You're on your own now, Frenchy. You know what to do."* Calling Gabe in the middle of the night would only raise questions at the prison. Bad idea, Gabe.

Then a really stupid idea took shape. I took out my billfold and pulled the slip of paper hidden under the so-called secret flap and stared at it for a long time before going to the phone and plugging in my dime.

After several rings a sleepy-sounding woman answered.

"I need to talk to Ernie," I said. Then, in the prolonged silence, I added, "This is a program call."

"Oh. Just a minute."

There were too many issues from which I needed to free myself.
I couldn't guess what he was going to say.

Ernie asked, "Have you been drinking?"

"No."

"Glad to hear it. Are you in a bar?"

"No."

Ernie was quiet into next year. "I've missed you, Frenchy."

"For four stinking days, I've been smelling beer, smelling it,
listening to it go down, tasting it in my mind, in my mouth. I'm
about to lose it."

"You did right to call. Do you want to come over?"

I had a car, could do that, but in my mental state I'd get caught
running a red light. Or worse. I chickened out. "That's not a good
idea."

"I'll come to you then."

Numbed by Ernie's generosity, I gave him directions. "I can't
believe you're doing this."

"What's a sponsor for? It'll take me twenty, thirty minutes."

I hung up, thinking I could drink the beer in the car before Ernie
arrived; Ernie would never know the difference. Who was I
kidding? That's when the honest-to-God, real heavy responsibility
landed: *Nathan needs me sober.* Only Nathan had known what
Jupiter needed and now I knew what Nathan needed. I had come
this far, hadn't I? This was no time to give up.

Ernie took one look at me, reached out, and hugged me. I
dropped my head on his shoulder and blubbered all the way to hell
and back.

"Well," he said, finally patting my shoulder. He removed his
coat and draped it over the banister, then placed his hat on top of it
and looked around.

Ernie moved into the living room and sat in the overstuffed
chair. I sat on the ottoman at his feet. We stared at each other.

"Uh . . ." I said. "Junior been to meetings?"

"Ye-ah," responded Ernie in that slow way of his. "Why?"

I bit my lower lip, looked at the ceiling. "Tell anybody about this and I'll blast your head off."

Ernie smiled his crooked smile. "More guts in tears than in fists."

I hadn't heard that one before.

"What kind of place is this anyway?"

"Halfway house for the mentally ill."

Ernie's face wizened into disbelief.

"I'm not one of 'em." I knuckled my mustache. "Right now that's the least of my problems." I took a deep, deep breath for courage and launched into the whole dismal story. By the end of it, I had paced enough to wear holes through my soles. "So," I said, "I have a car I'm not supposed to drive, and a cooler of beer I want to drink, and my social worker—" How could I explain this naive nun who had no taste in jewelry, who could and would, once and for all, end my chance at life? I didn't want to be done in by a woman. Not to mention Peso. There were too many people who thought it was their job to fix me. Ernie's leg swung over the arm of the chair, his foot tapped the air. He stroked his chin. I heard the rasp of his whiskers.

He asked, "Are you comfortable with your sexuality?"

"Jesus! What a question at a time like this! Weren't you listening? What do I tell my social worker? She needs signed proof that I attended meetings. Junior. What do I tell him?"

"Why tell him anything?"

"He thinks I was buying drugs for myself!"

"French, French." Ernie put his elbows on his knees and waved a hand to calm me. "It's not Junior's business to take your inventory and it's not likely he'll say anything. Crisis keeps you running from yourself so fast, you'll never catch up."

Ernie raised his hand to stop my protest. I had to listen.

"What Junior thinks isn't important. What *you* think is."

The carpet, dingy as my life.

"I suppose the big question—besides yourself—is your parole officer."

"Cover for me?"

"So you can get by with deceit, keep more secrets? Those things turn people crazy, Frenchy. That would be doing you no favor. I will honor the program."

I cringed.

"Have you been vulnerable with Sister Kathleen?"

"Are you nuts?"

Ernie looked like he was offering me this great gift on a platter I wouldn't take. "No vulnerability, Frenchy, no relationship. Without vulnerability, you won't, can't, open to receive whatever comes. There is crisis addiction. Maybe you have it. Try letting go, coming clean, and turning it over. Trust that if you change what you can, the rest will take care of itself, that you will surface whole and intact."

Turn over what? Lower my guard? Let go? Ernie was betraying me, too. The jerk. I felt even worse than I had thought possible.

"Frenchy, why not try it my way? Try taking it minute by minute. Have you ever done that? Why not just allow what's *best* for you to come through?"

Through what? I had spilled too much, left myself wide open, which was enough vulnerability to beat the band all the way to kingdom come, my funeral dirge.

Ernie's tone turned gentle. "Frenchy, befriend yourself. If you can fill that void inside of you with self-esteem and self-respect, with patience and kindness, instead of filling it up with booze—"

Sermons I could do without. I wanted to pop him in the mouth. Something in Ernie's eyes stopped me cold.

Ernie said, "Maybe you'll discover what happens if you don't meddle and create exactly the setup you're trying to avoid. Try waiting and see."

His eyes offered no judgment, no demand, no dare—only caring softness. I felt none of that terrible pull like I felt around my old man or around the police, around McMaster, Peso. Pullers were everywhere. Even my own mother pulled on me! Pullers took life out of you. Pullers drained your energy and sponged it up and slurped away your life. How did Ernie even know I felt empty?

I made eye contact, hoping for a clue, and felt disarmed and vulnerable, even unsexed—that is, attracted and repelled at the same time. I sensed, sure as a line marking where Ernie left off and where I began, some invisible boundary, a line that I was somehow forbidden to cross. Noting all this sent my body into uncontrollable shakes.

"I-I d-don't know wh-what's happening." I gripped Ernie's forearms and held on for dear life. Peering into his kind eyes, I saw Morton lying on the vet's cold steel table, those dead eyes peering up at me.

"What is it?"

Deep in my gut, *shazam,* something let go, something that had held me hostage for a long, long time. It released, I knew, never to return, except this time I didn't hold back the grief that flooded into my big void.

"Tell me," Ernie said, watching, waiting, holding onto me. "Are you ... surrendering?"

Surrendering? Suddenly over self-conscious, I let go of him. He was right! Like a weasel. Like a no-count pissant I'd surrendered, let go of control. I shoved my hands into my pockets, feeling stupid and defenseless.

Ernie watched me in silence. Reluctantly I met his gaze. No words could describe the understanding and compassion I saw there. Humility, the big H. *Oh boy.* Here I was, one sorry, sexless, lonely, powerless runt lost in time, out on some strange, bigger-than-life field playing a game in which I didn't even know the moves, let alone the rules.

"Well," Ernie said, exhaling. "I think you got what I came to give."

I felt prickly all over, as if, not only a hand or a foot, but my whole body had been asleep and was just waking up. I sure felt powerless. *Finding and admitting powerlessness. The first step!* I looked down, saw that my hands were steady.

"Tell you what I'm willing to do," Ernie said, picking up his coat and putting it on. "I'll return the car to Mrs. Waite."

"I-I better ask her. I mean, it's her car. What do you think?"

Ernie seemed big as a giant like my father.

"Okay. I'll take the brew," Ernie said. "It's okay. We keep liquor in the house for guests."

Never in three billion space years would I ever be able to do that. Gratitude flooded me. There was no hint of pull in the air. This man had never steered me wrong.

"With Sister Kathleen," Ernie said, sounding like a teacher, "the closer you stay to the truth, the easier it'll go. Act like you believe everything will be all right and it will. Trust me," he said. "As for sexuality, that'll haunt you until you own whatever it is." He extended his hand. "Keys? For the beer."

I watched him transport the cooler to his car. When he returned the keys, I thought about asking him to take the toilet paper, too, but didn't. The void inside me buzzed. It didn't feel like anything I would call power; no, it felt busy AND quiet—an oxymoron Peso would say.

Lying on my bed, hands behind my head, I envisioned Nathan and me making shelves, a cabinet, a chair—simple, salable stuff. A cat rubbed against Nathan's leg, which suggested Nathan might be willing to ditch his dumb harmony clock. Maybe we could build a milk carton boat and enter it in the Aquatennial. Wouldn't a dairy sell empty cartons? On meds Nathan could be good company, trustworthy. Maybe we could build a life together. I could earn enough for the two of us to live on. Separate bedrooms. Maybe together, each of us could learn how to be a friend.

Talk about fantasy! I had to get past Sister Kathleen and learn how not to create a crisis, how to wait for what developed, and didn't even know what any of that meant. I was thinking stupid because I was going to be locked up forever. Worse ... *only losers surrendered.*

CHAPTER FORTY-EIGHT

Nathan wanted to be anywhere but strapped to his hospital bed. In saner days, he had developed two strategies for survival—free-floating through space with his mind or the opposite—focusing on some tiny, tiny element like an extreme close-up lens. He wanted to be out of here.

The azure sky cast the peaceful Boundary Water lake into a diorama the way it reflected everything. Nathan watched heavenly reflections, a soaring eagle, an osprey, a blue heron. As the bird landed high in a majestic spruce, its wings closed. Nathan moved his gaze to a nearby birch, closed in on a white curl of bark until it uncurled. He scanned unbelievable colors of rocks on the bottom of the lake—charcoal, slate blue, rust, red, pink, amber. There, ancient earth glowed healthy and intact, ready and able to regenerate life. He focused on a fleck of shiny granite, enlarged it, walked around it, liked how it sparkled and disappeared in a flash of light. By an act of will Nathan forced himself to breathe, to come back, to not get lost in so small a fleck. Here he could canoe with a friend.

Sun glinted off granite deposits in the rocky bluffs. Frenchy sat in the bow of the aluminum canoe, his back already tan, as Nathan ruddered. The scar, which Frenchy usually kept hidden under a sleeve, shone with sweat. Frenchy couldn't sit still, kept dangerously rocking the boat.

"What're they doing, hey?" Frenchy asked, pointing to a pair of American mergansers.

The two ducks faced off, squawked, and circled each other. They flapped their wings, heads bobbing so fast that their heads looked like bouncing rust-colored balls.

"They're going to mate."

The male snatched her neck in his beak, dunked her under, mounted, and in a second, flapped across the water's surface into flight.

"I know a couple of fly swatters like that," Frenchy said.

Nathan didn't want to *be* a fly—he wanted—*to fly*.

Frenchy's amateur ragged stroke determined their rhythm and pace. Nathan J-stroked to keep them on course—J for Jesus, J for Jupiter, J for justice. Most people didn't notice beauty when they were right in the middle of it. They were moving when they could be flying. Energy lay stored in stillness, waiting to be tapped.

An insect floated upside down on the surface of the water, its frenzied legs going nowhere. Ducks preened themselves with oil to stay afloat. Everything he needed to survive was here—if only he knew how to take full advantage of it. The sun was high, the mosquitoes low. Nathan peered port side to the Canadian shore, then starboard to the U.S. shore. While the two borders appeared identical, some invisible line put you inside one country or the other. Paradox thrived. You could be serious and playful at the same time. Did joy work in tandem with responsibility? Nathan thrust the paddle and pushed down hard, turned a J-stroke.

Down-out. Down-out. Down and out.

In a different way, Frenchy was as bad off as he was.

He spotted the wooden portage marker ahead, with the distance burned in: 220 rods. Such measures kept them from getting lost in the middle of creation, helped them portage from one lake to another. Frenchy would like it here if he gave it a chance.

"Frenchy! Don't stand up! Don't!"

Frenchy harumphed with a look over his shoulder.

Frenchy had yet to learn that there was no more pleasant existence than losing yourself. Nathan intended to teach Frenchy, introduce him to the magic of beauty, the joy of immersing yourself to become one with it. They tied up on shore, unloaded Duluth packs, tents, and fishing gear.

Nathan instructed, "There are three ways to portage a canoe. Hoist it and walk under it like this, or rest the bow against a tree, then step under and take the yoke on your shoulders. Or, if it's on the ground face-up, take hold of the gunwales—this takes upper arm strength—lift it overhead, and ... walk. Only sixty-five pounds."

Frenchy's eyes grew as big as full moons.

"Balance is everything," Nathan said with the seventeen-footer overhead. He moved along the path. "Bring the rest of our stuff."

"Lackey all this! How many trips will that take?"

"That's your job."

Frenchy moaned and groaned. "How far is two-hundred-twenty rods anyway?"

"Not more than ten miles," Nathan said, chuckling. He stopped, backed up, and maneuvered the canoe between two trees. He hitched his shoulders to rebalance its weight, braced his knees, and took the hill.

"Won't someone steal our stuff?"

"How many thieves did you see?"

"Smart ass."

Nathan spotted a circle of stones with kindling ready to light, courtesy of the previous campers. "People in harmony don't steal," he said. "You can be a plus or a minus. People in harmony are pluses."

Nathan staked both their tents with incredible attention. Frenchy complained. Nathan started the fire. He dipped water from the lake into the coffeepot, then seined for minnows, and set bobbers on their lines. He baited the hooks, took their rods and reels up to the top of the huge rock, and cast out their lines, wedging the handles firmly in a crack in the rock.

"Time for a swim," Nathan said, shedding his clothes. He dove off into shockingly cold water. He watched as Frenchy, who said he couldn't swim, slipped and slid across moss-covered rocks, into water up to his waist.

Nathan moved away and swam until his muscles undulated with pleasant exhaustion.

"Hey," Frenchy called, still close to shore. "Come here. Look."

Nathan dog-paddled to him. A school of minnows nibbled at Frenchy's buoyant penis.

"Isn't this the damnedest thing? Tickles."

"Watch out for northern pike," Nathan said, biting his lip against laughter. "They've got long jaws and big teeth. After dark, walleyes."

Frenchy clutched his crotch in horror, hobble-flopped over slippery rocks toward shore. Nathan laughed, following, and splashed him. Laughter, like water, smoothed away rough edges, made for lasting friendship. Is that what they were, friends?

"God has a great sense of humor, Frenchy. Think about it. He made me. And you."

Frenchy pulled on his pants. "Risking your pecker's crazy!"

Suddenly Frenchy shrunk smaller and smaller. Disappointed, Nathan sat in the water, a child lost at sea without a paddle. He heard splashing, and turned toward it, saw a woman wearing white with water flowing over her hands.

"I'll shave you," said the apparition.

CHAPTER FORTY-NINE

Zero lost no time in attacking. "You don't look like you been sick."

My damn foot slid off the pedal.

"Got a doctor's note?"

Rebellion zapped me to hell and back. This boss was worse than a tick bleeding a dog dry. Surrendering had left me feeling powerless. I told myself, *Remember what's at stake. Cool. Keep cool. Sometimes you pitch in to help and get burned; sometimes you escape. Simple as that.*

I tried to ignore Otto Olson's presence, carefully placed the chip. There was no such thing as having someone you could count on, no real friendship. Peso had bought me; that's how he captured my friendship. Even Ernie exacted a price; I just hadn't discovered what it was yet. I didn't want to lose this job, stomped as if my life depended on it—which it did.

Zero's eyes gaped like astro doors waiting to chuck me out of the spaceship. Always one to rush in when smart people knew better, I said, "Olson, us drudges might do better work if you'd try mixing some of that huffing and puffing with an 'atta boy' or two." That's when others stopped working and looked at us. I became aware of my need to perform, except this time this need, this pull, wasn't coming from Olson; it was coming from ... *me!*

Too many lessons were coming too fast. I punted, said, "I try, Olson. I really try. Give me a chance. Don't kick me when I'm down, okay? Neither one of us makes it in the idiot department." Double Zero's cheeks turned red. He sputtered, didn't like not having the last word. *God.* How stupid could I get? I might just as well have sealed myself inside the casket with "Morton" and sent both of us to "Addressee Unknown." I stomped. "Listen," I said, stepping closer and lowering my voice, "why not just tell us when something pleases you? Nickel to nuggets, we'd improve."

"Bibideaux, You've got a lot of nerve."

Stupid, stupid, stupid. For sure, he was going to blow me off. I never learned.

Zero surprised me. He said, "I hate to admit it, but you've got a point, Bibideaux. While I roll it around in my empty head—" He pointed to the microchip on the frame and strode away.

Unnerved, I knuckled my mustache. Apparently Zero—Olson— didn't have an oversupply of compliments either. I noticed another feeling rising that I couldn't name.

Inside his glass office, Olson moved papers from one side of his desk to the other and back again. I wasn't paying attention to what I was supposed to be doing and ruined another chip. Guilty as hell, I noted he had seen me. I shrugged an apology. Olson nodded acceptance. My boss and I, two peas locked in the same proud pod. The two of us had just passed a crisis that I had, without a doubt, created. The feeling that I couldn't identify flooded like heat inside me. A glimmer of insight arrived: *Olson's fear of powerlessness had contributed to their differences, too,* and we both knew it. I placed the next microchip carefully and stomped the clip correctly. Olson had met me halfway. Peso never would. Nor McMaster. The house manager didn't deserve to inherit the toilet paper I had stored in his basement. Pack by pack, I intended to leave it in St.

Joan's rest room. I was making progress. Peso, what to do about Peso?

Telling your boss off when you wanted to hide plunked you in the spotlight. That's what I concluded waiting for McMaster to unlock the kitchen door. Some people created crises by rushing in too soon, or, now that I thought about it, the opposite—by avoiding any hassle. What if Olson changed his mind and came at me again? What if Nathan said something? Who would stand by him? And Sister Kathleen. What would she do? I wasn't home free yet.

Dinner was baked beans, creamed corn, and thimble-sized sausages. I filled up on bread and dread, mentally ticking off the people I had to face one by one—Sister Kathleen, Sister Angela, Nathan's so-called caregivers. Not to mention the one guy I couldn't get away from, short of croaking—me. When, how could I be sure about me?

Once inside the double-locked doors of Nathan's ward, I looked back over my shoulder because at the nurse's station ahead stood Sister Kathleen, Sister Angela, Mr. and Mrs. Waite, a nurse, and a man wearing a suit, holding a chart in his hand. I just won the lottery! I swallowed, shifted into the offensive, and advanced.

"What room's Nathan in?" I asked, shoving my hands into my pockets.

"Five-oh-two," the nurse said.

The guy in the suit touched her arm. She shut up. Mrs. Waite paled. I sure hoped Mr. Waite had advised her to keep quiet about my leaving town. There were so many ways I could be done in.

"I'm Doctor Etherby," the man said, extending his hand. The man looked worn out.

"How do you do?" I knuckled my mustache.

"Glad you're here," Mr. Waite said, shaking my hand while his other squeezed my shoulder.

"What happened?" the doctor asked me.

Nervous, I shifted my weight back and forth. Sister Kathleen studied me like I was the last egg on earth and she had to decide whether to protect it or peck holes in it. In her ear lobes, tiger's-eye studs. Sister Angela wrung her hands.

The doctor's attitude belonged to a funeral director. "Tell us what medications Nathan took. How much alcohol he consumed."

"Medications," I repeated, glad to be on safer ground. I didn't want to trip myself up, not say too much or too little. "His prescriptions are at the house. I could call the house manager and ask him to count pills or I can count them when I get home." Sister Kathleen's gaze bore through me like a drill. I pretended not to notice. How would I know about her? "I don't drink."

"The burns?" the nurse asked.

"Nathan's done that before," Mrs. Waite said, sounding meek and weak.

"Who drove?" Sister Kathleen asked accusingly.

"Nathan has a license," Mr. Waite said.

Sister Kathleen turned to him in disbelief.

Mrs. Waite mumbled, "It's my car."

I scratched my head, trying not to act out, feigning how difficult this must be for all of them.

"He's sunburned," Sister Kathleen said.

I withered. "S-s-sunburned?" I repeated.

"Where *was* he?" asked Sister Angela.

"Mr. Bibideaux," said the doctor, "Nathan's not able to help us. It's important that we know what happened."

Nathan hadn't said anything! Still, I felt like a ball tossed back and forth in a deadly keep-away game.

Mrs. Waite sniveled. She said, "We're afraid Nathan will walk out."

"He can't take care of himself!"

"I couldn't agree with you more," Etherby said.

"I've seen some pretty sick guys," I said, backtracking. "I can tell Nathan needs help, even if he doesn't want it."

Mr. Waite sounded angry, defeated. "We can't keep Nathan from leaving the hospital. The law."

The law, the law, the law. I smacked my palm with my fist. Heat fired up the back of my neck into the base of my skull.

Dr. Etherby said. "I'm in a bind. Nathan says, 'Give me the help I need or I'll harm myself,' then refuses my suggestions. He won't take his meds. He's in control."

Maybe fight was a good sign.

"I need control," the doctor said, turning to the Waites. "He's on seventy-two hour hold. Unless you move to commit him, I'll have to release him."

Commitment! Nathan would be lost forever!

"Get me a court order."

Nathan's parents, visibly desperate, looked at each other.

Had my risks been for nothing? "That's nuts!" I said.

The doctor glared at me with an expression that said: *Butt-out, Crapola.*

I turned to Mr. Waite. "Nathan burned his arms. Isn't that being harmful to himself?"

Tentatively Sister Angela said, "Nathan may never get past the insult. Couldn't we try something less drastic first?"

I was afraid to say anything. Dr. Etherby kept selling. "The procedure's humane. After serving Nathan papers, there'll be a court hearing within three days with a referee. Present will be the two of you, Mr. and Mrs. Waite, myself, Nathan, Sister Angela, and one or more doctors new to his case."

I didn't know one guy committed to St. Peter's who ever left. What could I say or do?

"You're right," the doctor said to me. "Self-inflicted burns prove he's harmful to himself, and there's accosting you in the hospital. Those should make commitment stick."

"Not St.Peter's! I'm not blaming Nathan."

The doctor narrowed his eyes at me, then turned to the Waites, faking compassion. "At best cases like this are heart wrenching," he said, sounding like a con. "It need not be Anoka State Hospital." He turned to me, "For people for whom there's hope, something halfway between Chance Place and St. Peter's."

That would end Nathan.

Sister Angela said, "I am hopeful."

She was the guard, the doctor, the warden.

I felt as desperate as when my old man pounded on me, saying, *Stop crying or I'll give you something to really cry about.* I got an image of Swede's blank expression and rage filled me. I challenged Etherby. "What's that hippo oath mean, 'Do no harm'? Seems the least anybody can do for the mentally ill ... the retarded ... even dumb alcoholics, is offer basic health care. Locking up Nathan when he needs understanding and kindness is the worst kind of harm, the worst! Forget those turf battles with lawyers if that's what you're into. Nathan needs patience, time, kindness. He'll rally if you give him a chance. I know he will."

"That *is* what Nathan needs," Sister Angela said.

Etherby said, "Time, I don't have."

You do, too, you double talker. The Waites looked as powerless as I felt. No doubt they had been through this before. Life was no-go for Swede, a maybe-go for Nathan. Compared to them, I had it easy. I said, "Nathan and I live together— We're ... buddies. Let me try. Give me a couple ... three days."

287

"I advise against that," the doctor said, as if with all those diplomas on his wall, I was competition. He added, "There's a limit to his hospital Medicaid days."

Why was he so quick to write Nathan off? To make life easier for himself? Mr. and Mrs. Waite peered at each other like they were about to jump off the same cliff together. Sister Kathleen wore a poker face. Sister Angela held her forehead.

Folding, Mrs. Waite said, "Dr. Etherby's spent a lot of time."

As if Nathan didn't deserve it!

"Please," Mr. Waite said to her, then to the doctor. "If you need to finagle time, we'll support you," he said glancing at her.

Mrs. Waite nodded.

Mr. Waite said, "Let's give Frenchy a week."

The doctor's eyes cut me like a scalpel.

"Hey," I piped, palms up, "what harm can it do?"

"Waste of taxpayers' money," snapped Etherby.

Mr. Waite said, "Doctor, Nathan's circumstance is exactly the kind of situation taxpayers intended welfare and Medicaid to fund. Don't prey on his mother's grief. If decision makers attended conferences like this one, they'd do a lot more."

Anger mixed with ego in the doctor's eyes. He clamped his jaw shut.

"Nathan deserves a chance," Mrs. Waite said, casting her vote.

The doctor walked away. The nurse followed him.

"I'll do my best," I said, already feeling blocks of heavy responsibility on my shoulders. Mr. Waite gave me a soft, caring Ernie kind of look.

"We know you will," he said. He touched Mrs. Waite's elbow and moved with her and Sister Angela to the door, leaving me alone with Sister Kathleen. I heard him say, "Frenchy's right."

Sister Kathleen said, "Nathan had a lot of money. Where is it?"

My toe traced the edge of a floor tile. "How would I know?"

I felt strained patience in her breathing.

"Frenchy, is there anything I ought to know?"

I didn't dare let down my guard. "Sister," I said, suddenly feeling overtaxed. "I live with Nathan. I like to think I'm family. If it weren't for family—"

CHAPTER FIFTY

Nathan lay swaddled like a mummy and strapped down. I closed the door softly and waited for my adrenaline to calm down. The room smelled like stale sickness. I had taken on too much, wanted to run away. Even after a lifetime of failures, I couldn't renege. This was one task I must not fail. I tried to slow my breathing, couldn't even tell if Nathan knew I was there. I edged forward, a slow-motion tortoise. Nathan's eyes fastened in a trance on the window.

Over the bed hung a picture of a cactus sprouting a yellow bud. I wondered if Nathan could hear and comprehend me. Loyalty and patience always happened to other people. Now I needed it for both of us. There was so much at stake.

"Nathan?"

Not the flicker of an eyelid.

"Nathan, the doctor wants you committed. Listen. I know you wouldn't hurt anyone. Not a dog, not a flea."

The way his eyes stared, Nathan could've been a corpse.

It's now or never. "Nathan I'm sorry for tricking you back here. Your parents are here. Your care is here. I-I wish you weren't ... strapped in. Nathan, the dice are loaded against you. That's the truth."

No sign of recognition. I listened to my own breathing. I watched Nathan's chest rise and fall.

"Nathan, if they lock me up, it'll be because I did stupid things; if they lock you up, it'll be because you wouldn't try. Claim yourself, man. Take hold."

I must be imagining that Nathan seemed to inhale when I did. Nathan's chest deflated as mine did. Maybe because I was trying too hard I was seeing things that weren't happening. An illusion? My hands formed fists of hope at my sides. I warned myself not to get too excited, held my breath, and counted to five.

Nathan stilled for the count!

I drew air.

Nathan drew air.

I got so excited I wanted to throw my hat in the air and yell. Instead I exhaled slowly, paused, counted to three, exhaled softly like blowing a kiss, making an easy sound—once, twice.

Weak, but a definite mimic. Nathan was with me!

"Okay," I whispered, forgetting not to make any sudden moves, swiping my mustache with the back of my hand. "Okay."

I measured what to do next, the same careful way I double-measured before sawing wood.

Ernie better be right. "Nathan. You don't want to end up warehoused. If we act like men, they have to treat us like men."

Where did that come from?

Nathan stopped breathing.

I hadn't anticipated Nathan holding his breath. I held mine until my chest hurt and I got dizzy and had to breathe. Nathan didn't. Still, Nathan wasn't turning blue. Some things—like breathing—a guy just had to do for himself.

"Nathan?" I tried to sound firm *and* gentle. "Breathe, man. You can do it. Take hold. Everyone misses you at Chance Place. Especially Jupiter. I … care about what happens to you. I want you to be my friend. If you don't want to be mine … that's okay. I respect you. I will respect you. That's a promise. I know what promise means. It's a promise."

Nathan breathed.

Thank you, God. Nathan's future lay in Nathan's hands. I would do my best to help him. Whatever happened, happened.

CHAPTER FIFTY-ONE

When Mrs. Waite came to retrieve her car, she held my hand and thanked me, and said this was the first time since Nathan's illness that she and Chuck had agreed on anything. She said Nathan was lucky that he still had thirty days of hospitalization left, even though he might need sixty. They would cross that bridge when they came to it. She didn't like Dr. Etherby any more than I did! She patted my hand like I was some kind of miracle worker, thanked me again and drove away.

A new robotics machine at my workstation, gave me more to learn and worry about. When one of the other workers explained how it worked I felt like part of the team. Olson didn't know much about new technology, so we all had that in common.

I visited Nathan twice a day. It felt like going to church. In between I hoped he was doing what he could do for himself. My mind ticked off hurdles I had already overcome: getting back, beer, car, Olson, Etherby. Taking responsibility—awesome.

Still I pondered what, exactly, was Ernie trying to teach me? That there was an alternative to fighting or running? "Be present," he had said. "Pay attention." I was paying attention and so far had successfully avoided creating a new crisis. Getting in the flow maybe? Is that what I was supposed to learn?

At AA the drunks clustered around and welcomed me back like I'd been gone for a couple of years. I didn't know what had happened to the cardboard puppets I had painted them out to be. Junior didn't seem nearly as concerned with me as I was with him. When my turn to talk came, I shared my worry about a friend in trouble and how absolutely powerless I felt wanting to help, not knowing exactly how I could. I said I was trying hard to trust that this friend could use his own higher power to find a way out of his serious situation. Ernie grinned at me like a proud father watching his son land his first good punch. That gave me enough courage to say, "I don't understand how this higher power stuff works."

Gramps said, "Don't try. It's not for understanding. It's a spiritual gift, something you simply allow to happen and accept. Most of us steep awhile in our own juices before we think we even deserve it. Sometimes we keep good fortune from happening. Once we surrender, though, higher power appears!"

Like a rabbit popping out of a hat? I still wasn't so sure. "Just accept?" I repeated. If ever anyone lay open and waiting for whatever happened, it was Nathan, and look at the condition *he* was in. This sure sounded like the dumbest advice I had ever received. When you go dredging up stuff inside yourself, might you not dig yourself in deeper? Or, digging deep could you strike gold? It didn't make much sense.

After the meeting Ernie pumped my hand. "Keep it simple," he said. "You're on the right track."

"You bet."

It took me a couple of days to figure that maybe higher power lay dormant like seeds in the bouquet Nathan had given Jupiter. Actually, Nathan knew a lot I didn't know. "Not dead," Nathan had explained. Given the right season and water and light and air, his field flowers would germinate. I didn't know much about plants. We *were* making progress. He breathed regularly with me now with a spark of recognition in his eyes. On one front though, I still had a ways to go. Apprehensive, hat in hand, I shuffled to Sister Kathleen's office.

There, I took the hot seat and braced for her accusations, turning my hat 'round and 'round, still afraid that tomorrow I would wake up and find myself in prison. I had little skill at what Ernie called essentials for a life well lived, starting with: Truth.

I tried. "This week, Sister, I don't have a slip from AA."

She pulled the edges of the sweater draped over her shoulders closer together. The paper in her hand fluttered. She turned to the form, without looking at me, and began asking the questions she asked every week. I could tell she knew something wasn't cricket. Tension made it hard to breathe. I didn't want to betray her. I was beginning to believe betrayal most hurt the betrayer.

Sister Kathleen didn't make one check mark. When she finished, she picked up her pencil, hesitated, then check-check-checked all at once. She fingered the corner of the form with such fire in her eyes that I expected the paper to ignite. When she finally looked up, she asked in a nervous, edgy tone, "How are you and Mr. Olson getting on?"

Olson had called her! Despite my anxiety, I took time and effort and tried to go with the flow; I worked to stay open to whatever would come, easier said than done. I uncrossed and recrossed my legs, resisted an image of Nathan's ditzy clock, and said, "Mr. Olson and I ... we've arrived at a kind of harmony. It's not exactly comfortable, but it ... ticks." I swallowed, didn't know where that had come from.

She *flip-flip-flipped* the corner of the paper between her thumb and index finger. Waiting for her final judgment, I realized how Nathan could be so sensitive to sound; the simple sound of that paper flipping irritated me no end.

"About Nathan," she said.

Alarms, sirens, whistles went off inside me. I pressed my lips tight. She was going to dunk me.

"Fear of closeness, it's awful," she said. "Comes from a sense of abandonment."

Who had abandoned Nathan? His parents? His girlfriend? It was hard for me to accept how Mr. Waite and Mrs. Waite had stood by me. I had felt abandoned lots of times.

Sister Kathleen said, "Friendship requires trust and hard work. That's especially difficult for someone suffering schizophrenia." Her eyes seemed to delve into my soul. "It's a different kind of commitment," she said.

I felt stung, dropped my hat. Trust and that kind of commitment were hardly my strong suits.

"What about alcoholics?" I asked, looking at my hat. "Is friendship hard for alcoholics?"

"With oneself," she said.

I winced.

She said, "Anything worth having is worth the extra effort."

Sister Kathleen's confidence made me shifty-assed. What had I done to deserve this? Her hand rested on her cross. Her eyes offered warmth. The blitz of truth: When it came to the skills of friendship, neither Nathan nor I scored very high, but we had connected out of some mutual understanding of abandonment. Nathan knew how to work hard. So did I. That could count. Did that mean we could become friends? Maybe, maybe not. I bowed my head and accepted this gift she had given me.

CHAPTER FIFTY-TWO

On Saturday when I usually visited Peso and didn't, I knew something BIG inside me had changed, even though guilt plagued me. Before the afternoon was over, I rationalized a lame reason to call him and plugged a coin into the phone. Peso cut me off before I said much.

He said, "I'm being paroled. You want your old job back, you got it."

I froze, felt like a hot fudge sundae, hot and cold all over at the same time.

He said, "I intend to travel some."

If you turned on Peso, Peso turned on you. I coughed, was quiet for a long time, feeling old stirrings in my groin, pleasure, shame, gratitude, guilt, all kinds of mixed-up feelings. Peso and I had shared histories. I owed him more than I could ever repay. Peso owned me, too! Whoring for money, I was no different than his girls. I shuddered with the willies, knew what I had to do, probably the hardest thing I would ever do. "P-Peso— I'm doing fine. Thanks for everything, but don't send ... any more money."

I braced for the worst.

Peso sighed, said, "Frenchy, you're the best."

He was cutting me slack? This was not the Peso I knew. I couldn't believe it!

"After that last phone call, Frenchy, I knew you were a lost cause. Well, Baby, take no wooden nickels."

Well, what d'ya know? Peso had let me draw a line. He did care. I had to say something quick.

"Peso, you've got big antlers. The heart of a moose. I'm ... grateful."

He was quiet. I didn't know what more to say.

He said, "Don't go soft now, hear? *Ciao.*" The phone clicked. Over and out. The end. Kaput.

I trudged up the cemetery hill to plat 789, which I was told lay in the shadow of a huge white oak. I wore a light windbreaker, was again toying with the idea of dropping in on Mom, to let her know I was all right. No one needed to worry all the time; at least she could stop worrying. The small rose granite marker said: Morton d. May 3, 1963.

Once I checked to be sure I was alone, I removed my hat and knelt on one knee. Vulnerability burned like a fresh open cut inside me. I forced myself to speak the words so I would hear them. "You and me, we're free now, Morton. Free. You were my best friend and I let you down. I know this wasn't exactly what Gabe had in mind when he said to put you to rest, but it's the best I could do to make amends." I clamped a hand over my eyes against stupid tears. They came anyway. The grudge against my father had been so heavy to carry.

I don't know how long I knelt there—long enough to feel drained and fatigued. I had been running on empty for a long time, my whole life maybe. Finally I blew my nose and wiped my eyes and ambled back to the bus stop. Open now to whatever happened, I expected I would feel vulnerable more often, but hopefully not all the time like Nathan.

On the bus my gaze landed on the swaying hips of a young woman as she moved up the aisle to get off. It was pleasant to watch hips sway. I couldn't help but wonder if a wife, a child, might be in my future. My eyes followed the woman as she crossed the street and disappeared around a corner. I saw a bumper sticker that said: I'm straight, but not narrow. That made me smile. It no longer mattered if I proved to be gay or straight. It had simply become more important to be honest with myself. Ernie said honesty required practice, practice, practice. AA had proved nothing short of the heaviest dose of self-truth anyone might tolerate. *Let go and let God,* that was the slogan I was working on now.

For some reason my mind turned to Swede and then to Nathan, who was free of physical restraints now, but running out of time. *We* were running out of time. It would take a miracle to save him and when it came to miracles, I was positively, definitely, beyond a doubt, powerless.

For some reason the idea for how to help Nathan sparked in this instant. It wasn't a whopper of an idea, not a sledge hammer hit, more like a gentle nudge that slid into my mind, a notion that had I not been paying attention I surely would have missed. Could something so difficult really be so simple? I resisted judging the idea, even tried to shrug it away. The idea, however, refused to diminish, defuse, or change. Because I had no other option in mind, I figured, Why not try it? I deboarded with a definite purpose, with a real plan in mind.

CHAPTER FIFTY-THREE

Geoff unlocked the ward door and let me in. "I didn't recognize you," he said.

I grinned self-consciously, said, "You're not the first. I don't have anything sharp to leave at the desk, just this." I held Nathan's red spiral notebook in front of my chest like a billboard. My checked jacket was too warm for spring weather.

"Nathan's Mindbook," read Geoff.

"I thought he might like to have it."

"Guess it's okay, if you take it when you leave. That wire spiral—"

"I will. Any change?"

He shook his head. "No. Just sits there."

"Thanks." I hurried away holding the notebook high over my chest. I closed the door to Nathan's room soundlessly and leaned my back against it, my breath shuddered with fear. I couldn't believe I had gotten this far, felt anxiety clawing inside my chest, an animal trying to get out.

Nathan sat in the corner chair. He had not acknowledged my presence. I took time to calm myself. It would be a long, slow trek to the dresser. I inched, inched, inched there and silently set down Nathan's book. Like stepping into the middle of some unknown dance, I pretended that Nathan and I were Siamese twins relying on a single pair of lungs. I accepted the rhythm of Nathan's breathing, forced myself to notice only that.

Once our breathing synchronized, I spoke softly, pacing the words slowly. "I brought your notebook. I thought you might like to have it. You know, for memories. Geoff said I have to take it with me when I leave." I unbuttoned my jacket. "I brought something else, too." I glanced at the closed door, bent forward—slow, slow. We breathed. "Don't get frightened, hey."

I cradled the gray kitten and pulled it out. The poor thing was shivering with fright. I cuddled it, stroked, cooed, inched closer to Nathan, all the time breathing with him.

"Hope she doesn't pee or scratch," I said. "It's a girl." I eased the kitten onto Nathan's lap. Its back rose and bristled. "It's okay, okay," I reassured, petting it. Slowly I backed away to give them space.

"I wanted the color you said yours, uh ... Debbie's, was. They didn't have a gray male."

The kitten's tail moved like a charmed snake. It turned its face up to Nathan's and mewed a plaintive sound. I've felt like that lots of times. I feel like that now.

"I think she's afraid to trust or let anyone get close," I said. Then I added, "Like us."

Nathan's breathing caught and held.

I held mine, too.

The kitten rubbed the top of its head against Nathan.

I concentrated. It wasn't easy to copy Nathan's ragged breathing.

The kitten kneaded Nathan's thigh with its claws, circled, then settled down proud as a lion guarding King Tut. It flicked an ear, half-closed its eyes and *purrrrrrred*. That's when Nathan's index fingertip rose and lightly stroked its fur.

I could hardly contain myself. Forgetting that I should make no quick moves, joyous, I knuckled my mustache, surprised once again that it wasn't there, only smooth shaven skin.

I said, "With so much love around, she shouldn't be cooped up at the Humane Society. Nathan, when—when we get our act together— maybe you and I, maybe we can share an apartment?" I paused, was talking too much, too fast. "We could give a home to a kitten or two? A dog even?"

I felt a shift in the energy in the room. An unmistakable change. Nathan's breathing quickened. The *purring* got louder. I cautioned myself to accept whatever happened. I extended my finger and petted the soft fur, too. It was too much to realize. My father had taught me how to be mean. Peso had bought me with clothes and food. Ernie had taught me to pay attention to what was going on inside. Now Nathan was teaching me ... to care.

Nathan's expression softened. In his eyes I saw ... presence. Nathan's finger lingered over my hand, then touched it. I looked up and smiled at him, then gently withdrew my hand, hoping he received both messages—that I cared and that I wouldn't violate his friendship again. Love was, after all, about a lot more than sex. Nathan and I were two sides of the same coin—opposites who had somehow struck a tethering, but acceptable, balance. Maybe that's what life was really about, finding balance. We were buddies now and maybe—in time—we could be ... brothers.

When will Thou save the people?
O God of mercy, when?
Not kings and lords, but nations!
Not thrones and crowns, but men!
Flowers of Thy heart, O God, are they;
Let them not pass, like weeds away—
God save the people!

Corn Law Rhymes 1828

About the Author

Frankie Schelly has published numerous short stories and articles in magazines and journals. She enjoyed a career as an advertising manager and as associate creative director of an advertising agency. In 1984 she earned her CCDP—certified chemical dependency practitioner—in Minnesota, and volunteered as a facilitator to groups in recovery from addiction. Mother of three children, she lives with her husband in the Blue Ridge Mountains of North Carolina. *Chance Place* is her second novel.

If you enjoyed *Chance Place*, please go to Amazon.com and Barnesandnoble.com and type: Frankie Schelly in the search box, then follow instructions to write a customer review. To e-mail Schelly, go to her website: http://www.firesignexclusives.com.

Praise for Frankie Schelly's *At the Crossroads*

For a sneak peek of Frankie Schelly's At the Crossroads, Honorable Mention Winner, Mainstream/Literary Fiction, *Writer's Digest* 9th National Self-Published Book Awards, read on. Here are just three of many complimentary reviews of this novel about four contemporary nuns facing feminist issues.

A deftly written, powerful novel of modern moral dilemmas facing four postmodern nuns who are caught between the beliefs they have long cherished and modern feminist values. From the divisive issue of abortion to infertility treatments to a contested living will, *At the Crossroads* explores the hot-button social issues that come uncomfortably close to home for men and women today. Highly recommended reading from first page to last. –James A. Cox, *The Midwest Book Review*

The nuns have not been sheltered from events and issues of the larger world. Their spirituality has not been an escape from it, but is a guide and resource for dealing with the tough choices they face. This spirituality gives an added dimension to the treatment of contemporary issues. The nuns' actions disclose new shades of involvement, concern, and effectiveness, with respect to circumstances and events of contemporary life facing all thoughtful persons. The reader becomes absorbed in following the characters as they struggle to make up their minds about what to do in their changing circumstances. –Henry Berry, *The Small Press Book Review*

Sister Vivian Tiamet is torn between the past and the present in her role as principal and superior of St. Anthony School and Convent in Sleeder, IL. She became a nun in a faltering attempt to expiate her guilt about having an abortion when she was a teen, and now a teen in a similar situation needs her help. The depictions of sex are more graphic than usually found in Christian fiction, but Schelly's novel grapples with topics of current interest. A strong contribution for most library collections. –Melanie C. Duncan, *Library Journal*

CHAPTER ONE

The floor-to-ceiling, white marble altar looked like
an overfrosted wedding cake. In the central niche stood the statue
of St. Anthony, the saint to whom you prayed to find what was
lost, while Matthew, Mark, Luke, and John upheld gospel truth
from the four overfrosted outer reaches. In the front pew, Vivian
Tiamet nervously shifted her weight.

She was a slender, small-boned woman with angular features in
her mid-forties. She felt hot and heady with her navy blue woolen
coat over her gray woolen suit. Though PTA mothers teased her
about her virgin-blue eyes and her graceful gestures, in this
moment she felt no grace. Father Rupert had given yet another
homily on: In marriage avoid the sins of sex. Irritated, anxious to
exit, Vivian edged toward the aisle. The scent of stale incense
made it hard to breathe. The priest turned to the congregation,
raised his hand and blessed them, making the sign of the cross,
saying, "Go in peace."

Vivian moved into the aisle, nodded a token bow toward the
altar, and hurried toward the door. She felt nauseous. She reached
up and pushed back the right side of her blunt-cut hair, should

1

never have agreed to a cut that hid some of her view, even if the style suggested that her gray streak belonged there.

Whatever did Father mean when he said, "Purity of intention renders the conception of a child holier?" She gripped and squeezed the figure of Christ on the pectoral cross hanging between her breasts. *Not once did he mention pleasure. Not once.* Caught up among others now, she moved slower. Surely the priest knew that kind of sermon put struggles in the minds of wives and mothers. They brought them to Vivian's principal's office and expected her to come up with solutions. He had actually encouraged couples to deny sexual pleasure in marriage. Lest anyone ask her opinion of the homily and she betray her disdain, Vivian kept custody of the eyes, kept her eyes downcast.

Outside it was predawn, still dark. She stepped gingerly over a thinly iced puddle and off the curb into the street. Behind her, a woman screamed. Brakes screeched. A car horn blared. Vivian found herself illuminated in the beam of headlights, hands clutching her ears. *What on earth?* The car's radiator blasted heat and looked like a confessional grill.

Rankled—she could have been killed—Vivian chopped a hand behind her at those watching, to say, "I'm all right," and waved the driver on. Once safe and shuddering on the other side of the street, she drew her lips into a thin, pinched line, and strode determined to hold her own against the priest's ignorance. She trembled at her near miss as she passed the school, moving toward the house that was their convent. Despite tremors, her thoughts invaded. *Imagine a wife saying to her husband in that most intimate of moments, "Darling, remember, self-denial!" If sexual pleasure doesn't compensate for all those wakeful nights with a colicky baby, for all those times when a mother sets a child firmly on the moral path, what does?*

How convenient for Father Rupert if she had landed in the hospital or ... worse. Her heart pounded. As she approached the back door of the convent, she realized how much it would upset Sister Dominic to see her this way, and turned and paced on the asphalt playground between the convent and the school.

From day one Rupert had scotched every visionary plan she proposed until his dumb decisions brought them to the brink of their current financial troubles. He meddled, couldn't seem to remember that she answered to him only in parish matters, that the other three sisters answered to her, and she to Reverend Mother Philip Neri, who lived in the motherhouse, in Sisters of the Immaculate Heart of Mary headquarters in Brandenburg, Indiana. Mother's lack of support disappointed her. Men believed in control; priests were men. That was the nub of it. Why in the world had Mother ever sent her here to Sleeder, Illinois to save St. Anthony School if it couldn't be done?

Damn. Sometimes couples marry to avoid the sin of sex. They do.

If Vivian had known her life would become as spiritually and financially bankrupt as the lives of the women who confided in her, never would she have entered the convent in the first place, not that she had felt she had much choice back then. She fumbled in her pocket for her key, drew a deep breath of cold air, and opened their back door.

The kitchen's bright fluorescence always reminded Vivian of the transfiguration. Sister Dominic looked up from the batter she was mixing in the stainless steel bowl and smiled. Vivian nodded and hung her coat on the coat tree beside the sewing machine in the corner. Like many sisters after Vatican II in the late sixties had urged religious orders to modernize, their housekeeper chose to keep wearing her black habit, and to keep her sister title. Sister Dominic just said, "There will be no ankle showing or jewelry wearing for me."

3

"What was the commotion I heard?" the old woman asked, pushing her trifocals higher on the bridge of her nose. Before her shoulders bent, Sister Dominic stood a shy five feet. The corners of her mouth perpetually turned upward as if she had just grasped some delightful cosmic joke. People said they experienced awe in her presence.

Vivian touched the spot in her chin where her old starched guimpe had dented it so deeply she thought it would never go away, but it had. Unnerved, not wanting to admit her own stupidity, Vivian said, "Someone didn't look before entering the street. The fool could have been killed," she muttered. "Thankfully, the car stopped in time."

She entered the ill-placed bathroom they had added near the back door after climbing stairs became too difficult for Sister Dominic's arthritic knees. Though inconvenient, the plumber claimed it was the most economical location. For modesty the bathroom had two doors. When the second one closed, the vacuum between the two sounded a grand *phuff*, calling attention to you when you least wanted it. By the time Vivian came out she had breathed herself into some calm. The red light on the waffle iron glowed.

"You have a visitor."

"Who?"

"Mrs. Suges and her daughter."

"Jennifer? Jennifer Suges?"

The girl had graduated from Vivian's eighth grade class two years earlier. "I wonder what she wants. That priest," Vivian said, seeking comfort. "Picking up his psychological litter makes me feel like a wife picking up a husband's dirty socks." They exchanged conspiratorial smiles. Vivian sighed. She loved this dear woman whom she could count on for comfort, wisdom, balance.

Sister Dominic pushed her trifocals higher, said, "Kimberly's staying in church a bit."

"Well," Vivian smiled suggesting Kimberly could use a bit of extra prayer. She tugged the hem of her jacket and straightened her cross, wanted to say, *I love you*, but, of course, couldn't; tradition discouraged any show of affection. "I'll see what the Sugeses want. Thanks for the waffles. My spirit could use a lift."

"I can tell."

Vivian moved through the hall, past the small telephone table, past the closed door of the reception room they had turned into a bedroom for Sister Dominic, and arrived in the entry hall. Behind the closed music room door, Mary Ruth was playing the piano, Bach. The room had been a formal dining room before they sealed off the archway to the kitchen and turned it into the piano lesson room. If only Kimberly were as malleable as Mary Ruth. Her task of coaching this only child of a doctor and his socialite wife into manners and behavior becoming to a religious would be easier. Vivian lightly tapped her plain gold wedding band on the parlor door and opened it.

Mrs. Suges rose. "Sister, I hope you don't mind us dropping by." Mrs. Suges was one of few parishioners who refused to drop the sister title. "Sister, I been threatening to bring Jennifer for some time. You're the only one Jennifer ever listened to."

"No. No. Of course not." Vivian said, closing the door, not liking the idea of being used as a threat. Tension between the mother and daughter was palpable. The woman's pudgy knuckles whitened on her clutch purse. Dark puffy crescents under Mrs. Suges' eyes suggested the woman carried germs of worry there. The problem was serious.

The girl wore a yellow sweatshirt with rhinestones on it and her hair had been died a brassy strawberry color. Dark eyeliner exaggerated her eyes like a doll's. Underneath all that eyeliner Vivian could tell Jennifer's eyes were red and swollen from crying.

5

Vivian said, "It's nice to see you, Jennifer," and offered a warm smile.

The girl turned her gaze away.

"Please sit down. What can I do for you?"

"She don't come home, won't listen, won't mind, stays out too late." The woman sat on the edge of one of the two Queen Anne chairs, drumming her fingers on her purse.

Vivian wanted to help. Humbled by their confidence, needing to pull out the problem, she turned to Jennifer and tried a tactic that worked in the classroom. "That doesn't sound like you, Jennifer, not like the young woman who stayed home and cooked for farmhands when your mother had pneumonia, and then worked doubly hard to make up lessons. Not the Jennifer who nursed the new calf for nearly fifty hours after everyone else had given up on it."

The girl peeked at her mother, seeking approval. Not receiving it, she slid one soiled sneaker over the other and stared at her toes.

Vivian wanted to reach out and squeeze the girl's hand, say something reassuring, but she dared not take sides. She waited. When the girl said nothing more Vivian turned to Mrs. Suges and said, kindly, "Maybe Jennifer doesn't want my assistance."

"She doesn't listen! Somebody's got to help!"

"My brothers stay out all night."

"They're not girls!"

Trying to persuade Mr. Suges would be like going up against the old Soviet Union—a cold war. Vivian's own family had settled squabbles by not acknowledging them. At least Mrs. Suges was trying to confront whatever it was. What would possibly make Jennifer so inconsolable? Vivian experienced a sudden visceral dread followed by a drain of energy. Her heart dissolved into fear. *That* problem still ruined a girl's life. Her hand moved to her abdomen. She swallowed.

Jennifer muttered, "S'ster, my dad's mad 'cause of geometry. That's all."

Vivian wanted to reach out and hug Jennifer. She softly signaled the girl with her hand to say, Save this conversation until we're alone. She could hold her. The girl blinked understanding. This pact happened so instantly that Vivian questioned whether it had even occurred. She became aware of eyes in the portrait of the founder of their order, the eyes of Mother Mary Gertrude, watching, and felt the weight of authority. *Jennifer doesn't need self-righteousness*, her mind protested, *Jennifer needs compassion.* Vivian fairly brimmed with it.

She drew in a quivering breath, turned, and addressed Mrs. Suges in an overly light tone. "Mrs. Suges—Clara, Jennifer wouldn't be the first student stumped by geometry. If you like, if *she* likes," she said, smiling, then addressing the girl, "I'll tutor you."

Jennifer peered into Vivian's eyes, then away. She shrank into what looked like shame, pulled her mouth to one side, bit on her lower lip.

In a small farming town of twenty-five thousand like Sleeder, Protestants outnumbered Catholics two-to-one. Everyone knew everyone else's business. Protestants never failed to point it out when a Catholic teenager got pregnant. It would be difficult for Jennifer; she wanted so much to be popular. *Maybe I'm wrong,* Vivian told herself. *Please, God, let me be wrong.*

Mrs. Suges raised her purse and set it firmly on her lap as if sealing some agreement.

"It's a start. A start," she said.

Vivian experienced the same kind of betrayal she had felt when her mother acted as if Sister Rosella, her eighth grade teacher, were all knowing and *she* no-count. Jennifer's toe traced the blue geometric border of the rug.

Vivian rested her hand on the girl's and said, "If that's what you want. Only if that's what you want."

"Okay," Jennifer breathed. "Okay."

Mrs. Suges stood. Vivian and Jennifer followed suit. The woman said, "You're too good to the children, Sister. Too good. We wish you could be here forever. We, my husband and me, we want you to know we are grateful."

The decision was made. Vivian tried to smile and extended her hand.

Mrs. Suges held on and patted it.

"You're welcome," Vivian said, feeling a tinge of guilt for her complicity with the girl against her mother. As they walked to the door, Vivian put her arm around Jennifer's shoulders and tried to draw her close, but Jennifer tensed and resisted. Vivian knew full well the girl's awful anxiety.

"Dear, when would be a good time?" Vivian asked.

Without looking at her, Jennifer said, "I have to check my schedule. I'll phone," and shrugged free.

Will you? "I hope you will." Don't let the problem grow." *Terrible choice of words.* "I mean, it's better to deal early with any problem."

Jennifer looked into Vivian's eyes. Vivian sensed Jennifer knew that she knew.

Now shame engulfed Vivian. *How will I ever keep my own guilt and shame out of this?*

She took the girl firmly by the shoulders, said, "Trust me. It'll be okay, Jennifer. It will." Mary Ruth was playing *"Clair de Lune."* Vivian turned to Mrs. Suges and said, "We'll do whatever Jennifer needs, whatever she wants. That's a promise," she said, turning to Jennifer. To both of them, she said, "Thank you for your confidence."

Through the shaved head of St. Anthony in the stained glass panel in the door, Vivian watched them get into their rusty green

8

station wagon and drive away. "Call. Please, call," she said to the empty parking space. When Sister Dominic rang the breakfast bell, Vivian was still standing there with her hand on her abdomen, praying, *St. Jude, patron of the impossible, help me here.*

* * *

Order *At the Crossroads*: http://www.booklocker.com/crossroads or from bookstores using ISBN 1-931391-32-7. Bookstore fax orders: 207-262-5544.

Order *Chance Place*: http://www.booklocker.com/chance or from bookstores using ISBN 1-59113-220-7. Bookstores fax orders: 207-262-5544.

You may e-mail author Frankie Schelly from her website: http://www.firesignexclusives.com.